LAST BUS TO COFFEEVILLE

LAST BUS TO COFFEEVILLE

J. Paul Henderson

NO EXIT PRESS

This edition first published in 2015 by No Exit Press,
an imprint of Oldcastle Books Ltd,
P.O.Box 394, Harpenden,
Herts, AL5 1XJ, UK

coffeeville.co
noexit.co.uk
@noexitpress

ISBN
978-1-84344-265-3 (B format)
978-1-84344-266-0 (epub)
978-1-84344-267-7 (mobi)
978-1-84344-268-4 (pdf)

2 4 6 8 10 9 7 5 3 1

Typeset by Avocet Typeset, Somerton, Somerset
in 10.75pt Minion
Printed and bound by CPI Group (UK) Ltd, Croydon, CR0 4YY

In memory of Amanda and Stanley

Acknowledgements

I would like to thank Val Henderson and Richard Farrar for keeping the faith; John C. Henry for driving the car and answering questions (many); Keshini Naidoo for reading the manuscript and making it better; Trevor Armstrong, James Fletcher, Steve Hardman and Madeline Toy; Jinny Frank, Virginia Haizlip and Michael R. Darby. I owe an especial debt of gratitude to Steven Mair and John Lea for getting the bus out of the ditch and back on the road again; and to Ion, Claire, Alexandra and Frances of Oldcastle Books for making it happen while keeping it fun.

Contents

Prologue

'It's started, Gene.'

The voice was deeper than he remembered and older sounding, but there was no mistaking whose voice it was. In the same instant he also understood the meaning of what she said.

'I'll be right over, Nancy,' he answered.

It was only after he put the phone down that he realised he had no idea where Nancy was.

Eight word conversations can have their limitations.

Part One

DISLOCATIONS

1

Gene and Nancy

Doc's Birthday

Eugene Chaney, or Doc as most people called him, sat on the back terrace of his house drinking coffee and wondering if the birds were singing off-key. He decided they were and shouted at them: 'Keep your damn beaks shut!'

In truth the birds sang no differently, neither better nor worse than usual. They stared at Doc as he settled back into his chair. They were used to his moods, but today he seemed different. Today he was: it was his seventy-second birthday.

Eugene Chaney III had retired from practice seven years earlier and eased himself effortlessly into a life of what his neighbours described as misanthropy. Doc would have balked at this description. He was unsociable yes, and made no effort to meet new people, but a misanthrope? No.

On the day he retired, Doc threw away the suits and bow ties that had characterised his professional life and replaced them with plaid shirts and corduroy pants. His white hair had grown long and was combed back in the style of Grandpa Walton, a character in a television series of his younger years. He had also grown a thick moustache in the fashion of Frank Zappa, a rock musician of his youth, and started to smoke again.

Daily life for Doc was no longer exacting. He would wake on a morning, walk downstairs and turn on the television. Most days he would read. Sometimes he would walk or drive places. He did things to fill time, to kill it stone dead. In the evening he would drink two glasses of red wine, impatient for the day to end, and at night sleep fitfully, his dreams disturbed. He was tired all the time.

The anniversary of his birth, however, always took a different turn. It was the one day of the year he allowed himself to look back on his life and consider its limitations. It was a dangerous, if necessary, safety valve.

He would question how a man could reside on a planet for seventy-two years and still live only ten miles from where he was born. He would meditate on a lifetime of helping others while unable to help himself, and ponder why he now preferred his own company. Above all, he would reflect on life's fragility, its lack of rhyme or reason, and the unbearable pain of loss.

Eugene Chaney had become a doctor by default, through lack of imagination.

Doc came from a long line of doctors. His great grandfather, Robert Chaney, although having no medical qualifications per se, had made a name for himself and something of a small fortune for his family by selling what amounted to little more than snake oil. On the proceeds of Robert's sales, his grandfather, Eugene Chaney, had gone to medical school and become a legitimate general practitioner, as had his own father, Eugene Jr.

In the small town where the family lived, the name Eugene Chaney became synonymous with medicine, and it was fully expected that Eugene Chaney III would also follow the well-trodden family path. Doc didn't disappoint. If not filled with a burning desire to help people, he was at least interested in maintaining an accustomed standard of living and, if honest, coveted the social standing conferred by the title doctor.

With a natural and easy understanding of all things scientific, and with no other career in mind, Doc enrolled at Duke University's School of Medicine in the fall of 1960. He drove to North Carolina in a brand new car, a present from his parents. Life was good and life could only get better. For a time it did but then it didn't. How true to life, life can sometimes be!

As it transpired, Eugene Chaney graduated from Medical School with little or no interest in either maintaining his accustomed standard of living or achieving the social standing he'd once desired. He did, however, leave university with an almost obsessive need to wash his hands and, after the trauma of dissecting his allocated cadaver, an aversion to eating beef that lasted four years.

Of more concern for a man who would be a doctor for the next forty years of his life – and potentially more so for the communities he served – was that he graduated with absolutely no interest in medicine. Fortunately, this lack of concern was compensated by a basic competence on Doc's part, and an awareness of his own limitations: he was happy, if not relieved, to refer patients to specialists when unsure of the correct diagnosis.

Patients came to him in differing states of vulnerability. Doc saw parts of their anatomy he preferred never to see again, and on a daily basis witnessed the corrosion of once healthy bodies now racked by disease and old age. The position of power he enjoyed and the onus of responsibility he suffered time and again overwhelmed him. He was expected to change lives for the better, but more often than not found himself managing expectations, explaining to patients the chronic nature of their conditions, and on occasion having to break news of the worst possible kind.

Unlike his patients, Doc appreciated how inexact a science medicine actually was, and likened himself to no more than a small-town garage mechanic who tried to figure out electrical faults on high-ticket European imports. In fact, no one was more surprised than he was when one of his patients actually recovered. His greatest and only fulfilment was syringing ears filled with wax.

Although Doc would have never been described as unsociable at this stage in his life, neither by any stretch of the imagination would he have been considered a people person. It might be surprising to learn, therefore, that amongst his patients he enjoyed the reputation of a kindly man, and was credited with a sympathetic manner; all remarked on the calm and reassuring nature of his voice. It was his patients, in fact, who had started to refer to him as Doc, rather than Doctor, and the moniker had stuck.

Doc's first full-time position was in a small town in Maryland, located at the base of the Catoctin Mountains and surrounded by apple orchards. Ominously for future repartee, the doctors in the practice all quipped that they were MDs in MD.

The small town boasted *Ten Police Officers for Every Man, Woman and Child*. After his own recent experiences with the police, Doc wasn't sure whether to feel reassured or threatened by this statement, and for many years would wonder where the supposed twenty officers assigned to his wife and child had been on the day of their deaths. Certainly not protecting them.

Four years after arriving in Maryland, Doc fell in love for the second time in his life. It also proved to be the last time. Her name was Beth Gordon, a twenty-five year old florist who operated a small concessionary close to where he worked.

Doc had been invited to dine at the house of another practice doctor, and had thought it fitting to take a bouquet of flowers for his colleague's wife. He didn't look forward to the evening and could predict from experience how it would unfold. The doctors from the practice would talk matters medical and debate plans expansionist, while their wives would talk amongst themselves, swap recipes for apple desserts and suggest suitable matches for Doc. (Doc was the only unmarried doctor in the practice and therefore considered eligible.)

There were two people working in the florists when Doc walked through the door, but it was Beth who'd greeted him: 'Hi, how can I help you?' she'd asked.

'I'm looking for some flowers,' Doc had replied.

'Well, you've come to the right place, then. This shop is full of them.'

Doc had immediately liked her. He'd explained what the flowers were for and asked her to choose something appropriate. As Beth busied herself picking out flowers, matching their colours and choosing background foliage, they chatted easily –

sparring with each other rather than aimlessly chit-chatting. Finally, Beth wrapped the flowers in cellophane and completed the presentation bouquet with a bow ribbon. As Doc was leaving – and halfway through the door – he turned to Beth and asked if she'd like to accompany him to the dinner party that evening.

'Sure, why not,' Beth had replied.

'Well, just try and make something of yourself, then. No jeans! I'll pick you up at seven.'

Two years later they were married.

'I don't suppose you want to get married, do you?' Doc had asked.

'Sure, why not,' Beth had replied. 'Who to?'

Doc had then slipped a ring on her finger. The next day they returned to the jewellers and exchanged it for something Beth thought more suitable.

'Okay with you?' she'd asked.

'Okay by me,' he'd replied. 'By the way, you do realise I'll be the titular head of the family, don't you?'

'Sure darling, and all the emphasis will be on the *first* syllable,' Beth had replied.

Beth was pregnant within the year, and nine months later Doc became father to a 7lb 3oz girl – Esther. How something so small could bring so much happiness into their lives sometimes baffled him. Often, when he looked down on his daughter's still and sleeping form, he thought his heart would literally burst. The unfulfilment of Doc's professional life paled into insignificance as he now gloried in the completeness of his family life.

Such feelings, however, would last for no more than a year. Shortly after his daughter's first birthday, Beth and Esther were killed by a giant donut.

The accident happened on an autumn day custom-built for convertibles: the temperature was warm, the air still, and the humidity non-existent. The Chaneys' blue Corvette Stingray was usually driven by Doc but, at Beth's request, he'd taken the family station wagon to the surgery that morning: she needed to run errands and wanted to make the most of the weather before it turned.

Beth rolled back the car's roof, secured Esther's chair firmly to the passenger seat and headed downtown. The warmth of the sun on her face and the breeze that rustled her newly short hair felt good. Beth had driven the route a thousand times before and could probably have driven it blindfold. At the intersection near the heart of the downtown district, she slowed to a halt, looked left, looked right, left again and then pulled out. Neither driving school nor her own driving experiences had ever suggested that she look upwards to check for falling donuts. Perhaps this was an oversight.

The giant donut had slipped from a crane in the process of attaching it to a tall advertising pylon adjacent to a donut shop. Without warning, it crashed down on the Stingray and crushed the car. Death for both Beth and Esther was instantaneous. Death for the doctor, however, would be prolonged and extend over a period of forty years. Their memory would be a constant in his life: as fresh as daisies and as dry as old leaves.

No words or damages paid can ever alleviate such loss, and at times like these God wisely removes himself to the sidelines – an anonymous spectator hoping to pass unnoticed. All that had been important to Doc had gone, and that day his soul died. The same day, he also lost his appetite for donuts.

Maryland and its memories began to suffocate him. He broke into a cold sweat every time he passed the intersection where the accident had happened, and involuntarily clenched his fists when he saw the giant donut – a new one – affixed to the pylon. Beth and Esther turned up in too many places for life to be comfortable, and when his father phoned to tell him of his decision to retire and inquire of his son if he'd be interested in taking over the practice, Doc readily agreed. The day he left Maryland was the last time he saw the town; he never set foot there again. He carried with him the remains of his erstwhile family: two small urns, one smaller than the other.

Doc's parents had aged comfortably over the years, and he

again looked forward to spending time with them. The occasion he'd last seen them had been Thanksgiving holiday of the previous year, and then they had still appeared as the archetypal old couple: the kind that telephone companies might use to encourage sons and daughters to phone home, or travel companies feature as model senior citizens journeying to visit grandchildren. Arriving to take over his father's practice, however, Doc had been shocked to find them old people.

It had happened suddenly, and nothing had prepared him for the change. The phone calls and letters of the intervening year had given him no clues, signalled no warning. He wondered if signs of their decline had already been visible on that Thanksgiving visit, but that he'd been too consumed by his own grief to notice. There was no mistaking now, however, that his mother was seriously ill.

Aware of their son's own pain, neither she nor his father had mentioned her cancer to him. The cancer proved terminal, and Doc and his father could only watch as it cruelly ravaged and consumed her body. As his mother faded, so too did his father's spirit. The humour that once characterised and defined the man's being disappeared and he shuffled around the house a mere shadow of his former self. Three years after his return, Doc's mother died of a broken body and, six months later, his father of a broken heart. They now lay buried side by side in a small cemetery behind the Episcopal Church they'd attended, the church in which they'd been married and the church in which Eugene had been baptised.

In little more than an eight-year period of his young adult life, Doc suffered losses that would, for most people, have been spread over a lifetime, or never happened at all. Whether consciously or unconsciously, he withdrew from the world and into himself, protected from further loss by a shell of gruff exterior. For the next forty years, he would shed no fresh tears.

As the sun rose in the sky and the day of his seventy-second birthday grew hotter, Doc moved his chair into the shade, poured himself another coffee and lit a cigarette. Having unravelled the threads of his life, he now drew them together and refined them into a litany of advice he believed all fathers should impart to their children. Children, he maintained, should be prepared for everything that life might throw at them.

He believed they should be told that their lives would probably get worse rather than better, that they would encounter more difficulties than easy streets, and should learn to come to terms with disappointment. They should be told that they would fail more times than they would succeed, that they would be lucky to find careers that fulfilled them and would, in all probability, be bored stupid for much of their professional lives. Their hearts would be broken, and they would endure relationships that went up in flames or collapsed into rubble; sometimes they would know why, but most times they wouldn't. They would suffer bereavement and loss, and for long periods of time simply exist. For all these experiences they wouldn't be a better or worse person, only a changed person.

Once old, they should compare photographs of themselves as a child with how they were then. They should focus on the eyes: it would be their eyes that would tell the real story of their lives, not the lines on their faces or the loose skin hanging from their chins. Assuredly, their eyes would be sadder; there would no longer be a twinkle there but weariness, a hunted look.

Doc believed that if children knew such cataclysms were possibilities that could strike their lives at any time, the lucky ones would more likely appreciate the providence of their blessed lives, while the unlucky would learn to savour the fleeting moments of happiness allowed them. In particular, he would urge both groups to remember and appreciate the people who had shared in, and were often the reason for, their happiness. Always remember to take photographs, he would have advised them. Don't forget the photographs!

And then, five years ago, Nancy had unexpectedly phoned and renewed a relationship that had ended close to forty-five years earlier. In all probability it would end again within the year, and once more at Nancy's choosing.

Uncivil Times

When the clock struck midnight on December 31, 1959, few could have foreseen the troubled years that lay ahead for the nation or prophesied the forces about to be unleashed. The time of Eisenhower had been one of consensus, and its spirit unquestioning and complacent. The parents of Doc and people their age had little appetite for self-criticism. They had lived through the Great Depression and fought a World War, and their lives were now comfortable. They had every reason to celebrate rather than criticise the America of their birth.

Change, however, was in the air, ruffling the growing hair on their children's heads and tapping into their consciences. By the time Doc enrolled at Duke University's Medical School, his generation was already starting to question the nation's values, especially in the area of race. Negroes, they noted, were still discriminated against in almost all walks of life, and stores, restaurants and hotels remained segregated. They intuitively recognised that racial prejudice was wrong, an unquestionable evil.

Before arriving in Durham, Doc had experienced little of the prejudice that Negroes endured on a daily basis. The town he grew up in had been essentially white, and consequently there had been no racial divide. His early life had also been sheltered, and the success of the high school football team or finding a date for the prom had always taken precedence over any national issues that might have stirred the day.

Duke University changed this. Friends he made there were of the intellectual variety, people who placed emphasis on creativity and originality. By nature, they were more disposed to question and reject traditional and dominant values, and Doc came under their sway. Two friends, in particular, were instrumental in steering him down the path of civil rights activism. Galvanised by a black student sit-in at a segregated Woolworth's lunch counter in nearby Greensboro, they joined the Congress of Racial Equality and, in conjunction with another student called Steve Barrentine, started to organise regular meetings and activities on campus. It was at one such meeting that Doc met Nancy.

Twenty people were gathered in Steve Barrentine's apartment that night. It was the first meeting Doc had attended, and the only two people he knew there were his friends, neither of whom had thought it important to mention that, as a new arrival, he would be expected to describe his own experiences of racial discrimination and suggest ways of combating the unconscionable status quo. Consequently, when called upon to do so, Doc was taken by surprise.

Flustered by having to address the meeting with no thoughts prepared, he started by sensibly admitting that he had few experiences of racial discrimination to recount. He then joked that he'd have probably befriended more Negroes had they had air-conditioning in their houses. 'All the Negroes I knew were poor,' he said, 'and let's face it, who needs poor friends when it's ninety-eight degrees in the shade?'

There was a stunned silence. People let out small gasps of air, shook their heads and examined their shoes in particular detail. Doc noticed only one person in the room stifling a laugh: a scrawny-looking girl sitting cross-legged on the floor smoking a cigarette. The silence was punctured – and Doc saved – by a loud and deep guffaw from the kitchen. A well-built Negro came into the room and walked towards Gene with his hand outstretched.

'I don't know who you are, man, but I think you jus' nailed it. I ain't got no air-conditionin' an' I ain't got no civil rights, neither. Ain't no way they not linked. Hell, if the governmen' jus' give me an' my people some o' the ventilation you white folks have, we'd be on our way to equality!'

As the man who'd spoken these words was the only black person in the room, the others started to smile and nod their heads. 'Good thinking, Bob,' Steve Barrentine said. 'I think we should make that a discussion point for our next meeting.'

Doc imagined that if mud ever became animate, then it would sound like Bob Crenshaw: he'd never heard such a deep and resonant voice. He took Bob's proffered hand with a greater enthusiasm than he usually accepted hands, and made a mental note not to wash until back in his apartment.

'Glad to meet you, Bob – and thanks for speaking up when

you did. I was beginning to feel like Jesus on the cross out there. They appear to hold you in some regard.'

'Only reason they do is cos I black, an' they ain't,' Bob smiled, taking Gene to one side. 'I could say any ol' damn shit an' they'd still agree with me. By the way, what you said then was jus' plain dumb, man. This ain't no audience fo' jokes, Gene. Folks here is humourless – well-meaning, but too worthy fo' their own damn good. You wanna get a drink an' be humorous some place safe?'

'Sure,' Gene said (as we'll call him during his time at Duke; just as we'll call black or Afro-Americans, Negroes – as they too were called at the time).

'Hey, Nancy,' Bob called over to the scrawny girl. 'We're goin' fo' a drink. You comin'?'

Nancy nodded and went to get her coat. 'Let's go to my place,' she said.

The three of them left together, and Gene, who had arrived at the apartment on foot, climbed into the passenger seat of Bob's battered old car.

'This the firs' time you been in a black man's car?' Bob asked.

'First time,' Gene replied, 'so drive carefully. I have a promising career ahead of me.'

Bob let out one of his deep guffaws: 'Ha!'

Nancy lived in a house rather than an apartment, and unlike most students at the university didn't share with others. She threw her coat over an armchair and took three beers from the refrigerator. When she handed one of the bottles to Gene, she introduced herself as Nancy Travis.

'This is a really nice house, Nancy,' Gene said. 'It's the size of my parents'!'

'Nancy's a rich girl, ain't you, Nancy,' Bob teased. 'A rich girl from Miss'ippi. How would yo' daddy feel if he knew a black man was sittin' on yo' couch, Nance?'

'He'd be fine with it,' Nancy replied, with what Gene took to be a hint of exasperation in her voice. 'Black people come and go in our house all the time.'

'Yea, but I bet they's servants.'

'They're also friends, and some of them we look upon as family. That's what people here don't understand. They simply see Miss'ippi as a boogey man. It's a lot more complicated than that.'

'I jus' messin' with you, girl. No need to get antsy.'

'Who's antsy...?'

'You two seem to know each other well,' Gene interrupted. 'How did you meet?'

'At one of the meetings,' Nancy answered. 'A girlfriend of his brought him and then dropped out of the group. We got stuck with him. She dropped him too, by the way, and I can't say I blame her.'

Bob excused himself to use the bathroom. 'How you know I didn' drop her?' he called out.

'But you're friends, right?' Gene asked.

'I guess so,' Nancy laughed. 'But there are times when he drives me nuts!'

Bob came back into the room and picked up the phone. 'Okay if I use the phone, Nance?' Nancy nodded her approval. Bob dialled a long number, grunted a few times into the mouthpiece, hung up and then announced he had to leave: some urgent business had come up. 'You okay to get back by yo'self, Gene?'

Gene looked at Nancy to make sure it was okay for him to stay.

'I'll take him back,' Nancy said.

'Will you be at the next meeting?' Gene asked him.

'Hell no,' Bob said, as he pulled on his coat. 'I can think o' better things to do with my time 'n listen to Steve Barrentine talk 'bout air-conditionin'. One mo' thing, Nance – you gotta stop wearin' that top. Looks like it's made outta some ol' bathmat!'

Gene was right in supposing that Nancy had been trying to suppress a laugh at his inappropriate comments during the meeting, but on closer examination proved to be nowhere near as scrawny as he'd first imagined her to be. She was in fact slim rather than skinny, about 5 feet 6 inches tall and really quite beautiful. She had large green eyes, expensively uniform teeth and thick strawberry-blonde hair. She also spoke with a seductively lazy drawl, and Gene found himself drawn to her.

When Nancy stopped the car outside his apartment building, he asked for a date. She paused before agreeing and then paused again. 'There's something you need to know about me, Gene,' she said. As he waited for her to continue his heart dropped, and he feared she was going to tell him that she preferred the company of women or was addicted to prescription drugs. But what Nancy said was this: 'I'm from the Delta, Gene. The most I'll ever be able to cook for you is a grilled cheese sandwich.'

The Delta

Nancy Travis came from a rich family that owned large tracts of land in the Mississippi Delta. The temperature on the day of her birth had been 100.4 degrees Fahrenheit – the exact same temperature as her mother's womb – and the day's accompanying humidity had made for an easy transition into the world. Her parents' money and privileged position similarly ensured that her passage through life would, in all probability, be smooth and uncomplicated.

The Travis family owned 6,000 acres of fertile land in the county of Tallahatchie, and grew cotton on topsoil estimated to be twenty-seven feet deep. The nearest small town was Sumner, and the nearest large town Clarksdale. The Travis family had moved there from Virginia in 1835, two years after the territory was opened for settlement, and with a cohort of slaves transformed the wilderness and swamps into some of the richest land in the state. In the nineteenth century they survived malaria, yellow fever, the Civil War, Reconstruction and the floods of 1882–84; and in the twentieth century embraced the new technologies of machinery and pesticides, and survived the floods of 1931 and 1933.

The family enjoyed a life of advantage, and a lifestyle that came with money. They gave lavish parties; flew to New York for opening nights and shopping trips; holidayed in Europe and the Caribbean; had a reserved suite at the Peabody Hotel in Memphis; and Hilton Travis, Nancy's father, went on safari to Africa. Black cooks prepared their meals; black maids cleaned their house; and black gardeners tended their grounds.

Nancy was the youngest of four children, accidental. Her mother, Martha Travis, had borne her first three children while still in her twenties: Nancy was conceived in her mother's forty-third year. (Bob, with his usual sensitivity, had told Nancy she was lucky not to have been brain-damaged.) There was a gap of some fourteen years between Nancy and her closest sibling. She had one brother and two sisters: Brandon, Daisy and Ruby. She became the centre of attention and, for many years, was treated like a family pet.

Brandon had attended the state's agricultural college in Starkville and now helped his father run the farm. Daisy and Ruby had married early and well, Daisy to a dentist in Memphis and Ruby, Nancy's favourite, to another farmer in neighbouring Leflore County. Nancy was the first member of her family to attend university.

Martha and Hilton Travis wanted the best for their youngest daughter. The first three of their children had grown up in times that placed greater emphasis on training in social and cultural activities than on academic studies – Brandon had attended college purely to acquire practical knowledge. They realised, however, that unlike that of her siblings, Nancy's future would much more depend on the schools she attended and the education she earned.

Before the Supreme Court ruled in 1954 that all public schools be desegregated, Mississippi's schools were already poor. The private academies opened by White Citizen Councils in response to that ruling only served to further weaken the standard of education in the state. At the age of twelve, therefore, Martha and Hilton Travis enrolled Nancy in a private girls' school in Richmond, Virginia; and in 1960, Nancy enrolled herself at Duke University. Herein lay the roots of Nancy's dualism when confronted with the issues of race and racial prejudice.

Nancy was a child of Mississippi but became a stranger to it. She loved the state of her birth, and the Delta more so. Above all she loved her parents and family. She intuitively knew her parents to be good people, and could never remember them treating the Negroes who worked for them with anything other than kindness and consideration. When she'd told Bob that household servants were considered friends – and some as part of the family – she hadn't been exaggerating.

At school and university, however, the environment was different. Many of the students were from northern states, whose families were politically more progressive or liberal by nature. They looked upon Mississippi as exotic, and Nancy was forever being placed in the position of being its spokesperson, and with increasing difficulty its defender.

The first – and worst – such occasion happened barely a year after Nancy had arrived in Richmond, when the badly beaten body of a fourteen-year-old Negro boy was pulled from the Tallahatchie River. His face had been mutilated: his nose was broken, his right eye missing, and there was a hole in the side of his head. The boy's name was Emmett Till. He came from Chicago and had been visiting relatives in a county adjacent to Tallahatchie. He'd either wolf-whistled a white woman or called her *Baby*; no one was quite sure.

It was decided by some, however, that Till had insulted the nearest thing to an angel walking God's planet. Condemned as an *uppity nigra* who didn't know his place, Till was dragged from his bed three nights later and brutally murdered. Those who killed him went to bed that night with their consciences clear, and the jury that acquitted them of his murder at the ensuing trial, similarly returned to their beds untroubled.

The murder of Emmett Till horrified Nancy and her parents as much as it disgusted the nation. She refused to defend the actions of those responsible or excuse the ignorance and bigotry that caused them to act the way they did. She believed they were uncharacteristic of Mississippians, aberrations. Eventually, however, she came to wonder if this was really so.

As Nancy spent more time away from home, she became increasingly distanced from the romantic memories of her childhood idyll. In succeeding visits to the Delta, the scales that blinded her while living there gradually fell from her eyes. She started to notice the poverty and the gulf that divided the lifestyles of the privileged white few from the unfortunate black many. She saw the Negroes' cabins for what they were – shacks, more suited to hens than humans: leaking roofs, broken windows repaired with cardboard, torn screens and no plumbing. She noticed too, the deep creases in the Negroes' faces, and the look of their being much older than their actual years. More disturbing still for her was the realisation that her own family's wealth was built on such poverty.

Nancy's parents were paternalistic in the best sense, but within that word lay the dichotomy. The relationship between them and their Negroes was never one based on equality. In reality, her parents viewed them as children whose care was their obligation. In return for this care was an unspoken understanding that Negroes would pay them certain dues: they would defer to their judgements, never speak back, contradict or – God forbid – sass them.

Privately, her father criticised the ways of Mississippi, bemoaned the fact that Negroes could never expect justice from white juries, and recognised the anomaly of black people being barred from exercising democratic rights in what, supposedly, was the world's greatest democracy. He would admit that change had to take place, but maintained that such change could only come from within – and that it would be slow. The worst thing that could happen, he argued, was if outside pressure was brought to bear on the state. He held that it was always easier for people to be influenced by principle the further they were from a situation.

Apart, however, from taking out a subscription to the *Delta Democrat Times*, the state's only liberal newspaper, her father appeared to do little if anything to bring about change. He protested the verdict of the Emmett Till trial, for instance, but only in private. In truth, Hilton Travis could never afford to be seen as a 'nigger lover' by the surrounding white communities. The decade of the sixties might have dawned in America, but in Mississippi the year was still 1890.

At Duke, Nancy joined in the civil rights movement, but with the proviso that she would never take part in any activities within Mississippi. Despite all her soul-searching and new-found insights, when the moment of truth came she proved as incapable as her father of taking any kind of action there. She believed such undertakings would be tantamount to throwing bricks through her parents' windows, and she could predict the hurt and embarrassment it would cause them. She was as much a prisoner of Mississippi as her father, tied to the place of her birth, her home and her family.

Freedom Riders

Gene and Bob struck up an unlikely friendship. Bob would swing onto campus in his worn-out car at no particular time, and with no prior notice. If Gene didn't have classes to attend or his cadaver to dissect, they would grab a bite to eat or drink a coffee together. Oddly for two people who'd met through a mutual interest in civil rights, they talked about anything and everything but civil rights: Bob's time in the army, the country of Vietnam where he'd been stationed and of which most Americans still hadn't heard; Gene's cadaver, their backgrounds, their hopes and Nancy.

Although Bob always arrived unexpectedly, there came a time when Gene could predict his arrival. The muffler on Bob's car was as old as the rest of the vehicle and could be heard from at least six blocks away; in its wake would trail a pall of blue smoke.

'Why don't you get yourself a new car?' Gene once asked him.

'Hell man, I'm black an' no job. I start drivin' roun' in an El Dorado or some such automobile, an' the police gonna think I'd stole it or was pimpin' girls. I prefer the low-profile approach to life, man: under the radar.'

'How can you possibly think you have a low profile when you're driving around making such a damned racket? Some of my friends in the Medical School already think you're dealing drugs and, what's worse, that I'm buying them from you!'

'Well that jus' plain racist! See what me an' my brothers have to put up with?' He paused for a moment and then turned to Gene. 'I don't suppose you in the market?'

'Give me a break, Bob! I don't want to get kicked out.'

'Jus' thought I'd aks.' He paused, and with a mischievous grin on his face said: 'Nancy smokes dope... bes' grade too. Gets it from me. She got no problem doin' business with a black man.'

'Nancy smokes dope? I didn't know that,' Gene said, unable to disguise his surprise.

'How long the two o' you been goin' out – four months?' Bob asked.

'About that.'

'An' you ain't never see'd her smoke pot?'

'No.'

'Well that's 'cos she don't. I was jus' foolin' with you, Med'cine Man. Ha!'

'Jesus, Bob! Why do you do that? Why do you always screw with people.'

'I guess it the black man's burden, Gene. I ain't got no choice in the matter, man. How else we gonna get things movin'? Gotta cause us a few waves or that tired ol' man rowin' his boat ashore ain't never gonna reach dry land.'

'Well, just make sure you don't sink him,' Gene said.

'You a one to talk,' Bob countered. 'People still aksin' me 'bout yo' air-conditionin' speech!'

Gene didn't take the bait. He'd learned from Nancy that sometimes the best way to deal with Bob was to ignore him. 'I'm off to class,' he said. 'See you at the meeting tonight. I gather it's an important one.'

'You bet yo' sweet ass,' Bob said. 'An' don't fo'get to bring Nance with you. She'll be scared shitless by this 'n. We talkin' Miss'ippi, man. Ha!'

As usual it was Steve Barrentine who took charge of proceedings. He explained to the gathered few (still no more than twenty attended these meetings), that the Congress of Racial Equality (CORE) had decided to test the effectiveness of a recent ruling by the Supreme Court that interstate bus stations could no longer discriminate against interstate travellers – whatever the local custom. Segregation of waiting rooms, restaurants and toilets had theoretically been ended.

'But we all know what theory is, don't we?' Steve continued.

'Theory?' Bob suggested.

'Exactly!' Steve replied, taking Bob's comment seriously. 'And if we don't challenge it, that's just what it's going to stay. We have to make sure it *does* become practice. For this reason, CORE's organising a bus expedition through the Deep South. It's leaving Washington in early May and then heading towards Mississippi and picking up additional activists on the way. Whatever the provocation, all responses will, as usual, be peaceful and non-violent.

'They've asked us to provide three volunteers, and I'm glad to say we have them. Bob, Nancy, Gene: take a bow will you. You have our thanks.'

The meeting broke into applause. Bob stood up with a big grin on his face and bowed theatrically. Gene and Nancy just looked at each other: it was the first either of them had heard of this. Bob winked and mouthed: 'I'll explain later.'

When the meeting finally ended, Nancy marched up to Bob. 'My place. Now!'

'How could you, Bob?' she shouted at him when he walked through the door. 'You should have asked us first! Gene and I still have classes to attend and assignments to turn in. We can't suddenly drop everything. And I've told you before: I'm *not* going to Mississippi.'

'Aw c'mon, Nance. It's almos' the end o' the semester. Classes an' exams will be overed with by then, an' if you ain't finished yo' work you can get extensions. We talkin' two, maybe three weeks o' yo' lives. This a chance fo' you – fo' the three of us – to do somethin' useful fo' a change, steada jus' jawin' the whole time. An' it'll be fun. You can get off the bus in Alabama, Nance. Ain't no need fo' you to go to Miss'ippi.

'An' Gene, yo' cadaver ain't goin' no place, man. He'll wait fo' you. Not like he's gonna miss you cuttin' into him, is he? He'll be prob'ly glad o' the rest: give him a chance to get his strength back!'

The three of them joined the bus in Richmond, Virginia. The first few days were uneventful: they got out of the bus, ate food at still segregated counters and then climbed back on to the bus; the only danger any of them could foresee was haemorrhoids. In North Carolina, however, things started to change. After the bus arrived in Charlotte, one of the black riders went into the bus station's barbershop and asked for a trim. Refused his haircut, he in turn refused to leave the premises and was thereupon arrested for trespassing. The bus rolled on without him, and in Rock Hill, South Carolina, three riders were attacked by a waiting crowd.

In Atlanta, the Freedom Riders – as they now called themselves – divided into two groups and headed to Birmingham, Alabama, in two separate buses: a Trailways and a Greyhound. Bob, Gene and Nancy climbed aboard the Greyhound bus, and Bob lay down on the back seat and fell fast asleep. When a rock sailed through a window six miles from Anniston, he remained sleeping; the incendiary bomb that followed similarly failed to wake him.

The riders quickly disembarked. Fending off blows from the Klansmen who now surrounded them, it took a moment for Gene to realise that Bob was still on the blazing bus. After checking that Nancy was in no immediate danger, he rammed a peaceful and non-violent fist into the nearest face and climbed back on to the Greyhound. He fought his way through the flames and smoke to the backseat, where Bob still slept. He slapped him hard on the face, yelled at him, pulled him to a sitting position and slapped him again. Bob woke up, and fortunately for both of them his reflexes kicked in. Together they scrambled off the bus and reached safety only seconds before it exploded. Nancy burst into tears and Gene put his arms around her.

'Man, that the las' time I takin' sleepin' pills!' Bob said.

It was a more sober group of people that continued the journey through Alabama. They were attacked again in Birmingham and three of them hospitalised. In Montgomery it got worse and, there, the journey came to its end.

The city police commissioner of Montgomery had refused to provide the Freedom Riders with any sort of protection, and when they arrived at the city's Union Bus Terminal they were immediately surrounded by a hostile crowd of some 3,000 people. Fist fights broke out and, once again, the Freedom Riders were forced to defend themselves. White women joined in the affray this time, swearing at the girl riders and swinging purses at them.

Nancy was hit but unhurt, and Gene and Bob managed to escape with only cuts and bruises. Black bystanders at the Bus Terminal were less lucky: some had their bones broken and some set on fire. US Marshals and the National Guard appeared the next morning, but by then the civil rights activists had already decided to call it a day. Gene, Nancy and Bob returned home. Mississippi, they figured, would be worse still.

Life for the three of them returned to normal. Their friends in the civil rights group hailed them as heroes and Gene, in particular, drew praise after Bob recounted how the Medicine Man had saved his life on the Aniston road. But for the time being they placed activism on hold. Bob returned to the business of being Bob, and Gene and Nancy focused on each other.

Androcles and the Lioness

'They're just two of the sweetest people, Gene. I can't believe they're so nice. You're sure they *are* your parents?'

Nancy and Gene had spent Thanksgiving holiday with Gene's family, and were now returning to Durham.

'I remember them hanging around the house a lot when I was growing up, so I'm guessing they are,' Gene replied. 'Anyway, why does their niceness surprise you? Are you saying that I'm not nice?'

'You're nice enough,' Nancy said, patting him on the knee. 'At least you don't get on my nerves. But your parents are more sociable than you are. You have to admit that.'

'It's not a matter of sociability. I just don't like small talk. I'm no good at it, and I always end up saying something stupid.'

'Tell me something I don't know!' Nancy laughed. 'And drive faster, will you? The movie's going to be over by the time we get home.'

'I'm driving the speed limit, Nancy, and I'm not getting a ticket just to make the start of some dumb art movie. Anyway, a snail has a faster pace than those films. We could turn up ten minutes from the end and still understand the plot.'

'It's not just the plot, silly; it's the meaning and the nuances. You're such a Philistine, Gene. Do you know that? I'm trying to bring some culture into your life and this is the thanks I get.'

'I've got enough culture in my life already. I'm going out with you, remember.'

'Oh hush! The only culture in your life is television. If it was up to you, all we'd ever do is stay home and watch stupid game shows. We wouldn't go to the theatre, we wouldn't go to museums or art galleries, and we probably wouldn't even go to concerts. How many times do I have to tell you that you can't live life on a couch or in a laboratory? There are too many places to see, too many other experiences to be had.'

'And how would any of that be of help to my patients? If they come to me and I can't figure out what's wrong with them, what am I supposed to tell them? "I'm sorry, Mrs Forrester, I can't quite put my finger on what's ailing you at the moment, but if it's of any consolation I could always tell you about the Fellini film I saw the other night or show you some of the snapshots I took when I was vacationing in London last summer".'

'Just drive, Gene! You might not have any interest in a life but I do, and I'm not prepared to waste mine stuck in a car with you.' She then prodded him in the ribs and Gene flinched.

'For God's sake, Nancy, don't do that when I'm driving! You'll cause an accident.'

Nancy started to laugh and prodded him again.

'I'm warning you, you do that one more time and I'll stop the car and make you walk. I'm not kidding!'

'Of course you are. You'd never do anything to hurt me. You love me too much.'

'I must have been drunk when I told you that.'

'You didn't have to tell me. I knew it already. I know you better than you know yourself – and I know for a damned fact that you can drive over sixty and not get us killed!'

'You've never said that you loved me,' Gene grumbled. 'Do you?'

'Maybe. You should know if a person loves you.'

'Why won't you say it, though?'

'Because,' Nancy teased.

'Because what?'

'Just because.'

She smiled at him, snuggled closer and rested her head on his shoulder. Gene bent towards her and kissed her on the forehead.

'I don't know if we'll ever get married, Gene, but I think you'll always be my friend. You'd do anything for me, wouldn't you?'

'Not right at this moment, I wouldn't.'

Nancy raised her head from his shoulder, kissed his ear and ran her tongue inside it. 'You're sure?'

'Don't, Nancy!'

They made it back to Durham in time for the film, and afterwards drove to a newly opened restaurant. It had a rustic feel to it, sawn-timbered tables and benches, and the food on the menu was down-home.

'Would you like to talk about the film, Gene, or would that embarrass you?'

'The only thing that embarrasses me is the fact that I shelled out five bucks to see it! I don't speak French, Nancy. How the hell am I supposed to discuss a film that I haven't even understood?'

'The movie was subtitled, Gene. You were supposed to read the subtitles!'

'I couldn't. I didn't have my glasses with me.'

'Why didn't you say something, then? We could have left early.'

'Because you were enjoying it – and *I* was happy to waste two hours of my life for the enjoyment of yours. Remember that next time you're *stuck* in a car with me, will you?'

Nancy smiled and pinched his cheek. 'You poor baby,' she said. 'Why do you put up with me? If you treated me this way I'd dump you in a lake.'

The meal passed in similarly discordant harmony, and when the check came Nancy took care of it. 'My treat,' she said. 'You paid for the film.'

They got up to leave and Nancy gave a short scream. 'God, Gene. Look at that!' she said, holding out her index finger. 'Do you think I should go to the Student Health Centre?'

Gene examined her finger. A large splinter had embedded itself in the flesh and the wound was bleeding. 'There's no need for us to go to the Health Centre. I can take care of this.' He wrapped Nancy's finger in a paper napkin and then helped her to the car.

'It hurts, Gene. I mean, *really* hurts! You wouldn't believe the pain I'm in. I think I'm going to faint.'

Gene kept his face straight and drove them to his apartment. There he had Nancy lie down on the couch. He took a pair of tweezers from a small case he kept in the bedroom, and holding Nancy's finger with one hand and the tweezers in the other started to pull the splinter, slowly, carefully.

'Ow-ow-ow, Gene! You're hurting me!'

'Stop fidgeting, Nancy! It's almost out. Please, just keep still!'

But Nancy didn't. She pulled away from him and the splinter broke off in the tweezers, leaving a small sliver below the surface.

'Shit, Nancy! I'll have to use a needle now. Why can't you just do as you're told for once?'

He saw tears welling in her eyes and involuntarily started to laugh.

'It's not funny, Gene!'

'I'm sorry, Nancy. I know it's not. But one day we'll look back on this and laugh.'

'You really think so? God, you can be such a jerk! It's *your* fault I got this splinter in the first place. It was you who insisted we go to that damn restaurant. Why did you have to take me there?'

'Because you were telling me in the car how much you liked new experiences. We'd never been to that restaurant before, and so eating there *was* a new experience. It's impossible to please you, Nancy. Have you ever thought about that?'

Nancy pushed her lips into a pout, and Gene went to the kitchen to retrieve a needle from a small sewing kit his mother had bought him when he'd first gone to university. While he was there, he poured a large glass of brandy for Nancy.

'This is how it was done in the olden days, before anaesthetic,' he said, handing her the glass. 'People had limbs sawn off and bullets extracted, and all they had to dull the pain was alcohol. I'm pretty certain a glass of brandy will do it for a splinter.'

'It's goddamn 1962, Gene! We're not living in the olden days! I knew we should have gone to the Health Centre. *They'd* have given me a local anaesthetic.'

'They wouldn't have even given you a beer! Now stop being such a milquetoast and drink it.'

He struck a match and ran the flame along the needle, and then waited for it to cool. Once Nancy had calmed, he took a firmer hold of her finger and carefully picked at the flake.

'I hate you, Gene. *Really* hate you,' Nancy slurred. 'I'm never going to be nice to you again.'

Gene smiled. 'Will I notice the difference?'

'You know you will, you big lug.'

Gene continued to work on Nancy's finger until no trace of the wooden fragment remained. He then dabbed the wound with antiseptic and covered it with a Band-Aid.

'You want me to drive you home?'

'No, I'll stay the night here. If my finger falls off I'll need someone to put it back on. And don't for a minute think that I've forgiven you, because I haven't.'

Rather than unpack her overnight bag, Nancy cleaned her teeth with Gene's toothbrush and then climbed into bed. Gene joined her there and she nuzzled up to him.

'I'm sorry for being such a wuss, Gene. I'm not very good with pain. And I didn't mean those horrible things I said to you. You know that, don't you? It amazes me how you cope with my moods; you do it so well. Anyway, thanks for saving me tonight. I'll always be able to count on you to save me, won't I? You're my very own Androcles.'

'Who's Androcles?'

Nancy rested on an elbow and looked down on him. 'You're telling me you don't know who Androcles is? You've never read the story of Androcles and the lion?'

'No. I've never heard of him or the lion.'

'God, Gene! This is what happens when you live your life on a couch.' She punched him on the arm and then rolled on to her back. 'You should be ashamed of yourself. And I'm definitely not being nice to you now!'

'I wouldn't expect any patient to be nice to me, Nancy. It's against medical ethics. I could get thrown out of school.'

'Well, in that case, get ready to be thrown out of school then, because my ethics are more than okay with it!'

There are billions of people in the world, and many millions of them in the 1960s lived in the United States. In theory, and with time, Gene and Nancy could have fallen in love with hundreds of other people. They did, however, fall in love with each other, and believed each to be the fulfilment of the other's life; the proverbial needle discovered in their own backyard haystack. They talked of a future together and of marriage.

Like all couples they argued – maybe more than most – but they felt comfortable arguing, and doubted the nature of any relationship characterised by a lack of argument. The sun set on many of these differences of opinion, and days would often pass without any sort of communication between them, until one or the other would break the deadlock with a phone call or a visit.

It was the occasional silences when they were together, however, that confused and worried Gene. They could be lying side by side, either touching or only inches apart, when Gene would suddenly sense a gulf between them of unfathomable and mysterious depth. Nancy would be in her own world, distant and unreachable, lost in thoughts she'd never share or admit to having.

'Penny for them,' he used to say.

'Nothing to buy,' she'd answer with a forced smile.

'You know I love you, don't you?'

'Of course you do,' she'd answer, and then move away from him. Gene would lie there uncertain.

In the summer of 1963, however, things between them were good, and Nancy invited Gene to spend the last week of August with her and her family in the Delta.

Oaklands

Gene and Nancy flew to Memphis and were met at the airport by Nancy's sister, Ruby, and the heat of an oven. While Gene struggled with the suitcases, the two sisters ran to each other and hugged. Catching up to Nancy, Gene held out his hand to Ruby, who brushed it aside and hugged him. She told him she was pleased to meet him after hearing so much about him for so long, and teased Nancy for not bringing him home sooner.

'I think she was afraid you'd fall in love with me,' Ruby said.

Slightly shorter than her sister, Ruby was also darker complexioned and had the blackest of hair. She also carried more weight than Nancy, but the kind of weight Rubens had been happy to immortalize.

Driving south into Mississippi, Ruby asked Gene what Nancy had told him about the Delta.

'Only that it's flat,' Gene replied.

'Oh boo, Nancy. Shame on you,' she said. 'You didn't tell Gene how it got its name?'

'No,' Nancy said. 'Are you going to?'

'Damn right I am, sister. Now listen up, Gene, because all your friends back home'll want to hear this. It's called the Delta because it's shaped liked a D. Delta's the Greek name for a D. Did you know that?'

Gene nodded.

'Anyway, it stretches two hundred miles from Memphis in the north to Vicksburg in the south – there's a big Civil War battlefield there – and at its widest point it's no more than eighty-five miles. So if you draw a straight line from Memphis to Vicksburg, and then a curved one from Vicksburg to Memphis taking in the widest point, you get the letter D. Now that's interesting.

'Mom and Pop live in Tallahatchie County, but there are eleven others. I live in Leflore County, that's another one, so that leaves ten. Nancy, are you going to tell Gene what the names of the other ten are?'

'No,' Nancy said. 'I doubt Gene's that interested.'

'You are interested too, aren't you, Gene? Your friends back home'll want to know this as well.'

Gene said he was interested.

'In alphabetical order,' Ruby continued, 'they are Bolivar, Coahoma, Humphreys, Issaquena – that's my favourite name – Quitman, Sharkey, Sunflower, Tunica, Washington and Yazoo. And do you know how many acres the Delta has? Four million! Did you know that, Nancy?'

'No,' Nancy said. 'I don't know why you just don't buy a bus and set yourself up as a tour guide.'

'I could do that,' Ruby laughed. 'I love this place. I wouldn't live anywhere else in the whole world – and I've been to lots of places too, Gene. I'm going to die here and be buried here. Make the soil even more fertile. You might want to make a note of this too, Gene, but the soil here is twenty-seven feet deep. It's the best soil in the whole damned country!'

'That's because Miss'ippi was the last state to emerge from the mud.'

'Oh boo, Nancy. Don't come bringing any of your eastern ways back home with you. You know you love it too. Say you do or I'm stopping the car right now.'

'I do,' Nancy said.

'That's what she'll be saying to you soon, Gene. I dooo. I dooo.' Ruby then burst out laughing and didn't stop for what seemed like three miles.

Nancy rolled her eyes, but it was clear she enjoyed every second of her sister's company. 'Don't take what she says too seriously,' she whispered to Gene. Gene smiled, but sat there feeling uncertain again.

'How's Homer doing?' Nancy asked.

'He's doing fine, doll. In fact, I'd go so far as to say mighty fine. He treats me well and buys me presents. If he'd just do something about his damned last name, life would be perfect.'

'Homer's last name is Comer,' Nancy told Gene.

'Can you believe it? Homer Comer! I'm Mrs Homer Comer, for God's sake! He was once stopped by the police in Memphis for going through a red light, and when he told them his name was Homer Comer they thought he was taking the P-I-S-S. Homer Comer! I ask you. He almost got his sweet fanny hauled off to jail that night. I mean, it's like you being called Gene Bean or Gene Mean, Gene. What parent does that to a child – and to their child's wife?'

The car had turned off the main highway and was now travelling through the Delta proper. Gene wasn't sure what he'd expected when Nancy had told him it was flat. The Delta wasn't just flat, it was prostrate; level beyond imagination and endlessly so. But there was also an unexpectedly strange beauty to it: the cotton globes covering the flat fields were of the purest white and shimmered in the sun's glare.

The conversation between Nancy and her sister turned more serious when Nancy asked how her Mom was doing.

'She's doing okay, I suppose,' Ruby answered, 'but she's still as forgetful. Maybe more so. She scared me the other week when the two of us were driving to Memphis to visit Daisy. We'd been chatting away, and all of a sudden she just turned to me and asked me who I was. I said: 'Mom, it's me – your daughter, Ruby!' And she looked so relieved and happy when I told her, I could have burst into tears. It's scary, Nancy. I'm wondering if she isn't going to go like Grandmamma. Daddy says she won't, and he's going to make sure she sees the best people. He's already taken her to doctors in Memphis and Jackson, and now he's got the name of a specialist in New York.'

'It just seems so unfair,' Nancy said. 'She's barely into her sixties. I hope to God she doesn't go like Grandmamma.'

For the next fifteen minutes or so, conversation in the car was sparse and eventually stalled into silence. It was a relief when Ruby squealed out: 'Oaklands!' The car passed through two large brick pillars set at either side of an entrance. *Oaklands* was written in large brass letters on one pillar and *Plantation* on the other. Large trees lined the drive.

'Oaks?' Gene asked.

'Yup,' Nancy said. 'Imagination's always been a Travis strong point. The memory's shit these days, but the imagination's still okay.'

'Nancy! Wash your mouth out!' Ruby rebuked. 'Don't let Mommy and Daddy hear you talking like that.'

'Sorry,' Nancy said. 'What I meant to say was S-H-I-T.'

Gene had seen photographs of houses like this in magazines, but had never supposed he'd ever be a guest in one. Six huge Doric columns rose from ground level to a hipped roof. The façade of the two-storey house was symmetrical, with windows evenly spaced. The second floor bedrooms opened on to a balcony that ran the width of the house, and below the balcony a covered porch similarly ran its width.

'Wow, this is some house you've got yourselves,' Gene said. 'How old is it?'

'The original house was built in 1853,' Ruby said, relieved to be back in her role as tour guide. 'It burned down in 1925 after a lightning strike, and when Grandaddy rebuilt it he decided to use bricks instead of wood – which the house was originally built from. He figured if, God forbid, there was another fire, the house would burn more slowly and the fire trucks stand a better chance of arriving in time to save it. Wood just goes up in no time. The pillars are original though: they're not wood. You'll see a lot of big houses like this in Miss'ippi, and they're all built in this ancient Greek style. Do you know why that is, Gene?'

Gene said he didn't.

'It's because ancient Greece represents the spirit of democracy – or that's what people at the time thought.'

Gene searched Ruby's face for a hint of irony, but didn't find any. *Spirit of democracy* juxtaposed with *Mississippi* had to be oxymoronic.

Two bird dogs came bounding from the side of the house. They ran straight to Nancy, who bent down and fussed with them, greeting them by name: Jefferson and Franklin. The door of the house opened and an elderly black lady walked out, dressed in a server's uniform and wearing a large white apron.

'What y'all doin' standin' out here in the sun? Nancy, come give me a hug an' introduce me to that gen'leman friend o' yo's.'

Nancy stopped playing with the dogs and ran to give the black lady a big hug, indicating to Gene that he should follow her.

'My girl, you all skin an' bones; ain't nothin' o' you to get ahol' of. They ain't feedin' you? How you gonna get chil' rearin' hips if you don't eat nothin'?'

'I've done all the growing I'm going to do, Dora, and my hips are just fine, thank you very much. And who said anything about me wanting children? Who's going to look after you if I leave and start a family?'

'Oh hush yo' mouth, girl. I don't need no lookin' after. What you think I married Ezra fo' – his good looks? Now introduce me to that fine lookin' man by yo' side.'

'Gene, this is Dora. Dora's been with us forever and a day, because Mommy and Daddy are too scared to fire her. Make sure you don't cross her or she might stick a fork in your back when you're not looking.'

Dora laughed and took Gene's hand. 'Mr Gene, I very pleased to meet you. I surprised you ain't bin scared off by Nancy's big mouth. Sure has a big one, fo' one so skinny.'

Gene smiled, and said he was pleased to meet her, too. 'Nancy's already told me about you, Dora. I hear your cooking's the best in the Delta.'

'Sure is, Mr Gene. An' I gonna make it my business to fatten the two o' you up.'

Ruby went to give Dora a hug. 'Don't go ignoring me, Dora, just because Nancy's home with her gentleman friend. I don't leave you for months on end, and besides, you've known me longer. Where is everyone, anyway? This place is quiet as a Sunday.'

'Yo' Daddy, Brandon an' Ezra's out lookin' for Miss Martha,' Dora said, more serious now. 'She went walkin' this mornin' an' she still gone. Missed lunch an' ever'thin'. They be back by the by, so no use you frettin' yo'self. It happened b'fore an' it'll happen again. Now get yo'selfs unpacked an' I'll fix you a drink an' a bite to eat. You must be wore out by all yo' travellin'.'

Ruby and Nancy looked at each other, and Gene looked at both of them; neither of them spoke. They picked up their cases and went inside the house. Nancy and Gene climbed an imposing staircase that led to the second floor rooms. Nancy put down her case outside her own room, and then showed Gene to the guest bedroom.

'What's wrong with your Mom, Nancy?' Gene asked her.

'Can we talk about this later?' she asked. 'I will tell you. I want to tell you. But when I do, I'll also want to ask something of you. Just let's enjoy the next few days. There's plenty of time for everything else.'

'Sure,' Gene said, 'Whenever you're ready.' The two of them then held each other in silence until a gong sounded.

'Time to go downstairs,' Nancy said. 'You don't want to get on Dora's wrong side on your first day. She's quite something isn't she?'

'Yes,' Gene said. 'I think it's safe to say that.'

Downstairs, Dora had laid out plates of sandwiches and a pitcher of iced lemonade.

'I want it all eaten,' she said. 'Ever' las' crumb! An' Mr Gene, I don't wan' no soft-shoe walkin' to Nancy's room in the night.'

'Dora!' Ruby shrieked. 'You can't say things like that. Gene's our guest.'

'An' I sure he'll behave like one, but if he anythin' like Ezra…'

'Maybe we're already doing it,' Nancy teased.

'Nancy!' Ruby shrieked.

'Well maybe you is an' maybe you ain't, but there ain't nothin' happenin' in this house,' Dora said. 'You hear me?' she said, turning to look at Mr Gene.

The front door opened and voices sounded in the hallway. Brandon Travis walked into the room, hugged his sisters and shook Gene's hand weakly.

'Daddy sends his apologies for not being here to welcome you, Gene, but he'll see you in the drawing room at seven for pre-dinner drinks and formally welcome you to Oaklands then.'

'Where is he now?' Nancy asked.

'He's taken Mom to lie down.'

'So what happened? Is she okay?'

'I guess,' Brandon said with a shrug. 'We found her wandering on one of the dirt tracks, about a mile from the house. She's forever disappearing these days and it's becoming a problem. I don't know why Daddy doesn't just put a leash on her or keep her in the paddock.'

'Don't talk like that about Mom,' Ruby scolded. 'She can't help herself!'

'It's okay for you and Nancy, Ruby – you're never here! It's not your lives that are being affected by her behaviour so don't go lecturing *me*! I've got more important things to do with my damn time than play hide-and-seek with my mother. I was supposed to be spraying crops today. Maybe the two of you should consider spending more time here and sharing the load a bit more.

'Anyway, I have work to do. I'll see you at seven.'

Five minutes before seven, Nancy knocked on Gene's door, and together they descended the staircase. The drawing room had an expensive formality to it, and an emphasis on antique furniture and animal death. The floor was spread with skins of exotic animals, and the walls were lined with an array of heads. In particular, Gene was drawn to a footstool made from the lower portion of an elephant's leg, and a giant bear skin that lay in front of the large fireplace. He wondered if there was now a three-legged elephant hobbling around Africa, and a bear shivering from cold somewhere in Oregon.

There were shelves against the far wall displaying ceramic and glass ornaments and stuffed birds, and a display case against another wall crammed with antique firearms and daggers. Reading matter displayed consisted of local and state newspapers and glossy magazines: the Charleston *Sun-Sentinel*, the Memphis *Commercial Appeal*, the Jackson *Clarion Ledger*, the Greenville *Delta Democrat Times*, *Harper's*, *Time*, *Life*, the *New Yorker* and the *Saturday Evening Post*. The family obviously read a lot, Gene concluded, just not books.

Ruby was already there, and shortly they were joined by Brandon and his wife Becky. Conversation and atmosphere nosedived immediately. Perhaps noticing this, Ezra assiduously attended to their drinks, ensuring that no glass was ever empty.

Gene checked his watch: Mr and Mrs Travis were running fifteen minutes late and he'd already drunk two gin and tonics. He was about to catch Ezra's eye to request a refill, when Hilton Travis walked into the room with a smiling Martha on his arm.

Hilton and Martha Travis looked every inch the couple. No one, Gene thought, would have ever raised an eyebrow to question why either one was with the other. Hilton was tall, slim and his features were pale but handsome. He had thick greying hair, worn longer than the norm for men of his age, and a striking aquiline nose. He wore an expensive linen suit and a striped military-looking tie.

Martha, on the other hand, had the dark complexion of Ruby, and the same dark hair that showed only traces of life's autumnal grey. Her face was tanned but relatively unlined, and she wore little make-up. She was dressed in a bright flowered dress with a shawl draped over her shoulders.

Nancy and Ruby went straight to their parents, hugged and kissed them. Brandon and Becky kept their distances. Gene stood there awkwardly waiting to be introduced, wondering if somehow they'd forgotten he was there. Ezra came to his rescue and handed him another gin and tonic.

'Mommy, Daddy, this is Gene,' Nancy said eventually. Gene shook hands with them both and, for some unknown reason, bowed his head Teutonic style as he did so.

'I'm very pleased to meet you,' he said.

'The pleasure's all ours, Gene,' Hilton Travis drawled. 'And I must apologise for not being here to greet you when you arrived. Martha decided to go for a walk today and got herself lost.' He smiled at Martha when he said this.

'Oh my,' Martha said, 'I don't know what I was thinking. I've walked this land my entire life and I've never once got lost. Why it happened today of all days I have no idea, but I got good and properly discombobulated. I guess this is what happens when you start to lose your marbles,' she laughed. 'But I tell you, when I saw Ezra, I've never been gladder to see a person in my whole life. I thought I was going to be out there forever with the snakes and mosquitoes.'

'You're not losing your marbles, Mamma,' Ruby said, 'and you've got to stop saying that. The doctor said that with the right medication you'll be fine.'

Martha smiled at her. 'You're so sweet Ruby – and you too Nancy: I know you worry about me as well. I hate to be a bother to you both.'

'Mom, you're not a bother!' Nancy said. 'If you were, I probably *would* put you out with the cottonmouths and bugs, but it's not going to happen!'

'Oh be whisht, Nancy,' Martha said, a beam stretching from one side of her face to the other. 'Sometimes you talk such foolishness.'

Gene imagined that Brandon stood there thinking it would be okay by him if his Mom got lost for good among the cottonmouths and the bugs; at least he'd be able to get on with his tractoring, or whatever it was he did on the farm.

Ezra had barely poured Hilton and Martha their drinks when Dora came into the room and told them dinner was ready to be served.

'Give us five minutes will you, Dora,' Hilton said. 'Miss Martha and I have only just made it downstairs.'

'Well, jus' don't go blamin' me if the food gets spoilt,' she said. 'Not as if I ain't got nothin' better to do wit' my time.'

'Boy, Ezra, you sure got yourself one cantankerous woman there,' Hilton said.

Ezra smiled. 'You bes' get yo'selves in there or it gonna be the worse for me, Mr Travis. Dora'll blame me fo' pourin' y'all too many drinks or pourin' 'em too slowly. Either way, I'll get it.'

'Okay everybody, let's go sit down and take our drinks with us,' Hilton said. 'We can't afford to lose Ezra just yet.'

Once everyone was settled, Martha rang a small hand bell placed next to her on the table and signalled that they were ready to be served. Dora, and a young black girl Gene hadn't seen before, came into the room with bowls of steaming soup. Everyone started to eat except Martha, who appeared to be staring at the mass of silver cutlery surrounding her plate. It seemed to Gene that she was unsure of which implement to choose.

'I'm no world's expert on cutlery, Miss Martha, but I find this one is probably best suited for the job.' He then placed a spoon gently in her hand.

'I might be losing my marbles, Gene, but I still know what a spoon is! I was wondering why there was no bread on the table.' She rang the bell again, and told Dora they needed bread.

Dora banged a basket of bread on the table without seeing any need to apologise for the oversight. Gene sat there embarrassed, wanting to apologise but fearful of making matters worse. Nancy and Ruby bit their tongues, while Brandon scowled.

'Nancy tells me you're going to be a doctor, Gene. Are you going to specialise in a particular field or become a general practitioner?' Hilton asked.

'General practitioner, sir,' Gene replied. 'I can't say I've found any particular field that interests me more than another, and I don't want to have to get involved with any kind of cutting. Surgery's my least favourite subject at the moment. It seems I have an aversion to the sight of blood.'

'Well, maybe we can talk about this more once the meal's over,' Hilton said. 'Nancy, how are your studies? Last time we talked, you were reading and enjoying the nineteenth century English poets. Wasn't it Dryden who was your favourite?'

'Hazlitt,' Nancy corrected. 'Hazlitt's my favourite.'

'What I don't understand is what you're going to do when you finish your studies,' Brandon said. 'I mean, what can you do with poems and books when you get down to it?'

'I'll probably write verses for the inside of cards,' Nancy replied. 'Something like: *Dear Brother, I Wish I Had Another.*'

'Now you two be nice to each other,' Martha said. 'Let's not spoil the meal, and remember we have a guest with us.' She turned to Gene. 'What's your name again, dear?'

'Gene, Miss Martha. Gene.'

Gene became further alarmed when Dora served the main course: particularly rare steaks. It struck him that Nancy had failed to mention to either Dora or her parents that since being given a cadaver to dissect, he could no longer eat beef without gagging. Gene looked to Nancy for help, but all she said to him

– rather sharply he thought – was: 'Eat it!'

Gene made willing and cut the steak into pieces, which he then moved around his plate while eating only the vegetables and potatoes. When conversation revolved around others, and no eye was upon him, he carefully picked up pieces of the meat with his fingers and placed them in his jacket pocket. At other times, he put pieces of steak in his mouth and manoeuvred them into his napkin while pretending to wipe his lips. He would then sanitise his mouth by taking a drink of red wine. By the time Dora and her helpmate came to collect the plates, his was as clean as any. 'Well done,' Nancy whispered. 'Mind over matter, right?'

Ruby said her goodbyes before dessert: she had a drive ahead of her and didn't want Homer worrying. As the meal came to an end for the rest of them, Hilton suggested the men step out on to the porch and smoke a cigar.

'One each, or are you going to share the same one?' Nancy asked.

'I think I can run to three,' Hilton said smiling. 'You and Brandon go on ahead, Gene. I'll take Miss Martha upstairs and get her settled. Nancy can give me a hand – unless you'd prefer to help Dora with the dishes?' Nancy pulled a face.

Internally, Gene also pulled a face. Although having promised Nancy to play a full part in the family's conversations, the idea of being alone with Brandon was a presentiment. His situation might have been eased if he'd removed the meat from his pocket before stepping out on to the porch, where Jefferson now lounged.

Smelling the meat, Jefferson raised himself from the floor and walked over to Gene. When Gene tried to push him away, the dog started to bark. Believing that the best way to extricate himself from another potentially embarrassing situation was to feed the meat to the dog, Gene took the steak from his jacket pocket and placed it on the porch floor. It was at this moment that Brandon chose to join him.

When asked by Brandon what he was doing, Gene had no option but to explain his aversion to meat, its origins, and his struggle not to appear rude at the table. It gave the two of them something to talk about, but Gene was left with an uneasy feeling that this wasn't the last he'd hear of the matter.

True enough, it wasn't. The next day, Brandon told Dora that her cooking reminded Gene of dead people.

The Field of Cotton

Gene found the days that followed long and increasingly slow to end. It wasn't simply the fact that it was high summer and the days were naturally long, or that Delta days were always slow to end, but more the strain of actually being there.

Gene had been apprehensive even before arriving at Oaklands. Nancy had given him a long list of pointers of what, and what not, to say. He was to address her father as Sir and her mother as Miss Martha. He was also to make no mention of civil rights unless her father originated the conversation, and he was certainly to make no mention of the bus they'd ridden to Birmingham – two years after the event, and still Nancy hadn't divulged this to her parents. It might also be a good idea, she added, if he made no mention of the fact that his best friend at Duke was an unemployed Negro.

Dora now cold-shouldered him and Ezra, though polite when they bumped into each other, was distant. Conversation with Hilton Travis proved difficult and faltering, and Miss Martha never seemed too sure of who he actually was. On one occasion, she'd reported him to Nancy and asked her to find out from him what his business in the house was.

He met some of Nancy's friends but warmed to none of them, and wondered why she'd befriended them in the first place. The only person he truly liked was Ruby. The atmosphere always lightened when she visited the house. Ditsy as hell and always full of fun, she couldn't have been more different from Homer, who struck Gene as a dufus.

It was while Gene and Nancy were staying with her parents that Martin Luther King stood at the Lincoln Memorial and told a crowd of 200,000 that he had a dream. 'So do I Martin,' Gene thought, 'Just to get out of here!'

The family sat around the television set and watched as King spoke. After only a few minutes, Brandon left the room. Hilton Travis continued to leaf through his newspaper. Dora, who was standing behind them, commented that Martin Luther King was a troublemaker and that no good would come from him stirring things up like this. Nancy watched but made no comment, while Gene pretended to wipe drops of sweat from his face when the occasional tear spilled from his eye.

The day before he and Nancy were due to leave Oaklands, they took a long walk. Nancy led him through the back garden, past the pecan and walnut trees and out to where the cotton grew.

'This is the most beautiful time of the year in the Delta,' she told Gene. 'After the cotton's harvested in the autumn, all that's left are dried stalks. Everything changes from white to brown, to monotony.' Maybe it was this talk of the life cycle that now led Nancy to talk of her mother.

'You might have noticed that Mom's not well.' She gave a deep sigh. 'She's displaying the early signs of Alzheimer's,' she continued, 'and it's only going to get worse. What do you know about Alzheimer's? Is it something you've come across in your studies, yet?'

'We've touched on it,' Gene said. 'All I know is that it's cruel and unforgiving – as much for the family as it is for the person suffering from it. Are you sure it is Alzheimer's? Your Mom seems a bit on the young side to be starting with it now.'

'We're sure,' Nancy said. 'The doctors in Jackson and Memphis don't have any doubts, and the specialist in New York that Ruby talked about would only be advising on treatment. The diagnosis has already been made. He won't be able to change that.

'I saw my Grandmamma suffer from the same thing and it was horrible. She started with the same confusion my Mom's showing. At the time it seemed funny, and even she laughed about the things she did – much like my Mom does now. But then she got depressed, and then irritable – really irritable. She couldn't understand what was happening to her and got scared. She ended up not recognising us, and started to look for people who'd been dead for donkey's years.

'Her personality changed, too. At one time she'd been my favourite of all the family, so sweet and so kind; but then she became abusive and started to say really hateful things and cuss – horrible words. I still don't understand how she ever knew them.

'She lived with us at Oaklands – in the room you're staying in – and Mom and Daddy looked after her for years. It was Dora who took the brunt of her insults though, and for all her foibles and occasional rudenesses, my parents would never dismiss her because of the way she cared for Grandmamma. She was kind and patient with her.

'Eventually, my Gran lost control of her bowels and became as helpless and messy as a new-born babe. It got too much for everyone and my parents had to put her in a nursing home. She lingered there for another two years, alive for the sake of being alive, and when she died, I was glad.

'I hated myself for thinking this, but it's true, I *was* glad. It put her to rest and it brought the nightmare she'd been living to an end. And her death stopped the nightmare for us, too. I still have difficulty remembering her as the person she used to be, rather than the person she became. It's so hard, Gene – really hard. And the same thing's going to happen to my mother.'

Gene listened as the words came pouring out of Nancy, a log jam of fears and emotions undammed.

'The same thing happened to my Grandmamma's mother too. We don't know of any others before then, because people tended to die younger in those days; but there's something hereditary going on – I just know it. And the same thing will probably happen to me.'

She made contact with Gene's eyes and held them. 'I never want to have children, Gene. If I inherit this dementia, I want it stopping with me. I don't want to pass it on to my own children!'

Gene took hold of her hand. 'From what I know, Nancy, Alzheimer's isn't hereditary. There's no documentation or any proof of that being the case. I know you're worried, but I think you're worrying for nothing. Even if it did happen, thirty years from now there'll probably be a cure for it, or at least medication to control it. Things are moving fast in medicine.

I'm sure any children you have would be okay.'

'I don't care what medicine says,' Nancy said, 'or any logic that says it won't happen to me. All I know is that it happens to people in my family – to the women of my family. Something's passed from one generation to the next. Maybe it is a strange thing to happen, and it doesn't fit with medical science, but it's a fact. You have to take my word on this.

'And now I have to ask you something, something I don't think I could ever ask another person.' She let go of Gene's hand and moved away from him, turning her back. 'If it happens to me, Gene, and I get Alzheimer's… I want you to bring it to an end.'

'Of course I'll take care of you, Nancy. That goes without saying.'

'You're not understanding me, Gene. What I'm asking you to do is bring my life to an end – prematurely. I don't want to live through it, and I don't want anyone who knows or loves me to have to live through it with me. There's too much hurt, too much damage. I want people remembering me for the person I was and not for the demon I'll become. Will you promise me, Gene, promise me you'll do this?'

Gene didn't reply immediately. He pulled a cigarette from its pack with his lips and lit it. As he blew the smoke upwards, he noticed white cumulus clouds floating high in the sky without a care in the world. At that moment, he wished that he and Nancy were those clouds.

'But if you feel so strongly about this,' he eventually asked, 'why wouldn't you just take your own life? Why would you need me to do it?'

Nancy now turned to face him. 'Because I don't think I'd be able to do it,' she said. 'A small part of me still thinks that suicide is a sin and that if I killed myself I'd go straight to hell. The larger part of me thinks that I'd never get the timing right – and I don't want my life to end before it absolutely has to. I could live through the early confusion, but once the disease progressed I'd probably lose all knowledge of what I'd intended to do. I wouldn't have a clue what was going on, and if I tried and botched it, I'd be worse off still and probably placed in a mental institution or something. And you'd be a doctor, Gene. You'd be able to judge when the time was approaching; when the time was right. And I know you'd make it painless for me.'

Gene thought about it. He was familiar with the Hippocratic Oath and aware that his intended role in life was to save rather than take lives. Saving lives, however, was one thing; prolonging nightmares another thing altogether. He loved Nancy. She was, and always would be, the priority of his life. He would never willingly allow her to suffer.

'Okay, I'll do it Nancy. You have my word. But don't live your life expecting the worst to happen. It might not. If it does, then I'll take care of it.'

'And whether we're still together or not? Even if we're not a couple, you'll do it? I'd still be able to count on you?'

A quizzical look crossed Gene's face. 'Yes, you have my word on it,' he said, and after a pause asked: 'You don't know something I don't, do you?'

'No,' Nancy said, 'but things happen in life. Bad things.'

That night Nancy did the soft-shoe walk to Gene's room and told him she loved him.

Five months later, Gene and Nancy were no longer a couple. She never returned to Duke after the Christmas vacation, and when Gene arrived back at the university a brief letter awaited him.

Dearest Gene,

I don't think we should see each other again. It breaks my heart to write these words, and I know you'll be just as hurt to read them. Please don't ask me to explain.

I hope you have a great life, darling – and I hope that I have a great life too. I just don't think we can have a great life together. If it's any consolation, and I hope that it is, please know that I'll always love you, and you'll never be far from my thoughts.

Please don't try and contact me. This is difficult enough.

Yours always,

Nancy

The letter came as a shock to Gene. He read and re-read it, puzzled over it for days before eventually placing it in a drawer. What the hell had happened? He'd recently and – to his way of thinking – magnanimously agreed to kill Nancy, and now she'd dropped him like a hat. What kind of gratitude was that?

Nancy was right, however. Reading her words did break his heart.

It would be another forty-five years before he understood them.

Hershey

Hershey is a small town in Pennsylvania, thirteen miles from the state capital of Harrisburg. Surrounded by cows and pastures, it nestles in the rolling hills of Dauphin County and is home to the chocolate manufacturing company of the same name. (The word *nestles* should be used advisedly in these parts, for fear of being confused with the name of the rival Swiss chocolate manufacturing company, Nestlé.)

The man whose name became an eponym for both town and company was Milton Hershey, a leading player in the late nineteenth century world of candy, and considered by many to have been the king of caramels. In 1893, however, Milton renounced this sweetmeat crown and became a convert to milk chocolate. He'd tasted the brown delicacy at a world's fair in Chicago that year, and thereafter lost all interest in caramels; he sold his company in Lancaster and embarked on a mission to bring the luxury of the rich to the taste buds of the ordinary. To this end, he built a factory at Derry Church.

A life in confectionary had sweetened not only Milton's tooth, but also his general disposition. As an employer, he embraced benevolence and exhibited a keen social conscience. Determined that his workers would enjoy the lifestyle of the middle classes, he built a model town for them; a utopia of his own design with schools, sports and leisure facilities. In 1906, the new model town slipped a ring on Derry Church's finger, and Derry Church changed its name to Hershey.

Seventy years later, the Vice President of Milk Production at the Hershey Foods Corporation slipped a ring on the finger of Nancy Travis, and she changed her name to Mrs Arnold Skidmore. In doing so, Nancy exchanged the paternalism of the agrarian south for the paternalism of the industrial north, Oaklands for Hershey. It was progress of a kind, she supposed.

Thirty-one years later still, Eugene Chaney III drove into the town that advertised itself as *The Sweetest Place on Earth,* and checked into a hotel for three nights. If life in cocoa producing countries was cheap, the room rates at Hotel Hershey were anything but.

Doc slept badly that night, worse than usual: a strange bed and thoughts of strange days ahead. He hadn't seen Nancy for well over forty years, and in that time both of them had grown old, married other people and been widowed. This, they had in common. But what of the feelings they'd once had for each other? Were they still existent? Would their history make for awkwardness or could they start out afresh: two friends renewing an old and easy relationship? He had no idea.

Although Nancy's letter had requested Doc not to contact her after her sudden departure from Duke, he had, nonetheless, tried on several occasions: he'd phoned her parents' house, tried to speak with Ruby and written letters. But the Travis wagons had been circled: if it was one thing Mississippians understood, it was defence! The answer was always the same: Nancy had gone away and couldn't be reached. His letters were returned unopened.

Bob proved a good friend during this time. He sympathised, but told Doc he should never expect to make sense of the Delta or its people, and should therefore stop trying.

'Let it drop, Gene. Fo' whatever reason, Nancy's gone an' there ain't no damn thing you can do 'bout it. Jus' make sure you don't lose yo' dignity, man. That's my advice. Control what you can an' let go o' what you cain't. Black pearls o' wisdom an' no charge.'

Doc remembered taking Bob's hand and grasping it firmly, thanking him for both his friendship and his thoughts. Bob had responded by asking Gene if he could borrow ten dollars.

As Doc dressed that morning, he thought about the conversation he and Nancy had had in the cotton field those many years ago. At the time, he'd been naively optimistic that a cure for Alzheimer's would by now have been found, that medication would be available to either solve or manage the condition. Medications had improved, but it seemed that little progress had been made finding a cure. Nancy, however, had been proved right in thinking that the condition might be hereditary in her family.

Although there was still no obvious inheritance pattern to Alzheimer's, clusters of cases in an extremely small number of families had now been documented, and it was agreed that genetic factors could play a role. A gene called Apolipoprotein E found on chromosome 19 was considered a risk factor, and other genes and pathological mutations had also been identified on chromosomes 1, 9, 10, 11, 14 and 21. Even for Doc with his medical training, these numbered chromosomes seemed more like the names of planets in a science fiction movie than anything to do with real life. He knew he would be unable to bring any medical solace to his meeting with Nancy – and that meeting was only two hours away. He finished dressing and went downstairs to eat breakfast.

Nancy had agreed to meet Doc in the formal lobby of the hotel at ten o'clock. She'd told him she was still fine to drive, and that the onset of her Alzheimer's was at a stage that didn't wholly interfere with her day-to-day life.

The lobby was one floor up from the hotel's entrance and designed, Doc supposed, to give the feel of a Spanish courtyard. A turreted balcony ran around its top, and the high ceiling was painted to give the impression of white clouds floating across blue sky. To pass the time, he picked up a brochure from the table nearest to him and read about the various treatments available in the hotel's spa. The therapies were all based on chocolate and roses, and ranged in price: he could have a Whipped Cocoa Bath for $45, a Chocolate Bean Polish for $65, a Mojito Body Wrap for $115 or a Chocolate Fondue Wrap for $120.

He replaced the brochure and looked at his watch: three minutes to ten. He wiped the moisture from the palm of his hand onto his pant leg. He was dressed in his usual attire – plaid shirt and corduroy pants – and started to wonder if he might have underdressed for his meeting with Nancy, especially when surrounded by such opulence.

Doc had always figured that Nancy's beauty would grow with her years, and in thinking this he'd been right. No one would have thought that the elegantly dressed woman who entered the foyer was anything but in the rudest of health. Her face, like her mother's had been at this age, was relatively unlined and there were only slight traces of grey in her hair. She wore a modicum of make-up, no more and no less than was called for, and was dressed in an expensive two-piece suit, emerald green in colour. Doc rose uncertainly as she walked towards him. 'Nancy?'

Nancy's face broke into a smile and she put her arms around him. 'Gene!' They hugged, as he remembered her hugging Ruby.

'You look beautiful,' he told her. 'I always said you'd look better the older you got.'

'And look at you, Gene,' she smiled. 'You look like an old tramp – just as my father predicted… a joke!' she added, when she saw the look of surprise on Doc's face. 'You did graduate though, didn't you? You weren't too broken-hearted when I left you that your whole life went down the pan?'

'I got through it,' Doc said. 'And yes, I graduated. Look at the register if you don't believe me: Dr Eugene Chaney III.'

'I'll take your word for it,' she smiled, 'though anyone can call themselves a doctor these days.'

They ordered coffee from reception and arranged to take it on the terrace. It was too nice a day to sit indoors, and besides, the terrace would afford Doc a good view of the town – its houses, parks, silos and smokestacks. Doc found a couple of rocking chairs at the perimeter of the rooftop, away from the geranium and petunia baskets attracting the bees and, more importantly, well away from the other hotel guests sitting there.

Nancy poured, and asked Gene to tell her about his life: what he'd done, had he married, did he have children, had he been happy?

Doc gave her an outline of his life: his final years in the civil rights movement with Bob, his time as a doctor in Maryland, his marriage to Beth, the birth of Esther, the death of Beth and Esther, his taking over his father's practice, the death of his parents and retirement.

Tears came to Nancy's eyes when he told her about Beth and Esther. She now regretted asking him if his life had been happy. How could it have been?

And now it was her turn, her time to tell Doc of her life. She started in the present and gradually returned to the past, the reason she left Duke. 'I was pregnant, Gene. Pregnant with your child.'

She described the panic that had taken hold of her the month she'd missed her period, and later, when the doctor confirmed her pregnancy. 'I couldn't go through with it, Gene, I just couldn't. I told you why I never wanted children, and I still don't regret having the abortion – especially now. I always wanted the Alzheimer's to end with me. Remember me telling you that?'

Doc nodded.

'But I also knew you wanted children. You were always talking about us having a family, and I knew that if I'd told you I was pregnant you'd have tried to talk me out of an abortion and persuaded me to keep the child. You'd have told me I wouldn't get Alzheimer's, and that if I did, by the time our children were grown up the disease would be a thing of the past. And you'd have been wrong, wouldn't you?'

Doc nodded again. He sensed that Nancy had braced herself for this conversation, had carefully practised the words she now spoke. He was also conscious of the strength draining from her voice.

'I knew when I decided to have the termination, that once I had it I'd never be able to look you in the eye again. If we'd stayed together, Gene, there'd have always been a dark secret I could never have shared with you. How could I? I'd have killed your child – and how would you have still been able to love me knowing that? You might say now that you would have done, but you wouldn't. It would always have been something that hung over us, and eventually it would have broken us. I never wanted you to know. I never wanted you to think of me, or feel about me, any other way than you did the last time you saw me.

'Even though I can forgive myself for doing what I did, I know that what I did to you was unforgivable. It was selfish of me to leave you the way I did, but I was never uncaring: I knew you'd be hurt. I wasn't lying to you when I wrote that I'd always love you. They weren't empty words, and it almost killed me to write them. You'd been the best thing that had ever happened to me. I'd have left Oaklands behind for you, Gene, I honestly would. But everything I did, I thought I was doing for the best, and I hope you can come to accept this – even after the tragedy of losing Esther.

'After you told me about Esther, I wasn't sure if I should go ahead and tell you all this or not, but I think it's important that I'm completely honest with you. You'd have made a great father, I know it, and I hate it that you've never had a full chance to be one – and part of that reason is me. I'm sorry Gene, so very, very sorry. I hope you can forgive me. It's… it's important to me that you do.'

Nancy fell silent and stared down at the hands in her lap, which played together nervously. Doc took hold of them. He couldn't speak. Not once had he ever suspected this to be the reason. He could now only imagine how hard it must have been for her at the time, the intrusive indignity of the procedure she'd undergone, and how scared and alone she must have felt; he should have been there with her. Finally, he whispered: 'It's okay, Nancy, it's okay.'

It was a relief for both of them when the topic had been raised and excised. They were now free to enjoy the days that followed unencumbered by its burden. They strolled down the avenues of Chocolate and Cocoa arm in arm, and explored the lesser streets named after varieties of cocoa beans. Nancy pointed out the brown and silver street lamps made in the shape of Hershey

Kisses, and the sweet smelling mulch made from cocoa husks that protected the roots of the town's plants and hedges. They drank coffee at Fenicci's, visited the town's Grand Theatre at the rear of the Community Centre and, at Nancy's insistence, drove to Chocolate World to experience The Great American Chocolate Tour.

They walked into the building's foyer and down a dark ramp. Under the watchful eye of two young attendants, they climbed carefully into one of the small cars attached to a continuously moving belt, and moved slowly from one illustrated process to the next. They saw how cocoa beans were cleaned, screened, blended, roasted, shattered and milled before milk was added to the mix. Three mechanical cows called Gabby, Harmony and Olympia wagged their tails and sang a song about the importance of cows – and the commentator's voice backed them up: the factories, it said, used a quarter of a million gallons of their milk every day! At the end of the tour, each of them was handed a miniature candy bar: Doc got a small piece of Hershey Milk Chocolate, and Nancy a miniature Heath Bar.

Doc left Chocolate World with no real memory of how chocolate was made, but with the cows' song stuck firmly in his head. What he'd really wanted was a tour of Nancy's missing years.

He didn't have long to wait.

The Missing Years

The abortion had been performed by a doctor in New York City and arranged by her father. Hilton Travis had come into his own during this episode in his daughter's life, and was the only member of the family to ever know of Nancy's pregnancy – or her reasons for termination. Initially, the news had shocked him, but he didn't shout and he didn't scream. Instead, he regarded the problem as if it were a farming complication and proceeded to solve the matter in a practical manner.

Nancy had been only a few courses short of graduating when she'd left Duke, and after the abortion chose to complete her studies at Vanderbilt, a reputable university in Nashville. She then travelled for a year in Europe, spending most of her time in Italy and learning to speak its language. She returned to Oaklands bronzed and refreshed, only to evidence a marked deterioration in her mother – a decline the rest of the family had observed only gradually.

Nancy qualified as a grade school teacher, and after holding positions in the Memphis school system for three years applied for an opening at a private school in Pennsylvania. A friend from her Vanderbilt days, now living in Philadelphia, had forwarded her the advertisement, commenting in an attached note that the post would suit her down to the ground. The school was the Milton Hershey School, and the vacancy was for a teacher of English Literature. Nancy was successful in her application and moved to Hershey.

The Milton Hershey School was funded by a trust established by Milton and his wife Catherine. An expression of their benevolence and childlessness, the school provided a home as well as an education for children of families in financial and social need. Its mission was to nurture these children, build their character and provide them with the necessary skills for future success. The school's *raison d'être* appealed to Nancy, played to her social conscience and salved her self-imposed childlessness.

Nancy proved a born teacher. She developed an easy rapport with her students, inspired in them a love for the written word, and encouraged their creativity. She also took an interest in their welfare outside the classroom, sympathetically listening to their problems and proffering advice when able. She continued to teach at the school after she married, and retired at the age of sixty. Old students would drop by her house and some, after her husband's death, became her friends.

Nancy met her husband-to-be in a road accident. Arnold Skidmore had been driving home from a visit to one of the Mennonite dairy farms contracted to supply milk to the factory. He was smoking a cigarette and, at the time of impact, trying to insert a cartridge into an eight-track player the dealership had recently installed in his car. He didn't notice the brake lights flash on the car in front until it was too late, and although he managed to swerve and avoid colliding with that car, he mounted the sidewalk and shunted Nancy a good two feet back towards the shop door she'd just exited. Nancy fell to the ground, and Arnold rushed to her assistance.

Property was always uppermost in Arnold Skidmore's mind, and before asking Nancy if she was hurt he gathered together her belongings – shopping bags and purse – and brought them to her side. No bones appeared to have been broken, but Nancy was in shock and Arnold insisted on driving her to the hospital. She lay on the backseat of his car listening to the atonal drone of music she didn't recognise. It wasn't the kind of music to hasten anyone's recuperation.

'What is this?' Nancy asked.

'Captain Beefheart,' Arnold replied.

'Well it's *awful*,' Nancy said. 'Can you turn it off please: it's giving me a headache! I thought you'd have been more of a Lawrence Welk and his Orchestra man.' Arnold had been offended by such a suggestion but, from a position of weakness, complied.

Theirs hadn't been the most propitious of first meetings but, surprisingly, they started to date. Nancy often wondered if Arnold had asked her out after the accident simply to avoid the possibility of having to pay damages; despite the expensive car he drove, there was a thrifty, almost penny-pinching side to his nature that she never fully understood.

Arnold would disguise his frugality by attaching it to one or another lofty cause, in particular the conservation of natural resources. 'One day the planet will thank me, Nancy,' he told her. His conservation measures included flushing toilets in the house only once a day, and at its end, providing the bowls held nothing more than urine. When she first visited Arnold's house, Nancy had been shocked to find a pool of amber liquid in the downstairs bathroom, and even more shocked when Arnold became agitated after she flushed it away. 'Water, Nancy! We have to conserve it!' he shouted through the cloakroom door.

Arnold's concerns similarly ran to toilet paper. If guests visited the house for overnight stays, he would remove the roll from the bathroom and leave on their pillows only what he considered to be a sufficient amount of paper for their stay: neatly folded strips, each one no longer than two perforations. When she asked him why he did this, he replied: 'Trees, Nancy! We have to conserve them!'

After she married Arnold, Nancy saw to it that these strange practices came to an end. The marriage, however, came after the deaths of Arnold's parents and too late for her to do anything about their funerals – or lack thereof. Arnold had persuaded both parents to leave their bodies to medical research, telling them that he planned to do the same when he died. It was, he explained, an opportunity for them all to help save the lives of future generations – generations that might well number their own grandchildren, even though his parents might well be dead by the time they were born and in all likelihood never get to meet them.

When Nancy asked him nearer the time of his own death if he wanted his body donated to medical science, Arnold had responded: 'No way, Nancy! I don't want some kid rummaging around in my insides.' It then dawned on Nancy that Arnold had donated his parents' bodies to medical science purely to save him the expense of burying them.

Nancy told Doc that although Arnold was the most complicated, inconsistent, irrational, and often infuriating person she'd ever met, there was also an ever-present kindness to him. For all his foibles, he was a good man and she'd genuinely loved him. He was fourteen years older than her, fifty when they married, and had no interest in becoming a father. This too suited Nancy, and although she might have secretly wondered if Arnold's aversion to fatherhood had something to do with the cost of bringing children into the world, never once pursued the matter with him.

Arnold loved his job. As Vice President of Milk Production at the Hershey Foods Corporation, it was his responsibility to secure regular supplies of milk for the factory; without milk there could be no milk chocolate, and hence, he told her, his position was pivotal. Ensuring the quality of the milk was as important a part of Arnold's job as contracting the dairy farmers to provide it: the Hershey factory had no use for milk that tasted unnaturally sweet, aromatic or bitter.

'The milk that comes out of a cow is only as good as the food that goes into it,' he'd explained to Nancy over dinner on their first formal date. 'The farmers have to make sure that their pastures are clear of weeds such as buckhorn, ragweed and wild dog fennel, because those are the kinds of weed that flavour milk. They also have to be careful not to feed clover, alfalfa or soybean silage to the cows immediately before milking. Strong-flavoured feedstuffs like these can make the milk taste as bad as the weeds do. And sure as icicles melt, they should never feed them vegetable crops: nothing tastes worse than milk flavoured by cabbages and turnips!'

'What about thistles?' Nancy had asked him. 'Do they make milk taste funny?'

Nancy recalled for Doc the look Arnold had given her: 'He made me feel as if I had special needs or something. "Cows *avoid* thistles!" he said. I told him if he ever looked at me like that again, I'd deck him.'

Arnold died in his seventy-second year with Nancy at his bedside. Shortly before he breathed his last, he gestured to Nancy that he wanted to say something to her. Presuming Arnold wanted to tell her how much he'd loved her, she drew closer to him. 'Dust, Nancy,' he whispered. 'Where does dust come from? And money, where does money go?'

The funeral he'd arranged for himself had spared no expense. The coffin was the most lavish model the funeral home stocked and made from the finest mahogany – ironically, the most endangered tree on the planet. The music he'd chosen for his exit from the world had been as eccentric as the life he'd lived – and equally as puzzling as his final words. The opening hymn was *Good King Wenceslas*, a Christmas Carol about a king going out in the snow to give alms to a poor peasant, followed by *When Mothers of Salem*, a hymn about children. For a childless man who never gave to charity, as Nancy could recall, these were enigmatic and arcane choices.

Arnold Skidmore had also chosen two contemporary pieces of music for the service: *The Heartache* by Warren Zevon, a sad song about unrequited love, and *Pachuco Cadaver* by Captain Beefheart. If Nancy had been mortified by Arnold's death, she was even more so by these choices of music. Anybody hearing the lyrics to *The Heartache*, she told Doc, would have been convinced that the real love of his life had been someone else, certainly not her. She recalled people leaving the church and giving her their condolences, but few actually looking her in the eye. Nancy also wondered if by choosing a piece of music by Captain Beefheart – music she'd never allowed him to play in the house if she was present – Arnold wasn't also cocking a final snook at her.

The minister had also taken exception to Arnold's last choice of music. Written down on a service sheet, the title *Pachuco Cadaver* conjured in the minds of the unknowing – and this was the entirety of the congregation – a piece of seventeenth century European funereal music, when in fact it was a discordant four-and-a-half-minute song about a Chicano who wore zoot suits in the 1950s. From the opening and endlessly repetitive chord sequence, the minister decided that this was music that should never be heard inside a church again.

The intervening years had also taken their toll on Nancy's family, its members and its fortunes. Martha Travis had been the first to die. From the time of Doc meeting her, Miss Martha's condition had deteriorated unabated, and with a speed that had taken the family by surprise – much faster than Martha's own mother's decline had been. News of her mother's death reached Nancy shortly after she'd moved to Hershey. She didn't dwell on the details of her mother's final years, but told Doc she took solace in the fact that her mother had died at Oaklands and not in some soulless and amorphous nursing home. Hilton had promised his wife such an ending and, despite the distress it caused him, had kept to his word.

'I know you and my father never really hit it off, Gene, but he was quite a man. I couldn't have asked for a better father, or my mother for a better husband.'

'I presume he's dead too?' Doc asked.

'Well, if he isn't, then he's well over a hundred and living some place I don't know about,' Nancy replied. 'Yes, he's dead; Daisy and Ruby too.'

Doc had never met Daisy, but news of Ruby's death stung him. Apart from Nancy, she'd been the only member of the Travis family he'd actually liked. 'What happened to Ruby?' he asked.

'She died in childbirth when she was forty-five,' Nancy replied, tears welling in her eyes. 'She should never have been trying for a child at that age. It was Homer who was insistent, and Daddy never forgave him for Ruby's death. There was no trial or anything, but everyone pretty much assumed that Daddy killed him.'

Ruby and Homer had started trying for children soon after they were married, but for many years Ruby had failed to conceive. When eventually she did become pregnant, the parturition proved a difficult one, and the baby (a girl) was delivered still-born. Doctors warned both her and Homer that any future pregnancy might well put Ruby's own life at risk: apart from her already advancing years, she was now beginning to show signs of diabetes and high blood pressure.

Homer, however, set upon the continuation of the Comer name, reminded Ruby that her own mother had given birth to Nancy while in her forties. He persuaded Ruby to try for a child one last time, promising her the best medical care available, whatever the cost. Things, however, hadn't worked out quite the way Homer had hoped, and his wife and future heir (a boy) ended up on mortuary slabs in the Memphis Baptist Memorial Hospital.

Still grieving the loss of Martha, Hilton Travis was totally unprepared for the loss of Ruby. He could understand the death of his wife, but not the death of a daughter, and in his mind he knew the person responsible for it: Homer F Comer. (And the F he placed between Homer and Comer didn't stand for Fred – Homer had no middle name.)

For the sake of his family, however, Hilton made heroic efforts to disguise the feelings of contempt he now bore his son-in-law, but in doing so often failed miserably. During one of her regular visits to Oaklands – and several months after Ruby's body had been laid to rest – Nancy had asked him casually how Homer was doing. Hilton had looked up from the newspaper he'd been reading and said matter-of-factly that for all he cared Homer could be crawling across the Tallahatchie Bridge with a knife stuck in his back.

Hilton's disdain for the man only grew after Homer remarried. The insensitivity of this act had appalled him, and caused him to doubt the sincerity of the man's grieving. Another year was to pass, however, before he actually decided to kill his son-in-law.

When Hilton suggested to Homer they take a hunting trip together and get reacquainted, family and friends were surprised. Surprise, however, turned to shock when Hilton returned from the trip with the body of Homer sprawled on the backseat of his truck. 'Terrible business,' Hilton had said, somewhat perfunctorily. 'Shot him by mistake.' That night, and for the first time since the deaths of Martha and Ruby, Hilton could be heard wandering around the house whistling.

It was quickly settled that Homer's death had been an accident, that he'd been killed by a single shot to the back of the head after Hilton had mistaken him for a buck. Even though the sheriff thought the damage to Homer's skull suggested that the bullet had come from much closer range than that described by Hilton, he readily accepted Hilton's story. Hilton Travis, after all, was a friend and, moreover, the person who had been most instrumental in securing his election as sheriff in the first place.

Though Hilton knew his actions would never bring Ruby back to life, he was consoled in his final years by the knowledge that Homer had now joined her in death; buried in his own county far away from the Travis family plot. Still an elegant man in his old age, Hilton dated occasionally but told his children he would never remarry. He died of a heart attack in his eightieth year and was buried next to his beloved wife.

'Jesus, Nancy, that's some story,' Doc said. 'No one could ever accuse your family of being dull.'

'True,' Nancy replied, 'but on reflection, dull would have been preferable. Dull and ordinary. No major ups and no major downs. No tragedies. But that's not the way life is, is it? You know that as much as I do.'

Doc nodded. 'You know who I've often thought about over the years?' he asked. 'Dora. I never met anyone quite like her. She still brings a smile to my face.'

Nancy laughed. 'Well, Gene, you might like to know that she never forgave you for what you said about her cooking. You sure wiped the smile from her face.'

'That was your damned brother's doing,' Doc said. 'I hope to God he's dead – sorry, Nancy. Just a figure of speech. Of course I don't hope that. How is he?'

'Alive,' Nancy said, 'though I don't have much to do with him these days, and can't remember the last time I actually saw him. It might have been better if he had died. Maybe then, Oaklands would still be in the family. Do you know where he's living now?' Doc indicated he didn't. 'In an apartment complex in Clarksdale!'

Hilton had left Oaklands equally to his three surviving children. Brandon had been charged with its stewardship on the understanding that all profits would be shared with his siblings on a yearly basis. Neither Nancy nor Daisy had minded when Brandon moved his family into Oaklands: from a farming perspective it made practical sense, and as both daughters had established lives outside the state, neither had any interest in moving back to Mississippi. For the first few years Hilton's arrangements ran to plan, the estate continued to prosper and dividends were deposited into Nancy and Daisy's bank accounts. But then things took a turn for the worse. Apart from his personality, Brandon had one other weakness: he was a gambling man and, ultimately, an unsuccessful one.

During his father's lifetime, Brandon's gambling had been controlled and hidden from the rest of the family by the finite salary he received and his lack of any real collateral. When he moved into Oaklands and took control of the estate's finances, however, all constraints were removed and the wagers he ventured grew larger as his trips to Las Vegas became more frequent. His reputation as a high roller crystallized in the city, and casinos vied with each other to fly him free of charge to their desert lairs and accommodate him, at no cost, in their best hotel suites. Brandon was too dumb, too addicted to smell a rat. All he smelled was money and, eventually, his own stale sweat.

'Brandon gambled Oaklands clean away. The estate had to be sold to repay his debts and what was left, which wasn't much, Daisy and I shared. Brandon's wife left him and took the children with her. He got a job as a farm manager, and ever since he's rented a place. He's supposed to have gotten treatment for his addiction, but I still hear stories of him bumming rides to Tunica and catching the bus to the casinos on the Gulf Coast.

'He's started calling recently, asking me about my health and feigning concern. He's waiting for me to go like Mom, thinking he'll get my money when I die, but that's never going to happen. He doesn't know it, but I've already made my will and he gets squat. He'll contest it, of course – if he's still alive – but the lawyers have told me that the will is water-tight, and I also have doctors on record attesting to the fact that the state of my mind was sound when I wrote it.'

Nancy's story unfolded over the two days they spent together in Hershey. The first evening of Doc's visit they ate at his hotel. Aware of the formality of the hotel's elegant Circular Dining Room, Nancy had brought him one of Arnold's suits to wear. Doc agreed to wear the jacket but told Nancy that if it was okay with her, and with no disrespect to Arnold intended, he'd stick to wearing his own pants.

On the second evening, and the night before Doc was scheduled to return home, Nancy cooked a meal at her house. After they'd eaten, they retired to the living room and Nancy poured brandy into two snifter glasses.

'That was a damn fine meal, Nancy,' Doc said. 'Not bad for a girl who could only cook grilled cheese sandwiches when I met her.'

Nancy smiled. 'Do you think the elephant enjoyed his meal, too?'

'What elephant?'

'The one in the room, Gene. We've spent two lovely days together – and I mean that – but we've both been avoiding the one subject we have to talk about, the reason I phoned you.'

'I presume you mean the promise I made to you at Oaklands?'

'Yes,' Nancy said. 'I need to know if you're still prepared to keep it.'

It was the conversation Doc had dreaded.

The Promise

Like most decisions Doc made in life, his promise to help Nancy had initially come from the gut. It was a decision-making process that generally worked well for him. His track record for getting things right or wrong was no better or worse than those of his more cerebral-minded peers who, no doubt, would have dismissed his two-cigarette decision as hasty and ill-considered. In Doc's mind, however, he could have stood in that cotton field for another two years and still come to the same conclusion; all the reading and subsequent thought he'd given the matter had in no way changed his mind.

Doc believed that death was a part of life's course, natural and unavoidable. Sometimes, it was a bad thing, as in the case of Beth and Esther, but other times it could be a good thing, a blessing. After a lifetime spent ministering to the sick and dying, it was difficult for him to think any differently. He'd watched terminally ill patients inch their way towards painful and undignified deaths too often, and it had been impossible for him not to register their sufferings. On occasion, he'd given them drugs to reduce their pain, even though he knew – and, if truth be told, often hoped – that the drug itself would cause the patient to die sooner. He had felt no guilt.

In Doc's opinion, any person with no hope of recovery and no quality of life had the right to decide the circumstances of their own death, when it would happen and how it would happen. He saw no reason for a person to go on living against their wishes and exist for the sake of existence. Moreover, Doc wasn't a religious man, and so wasn't swayed by the argument that only

God could determine the length of a person's life and how that life ended.

Doc knew that Nancy's request to die was of her own volition and that she'd considered it well. No one had pressurized her into making this decision, and no close family member now remained to be affected by her premature death. He knew, too, that the future she faced was one of wretchedness and indignity, a future without hope.

In light of this logic, the answer to Nancy's question should have been a simple yes, but it wasn't. He should never have hesitated in granting her wish, but he did. When it came down to it, Nancy wasn't an abstract idea – she was a living friend. He hated the idea of losing her again.

'You're sure about this?'

'Yes,' she replied. 'One hundred per cent sure. Anything I say to the contrary after this evening, you should ignore.'

'But what if I promise to take care of you instead; swear to you that I'll never put you in a nursing home?'

'No, Gene, I don't want that! I don't want that for me and I don't want that for you. And besides, you might die before I do, and where would that leave me then?'

Doc was silent for a moment and then looked Nancy in the eyes. 'Okay, you still have my word on it. When I judge the time's come, I'll take care of it. You won't suffer.'

In that moment, he honestly believed he was telling her the truth.

Nancy breathed an audible sigh of relief. She'd worried that her long-ago desertion of him might have changed his mind and in some way negated the promise he'd made to her at Oaklands. She hugged him and started to cry, while Doc stood there feeling numb.

Nancy composed herself and returned to the matter at hand in a business-like, almost detached manner. She told Doc she wanted to die in Coffeeville. Doc's job was to get her there and, after her death, contact a firm of attorneys in Hershey who would then take matters in hand. Her will, she said, stipulated that she was to be buried in the family plot close to Oaklands, alongside

Ruby and her parents. Once settled, her estate would be divided equally between Milton Hershey School and Alzheimer's Research; there were to be no other beneficiaries.

'Before we have to leave Hershey though, I'd like you to choose something of mine; anything at all that might remind you of me after I'm gone, and hopefully bring back fond memories.'

'Not one of Arnold's suits, then?'

'Hah! Did I tell you that Arnold was a Republican, Gene? No? Well he was. Last night you wore a Republican's jacket! How about that?'

Doc smiled. 'Why Coffeeville, Nancy, and where the hell is it?'

'It's in Mississippi but away from the Delta. It's maybe forty miles or so from Oaklands, but in another county – Yalobusha. It's small: only a few hundred people live there. My father owned a farm on its outskirts, for tax reasons as much as anything, and he left it to me and Daisy when he died. It's secluded and not even Brandon knows about it. I became sole owner when Daisy passed, and Brandon thinks I sold it. I did, but only to Arnold. He put it in the name of a limited purpose corporation and leased it to a management company in Memphis that sold hunting rights. The lease expires next year and from that time it will be empty. Ideally, I'd have liked to have died at Oaklands, but that's no longer possible. This is the next best thing. After all this time and I'm still a Miss'ippi girl. Can you believe it?'

'I can believe anything of you and your family, Nancy. Strangest bunch of people I ever met… I'll take the portrait, by the way.'

'Of Arnold?' Nancy asked, somewhat surprised.

'No, of you, you clutz. It's hanging right there above the fireplace.'

'Sure,' Nancy said. 'If that's what you want. I never thought it was all that flattering of me, to tell you the truth. The nose is nothing like mine. I think the artist spent more time painting the bowl of fruit on the table than he did considering my face.'

'I think it captures you just fine,' Doc said. 'But do me a favour, will you: can I take it with me tomorrow?'

Doc had reason to ask for it now. Once Nancy was dead, he

wasn't sure if he'd need anything to remind him of her.

The next day, Doc drove home with the portrait of Nancy propped on the backseat of the car and the cow song going round in his head. For some reason, Arnold's final words also kept popping into his mind: 'Dust, where does it come from? Money, where does it go?'

A Visit to the Doctor's

Doc made two more trips to Hershey and then Nancy visited him. He picked her up at the airport.

'Good journey?'

'So far,' Nancy replied. 'Don't you think you're driving a bit close to that car in front?'

'What car?' Doc asked.

'God in Heaven, Gene! How bad *are* your eyes? I don't want to die just yet!'

'You won't die with me at the wheel, Nancy. This car's got the best airbags on the market!'

While Doc manoeuvred erratically through the afternoon's traffic, Nancy glanced at him nervously and held on to the door handle. She gave a sigh of relief when, eventually, he pulled into his driveway.

'Oh shit!' Doc said. 'Frisbee's out front. Don't make eye contact!'

Dennis Frisbee was Doc's next-door neighbour and Doc had disliked him from first meeting. It wasn't the man's stupid comb over or loose bottom lip that caused Doc's aversion – though, in truth, neither of these helped – but the fact that Frisbee was a crashing and self-centred bore, inconscient and uncaring of the discomfort his rambling monologues caused others.

'Hey, Doctor Chaney,' Frisbee called out to him. 'Are you going to introduce me to your lady friend?'

'No!' Doc said. 'And I've told you before: either muzzle that dog or I'll have it put down!'

Doc took Nancy's bag from the trunk and ushered her into the house.

'That was a bit rude of you, wasn't it, Gene?' Nancy said. 'All the man wanted to do was say hello.'

'Believe me, Nancy, I did you a favour. That man's a menace, and so too is his dog – the damn thing bit me last year.'

'What kind of dog is it?' Nancy asked.

'Part pit bull and part West Highland terrier, but don't ask me which part is which because I haven't a clue, and I doubt Frisbee has either.'

'He's not invited to the barbecue, then?' Nancy smiled. 'Who will be coming?'

Doc looked at her puzzled. 'Just you and me, Nancy. There is no one else to ask.'

Doc carried Nancy's bag upstairs and showed her to the guest room. At Nancy's request, he then reluctantly gave her a tour of the house. 'They're just rooms, Nancy. You'll find the same in all houses.'

'Stop being so stubborn, Gene, and just show me!'

Gene led her through the house and ended the tour in the living room. 'So, what do you think?'

'I can't get over how neat and tidy everything is. Maybe I'm misremembering how you used to be, but I thought you'd be living more like a slob, especially when you dress the way you do.'

'Give me a break, Nancy! There's nothing wrong with the way I dress. Coffee?'

They stood for a while in the kitchen and then took their cups through to the living room, where Nancy's attention was drawn to the framed photographs arranged on the sideboard. She moved towards them and picked one up.

'Oh Gene, this is beautiful! Is this a photograph of Beth and Esther?'

'Yes,' Doc said. 'It was taken on Esther's first birthday, shortly before the accident.'

'It must have been awful for you. How did you hear of the accident – or would you prefer not to talk about it?'

'No, it's okay,' Doc said. 'I was at the surgery when the call came through, getting ready for some home visits. I don't know why, but I had a feeling it was bad news even before anything was said. I couldn't let go of the phone – another doctor had to prise it from my grip. Damn near broke my fingers.

'But, you know what they say: life goes on. And it did, but it's never been the same, and I never expected it to be.'

Nancy stroked his back comfortingly, and then carefully replaced the photograph. She moved on to the next one, hoping for happier stories. 'Who are these people?'

'The old guy's Sydney Guravitch, and the young one's his son – and my godson – Jack.'

'Couldn't they come to the barbecue?' Nancy asked.

'Jack lives too far distant, Nancy, and Sydney's tied up at the cemetery these days.'

'Is he a groundskeeper there?' Nancy asked.

'No, he's a resident,' Doc explained. 'He was my best friend, too. Died of a heart attack the same year you phoned. It's a pity the two of you never got to meet.'

Sydney had been two years younger than Doc and displayed none of his friend's academic ability or ambition. He'd followed his father into portrait photography and continued to work in the studio after his father had died. His world view was finite; he'd stayed local and married local. He'd been there when Doc went away to university and there when he returned; there when Doc left to practise medicine in Maryland and still there when Doc returned from Maryland. Sydney had, in fact, been the only constant in Doc's life, and Doc told Nancy how much he missed his old friend: the ease of his company, the minutiae of their conversation and the unreserved nature of his loyalty.

'I'm sorry, Gene. I didn't realise. What about Jack? Are you close to him, or is it just the usual godparent–son relationship? You said he lived far away.'

'He does. He lives in Arizona, but we're still close. He's a good kid, a friend more than a godson. It's a good relationship.'

'Shall we move away from the photographs?'

'Yes, let's do that. It's not wise to have more than one dead person ganging up on you at any one time.'

'What a strange thing to say. Are you mad at me for asking about them?'

'No, of course I'm not mad at you, Nancy. It was just a throw-away comment. I didn't mean anything by it.'

He changed the subject. 'I've booked a table for eight o'clock, so you have time to shower if you want.'

Nancy went to her room, and when Doc heard the sound of running water he returned to the sideboard and stared at the photographs.

They ate in an Italian restaurant, small and noisy. They talked easily but aimlessly during the meal, and it was only after the dessert dishes had been cleared and coffee served that Doc asked Nancy if she'd noticed any changes.

'It's words mainly,' Nancy said. 'I see objects I've seen all my life and I find myself struggling to remember what they're called. It could be something as simple as a pan or an ice-cream scoop. I keep misplacing things, too, and God knows how many times I've keyed the wrong code into the alarm system. I'm thinking it might be easier just to have it disconnected. It's frustrating, but at the moment that's all it is. It's manageable.'

'Sometimes it's difficult to know what's caused by Alzheimer's and what's caused by old age,' Doc said. 'I have to search for words these days too, and I've lost count of the times I've gone into a room and then wondered why I was there. I wouldn't worry too much about it, if I were you. Are you on any kind of medication?'

'The doctor wrote me a prescription, but I don't know if the pills are helping or not. Don't worry though, Gene, I still have a few good years in me yet.'

'I hope so,' Doc said. 'It's nice having a friend again.'

Nancy smiled and took hold of his hand. 'It is, isn't it? It was only after Arnold died that I realised how important it was to share an experience with another person. If I hadn't been there with Arnold, I'm sure the Grand Canyon would have been no more than a big hole in Colorado and Venice just a crumbling and waterlogged city in Italy.'

'Nicely put, Nancy. It's as if you studied literature at university. You didn't by any chance read the works of the nineteenth century English poets, did you?'

'If you value your shins, Gene, I suggest you don't say another word! Now pay the check and let's go. I've had enough of you for one day!'

Doc smiled broadly – and then did as he was told.

'You have to bear in mind, Nancy, that this town isn't Hershey. There's not much to do here but potter.'

'Then let's potter. We can go for a walk.'

They were about to leave the house when Doc saw Frisbee emerge from his front door. 'Hold your horses, Nancy! Let's wait till he's gone.'

'Oh really, Gene! Don't tell me you're a prisoner in your own house because of that man. What if he stays there?'

'He won't. He's already climbing into his car – probably going to visit that new girlfriend of his.'

'What's she like?' Nancy asked.

'I think he dug her up at the cemetery,' Doc said absent-mindedly

'Gene!'

Doc took Nancy to a small park he occasionally visited. They walked for a while, and then sat down on one of its old wooden benches and watched children play softball. Doc's eyes closed and for a few minutes he dozed, jolted awake by a cheer from watching parents. He glanced at Nancy. She was lost in thought, staring into a distance of a thousand yards.

'Penny for them,' he said.

Nancy turned to him and smiled. 'You used to ask me that all the time. Do you remember? It used to irritate the hell out of me, too.'

'I might well have done, but from what I remember you never once gave me a straight answer. You used to shut me out – remember? It's me that should have been irritated.'

'I wasn't consciously shutting you out, Gene. It's just that there were some things I didn't want to talk about. It was difficult enough just thinking about them.'

'So, are you going to tell me now?'

'I was thinking about children, if you must know. I suppose it's sitting here with so many parents watching their own children at play. They all look so happy, don't they? I was just wondering what it would be like to be them; what it would have been like if the two of us had married and had children, been able to lead normal lives like everyone else. I'm being silly, I know, but sometimes I get like this.'

'Do you regret not having children?' Doc asked.

'I don't regret the decision not to have children – but yes, the biggest regret in my life is not to have been a mother. There's not a day goes by that I don't consider it.'

Doc took hold of her hand, and Nancy rested her head on his shoulder.

'Do you hate me for having the abortion?' she asked quietly.

'Of course I don't hate you. What you did was selfless – it wasn't an act of convenience. I wish you'd have told me at the time you were pregnant, though, and not just disappeared the way you did. It was my child as well as yours and we should at least have discussed it. In all likelihood, I would have tried to persuade you to keep the baby, but for reasons probably no less selfish than Homer wanting Ruby to have his child.

'At the end of the day I'd have gone with whatever you decided, though. It was your body, so it was always your right to choose. If you'd decided to go ahead with the abortion after we'd talked, then I'd have supported you in that decision. You should never have doubted me on that, and you should never have gone through the abortion on your own.'

There was a lull in the conversation, and then a shout of warning as a ball came sailing towards them. With reflexes Doc was no longer aware of having, he caught the ball one-handed, and to cheers from both children and parents, threw it to the nearest player.

'Well done, you!' Nancy said admiringly.

'It was either catching it or getting zonked on the head!' Doc said. 'Let's move before a ball comes our way that I *can't* catch. I don't want you going back to Hershey with a black eye!'

Nancy took his arm and they walked from the park.

'You know what you were saying about us getting married if things had been different? Did you mean that?'

'Yes, I think we'd have married,' Nancy replied. 'I'm not sure my father would have approved, and Brandon certainly wouldn't. He told me if I married you, he wouldn't come to the wedding – but that was more of an incentive *to* marry you!'

'How come your father never warmed to me?'

'My father never warmed to any of my boyfriends. I'm not sure he even liked Arnold for that matter, but by that time he was more concerned that I wouldn't get married, rather than who I married. How did you get on with Beth's parents?'

'Not a whole lot better, come to think of it. We stayed in touch for a while after the funeral, but not for long. Beth and Esther were the only things we had in common, and I suspect that deep down they blamed me for their deaths. Beth's mother – she was the force in the family – once told me it should have been me that had been killed. She was drunk at the time and apologised later, but I think she meant it. In my experience, people usually say what they mean after a few drinks.'

They came to a halt in front of a small stone church and Doc pushed open the gate. He took hold of Nancy's hand and led her to the churchyard at its rear, where his parents and Sydney lay buried.

'I think this is the first time I've been taken to a cemetery on a date, Gene. You sure know how to show a girl a good time.'

'It's pretty here, Nancy – peaceful too. Some days I bring a sandwich and eat lunch.'

'Are Beth and Esther buried here?'

'No, they were cremated. I keep their ashes in the house.'

'They're not in my room, are they?' Nancy asked, slightly alarmed by the idea.

'No, the urns are in the garage.'

'Don't you think you're being a bit morbid?'

'No,' Doc replied, slightly baffled by the question. 'I keep them next to the six-inch nails.'

'But why would you want to keep them at all?' Nancy pressed.

'Because when I die I'm going to be cremated too, and I've arranged for all the ashes to be scattered in a sandy area of Zion National Park – it's where Beth and I honeymooned.'

'You'd look well if there is a spirit world,' Nancy said. 'The only people you'd meet there would be Paiute Indians, and I doubt you'd understand a word they said! Anyway, let's go. All this talk of death is starting to depress me. We could go to a matinee, if you like – maybe take in a comedy.'

Doc slept through the movie but Nancy enjoyed it, laughing at all the contrived slapstick. They drove home and Doc prepared the barbecue he'd promised her.

'Does the dog next door always bark this much?' Nancy asked.

'Yes, and if I had a gun I'd shoot it!'

'I can't even envisage you holding a gun, Gene,' Nancy laughed. 'Arnold had a big collection, though. I gave them away when he died.'

'To the police?'

'No, to the school children. Of course I gave them to the police!'

After the plates had been cleared Doc excused himself, explaining to Nancy that he had meat stuck in his teeth. He went to the bathroom and flossed, and then returned to the living room where Nancy was sitting. 'If I was a pharaoh, I'd forego the ornaments and treasure and insist they bury me with a box of dental tape in my sarcophagus: there's nothing worse than having food stuck in your teeth.'

Nancy smiled. 'You're not a pharaoh though, are you, Gene, and seeing as how you're going to be cremated when you die, it would be a waste of everyone's money. Now tell me, where did you get that piece of artwork above the fireplace?'

'*The Barbed Wire Flag*? It was a present from a friend.'

'Well, he must have known you well. I suspect that the metal bars and barbed wire are meant to be representations of separation and containment, and that's you Gene. That's your life.'

'I'd be surprised if the artist was thinking that deeply,' Gene replied with a smile. He shook a cigarette from its pack and moved towards the door.

'Where do you think you're going?' Nancy demanded. 'I'm

talking to you! And don't think I haven't noticed how you use cigarettes to escape people and conversations you don't want to have. Now sit down and listen to me!'

Gene sat down and poured himself a large measure of red wine.

'And that's another thing. I've noticed you drink to be with people, too.'

'Jesus, Nancy! I drink to be with myself. What's all this about?' Nancy moved to sit next to him.

'I'm talking to you as a friend now, Gene, and not someone trying to hurt you. One day my mind is going to go, and when it does I won't make any sense; but while I still do, please listen to me.

'For most people life is too short, but for you – it's as if it's been too long already. There's no reason why your life has to be so empty and solitary. You're not the first person to have suffered tragedy and you won't be the last. People bounce back from such misfortune, and it's okay to do that: it's not a betrayal of the people who are dead. Beth would have wanted you to enjoy life, to live it to the full!'

Doc listened impassively, disbelieving that Nancy might consider he hadn't turned these thoughts in his mind a thousand times already.

'Doesn't it ever strike you as odd,' she continued, 'that I've still managed to lead a meaningful life while knowing the worst is yet to happen, while you appear to have led a meaningless life after the worst has already happened?'

Doc shifted uncomfortably. 'I don't feel sorry for myself, if that's what you're thinking. Besides, I think there's a self-limiting gene in the Chaney DNA: I remember my father withering on the vine after my mother died.'

'That's nonsense, Gene, and you know it. The only self-limiting gene in your family is you, Gene!' (Or had she said Eugene?) 'I worry about you, do you know that? I worry what will become of you after I'm gone.'

'I'll be fine, Nancy. I'll potter about for a while, and then go blind.'

'What are you talking about?'

'I have macular degeneration. I'm losing my sight.'

'Well, that explains your driving then, but I can't see it being responsible for all this pessimism of yours. You're wandering around in a world full of minor chords. Do you know this? Your glass is always half empty, never half full.'

Doc pretended to give the matter serious thought. 'I don't know about you, Nancy,' he said eventually, 'but I've always found that a cliché is as good a place as any to leave a conversation. I'm going to smoke that cigarette now!'

'Ugh, Gene, I give up, I really do!'

Doc smoked his cigarette and returned to the room where Nancy was sitting with her arms folded. He kissed her on the cheek. 'I'm sorry, Nancy. Thanks for what you said.'

'I doubt my words have done a scrap of good!'

'Probably not,' he smiled. 'But let's look on the bright side – there's always tomorrow!'

Nancy punched his arm.

Conversation returned to less controversial topics and Doc refilled their glasses.

'Where's that, er, square thing you took from my house? The thing with me in it?'

'Your portrait?'

'That's the word! See what I mean? A simple word and I forget it!'

Doc led her to the study and showed it to her. It was on the same wall as an autographed photograph of Martin Luther King.

'Did he sign this for you personally?' Nancy asked.

'No, I bought it in a shop,' Doc said.

'When did you leave the civil rights movement, by the way? After they locked you up in Jackson?'

'About that time. It wasn't so much the arrest as the music, though. *Michael Row the Boat Ashore* was bad enough, but nothing compared with *We Shall Overcome*. I grew to hate that song with a passion and, if you want to know the truth, I got sick of the sanctimony of the people who sang it.'

Nancy laughed. 'What happened to Bob? Did he have musical differences with the movement too?'

'He was killed in action in 1965,' Doc said, secretly pleased to be able to wipe the smile from Nancy's face. 'Having said that,' he continued slowly and deliberately, 'he gave me *The Barbed Wire Flag* you were admiring, just five years ago.

'We could pay him a visit if you like…'

2

Bob

Mississippi

The last occasion Doc had spent time with the man known as Bob Crenshaw was in the summer of 1964, in Hinds County, Mississippi, to be precise. It was the final days of their civil rights activism, and Doc was still called Gene.

Two years had passed since the time of the Freedom Rides, and the civil rights movement had gathered momentum. The national spotlight now oscillated between the states of Mississippi and Alabama, the towns of Oxford and Birmingham, and Governors Ross Barnett and George Wallace. It illuminated their dark and shabby corners, and captured on film the brutality of methods used to stem the threatening tide: electric cattle prods, clubs, high-pressure water hoses and savage dogs. It recorded bombings and burnings, bullets fired and Molotov cocktails thrown, white-sheeted Klansmen and burning crosses. And then came the summer of 1964 and the fateful decision to drive the registration of black voters in the state with the lowest registered percentage – the state of Mississippi.

'C'mon, man, one las' trip; one mo' try to get the black man on the ladder,' Bob said to Gene.

Gene didn't need much persuading. His student days were coming to an end, and very soon he'd be stuck in full-time employment with his freedom effectively curtailed. There was also the possibility that he might bump into Nancy.

'Okay, let's do it. When do we go?'

'Two weeks,' Bob said. 'I jus' need time to sort some things out b'fore we go. We'll take my car. One place it'll fit right in is Miss'ippi; they all poor as dirt down there.'

Gene and Bob arrived in Mississippi in the second week of July and reported to a small black church on the outskirts of Jackson. At the evening's orientation meeting, they were told of three activists who'd gone missing in another part of the state while investigating the burning of a black church. 'Be careful,' they were warned. 'Stick together, vary your movements and steer clear of the local police.'

Over a drink that night, Bob said to Gene: 'Let me aks you somethin', Gene?'

For some unknown reason, Bob had developed the habit of prefacing any question he had for Gene with a question to ask it, or to Gene's hearing of the word, *axe* it.

'Axe, Bob? Axe? It's ask, there's no X in the word! No wonder white folks are scared to death of you and your brothers when they hear you talking about axes all the time. They probably think you're going to creep up in the night and chop them into little pieces. Have you ever stopped to think that maybe the black people's worst enemy is their own diction?'

'You too much, man, too much,' Bob laughed.

'So what's your question?'

'I ain't aksin' it now. I takin' offence on behalf o' my people.'

'Suit yourself.'

A few minutes later, Bob spoke again: 'Let me aks you somethin', Gene?'

'What?'

'Same question I was gonna aks you b'fore.'

'Okay.'

'What you think o' my hair?'

Bob had spent the last two years of his life growing an Afro and it had become his pride and joy. He'd comb it over and again, taking out tangles and ensuring its symmetry with a wide-toothed comb he kept lodged in his hair.

'I think it looks good,' Gene said, somewhat nonplussed. 'Why do you ask?'

''Cos you ain't never said, not once mentioned it.'

'Well, I think it suits you. What does it feel like?'

'Well it don't feel like no Brillo pad, if that what you thinkin'! I get tired o' that ol' ches'nut. It soft and springy if you really wants to know.'

'Can I touch it?'

'You ain't turnin' fruity on me, are you, Gene? Cain't says I see'd you with a girl since Nancy hightailed it.' He laughed and then gave Gene permission: 'Don't go messin' it!'

'It's like moss!' Gene said surprised. 'It feels good.'

'Well remem'er it, 'cos you ain't touchin' it again. Clumsy hands like yo's'll probably do it a mischief. If you likes it so much, you oughta grow one yo'self. You could become an honorary brother. You wan' me to put a word in fo' you?'

'I'll stick to being white, thanks. It's an easier life.'

Registering the black vote was slow and often frustrating. It helped if out-of-state volunteers were accompanied by black activists native to the state, but even then they were often viewed with suspicion. Worse was the reaction of white Mississippians, who resented outsiders coming to their state to change it: unsurprisingly, some volunteers were beaten and hundreds more arrested. The news that the three missing activists had been found murdered, however, came as a shock.

The three bodies were discovered buried under an earthen dam near the small town of Philadelphia. Two of the dead were white and from New York, and the third was a twenty-one-year-old local Negro from Mississippi called James Chaney. (Nancy would later tell Gene that she misheard the name when it was first read out on the news, and for two hours thought it was he who was dead.) Two bullets were found in each of the white bodies and three in Chaney's, which had also been badly beaten; as always, Mississippi was more generous to its own – if also less forgiving. The nation was appalled by the outrage, and the government sent the FBI to investigate. It was their presence in

Jackson that probably saved Bob and Gene from similar fates.

It was late afternoon, and the two of them were driving to eat at a friend's house in Jackson. There was little traffic on the road and Bob was driving within the speed limit. It was Gene who first noticed the flashing blue lights behind them.

'Shit,' Bob said. 'What you suppose they want?'

'God knows,' Gene replied, 'Probably just to mess with us.'

When Bob failed to stop, the police car pulled alongside him. The cop on the passenger side rolled down his window and shouted: 'Pull over! Pull over!'

'I ain't wearin' no pullover, man,' Bob shouted back at him. 'It's a jacket, seventeen dollars an' change from Sears, Roebuck.'

'Jesus Christ, Bob,' Gene said, 'Don't fool with the man. Do as he says. There's another police car behind us now!'

Bob checked the mirror to confirm what Gene had told him, and then slammed his foot on the brake. The police car following was taken unawares and smashed into the back of them. There was no way, Gene thought, that Bob hadn't intended for this to happen.

Bob got out of the car and walked to its rear to survey the damage. He turned to the driver. 'Yo' gonna have to make restitution, sir. *You* went into the back of *me*. It's the law o' the land, I b'lieve.'

'Fuck the law,' the policeman said, 'You've broken my damn nose, you fuckin' nigger!'

One of the cops from the first car drew his baton and clubbed Bob on the back of the head. In a knee-jerk reaction, Bob turned and punched the cop on the jaw, knocking him clean out. The third and fourth policemen drew guns, and only then was order on the roadside restored.

As only one of the three vehicles was now capable of being driven, all six men crammed into the surviving police car and drove into downtown Jackson, with Gene and Bob in handcuffs. 'Cain't help thinkin' six in a car's illegal,' Bob said to no one in particular.

'You're lucky we don't stuff yo' damn nigger ass in the trunk,' the policeman with the broken nose said.

Bob was charged with resisting arrest, assaulting a police officer (two), dangerous driving and reckless endangerment, while Gene was charged with being his accomplice. They were processed together, but then separated: Bob was taken to a holding cell reserved for blacks, and Gene to one reserved for whites; oddly, both cells were painted lime-green.

Alone in his cell, Gene was unashamedly scared; a prisoner in a foreign land whose language, judicial system and customs were alien and unintelligible. He took deep breaths, waited for the feelings of panic to subside, and wiped the palms of his hands on his trousers. What the hell had got into Bob?

He thought of his parents, of Nancy, and wondered when, or if, he'd ever see them again. He worried about being sent to the notorious state prison and his chances of survival there; if he was falling apart now, how on earth would he survive in Parchman Farm? He doubted that a civil rights activist would be given the friendliest of receptions there, either by guards or inmates.

He paced the small cell for a time and then tried to distract himself by exercise: push-ups and sit-ups. Eventually, he lay down on the small cot and stared at the ceiling, listened to the sounds of the building and the occasional muffled voice. At last, he fell into a sporadic and disturbed sleep, resigned to the worst.

When the cell door opened the following morning Gene was already awake, but, when told he was now free to leave, wondered if he was still asleep and dreaming. 'I can go?' he asked.

'I don't know who your nigger friend is or who *his* friends are, but we been told we cain't hold you. I don't know how many lucky days you had in your life, young fellah, but I doubt you'll have one lucky as this again. Now get your ass into gear and follow me.'

Gene was led to the reception area and handed over to two FBI agents.

'You know the deal?' the Chief of Police said to the agents. 'He's on the next bus out of the state or we re-arrest him. You got that?'

One of the agents nodded, and took Gene to a waiting car.

'Where's Bob?' Gene asked. 'Shouldn't we wait for him?'

'He's already gone,' the agent replied. 'He told us to tell you that the deal cost him his Afro – if that means anything to you.'

Under the Radar

Bob Crenshaw was born into a loving family, but the love soon ran out.

Moses and Clarissa Crenshaw did everything in their lives early: they married early, became parents early and died early. The dreams that would eventually separate them from each other and Bob, however, formed late in their young lives and were no more than opaque desires on the day they exchanged vows. They set up home in Atlanta. Mo went to work at the Coca-Cola bottling plant and Clarissa found work as a seamstress. Their lives were comfortable and, until the birth of Bob, uncomplicated. It was Bob's unanticipated arrival, however, that catalysed their opaque desires into transparent dreams.

Barely out of their own childhoods, and now with a child of their own to look after, Mo and Clarissa started to feel trapped. It was at this juncture that Mo realised he'd always wanted to travel the world and Clarissa that she'd always wanted to be a jazz singer. The cruelty of these realisations became all the more unrelenting after Mo and Clarissa accepted that their dreams would never be fulfilled. But then the United States declared war on Germany and Mo, at least, got his chance to travel.

Mo was taken by train to New York and then by ship to Liverpool, England. From there he was transported to a training camp on the Isle of Wight, where he and other recruits prepared for the planned invasion of Europe. He wrote letters home describing his journey, the English countryside, its climate and its people, and the new friends he'd made. He told Clarissa that he didn't think it would be too long before he'd be returning home, and that he loved and missed her and Little Bob. What he didn't tell her in these letters was that he was having the time of his life. What he also didn't tell Clarissa in these letters was that his life was nearing its end – though this, he himself didn't know at the time.

D-Day arrived and Mo's company set sail for an area on the coast of Normandy designated Omaha Beach. They were promised a display of precision bombing that would decimate the German defences and allow them a Sunday morning's stroll along the beach and, in all probability, an early breakfast of coffee and croissants in one of the local cafes. As it transpired the precision bombing was anything but precise, and the bombs missed their targets completely.

The troops were now faced with having to cover three hundred yards of open sand under heavy fire. Some of them thought it a challenge, others an opportunity, but whatever their thinking they ended up dying in droves, their bodies strewing the beach like clumps of red seaweed. Mo lasted no more than thirty-seven seconds before his travelling days came to an end, his soul departing the beach long before his body was dragged from it. Moses Crenshaw now lies buried in a cemetery overlooking the sea, popular with thousands of other American corpses.

Clarissa took the news of Mo's death badly. Having already found single parenthood difficult, his death not only robbed her of a husband she'd loved, but, in her increasingly fragile state of mind, seemingly fated her to an eternity of being alone with Bob. It wasn't as though she didn't love her son – she did – and it wasn't as though Bob was a difficult child – he wasn't – but he was always there, always. She never had time for herself, and eventually came to resent his constant and suffocating presence.

She knew she had talent. On those rare occasions she managed to persuade family or friends to take Bob for the night, she'd visit jazz clubs in the city's underbelly and guest with various bands. All who heard her voice, its cadence and velvet tones, were impressed, and at least two bands had offered to take her on tour with them. But she'd always had to say no, and explain that she had a young son waiting for her at home. 'Then ditch the kid,' one alto-saxophonist once said to her. At first she'd thought he was joking, but then realised he was deadly serious. The thought started to gnaw away at her, and thinking about it day after day and month after month eventually led her to act upon it. Her decision to abandon Bob and follow her dream fated him to a life spent in the company of his mother's sister, Selena.

On the second of July's two Dismal Days, she and Bob rode the bus to Aunt Selena's small house. It was a Sunday morning and Clarissa knew that Selena would be in church. She carried a suitcase packed with Bob's clothes and a few toys, and a letter of explanation for her sister. Selena's door was locked, and Clarissa told Bob to wait for his aunt on the porch and hand her the letter when she returned from morning service. She had an errand to run, she told him, but would return in an hour or so. She gave Little Bob a hug and then walked away. Bob stared after her, but she never looked back. It was the last time he saw his mother.

Selena Priddy was a spinster, and no more than four feet two inches tall. She was four years older than Clarissa, and as a growing child had been considered the prettier of the two sisters. Then, at the age of ten, something went wrong with her growing. When the Priddys eventually took their daughter to see a doctor, they were told she had a severe form of scoliosis, or curvature of the spine. Both the family and available treatment at the time were poor, and Selena's growth was effectively stunted. The upper part of her spine continued to curve to the right, while her ribs and shoulder blade started to stick out on the side of her back like a hump.

Returning from church that Sunday morning, Selena was both surprised and overjoyed to see Little Bob sitting on her porch steps. Bob's eyes lit up too when he saw his favourite aunt appear. He ran to kiss her and hand her the letter his mother had written. Selena took the letter and opened the house door.

'You had anythin' to eat, L'il Bob?' she asked.

'No, Ma'am. Nothin' since breakfas'.'

'Well, sit yo'self down an' I'll make us both a san'widge.'

She knew what was in the letter before she even read it. Her sister's behaviour had been getting stranger by the day. All that talk about jazz and how Bob was holding her back. She wondered sometimes if Clarissa wasn't popping some kind of pill, or taking powders when she went to those nightclubs. The letter said she'd be back for Bob in a couple of weeks, but Selena knew it was a lie. 'Looks like it jus' you an' me, L'il Bob,' she murmured to herself. Secretly, she was pleased.

Selena showed Bob real love, the kind of love a small boy of seven should have expected from his mother. Early in their time together, Bob asked her about his mother, if she loved him and when she'd be coming home, but soon stopped asking these questions and appeared to forget about her altogether. He seemed to accept that Aunt Selena was now his new mother, and wasn't unhappy with the situation. He made friends with children in the neighbourhood, started school there and ended his schooling there.

When Bob was small, he and Selena – forever limited to the fashions of the very young – shopped for clothes in the same children's department store, but it wasn't long before Bob grew taller than his aunt. He'd stand next to her and proudly point out this fact. He never saw the hump on her back or the crookedness of her small body; all he ever saw was someone he loved more than any other person in the world. For her part, Selena was thrilled to have Bob in her life. Apart from her work in the mill during the week, and attending church on the Sunday, hers had been a relatively lonely life. She knew men didn't find her attractive and that she'd never have a husband, but now at least she had her own child. She hoped Clarissa would never return.

Clarissa didn't return: she followed her dream for two years and then died of a heroin overdose. She was found dead in a cheap hotel room by the man who'd introduced her to the drug, the very same man who'd advised her years earlier to ditch Bob. Selena arranged her sister's burial, but for many years made no mention of the matter to Bob.

Bob was a bright child, inquisitive and naturally mischievous; he was also lazy. Miss Priddy lost count of the times she was summoned to the school by his teachers. On her return she would scold Bob, but all he did was smile his big goofy smile at her. Bob did, however, excel on the baseball field: he had a keen eye and an accurate throw, and every year was chosen to pitch for the school team. Nothing made Selena prouder than to see him on the field wearing his baseball uniform, or when Bob took her hand and walked her home after a game.

Bob and Selena walking together made for an incongruous sight. At six feet two, Bob dwarfed his aunt, and from behind it was difficult to tell who the adult was and who the child. Bob, by now, had come to look upon himself as his aunt's protector. He didn't have to rescue her from fist fights, but he couldn't help but notice the snide looks as they walked through town, or hear the cruel jokes made at her expense. Despite Selena telling him to ignore these people, he never hesitated to confront them. These confrontations often led to altercations and, occasionally, an overnight stay in jail. After one such fracas with a white grocer, Bob was given the choice of going to prison for a short spell or joining the army. Both he and Selena opted for the latter.

Bob proved a natural soldier. He was big, strong, naturally athletic and surprisingly – under direction – exceptionally disciplined. He also looked the part. What really caught the eye of his superiors, however, was his *eye*, and shooting ability. He had twenty-twenty vision and accuracy honed on the baseball field, and years of sitting quietly in a chair watching cartoons on the television had also equipped him with a natural stillness. Bob, they decided, was a natural born sniper.

For his part, Bob delighted in his new-found skill and the elite status he now enjoyed. He boasted of both to his Aunt Selena, and she was the first to know of his posting to Vietnam, though neither of them was too sure just exactly where Vietnam was. The French had known where the country was for some time, and until 1954 had made it their home away from home. In that year, however, their forces were defeated and expelled. What had once been one country, now temporarily became two, split by the Geneva Accords at the seventeenth parallel until elections could be held.

The United States viewed the nationalists in the north of the country as communists, and Ho Chi Minh as no less than a thinner version of Mao Tse-tung. Consequently, to ensure the creation of a non-communist government that would act as a bulwark against communist expansion from the north, it poured vast amounts of financial and military aid into the south. It also sent people. They were amorphously termed advisers or technicians, and their duties were similarly irregular; one of them was Bob.

Bob arrived in Vietnam in 1958. Insurgency in the south had targeted government officials, school teachers, health workers, agricultural officials and village chiefs; Bob's brief was to target the insurgents. For the next two years he rarely moved, spending his time motionless in trees, on the ground or on the roofs of buildings. He stopped counting the bodies at fifty.

Bob's rifle became his best friend. Unlike other snipers stationed there, who preferred the newer and semi-automatic M1D rifle, Bob stuck with the M1903A4 Springfield. It was a pound or two heavier, but its bolt-action made for greater accuracy and range; mounted with a Stith-Kollmorgen Model 4XD scope, Bob could kill a target at 1,200 yards. He called it Old Mo, in memory of his father.

Though he personalised his rifle, Bob never personalised his targets. They always remained targets, and never became living people. The scope allowed him such detachment. Every killing was at a remote distance, and he never had to witness the results of his handiwork at close quarters. Bob felt no guilt, no remorse; in his mind killing was no more than a regular nine-to-five job sanctioned and paid for by the government. If the US government viewed communism as an evil, then communism *was* an evil.

Bob made friends among the other advisers, but most of his free time was spent alone; he preferred to explore the strangeness of the country he was there to defend, rather than joining them in their search for what they crudely called chicken-chow-pussy. Vietnam, in fact, fascinated him. More people should come visit here, he thought, and within a matter of years they did – hundreds and thousands of them, all soldiers. Unfortunately, it wasn't the kind of tourism Bob had had in mind.

After two years in Vietnam, Bob returned home to serve out his final months at the Fort Bragg army base in Fayetteville, North

Carolina. Shortly before his discharge, Bob was summoned to base headquarters and introduced to Colonel William B Fogerty, a man who appeared to live life in the shadows. Even when asked, Fogerty never directly told Bob which agency or branch of government he worked for.

'It doesn't matter, son,' he told Bob. 'The mere fact we're having this conversation on base tells you I'm legit, and that my business isn't just army business but government business.

'You did a hell of a job in Vietnam, Crenshaw; killed more gooks than the rest of the other snipers put together. You're blessed, kid. God has given you a talent for putting lead into people when they least expect it, and it would be a crime to waste it, a sin. Now here's the deal...'

The deal was that Bob would work for him – and therefore the government – on an informal and freelance basis. There would be no contract or written paper trail; he could tell no one what he did or where he went. In return, he would be paid a monthly retainer for – as Fogerty put it – essentially sitting on his butt, and larger sums after completing missions.

Bob took the deal. He'd had little idea of what to do after leaving the army anyway, and this option appeared to allow him the part of being in the army he enjoyed, without the rest of it. Besides, he needed money: Aunt Selena's health had deteriorated. A relatively short lifetime of hard work and deformity had taken its toll, and she'd suffered a stroke; her beautiful face was now as crooked as the rest of her small body.

His decision pleased Fogerty. Apart from one trip to Laos in the three years that followed, the majority of Bob's missions were to Central America: Haiti, Guatemala, Ecuador and the Dominican Republic. Wherever Bob went, dead bodies were left in his wake.

'What you do, Bobby?' Aunt Selena once asked him. 'You never rightly say.' She was in a nursing home now, sitting in a chair propped up with cushions, her small legs sticking out parallel to the floor.

Bob hesitated. 'I work fo' the governmen', Aunt Selena. Take care o' problems o'erseas.'

'But you do good, right?'

He hesitated again. 'I figure so,' he said uncertainly.

He found her questions unsettling. There were official reasons why he could never tell his aunt the truth, but there were also personal grounds. If he told her he killed people for a living, she'd be shocked and more than disappointed in him; and the realisation that he could never tell her the truth also shocked and disappointed him.

He'd been proud of his achievements in Vietnam and had understood the nature of his task there, but now he had no idea of the rights and wrongs of his actions and an uneasy feeling started to eat away at him. He began to question the nature of what he was being asked to do, and over the months that followed reluctantly concluded that it was no more than blood money that allowed his aunt the comfort and care of a nursing home. If she'd known this, Aunt Selena would have left immediately.

His decision to leave his vocation was made all the easier after his aunt's death. Selena's body had never been strong, but her will and spirit had always appeared to Bob to be indomitable. After her stroke, he knew her time on earth would be limited but, even so, was still surprised she died as soon as she did. The second stroke was massive. For two days, Selena lay in a coma, twitching and flinching, her body in the throes of a spasm that looked to be trying to straighten its own misshapen form. And then she died.

Bob had visited his aunt regularly after her first stroke. Her once beautiful smile had become lop-sided, but the light that radiated from her face never dimmed. She still laughed at his stupid jokes, listened to his stories and told him she was proud of what he'd made of himself.

'All this travel o' yo's, Bobby,' she'd once said to him. 'Yo' daddy woulda been jealous. All he ever wanted was to travel the worl'. It prob'ly in yo' blood, boy.'

'If you'da had a chance to travel, Aunt Selena, an' you coulda gone any place in the worl', where would you o' gone to?'

Without blinking an eye, she answered straightaway: 'China, Bobby, I'da gone to China.'

'Why China?' Bob had asked her, somewhat taken aback.

''Cos ever'body there little. No one woulda given me no mind. No one woulda looked twice at me there.'

Bob sat by her bedside stunned into silence. It was the first time his aunt had ever indicated she didn't like the way she looked, or that her appearance had made her life a trial. Because she'd never complained, and seemed to accept the way she was, he'd wrongly presumed it didn't matter to her. Obviously, he'd been wrong, very wrong.

Tears from a six foot two inch man are no larger than those shed by a woman of four feet two, and they still fall – just a lot further.

Aunt Selena died with Bob holding her hand.

The Congo

It was now 1965 and Bob straddled a tree branch in the eastern Congo, the Springfield carefully balanced across his arm. More than a year had passed since he and Gene had been arrested and thrown into jail.

He still kicked himself for getting the two of them locked up, and felt particularly guilty for involving Gene in the roadside altercation. Even at the time he knew he shouldn't have been messing with those police, but something outside his control had driven him on. Maybe it was as simple a thing as a man being programmed to take only so much bullshit in one lifetime, and that by the time the police had pulled him over his quota had been filled. Maybe. He couldn't say for sure. Whatever the reason, he'd managed to get both of them in deeper shit than he could dig either one of them out of. It was then he'd remembered Fogerty and the colonel's last words to him when he'd told him he was quitting.

'You ever change your mind, son, or find yourself in some kind of predicament, call me on this number. I warn you now there'll be a price to pay, because there's no such thing in life as a get out of jail free card – but we can talk about that then.' He'd then written a telephone number on a small blank piece of paper and, for some reason, Bob had placed it in his wallet and kept it. (Bob still thought it strange that Fogerty had used the expression 'get out of jail free card'. How had he known?)

Bob remembered the colonel's words while being led to the cell, and insisted he be allowed the one phone call that was his due. The number Fogerty had given him had rung and rung, and Bob had grown nervous; but then came the familiar click of a phone being lifted from its cradle and the sound of Fogerty's gruff voice.

'You believe in God, Crenshaw?'

'Yes sir, I do.'

'You ever seen Him?'

'Cain't says I have, sir.'

'You ever heard His voice?'

'No sir,' Bob said, wondering where the conversation was heading.

'Well, you're hearing it now, son, and when you see me, as far as you're concerned you'll be seeing Him. From then on, you'll be beholden to me. You got that?'

'Yes, sir.'

'Okay. I'll see you in the next day or so. What's the name of this other clown you want out?'

'Chaney, sir. Gene Chaney.'

Fogerty hung up. Six hours later, Bob was handed over to the FBI and put on a plane for Washington, DC.

The Congo had become independent from Belgium in June 1960. Scarred by the savagery of its colonial experience and cursed by vast mineral wealth, the Democratic Republic soon spiralled into chaos. That the United States judged its first prime minister anti-western also didn't help matters; Patrice Lumumba, they told anyone prepared to listen, was a communist.

The bulk of the nation's wealth – cobalt, copper, gold and uranium – lay in the province of Katanga. Under the leadership of Moise Tshombe, and supported by Belgium and the United States, Katanga seceded from the republic. Patrice Lumumba, meanwhile, was overthrown in a US-inspired military coup led by Joseph Mobutu and, in January 1961, assassinated. Three years later, his ideological heirs rebelled and the United States despatched two hundred advisers and technicians to support the established government, now headed by its old friend Tshombe. Among them was Bob.

Bob had been grateful for Fogerty's intervention in Jackson, but now felt trapped by it. He'd escaped prison in Mississippi only to become a prisoner of the colonel, serving a non-determinate sentence in cells overseas – the Congo being the most recent of a series of such cells. He was wondering how long this situation would prevail when his attention was caught by the glint of sun striking either glass or metal.

He looked through the scope and saw a white man with a trained rifle. The weapon he was holding was an M1D, but had no cone-shaped flash hider; Bob quickly surmised that the man was therefore one of the mercenaries operating in the area, and not an American. He followed the direction of the man's rifle and made out the crouched figure of a dishevelled-looking Hispanic man in the process of emptying his bowels on to the baked Congo soil.

Bob had to make a split-second decision: did he let the mercenary kill the man, or did he save the man and kill the mercenary? He disliked mercenaries and resented their contempt for the Africans whose country they operated in; he also thought it unfair that any man be shot in the middle of a bowel movement. It was another thought crossing his mind, however, that ultimately won the day for the Hispanic. As the mercenary's finger closed on the gun's trigger, a bullet from Bob's Springfield hit him square in the temple, and the mercenary slumped to the ground.

Bob walked towards the Hispanic with his arms held in a gesture of surrender. The crack of rifle fire had disturbed the man mid-motion, and he trained his pistol on Bob. When Bob saw that his presence had been noted, he carefully took the rifle from his shoulder and placed it on the ground. He then looked away while the man cleaned himself and gathered his trousers.

When the man came towards him, Bob motioned for him to

follow. They reached the body of the mercenary, whose arms were heavily tattooed. 'He was gonna shoot you,' Bob said.

'Espanol?' the man replied.

Fortuitously for Bob, the only Puerto Rican family in the whole of Atlanta had lived next door to his Aunt Selena. He'd made friends with the son, and tiring of ever making himself understood in English started to learn Spanish word equivalents. The result was that his friend learned to understand and speak English, while Bob learned to understand and speak Spanish with an almost perfect accent.

'He was going to shoot you,' Bob repeated. 'He's a mercenary.'

'What's your name?' the man asked.

'Bob Crenshaw.'

'American?' Bob nodded.

'Ernesto Guevara de la Serna. I'd give you my hand, but in the circumstances I doubt it hygienic. I'm interested as to why you saved me?'

The part of his name that struck a chord of recognition in Bob's mind was Guevara, and his eyebrows rose. 'Guevara as in *Che* Guevara?' he asked. It was Che's turn to nod.

'Well, I don't like mercenaries, Che.' Bob said, 'But I was also hoping you might be able to help me out. I'd heard there were Cubans operating in the area and figured you were one of them.'

'Argentinean,' Che corrected him. 'I recently renounced my Cuban citizenship. But help you? How?'

Bob explained his idea. During the endless hours he'd spent in his own company, he'd daydreamed elements of a plan, but the final part had only slipped into place after he'd caught sight of the mercenary and Cuban that morning. His intention had always been to somehow disappear and return to the United States with a new identity, but there had been logistical holes the size of planets in his scheme. By placing the Cuban in his debt, he was hoping to fill at least one of these holes and hitch a ride to Cuba; Cuba, at least, was a lot nearer to home than the Congo.

'And how were you going to disappear? Simply evaporate?' Che asked.

'I was hoping they'd think I was dead,' Bob replied.

'That's no good. Your superiors will want proof. Do you have dog-tags?'

'Not dog-tags as such, but this chain around my neck would identify me to a commanding officer if I got killed.'

'Okay, follow me,' Che said after a few moments thought, and led him to the Cubans' encampment.

'Go get Raoul's body!' he ordered two of the soldiers with hair as long as his. 'Put it on a stretcher, get some gasoline and then follow me.'

The four of them walked back to the tree where Bob had positioned himself that morning, unwrapped Raoul's body and placed it on the ground. Bob saw then that Raoul was Afro-Cuban and pretty much the same height and build as himself. Without being asked, but knowing what he was supposed to do, he took the chain from his own neck and placed it around Raoul's. Che nodded his approval. The mercenary's body was brought to the same spot, and gasoline poured over both.

'It's your death,' Che said to Bob. 'You do the honours.'

Bob struck the match Che passed him, and tossed it on to the bodies. There was a whoosh as the gasoline caught fire and Bob's identity disappeared in flames.

'Now *that's* how you fake your own death,' Che said, a look of satisfaction on his face.

A sudden thought crossed Bob's mind. 'What were Raoul's teeth like?'

Che looked at him. 'I was his commander, not his dentist. How the fuck should I know?'

'It's just that the US army takes teeth seriously.'

'Why? Do you need a perfect smile to join your army these days?' Che sneered. 'I thought you Americans only needed good teeth to run for political office or enter beauty pageants. We have no time for such fripperies in Cuba. We don't have beauty pageants and we don't have elections.

'So tell me Senor Crenshaw, why *does* the mighty US army take such an interest in the teeth of its soldiers?'

'It keeps dental records for purposes of identification,' Bob said. 'If they recover a body that's been dead for a long time, or mutilated and unrecognisable, they look at the teeth.'

They waited for the flames of fire to lick their last bone, and then poked around the skeletons of Raoul and the mercenary. It became immediately apparent that Raoul's teeth would never pass for Bob's: the central four teeth of Raoul's upper jaw were completely missing.

'Now what?' Bob asked.

Che handed him a machete, kept in a leather scabbard attached to his belt. 'Cut off both heads at the neck and bring their skulls.'

Bob took the machete and did as instructed. He returned the heavy knife to Che and then threaded a piece of thin rope through the eye sockets of each skull. He tied the two ends of the rope together to form a handle, and followed Che and the two Cubans as they headed back in the direction of their encampment. After about a mile Che halted, and ordered one of the Cubans to dig a hole four feet deep.

'Why so deep?' Bob asked.

'To make sure no animal gets a scent of them,' Che replied. 'I think you'll agree that it's best these bones never see the light of day again?'

Bob agreed and, after a while, relieved the Cuban using the spade and finished digging the hole himself. He placed the skulls at its bottom, packed the soil firmly around and above them, and then placed fallen branches and loose vegetation over the disturbed area.

'Congratulations,' Che said to him. 'You are now dead. All we have to do is get you to Cuba.'

For the rest of the day and deep into the night, Bob and Che talked; it was natural that two people now beholden to each other would want to learn more about each other's lives. Che talked about growing up in Argentina, meeting Fidel in Mexico and travelling to Cuba; he talked of the time he'd lived in the Sierra Maestra Mountains fighting Batista and, with less enthusiasm, about his time in government. He told Bob about the disagreements he had with Fidel, how the man was a fool to trust the Soviets after the way they'd betrayed Cuba during the Missile Crisis, and of his decision to leave Cuba and offer his services to the revolutionaries of the Congo; revolutionaries, he lamented, who'd turned out to be little more than a jumble of in-fighting splinter groups with no discernible revolutionary programme. Disheartened by their incompetence and debilitated by asthma and dysentery, he'd already decided to leave the Congo to its own devices.

In turn Bob told him of his life and Che listened intently.

'For young men we've both led interesting lives,' Che said. 'More interesting things will happen to us and, when they do, we should think of each other and remember the time we spent together in this hell-hole.' He then gave Bob his beret with the single red commander's star sewn on to it. 'A present,' he said. In return, Bob gave him the Springfield, and told him its name was Old Mo.

Che explained to Bob that he wouldn't be travelling to Havana with him, but would write a letter of introduction for him to give to Fidel; Fidel would see to it that he got to the United States safely. When Bob asked him why he wouldn't be returning to Cuba, Che turned downcast.

'I've never failed at anything in my life, Bob. Okay, I never got a permanent position as a doctor and, come to think of it, I've never done too well as a husband or a father for that matter, but apart from these things, nothing. Failing as a revolutionary is a hundred times worse than failing on the personal level. It would be humiliating for me to go back to Cuba after making such a furore about leaving the country and devoting my life to world revolution. I'd be looked upon as a dog with its tail between its legs. They would never understand how impossible it's been here, how futile.'

'I think they'd understand,' Bob said. 'Surely the others would vouch for you?'

'That isn't the point.' Che said. 'I don't want anyone vouching for me! Maybe in a few months, I'll return. Maybe.'

When the two of them said their goodbyes, they shook hands and embraced.

Cuba

'I can't read this scrawl!' Fidel shouted, after Bob gave him Che's letter. 'It may as well be a fucking prescription. We'll have to wait till he gets back and verifies your story.' He walked to within two feet of Bob and looked him in the eyes. 'You know who I am, don't you? But I don't have a fucking clue who you are, gringo. You see my point?'

Fidel left Bob alone in the room and shouted instructions to an official sitting at the desk immediately outside its door. The official immediately made a phone call and, half-an-hour later, took Bob by the arm and escorted him downstairs to a waiting jeep.

'Where are we going?' Bob asked.

'Out of the way,' the official replied, and climbed into the backseat.

Out of the way proved to be a remote farm in the mountains of Pinar del Rio called San Andres de Caiguanabo. An old man and woman lived there as caretakers, and showed Bob to a small cabin close to the main house. The official told him the old couple would look after him, feed him and take care of his laundry; in return, he would be expected to perform farm chores. 'Everybody works in Cuba!' the official informed him.

While Che stayed in Dar-es-Salaam and then Prague, Bob helped with the tobacco crop, fixed fences, chopped firewood and painted the house and outer buildings. He ate well, smoked good cigars and enjoyed the company of Bebo and Hilda, the old caretakers. He also found he enjoyed the manual nature of his work. What he didn't particularly enjoy, however, were the visits of Fidel, the man's endless and meandering harangues and the questions he'd ask and then always answer himself.

'How tall are you?' he asked Bob on one of these visits.

'About six two.'

'I don't think so, gringo. I'm six foot two and I think I have the edge on you. I could have been a professional basketball player. Did you know that? What about you, did you ever play?'

Bob thought that if Fidel took off his boots, they'd be exactly the same height, but said nothing. 'I shot a few hoops,' he said, 'but baseball was my game. I used to pitch for the school.'

'For the school? Ha! I was one of the *country's* top pitchers,' Fidel retorted. 'I doubt you'd have been my standard. I could have made a living playing either baseball *or* basketball, but I didn't, I chose not to. I set aside my own ambitions, sacrificed them and myself for the good of the country, for the people of Cuba. Have you ever done anything like that? I didn't think so! You Yankees like making money too much. But do you give it to poor countries like Cuba?

'I once wrote your President Roosevelt asking him for a ten dollar bill. You think he sent it? Fuck no! All those millions and he couldn't spare ten dollars for a small Cuban schoolboy. Even Batista wasn't such a tightwad. He came to my first marriage, did you know that? Gave me and Mirta $1,000 for our honeymoon. Probably knew I was going to topple him one day and thought he could buy me off. The bastard got it wrong, though. No one buys Fidel off: not the Americans, not the Soviets and not the Chinese. If ever a man was his own man, then that man has to be me: Fidel Fucking Castro.'

'I don't suppose you've heard anything from Che, have you? Is he coming home any time soon?'

'You know something that's funny, gringo? People think they're all chummy with Guevara when they get to call him Che. He ever tell you his nickname, the name his real friends call him? No, I didn't think so. Telling you would have been too much of an irony. It's Sniper! Sniper Guevara. Ha!'

'Did he used to be a sniper?' Bob asked.

'Not in your sense of the word. The name comes more from his lack of social graces, the way he talks to people, assassinates them mid-sentence if he doesn't think their argument's worth a shit.'

'So, is he coming back any time soon?' Bob asked again.

'A month, two at the most. He's in Europe now, but thinking Latin America. He thinks countries there are ripe for revolution just like the Congo was. Gets it fucking wrong every time. He ought to listen to me more.

'Was he still wearing his hair long in the Congo? He was? I thought as much. I can't get it into his head that he's not a rock star or one of those fucking hippies. I don't mind the beard, we all wear those, but his hair's a mess. Makes him look too much like a pretty boy.'

'He'll be staying here when he gets back and you'll see him then. He'll like the place. You've done a good job fixing it up. The fences look particularly good.'

Bob had barely finished thanking him for his comments when Fidel launched into what he obviously considered a related topic.

'You know the two things a man needs most of in life? No? Then I'll tell you. Rubble and wood! A man can never have too much. Rubble and wood always come in handy. And it's the same for a country. No country can have too much rubble or wood. They're the basis of a nation's economy.'

Bob never did figure out how a man who talked as much as Fidel ever found the time to accomplish anything, let alone run a country. The man talked for hours on end, and on all subjects. He had opinions on anything and everything. After taking three hours to answer a simple query about Cuban cigars, Bob learned never to ask Fidel further questions. It was strange how he ended up liking the man.

Bob was leaning against a fencepost and smoking his first cigar of the day when he noticed the plume of dust rising from the mountain road leading to the farm. Dust always signalled the arrival of a visitor, usually Fidel, and Bob braced himself. It was late afternoon and the month was June.

The vehicles came into view and Bob saw that it was a small convoy: two jeeps to the front, an old American sedan in the middle and two jeeps to the rear. His interest was aroused and he walked to the house where Bebo and Hilda were standing.

'What's going on?'

'Commandante Guevara has returned to us, Senor. He is to be our guest,' Hilda said excitedly.

'Well I'll be damned,' Bob said. 'I'd almost given up on the guy.'

The vehicles drew to a halt, handbrakes were applied and

engines extinguished. Sixteen soldiers dismounted from the two jeeps, and the driver of the sedan climbed out shaking his head. Fidel and Che remained in the backseat of the car, arguing and gesticulating furiously.

'Same old same old?' Bebo asked the driver, a broad smile on his face.

'You got it,' the driver replied exhaustedly. 'We'd barely left Havana before they got into it: People or Individuals, Soviets or Maoists, Agrarianism or Industrialisation. And then Fidel went and called him Wispy Beard and all hell let loose. You know how sensitive he is about his beard.'

The door of the sedan was suddenly flung wide open and the two revolutionaries came tumbling out, grappling with each other and trading insults. No one intervened and no one – apart from Bob – even showed the least bit of surprise. Hilda shrugged her shoulders and announced there was food waiting for them inside the house, and that they should eat it before it got cold. Everyone headed inside and sat down at the long table, leaving Fidel and Che rolling around in the dust, one moment the advantage with Fidel, the next with Che.

Ten minutes passed before the two men joined them at the table. They entered the room laughing, arms around each other's shoulders. Hilda put two plates of food in front of them and told them not to blame her if it was cold. She spoke to them as she would errant sons.

The meal ended and Fidel and most of the other soldiers lit cigars. Che took a pipe from one of his pockets, filled the bowl with tobacco and leaned back in his chair, disappearing behind a cloud of smoke.

'So, gringo,' Fidel said to Bob. 'Did you finish making the bunks?'

Bob said he had.

'So where are they?'

'Surprisingly enough, I put them in the bunkhouse,' Bob replied.

Fidel gave him a hard stare. Over the months, and when it had been just the two of them together, Bob had been allowed to speak to Fidel with familiarity. He interpreted the look as an indication that he should be more reverential when others were in the room.

'Show me them!' Fidel commanded.

Fidel followed Bob to the bunkhouse. He stopped at the door and surveyed Bob's handiwork from a distance: ten sets of two bunks, five against each side of the room perpendicular to the walls. He then walked the length of the room and inspected each bunk in detail.

'They're adequate, gringo, but I could have done better. At school, they said I showed the talent of a master carpenter. I could have been a fucking cabinet maker, you know that? Another Chippendale or a Hepplewhite. No one had seen such craftsmanship for two hundred years. They called me a woodworking prodigy!'

Che, who had followed them to the bunkhouse, interrupted Fidel. 'Then why did the bookcase you made wobble? You told me yourself it rocked from side to side. You laughed about it, remember?'

'It was sabotaged! I distinctly remember telling you that someone *sabotaged* it – and, for God's sake, stop creeping around like that, Guevara. You're not in the jungle now!'

'I laughed only at the pitifulness of the person who did it, the shallowness of the life he led, his mean and jealous spirit.' He turned to Bob. 'This person planed half an inch off one side of the bookcase's base. He sneaked into the woodworking studio at night like a thief, to steal from me, to undermine me. I promised Che that if this hedge-creeper was ever found, I'd allow him to execute the bastard. You like executing people, don't you, Guevara? Eh?' Che didn't react, and Fidel continued.

'If you'll excuse me, gentlemen, I now have to return to Havana. Unfortunately, the country won't run itself. I'll see you in two days.' He embraced Che and made to leave the room. As he drew level with the door he turned to Bob. 'Start packing your bags, gringo. Next time I leave here, so do you.'

After Fidel had left the room, Che burst out laughing. 'There'll be no execution,' he said to Bob. 'The truth is he got his measurements wrong: *that's* why the bookcase rocked from side to side. It's as simple as that. The man's got two left hands. Hell, if you gave him two pieces of wood and a nail, he'd be hard pressed to make a cross…

'Good bunks, by the way,' he added.

In the two days before Fidel returned, Bob saw Che only in the evenings. The Commandante and the sixteen soldiers would rise from their bunks before daybreak and spend the day trekking through the surrounding countryside, and returning only shortly before dinner. Che told him they were training for a new expedition which this time, he said, would be in Latin America. He also told Bob that his departure from Cuba was now in hand, and would happen after he returned with Fidel to Havana.

Fidel returned to the farm and stayed for two days. During this time training was suspended and conversation became the order of the day, sometimes meaningful and sometimes seemingly meaningless. Fidel talked about Bolivia, its history and geography; he talked about recent worker uprisings there and the country's unique positioning at the centre of the continent. Fidel, however, also spent time talking to Che about the way he brushed his teeth, the way he tied his boots and the way he poured beer from bottle to glass.

'Guevara, what are you doing?' he asked Che one morning, as the revolutionary rinsed toothpaste from his mouth. 'Use a fucking glass. Scooping water into your mouth with a brush takes too much time, valuable time. How would you feel if you failed in your mission because you'd spent too much time brushing your fucking teeth instead of fighting imperialists?'

'I've always cleaned my teeth this way,' Che retorted. 'Ten scoops of water and rinse; ten scoops of water and rinse; ten scoops of water and rinse. It suits me fine. I don't carry a glass with me into the jungle! Do you think I go there for a picnic, for a holiday?'

'Suit your damned self then,' Fidel shouted back at him, 'but don't come running to me if Bolivia goes tits up.'

Another time, Fidel saw Che in the middle of changing the

boots he wore inside the house for those he wore outside. 'Guevara, what are you doing? You have no boots on your feet. What would you do if enemy soldiers stormed into the camp and you didn't have boots on your fucking feet? It would be hard for you to make a run for it, and if you did, your feet would be cut to pieces. Change one boot at a time and make sure you always have a boot on each foot. It's common sense. You got any of that left, Guevara?'

Che ignored him.

As Bebo handed around bottles of beer before dinner on the first evening of Fidel's return, Che prised off the cap on the bottle and poured the beer into a glass. The beer foamed and he had to wait for it to settle before he could pour the rest of the bottle's contents.

'Guevara, what are you doing?' Fidel asked him. 'You should hold the glass in your left hand and pour the beer over the area where your thumb shows through from the outside of the glass. Your thumb warms the glass, and if you pour beer over warmth it won't foam. Look!' Fidel then poured a bottle of beer into his own glass without it foaming. 'Perfect!' he said.

Che stood up and started shouting at Fidel. 'I'm not taking any lessons from someone who puts fucking hair conditioner on his beard! Why do you think I renounced my Cuban citizenship? For the fun of it? No! I did it because the revolution in this country is dead. How could it be alive when its so-called President has fallen into such bourgeois habits?'

'Oh, back to the beard argument again, are we, Guevara? You're just sore because you never really qualified as a *barbudos*. How could you when you have such a wispy beard? I had a thicker beard than you have now when I was fourteen! The teachers made me shave it. They were jealous, of course, because I attracted the attentions of the senior girls and their own frustrated wives! They saw me as a threat. They were aware of my sexual power over women even then, and they were scared.' He then turned to the soldiers in the room and explained that it hadn't been his idea to use hair conditioner on his beard. The doctors had ordered him to use it: it was too dangerous for any man to have a beard as thick as his!

Fidel slept with Che and the soldiers in the bunkhouse for two nights. On the morning of the third day, he told Bob to gather his belongings and say goodbye to Che, Bebo, and Hilda. Bob embraced all three, but when he tried to thank them his voice broke, and Hilda started to cry.

'Save your tears for Cubans, old lady,' Fidel teased her. 'This man is a gringo – an American gringo.'

Fidel held his hand out to Che and, as Che made to grasp it, he took it away and flicked Che's nose.

'Hah! Get you every time, Guevara!' Che smiled, and the two men hugged.

On the journey back to Havana, Fidel asked Bob about Mississippi. 'You spent time there. What do you think of the people – did you like them?'

'Not the whites, no. They were mean people. Weaned on hatred, if you ask me; sucked poison from their mothers' teats from the day they were born.'

'Do you know how they reacted when President Kennedy was assassinated?'

'No,' Bob said.

'They laughed and cheered,' Fidel said sombrely. 'I was sadder than they were when I heard the news. If he'd lived, I think matters between our countries would have been different, that somehow we would have learned to live together.'

He paused in his conversation, and then asked: 'Will you be able to find a home when you return?'

'I hope so,' Bob said. 'Sometimes the thought of going back scares me, but it's where I belong.'

'You'll be an outsider in your own country – you know that, don't you? In this world, Cuba is an outsider too, but at least we have our own country to be outsiders in. And we also have ourselves.' He smiled. 'Maybe we should send each other postcards, gringo. Hah!'

Five days later, Bob flew to Mexico City as an attaché to the Cuban embassy there. The following week he left Mexico as Percy Collins, a chewing gum salesman from Chicago.

Dead or Missing in Action

Colonel Fogerty read the report on his desk with his brow furrowed: Crenshaw, or what was thought to be left of Crenshaw, had been found dead, his charred and headless skeleton discovered lying alongside that of a mercenary whose head was also missing. The only piece of positive identification found was Bob's army necklace. Fogerty's frown deepened: it wasn't just the missing head that puzzled him, but the fact that whoever killed him had gone to the trouble of cremating the body – as if they didn't want it to be recognised. Bodies were found all the time in the eastern Congo, sometimes suffering from the processes of decomposition, but always intact. He wondered if something in the Kingdom of Denmark wasn't quite right.

He looked through Crenshaw's personnel file and noted the next of kin was named as Eugene Chaney III. The name rang a bell. He read deeper into the file and found the reason: Chaney was the person who'd been locked up with Crenshaw in Mississippi, and whose release Crenshaw had asked him to arrange. He pressed a button on the intercom that connected him to an adjacent office.

'Get me the whereabouts of Eugene Chaney III,' he barked. 'He's a recent graduate from Duke Medical School, so you might want to start there.'

Two weeks later, Fogerty drove to Maryland in full uniform and knocked on Gene Chaney's door; it was eight o'clock in the evening. When the door opened, Fogerty saw a man wearing jeans and a T-shirt and no shoes.

'Are you Dr Eugene Chaney III?'

Gene acknowledged that he was and, for one awful moment, wondered if he was being drafted. He nervously asked Fogerty to step inside and offered him a drink. Fogerty declined.

'Robert Crenshaw has made you his next of kin. My question is: have you seen him recently?'

'Bob? Bob Crenshaw?' Fogerty nodded. 'What's happened to him? He's alright, isn't he?'

'If you'd just answer my question, Dr Chaney: have you seen him recently?'

'No… no, I haven't. The last time I saw him was over two years ago. We were locked up together in Mississippi for the night. When I was released the following morning he was gone. He just disappeared.'

'And you haven't seen or *heard* from him since?'

'No. I keep thinking he's going to get in touch, but he never does. What's happened? Has something happened to him?'

'Something *has* happened to him, but at the moment we don't know what that something is. I gather he's a friend of yours so I don't want to cause you any needless distress, but we think he might be either dead or missing in action.'

Gene thought that if his own bedside manner was somewhat lacking, Fogerty's was completely missing.

'I didn't even know he was in the army. I mean, I knew that he'd been in the army, but I didn't know he'd rejoined. Where is he missing? What country?'

'Vietnam,' Fogerty lied.

The Colonel watched Gene carefully throughout their short exchange, looking for any hint of a lie, any sign of deception.

'I mentioned to you earlier, Dr Chaney, that Crenshaw made you his next of kin. It appears you're the nearest thing he has to family. The investigation is still on-going but, once it concludes, do you want us to send his remains and personal possessions to you?'

'Yes, I'd want that. I'll make sure he gets a good burial,' Gene said.

'As you're his heir, you'll also receive a cheque for $10,000. It's standard payment.'

Gene didn't react. He sat in his chair unmoving, feeling as though someone had just given him a huge injection of novocaine. Fogerty stood up and went over to him. He took Gene's hand, shook it and then let himself out of the house.

Gene saw the half-eaten apple he'd placed on the kitchen counter after he'd invited Fogerty into the house. He threw it into the bin. It would be the last apple he ever ate. Thereafter, even the smell of an apple reminded him of death and loss. First meat and now apples. Little did he suspect that donuts were waiting for him just around the corner, biding their time until they too could join his growing list.

The Dentist

Bob passed from Mexico into the United States without incident. The border policeman examined the passport given to him by the Cubans, asked him a few disinterested questions about the chewing gum industry, and then waved him through. 'Home!' Bob thought, though just where home actually was, he had no real idea.

These thoughts turned in his mind as he drank coffee in Laredo; it was tasteless and disappointing but how else could it be after drinking Cuban coffee for six months? He could hear Fidel's voice in his head: '*Smell* the coffee, gringo. Your country *is* fucking tasteless and disappointing!'

He smiled briefly and took a small folder of documents from his case. Most of them related to his supposed employment as a chewing gum salesman, but amongst them were the names and addresses of two people given to him by an American he'd met at the Cuban embassy, and also a handwritten letter of introduction. One of the two names, Bob noticed, had been asterisked. He walked with his case to the bus station and bought a one-way ticket to Charlotte, North Carolina. 'Who the hell was Newton Ballard?' he wondered.

Three days later, he found out.

Newton Ballard was a white man in his late fifties, a successful dentist and property owner, and to all outward appearances a man of the Establishment. Lurking beneath the surface, however, was a dissident, whose moral code and political consciousness had been forged in the southern coalfields of West Virginia.

Newton's father – known affectionately to his friends as Pickaxe – had worked as a miner in Logan County, West Virginia. The company he worked for owned his house and everything else in town. Pickaxe leased tools and equipment from the company, bought food and other provisions at inflated prices from the company store, and paid rent to the company. All financial exchanges were made through the medium of scrip, and the company made sure that the scrip he received each week was always short of the scrip he already owed them. The family was forever in the company's debt, forever its prisoner. It was the way the company liked things.

The work was hard. Pickaxe spent his days stooped, kneeling in water and breathing bad air. Wages were low – below average for the mining industry – and conditions bad. He lived in fear of roof falls and gas explosions, and had a greater chance of being killed than an American soldier fighting in WWI. What the miners needed, he believed, was a union to represent them.

The United Mine Workers of America tried to accommodate Pickaxe and those of similar mind and, in 1921, 13,000 miners marched on Logan County to unionise the mines by force. They were met at Blair Mountain by a well-armed force of two thousand men – a mixture of deputies, detectives, state police and soldiers – and from positions on the crest of the mountain, these men fired down on the miners, expecting them to turn and flee. When the miners not only held their ground but gained new ground, they called on the government for assistance. The government obliged them by dropping bombs on the miners.

Although no doubt surprised by this turn of events, the miners remained strangely undaunted: discipline was maintained and the attack continued for a further three days until federal troops arrived in the area. Only then – and to avoid greater loss of life – did the miners' leaders call for a withdrawal. The battle had lasted a week, and a hundred miners lay dead. It had been the largest uprising in the United States since the Civil War. The owners had triumphed, and life for the miners of West Virginia returned to normality – feudal brutality.

Pickaxe Ballard had fought alongside the miners on Blair Mountain but had escaped injury and managed to avoid capture. He returned to the mine with his hopes extinguished and his helplessness confirmed. Three years later he was dead, killed in an explosion. His body was never recovered and the mine shaft where the methane gas had ignited was permanently sealed.

His wife, Bella, was evicted from the house – company property – and she and her three children moved to Raleigh, North Carolina. There she met and married Henry Perkins, the owner of a local convenience store. Henry fell in love with his new family, but reserved a special place in his heart for Newton. He encouraged his adoptive son to aim high and was pleased when Newton decided to become a dentist, and happy to pay for his education.

Despite his new life, Newton never forgot his old one – or that of his father. He remembered its hardships and the toll it had taken on the family – especially the toll it had taken on his father. Pickaxe had been thirty-seven when he was killed in the mine accident, but by that time had already looked like a man of sixty. In particular, Newton recalled his father's conversations at the dinner table, the way he'd railed against the mine owners, their exploitation of the miners who made them rich, and their callous disregard for all lives other than their own.

Pickaxe had made it clear to them that he had little time for governments. Whether state or national, he argued, governments would always side with the owners, the people of their own class. Rather than acknowledge abuses in the system, they would happily look the other way – and were probably paid to do so. Their concern wasn't for the welfare of the poor or the helpless: it was for stuffing their pockets with dollar bills and building their bank balances. No poor or working man could ever hope to get justice in a court of their law. The poor and the dispossessed had to look to themselves, and if necessary operate outside the law. (Unsurprisingly, Pickaxe's views on government became even more decided after the government dropped a bomb on him.)

Undeterred by his newly acquired status as a qualified dentist, psychologically Newton still looked upon himself as a dispossessed coalminer, and consequently sided with the causes of the poor and the helpless. To this end, he joined the American Socialist Party and remained an active member until Norman

Thomas, the party's leader, decided that future electoral activity by the party was pointless. Newton's social activism was now without a home and for a period fell dormant. It sprang back to life, however, on the emergence of the civil rights movement.

From identifying with the black faces of West Virginian coalminers, it was but a short step for Newton to identify with the black faces of people who were naturally black. He equated the abuses of their civil rights with those suffered by the miners, and saw no difference between the company owners' treatment of their employees and the segregationists' treatment of Negroes. As usual, the state and federal governments erred on the side of the powerful and upheld laws that were, to Newton's way of thinking, not only immoral but unworthy of respect. Consequently, when situations arose that demanded he step outside the law, he willingly took that step, and when Bob Crenshaw stood on his doorstep asking for help, he didn't hesitate in offering his help.

Newton lived alone and the two men talked into the early hours. He listened intently to Bob's story, smoking one cigarette after another and sipping from a glass of bourbon he occasionally refilled. He examined the forged documents Bob had been given and gave a low whistle.

'I know a man who'd be interested in seeing these,' he said. 'Very interested. They're good – some of the best I've seen – but to be on the safe side I think we should find you a new identity. I'll start working on that first thing in the morning after we get you fixed up with a place to stay.'

'I ain't got much money, Mr Ballard, so you need to make it cheap.'

'Don't worry about money, Bob – and I already told you, my name's Newton. I own a boarding house near downtown and you'll stay there as my guest. No one will bother you, and you'll find Miss Lettie to be a fine cook.' He looked at his watch.

'I suggest we call it a night. I'll give you a shout about seven. Sleep well, Bob, and – if I haven't already said so – welcome home!'

The boarding house was an old wooden structure but in good

repair. Newton knocked on the front door and walked in. 'Lettie?' he called out, 'Lettie? We have a guest.'

A large black woman bustled into the room, a big smile of welcome on her face. Newton introduced Bob as Percy and apologised that he couldn't stay longer: 'Root canals,' he explained. He turned to Bob and told him he'd return about seven.

'Set a place for me, Miss Lettie. I'll eat here tonight.'

The boarding house had six guestrooms on the second floor. Miss Lettie Williams showed Bob to the first one they came to and handed him a key. She pointed out the bathroom and toilet at the end of the corridor, and then led him back downstairs and showed him the lounge and dining areas. The lounge had a television which, she explained, he was welcome to watch anytime until 11:00 pm; at that time it had to be switched off. Breakfast, she informed him, was served at 7:30 am and dinner at 7:00 pm; a few minutes either way, however, was of no mind to her. She indicated her own rooms at the back of the first floor and told him to holler if he ever needed anything – but not after 11:00 pm.

Bob unpacked his case and put most of his clothes in the drawers of an old dresser; his suit, courtesy of the Cuban government, he placed on a hanger. He lay on the bed and started to relax; it seemed to him that things were starting to work out. After an hour or so, he stood up from the bed and splashed water on his face. He looked in the mirror and smiled. 'Bob Crenshaw,' he asked himself, 'what's gonna become o' you? Who you gonna be?'

The answer to that question came two weeks later when Newton brought him his new documents: Lucius Tribble. It wasn't the name Bob had been hoping for, and Newton sensed his disappointment.

'We never get to choose our parents in life, Bob, and consequently we never get to choose our names. If I'd had a choice in the matter, do you really think I'd have wanted to be named after a fig bar?'

Bob looked quizzical.

'Newton. I'm named after *Fig Newton*. My parents were trying to think of a name for me, and my mother's attention was caught by an opened packet of cookies on the table. She thought it had a certain ring to it and, for reasons I'll never understand, so too did my father.

'You're stuck with Tribble, I'm afraid, but you don't have to be called Lucius if you don't want. It'll always be your official name – and you can't get around that – but you can decide on a nickname for yourself and then get people to call you by that.'

Bob's mood lightened. It sounded like a plan – and plans, after all, were what he and Newton were supposed to be discussing that day.

'What I'm thinking, Bob, is that it would be a good idea if you moved out of North Carolina for the time being. The place is crawling with military, and though they don't have a base here in Charlotte, Fayetteville's a bit too close for comfort.

'The army still has you down as Missing in Action. Until they pronounce you dead and you get your money from that friend of yours, I'm afraid you're in limbo. I've got contacts who can tell me if and when your status changes, but it will likely take time.

'There's a small town in the Blue Ridge I suggest you go to. Crawford's the kind of place where they don't ask questions; you'll understand why when you get there. I know someone living there who's in a similar situation to you and can be trusted. He's renovating a house, and I know he could use some help. I've already talked to him, and in return for your labour he's happy to provide you with board and lodging. Of course, as soon as I hear anything about your status, I'll let you know.

'How does it sound, Mr Tribble?'

Lucius Tribble said it sounded fine to him.

That night Miss Lettie cooked Bob a T-bone steak for dinner. He looked at it admiringly, savoured its taste and then named himself after it. Lucius Tribble became T-Bone Tribble.

Crawford

The town of Crawford sat on a high plateau in the Blue Ridge Mountains. It was isolated and small – very small: it had one stop light and fewer than four hundred residents. It was the county seat of Crawford County, and where its two roads intersected stood a memorial to the Confederate dead.

For geographical reasons, all rivers and streams flowed out of the county, and from the late 1950s, and in search of a better life, so too did its population. Land and property prices plummeted and hippies moved into the small town. The new residents of Crawford wore their hair long and dressed in jeans, overalls and tie-dye T-shirts. Sweet aromas of incense and marijuana filtered from their houses into the streets, and the memorial to the Confederate dead became a meeting place for Confederate deadheads.

Newton stopped the car outside an old wooden house three hundred yards from the town's centre, but still at its outskirts. A tall thin slat of a man pushed open the screen door and walked out on to the porch. He stood there silently while Newton and his passenger climbed out of the car, and spoke only when both men had climbed the steps. Newton and Bob followed him into the house.

'Merritt,' Newton said, 'this is the man I was telling you about.'

The man held out his hand and introduced himself as Merritt Crow. In turn, Bob introduced himself as T-Bone Tribble. Merritt took three beers from the fridge and prised off the caps. He handed one to Newton and one to Bob.

'New beginnings,' he toasted.

'New beginnings!' Bob and Newton replied in unison and the three men clinked bottles.

Newton stayed long enough to ease the two men into their own company, and then headed back to Charlotte. Bob and Merritt drank more beer and Merritt made sandwiches. He apologised to Bob for not offering him a hot meal, but explained he didn't yet have a cooker. As they ate, Merritt asked Bob if he'd ever had a rum bun.

'Cain't says I have, Merritt. What's a rum bun?'

Merritt put down his plate. 'Rum buns are similar to sweet rolls – but different, much stickier. So far as I can tell, the buns are made out of dough and a cinnamon sugar mix, and then glazed and iced. From what people say, the secret's in the glaze and the kind of rum they add to it. It's the only thing about Washington I miss. They used to serve them in the seafood restaurants on the south-western waterfront: always hot and always before dinner. Hogate's restaurant had its own bakery and their rum buns were the best. If you ever figure out how to make them, I promise you, I'll be your friend for life.'

Merritt Crow, whose real name was John Driscoll, had been an analyst with the CIA. He'd been recruited during his final year at Princeton and had gone to work for the Agency straight after graduating. He'd majored in international relations and been considered the brightest student in his year; throughout his four years at the university he'd maintained an unblemished 4.0 average. Merritt's father had been a Vice-Admiral in the US Navy, and his family pedigree had been considered a plus by the CIA.

Merritt told Bob that for many years he'd enjoyed the work. It had been challenging and stimulating, and he'd proved adept as an analyst. In the seven years he'd spent dissecting information he'd been promoted three times, and by the time he left for the field was managing a team of six other analysts. It had been his decision to go into the field. He was unmarried and wanted adventure, a chance to do rather than read about what others had done, and a chance to put into practice plans he'd only been able to theorise about. His first (and only) assignment was Vietnam.

'When I worked as an analyst, T-Bone, I worked in an office. I was hermetically sealed from the real world. Everything was abstract, and all the abstracts were clear cut. There was black and there was white, right and wrong, good and evil. We were the good guys and our enemies were the bad guys. It was as simple and uncomplicated as that.

'And then when I worked in the field everything blurred; there was no black and there was no white. Everything came out of the wash grey. There was good and evil everywhere and no one side had a monopoly of either; there was as much evil on our side as theirs. I did things in Vietnam that were wrong – unjustifiably wrong.' Merritt paused and stared at the floorboards.

'I was in too deep to just resign though. I knew too much – and they knew I knew too much. I'm not saying they'd have put a bullet in my head, but I couldn't be sure at the time that they wouldn't.

'I got transferred back to the States and they gave me a non-job. Subtle threats were made – not just against me, but against my family. I got home one night and found my house broken into. The only things missing were the journals I'd been keeping and some documents I'd photocopied without authorisation. I left the house that night and never returned.

'And now I'm here. Thank God for people like Newton Ballard.'

'I'll drink to that!' Bob said.

Merritt's house was a mess. The roof leaked and the back part of the structure had collapsed. It took them six months to get the house back on its feet and furnished to a level of comfort both men found acceptable, and to celebrate its completion they threw a party and invited the town.

Merritt roasted a pig and guests brought bowls of salad, vegetable sides and desserts. Bob filled an old bathtub in the back garden with ice and crammed it with beer and wine. The music of West Coast psychedelic bands blared from speakers, and people danced, shared joints and laughed. The sheriff came by, drank beer and took tokes. Crawford, it seemed to Bob, was a good place to spend time when life was on hold; it was like being on holiday.

The following day, Bob and Merritt cleared debris and washed dishes. Merritt then went for a walk and left Bob to watch the evening news.

The report of Che's death came on Merritt's black-and-white television set, but hit Bob in Technicolor. His friend, the newscaster said, had been captured by Special Forces close to La Higuera in south-eastern Bolivia and executed the following day, shot nine times by a single soldier who took his pipe as a keepsake. Che's handless body had been flown to Vallegrande for display purposes, and his amputated hands to Buenos Aires for identification purposes.

Bob was one of the few people in the United States to be saddened by the news. He retired to his room and sat there thinking. He thought of Fidel and how devastated by Che's death he would be – and also annoyed: Che hadn't been wearing boots at the time of his capture! He remembered the beret Che had given him and took it from the polythene bag he kept hidden behind a chest of drawers. Che should have had a better ending, he thought, or no ending at all; not yet anyway. He put the cap on his head and shaped it the way Guevara had. He stood looking in the mirror for a long time and then saluted his old friend.

The date was October 9, 1967.

Che's death released the logjam of suspicion that had surrounded Bob's disappearance and kept his life in limbo. Among the objects found in the guerrilla's possession was an M1903A4 Springfield rifle with a Stith-Kollmorgen Model 4XD scope attached to it, and Fogerty had known instinctively that the sniper rifle had belonged to Crenshaw. Knowing snipers the way he did, the colonel also knew that the gun would have comprised too great a part of Crenshaw's being for him to have parted with it willingly. He concluded that Robert Crenshaw had been killed by Cubans while serving his country in the Congo. He closed the file and released his remains to Eugene Chaney III.

Newton gave Bob the news in person. He told him that he was to be buried with full military honours on December 22 – ironically, another Dismal Day.

Bob was laid to rest in Atlanta, in a plot close to his Aunt Selena. Six soldiers carried the lighter-than-usual casket, and as the coffin was lowered into the ground a volley of rifle fire tore into the afternoon's silence. The Minister, Fogerty, the soldiers and the handful of mourners who'd shown up for the service – Bob's baseball coach, a few of his friends who'd avoided going to prison, and three elderly women who'd been friends of Selena Priddy – didn't linger for long, and slowly made their way from the cemetery grounds. Three figures remained at the graveside: Gene, holding the folded flag presented to him by one of the soldiers, and Gene's mother and father. A fourth figure stood in the distance and out of sight.

"Bout damn time,' Bob thought, and smiled at the thought of Colonel Fogerty having just given full military honours to a Cuban guerrilla fighter named Raoul. He never did know Raoul's last name.

In early February of the following year, Bob paid a visit to his old friend.

'I hope you ain't spent my money, Gene.'

The ethereal voice came from the backseat of Doc's car. Doc gave an involuntary yelp and drove straight into a fire hydrant.

'Why in God's name didn't you just knock on my front door?' Gene asked.

'I gotta be careful, man. Wouldn' surprise me if ol' Fogerty ain't got an eye open fo' me yet – an' I never knows which way that eye pointin'. If I'da marched up to yo' house an' knocked on the door, who knows who mighta see'd me.'

Doc and Bob stood in Doc's closed garage looking at the damaged front fender. Doc looked at Bob and shook his head, unable to decide whether to punch him in the face or fling his arms around him.

'Goddamn son-of-a-bitch, Bob!' he shouted. 'Have you any idea what you've put me through? A guy in a uniform comes to my house and tells me you're missing in action, and then, six months later, that you're dead and recommends that I keep your casket closed. I just fucking buried you for Christ's sakes!'

Bob gave him a big smile. 'Look upon it as a miracle, man, an' be happy fo' me. No one give Lazarus shit when he come back from the dead.'

'Lazarus didn't come back from the dead in the backseat of a moving car, you dimwit! You could have got us both killed – and how ironic would that have been? Why didn't you contact me, tell me you were still alive instead of letting me believe you were dead all this time. Did you think I'd turn you in or something?'

"Course I didn' think that, Gene. You my bes' frien', man, but you a fuckin' useless actor. Fogerty woulda read yo' face like he was readin' a chil'ren's book; hauled yo' ass off to jail, too. Had to be this way; no other way it coulda been. Tell you what, though: as recompense fo' all the emotional upset I put you through, you can keep the flag they give you at my funeral. You can hang it out ever' Fourth o' July an' celebrate *my* independence!'

Doc scrunched and un-scrunched his face, clenched and unclenched his fists and then, without warning, threw his arms around Bob and pulled him towards him. He then surprised them both by bursting into tears.

'Man, you wettin' my T-shirt,' Bob said. 'An' all this cryin's makin' me thirsty – you got any beer in that house o' yo's?'

Doc's emotional turmoil gradually quieted, and as the evening progressed he relaxed once more into the easy company of his resurrected friend. Although he'd often wondered what Bob did the times he disappeared from Durham, he had never known about Bob's life as a sniper. He listened while Bob told him of his adventures, particularly intrigued by his tales of the Congo and his relationships with Che and Fidel. The story was too far-fetched to be invented, and Doc saw the pain in Bob's eyes when he told him of the day he heard of Che's execution.

Fortunately for Bob, the money Doc had received from the government was still intact, but the matter remained of how to transfer this money to his newly risen friend. Bob told him a man from Charlotte would contact him and arrange for the money to leave Doc's account without drawing suspicion; it would be some kind of investment plan.

Over breakfast the following morning, Bob warned his friend that contact between them for the immediate future would be difficult, and possibly unsafe. He told him to look out for postcards initialled TT.

Doc left for the surgery with Bob lying on the backseat. Two blocks from the surgery, Bob opened the car door and climbed out.

'You pull any shit like this again, Bob, and I'll kill you myself!' Gene said.

Bob laughed. His exit was unseen, and he walked to a car parked in an adjacent street with an air of nonchalance. The engine turned at the third time of trying. Bob pulled away from the curb and drove back to Crawford.

He left the town a month later – this time for good. He had $10,000 in his pocket and seemingly the world as his oyster. It therefore surprised Merritt when he learned that his friend had gone to work for a dry cleaner in Seattle.

The Dry Cleaner

If it had been Bob's decision to head for Seattle, the initial suggestion had come from Newton. One meeting, he asked Bob if he remembered him mentioning a friend of his who'd be interested in seeing the documents given to him by the Cubans. Bob had nodded that he did.

'The thing of it is, T-Bone, Morris is getting old and he could do with an assistant. He's the person I got your new identity from, by the way. He asked if I could recommend anyone to him and I immediately thought of you. A person in his line of work needs someone he's able to trust, and needless to say a person in your circumstances has the same need. He'd pay you well and you'd be as safe out there as anywhere. Is it something that interests you?'

Bob said that it might well interest him, but asked for a few days to think it over. His answer, when it came, was *yes*. He found himself in the same situation he'd been in when he first planned to leave the army and Fogerty had approached him: he had no idea of what to do next. There was also a part of him that believed in fate and the serendipitous nature of life: if something came up, then it probably came up for a reason. Seattle, he thought, might well be the destination that destiny itself intended for him.

Ballard made a phone call to Morris and arrangements were made. Two weeks later Bob boarded a flight to Seattle; it was the first time he'd been on a civilian airplane and was surprised to find no parachutes.

Bob took the bus to downtown Seattle. He ignored the light drizzle and decided to walk the few blocks to the address he'd been given. The city's economy was experiencing a periodic slide in its fortunes, and the neighbourhood of the dry cleaning store was similarly down-at-heel. Businesses either side of the dry cleaner's were boarded, and the people he passed in the street looked dishevelled.

As he pushed the door open, a bell rang. A man came from a back room and gave him a gentle smile.

'Good day to you, sir. How can I help?'

'My name's T-Bone Tribble, sir. I lookin' fo' Morris Fowler.'

'You've found him, T-Bone. I'm the man you want.'

He took Bob's hand and shook it firmly. He then walked to the door and changed the OPEN sign to CLOSED. Bob followed him behind the counter and into the back room.

Morris Fowler was a man in his late seventies. He wore black working boots that were badly scuffed and a pair of loose-fitting jeans, patched at the knees; above the waist he wore a thick woollen shirt and over it an out-of-shape cardigan. The glasses perched on the end of his nose had tortoise-coloured frames and thick tinted lenses. He was just short of six feet and looked to weigh around two hundred pounds. His shoulders were broad and his forearms big, suggesting an earlier working life that had demanded strength. His face was unshaven and a three-day growth of grey bristles contrasted with the smoothness of his bald head. He also walked with a pronounced limp.

Fowler poured Bob a coffee and asked him about Newton: was he well, and had he explained to Bob the nature of his work in Seattle? He also asked to see Bob's Cuban documents. He studied them carefully but without comment. He asked Bob if he could hang on to them for a while, and Bob told him he could.

The dry cleaning store was a front, and Morris Fowler turned out to be not only a forger but also a fixer. People came to him primarily for new documents and new identities, but they also came to him as a man who knew how to get things. It worked like this:

Although the store had the equipment to dry clean, none of it was in working order and the polythene-encased clothes hanging from the racks were purely for show. In the rare event that a customer actually left clothes for cleaning, they would be taken to another dry cleaner's and then returned to the store. White tickets would be issued for such transactions. It was, however, the pink slip transactions that were the lifeblood of the store.

Any person doing bona fide business with Morris knew to ask for a pink slip: that was the code. Such people would bring clothes to the store, usually a single jacket or coat, and within one of the pockets would be a note of what was required, and also payment. A week or even a month later, dependent on what had been asked for, the customer would return to the store with the numbered pink slip. He – rarely a she – would then be returned the clothes they'd brought in, and within a pocket would be the documentation or goods paid for.

The documents supplied by Morris ranged from passports and driving licences to birth certificates, social security cards, high school diplomas and degree certificates. For such products he determined his own prices. For the goods he supplied purely as a middleman – firearms, explosives, pharmaceuticals, machine tools, duplicate keys and risqué photographs – he added thirty per cent to the price charged him. It was a marketplace where questions were never asked, where paper trails were non-existent and the only medium of exchange was cash.

Bob worked front of house, taking and returning clothes from customers and giving out and taking back the pink slips. Every once in a while he gave out a white ticket, and took these clothes to an actual dry cleaners; even on these transactions the store made a profit. Other times, Morris would send Bob to churchyards and cemeteries, not just in Washington but in surrounding states: Oregon, California, Idaho and Nevada. This was the part of his job that Bob enjoyed most, driving on open roads through new countryside, and exploring towns and cities he'd never before visited.

The purpose of such journeys was to collect the names of children who never had the chance to grow old; children who had died at different times and in different decades. Morris gave Bob a list of his requirements: white children, black children, Hispanic and Chinese children; children with Polish names, Norwegian names, German names, and children who'd been born with true-blue Anglo-Saxon names. Bob was then to visit libraries and read old editions of newspapers to find out as much about these unfortunate children as possible, and also their equally unfortunate families. Morris then took this information and, by exploiting cracks in the system, brought them back to life as new identities for those wishing to escape old ones.

Morris lived in a large apartment immediately above the store, and Bob lived in similar quarters on the third floor. They spent most of their evenings together in one or another of the apartments. Sometimes Morris prepared the meal and sometimes Bob – though neither could have been described as a good cook. Morris came to look upon Bob as the son he'd never had, and Bob, upon Morris, as the father he'd never known.

One evening when the two men had finished eating and the pots been cleared, Bob asked him how he'd got started doing what he did. Morris poured a large measure of bourbon from the bottle that sat between them.

'It's a long story. You're sure you're up for it?'

'Sure,' Bob replied. 'Somethin' I been meanin' to aks fo' a while.'

'Okay, then.' Morris paused and drew breath. 'You ever heard of the Industrial Workers of the World, the IWW?'

'No, sir, cain't says I has.'

'In that case you probably won't have heard of Centralia – that's where I'm from. It's a small town over in Lewis County, not a place you'd visit unless you knew people living there. I got arrested there when I was twenty-nine and charged with second degree murder. I got acquitted, but it took 'em long enough to figure out I hadn't done nothing wrong in the first place. Even now, I get a bad taste in my mouth when I think about it.

'My best friend back then was a man called Wesley Everest. We were born in the same year, 1890, went through school together, worked as lumberjacks together and fought in World War I together. Both of us were lucky enough to get back in one piece, and we went back to lumbering.

'It was hard work but we didn't mind that. What we did mind though was the lumber company we worked for. It's not so bad these days, but back then companies played by their own rules. They were ruthless. Workers didn't have any rights, wages were piss-poor and people got hurt. If they didn't get killed outright in an accident, then they were maimed bad enough to wish they had been. There was never any compensation paid. Me and Wes thought it wrong, so we joined up with the Industrial Workers of the World.

'Anyone belonging to that union was called a Wobbly. Don't ask me why; something to do with the Ws is my guess. Anyway, if you needed help, the Wobblies were the best people to have on your side. If angels feared to tread some places, the Wobblies never did: they just rolled up their sleeves and marched right in. They'd do battle with scabs, take on the police and not one of 'em was afraid of going to jail. They were fearless, and that's why they were hated.

'It wasn't just the lumber companies who hated 'em neither – it was all the factory owners they tangled with. And when you messed with management in those days, you also messed with the local politicians and the newspapers. Always the best of buddies those people. And then, after the IWW opposed US entry into World War I, the government in Washington DC started to take an interest in 'em too, and tried to smash the union.

'Wobblies were arrested left, right and centre, and some of 'em imprisoned. The government accused 'em of being un-American and unpatriotic and, after the war, accused 'em of being Bolsheviks. They whipped up public opinion and got 'em to hate the Wobblies. Vigilante mobs took to the streets and attacked meeting halls owned by the union, and any Wobbly found inside was dragged out and beaten to a pulp.'

Morris paused to refill his glass and then started to recount the events of November 11, 1919.

'There was a parade that day to celebrate the first anniversary of the Armistice. The Wobblies knew it meant trouble for 'em, because the last time the town of Centralia had a parade their meeting hall was attacked and those inside it beaten up. This time though they decided to take precautions and armed 'emselves with guns. They weren't looking for trouble, but they'd just got 'emselves a new meeting hall and didn't want it destroyed. Me and Wes went down to help out – and if needs be – defend the place.'

'Was you armed?' Bob asked.

'No. I didn't even own a gun. Wes did though and he took his. If he hadn't, he might well be alive today…

'Anyway, the parade got set and started to move through the town: American Legion war veterans, civic groups and a bunch of thugs hired by the lumber companies. They stopped outside the IWW hall – only time the parade ever did stop that day – and there was the sound of gunfire, shots ringing out. I don't know who fired first, but if it was one of us then it would've been in self-defence. All hell let loose and the next thing I knew the doors of the hall were being kicked in and men were charging at us.

'I saw Wes fire his gun and hit someone, but that's the last thing I did rightly see. I got clubbed unconscious and woke up in a police cell. I heard later that Wes shot and killed two people and wounded a few others, but the man must have feared for his life to do this. Wes wasn't a violent man. Apart from when we were in the war, I never saw him hit another person once. Hell, the man didn't even cuss!

'He got brought to the same jail I was in, but he wasn't there long and I didn't get to see him. The guards turned him over to a mob that'd gathered outside…' Morris paused, collecting himself before he continued.

'The mob took a rifle butt to his teeth. Smashed 'em. Next they castrated him. Then they took him to the Mellon Street Bridge, put a rope 'round his neck and threw him over the parapet; not once, not twice. Three times. The last throw broke his neck and they left him dangling there, and used his body for target practice. By the time they got 'round to cutting him down his neck had stretched to around fourteen inches.

'You know what the coroner said the cause of death was? Suicide! Wesley Everest, he said, died at his own hand!'

Morris stopped talking and Bob waited until he was ready to finish his story.

'Twelve of us were put on trial for second degree murder. They dropped charges against two, and me and another man were acquitted, but the other eight got convicted and sentenced to twenty-five to forty years. Anyone but a Wobbly would have got the normal sentence in those days – ten years!'

Morris went on to explain that after his acquittal it was impossible for him to find work in Centralia or any place close by. He moved with his wife to Seattle, and through the IWW got a job as a stevedore. He worked on the docks for three years until a box of machine parts slipped from the unloading cradle and smashed the bone in his leg. He found himself out of work, a Wobbly who actually wobbled. And then his luck changed. He was walking towards Pike Place Market one day when he heard someone calling his name; it turned out to be the man he'd shared a prison cell with while waiting to be tried. Morris admitted to Bob that the man was an out-and-out chancer, but likeable with it.

'He'd always been impressed with the drawings I did to pass the time, and he used to get a kick out of me forging his signature. He said I had a natural eye for facsimile. I'd always been pretty good at signatures, I knew that. I used to forge my mother's when I was at school, and for a consideration I'd forge the signatures of other pupils' parents. Saved 'em from having problems, and it gave me extra pocket money. I never thought it was something I could do for a living, though.

'He brought me to the building we're in now, the same dry cleaning store. It operated pretty much on the same lines, but in those days we used to fence more goods. The man who operated it took a shine to me and took me under his wing. I became his apprentice and me and my wife moved into the apartment you live in now. When he died, the business transferred to me. It's worked out okay. I know what we do is illegal, but what governments do is often illegal; they don't have a problem breaking laws when it suits 'em, and there's no love lost between me and them. I'll tell you straight, T-Bone, I'd rather shake hands with Ho Chi Minh than I would Richard Nixon, or any of his like.'

Bob worked at the dry cleaners for twelve years. Returning from a week-long trip scouting the graveyards of North Dakota, he arrived back to find the door of the basement workshop wide open. He looked inside and found it empty. He went to Morris' apartment and Morris met him at the door. He smiled at Bob.

'I'm retiring, T-Bone, calling it a day. I'm ninety years old and feel like I've worked two lifetimes already. I have more money than I'll ever be able to spend, and for the rest of my life I'm going to sit back and relax, do nothing.' He noted the surprised expression on Bob's face.

'I've closed everything down, T-Bone, but I haven't forgotten you.' He handed Bob an old shoe box. 'In there, you'll find ten complete identities – in case you ever have need for a new one – and the deeds to the building: it's yours now! There's also $50,000 in cash. Call it severance pay, a pension, or what you will, but it's yours to do with as you like, and I don't want any argument. Tonight I've booked us a table at the best restaurant in town, and tomorrow I go to Florida. I hope you'll come visit me there.'

Bob ate his last meal with Morris at the Hunt Club in the Sorrento Hotel. A month later he flew to Jacksonville, hired a car and drove to Ponte Vedra Beach. There, he laid Morris to rest.

Having spent most of his life in a Seattle basement, Morris Fowler had no intimate relationship with the sun; he was ignorant of its power and unaware of sunscreen. Shortly after his arrival in Florida, Morris died of hyperthermia.

The sun he never knew cremated him, and the son he never had buried him.

The Barbed Wire Flag

When Bob returned to Seattle, he put the building he now owned up for sale. The decade of the eighties had dawned and gentrification was nibbling at the edges of the neighbourhood. The property sold easily, and if not rich, Bob was certainly now comfortable. He moved into a loft apartment in Pioneer Square and bought a small cabin in the Klamath Mountains of California. The money would run out eventually, but for the time being he had no need for a job. Rather, he spent his time reading, learning to paint and collecting pieces of barbed wire.

Bob had never been a reader. His youth and early adulthood had been times of physicality rather than cerebration, and spent playing baseball with friends or shooting dead the nation's enemies. He associated books with enforced study and had never once entertained the idea that a book might be an origin of pleasure, a source of enjoyment in its own right. Indeed, the only book he'd ever owned was a copy of the Bible given to him by his Aunt Selena on the day he joined the army, and although this book was still in his possession it remained pristine and unread. But now Bob had time on his hands, a cabin in the Klamath Mountains with no television, and a new girlfriend who worked in a bookstore.

Marsha Hancock's first impression of Bob wasn't favourable. In fact, she thought he was as dull as a paintbrush. She'd noticed that he only came into the bookshop when it rained and made no pretence of even looking for a book. Rather, he would sit eerily still in one of the store's easy chairs and hum tuneless drones to himself, only ever stirring to check on the progress of the rain outside; when the rain let up, like clockwork he would leave.

One day, Marsha confronted him and asked why he didn't just buy a damned umbrella. Bob mistook her question as a sign of romantic interest and immediately asked her for a date. She snorted disdainfully, and told him he should ask her again once he'd read *War and Peace* – which to her way of thinking was the same as replying: *not before hell freezes over, buddy!* That Bob then purchased a copy of the book both surprised and disquieted her.

The size of *War and Peace* similarly surprised and disquieted Bob. Had he known that within its pages five hundred and eighty characters lay in wait for him, it is doubtful the transaction would have been completed and their future together ensured.

He returned to the bookstore six weeks later. Ominously for Marsha, the day was one of blue skies and streaming sun. Bob walked up to her holding an umbrella in one hand and a well-thumbed copy of *War and Peace* in the other.

'You owe me *least* one date fo' readin' this mutha,' he told her.

Against her better judgement, Marsha agreed – but for one date at *most*, she told him. One date, however, led to another, and passing acquaintanceship became intimate relationship.

Marsha Hancock was thirty-one, ten years younger than Bob, and happily divorced twice. Her father was a mid-level manager at the Boeing plant, and her mother a teacher in the city's school system. She had two older sisters and a younger brother. She had studied at the San Francisco Art Institute for four years, but had subsequently failed to make a living as an artist. Critics described her work as competent but derivative, and hence her job at the bookstore.

'What 'bout the two guys you divorced? They happy?' Bob asked.

'I hope not!' she replied. 'And that's all I'm saying on the subject. What's past is past. Concern yourself with the present and count your blessings that you have a date with the most beautiful girl you're ever likely to date.'

Bob laughed out loud. What Marsha had said was true: she *was* the most beautiful girl he'd ever dated. She was statuesque in appearance and had striking looks. Her hair was cropped close to the head and her cheekbones were high and chiselled.

Tolstoy, or T-Man, as Bob called him, hadn't been the easiest of introductions to the world of reading, and neither was Marsha's second choice: *Crime and Punishment* by D-Man (or Dostoyevsky, as the Russians and the rest of the world called him). Melville and Hawthorne, despite being American writers, proved even worse. One night, while he and Marsha were lying in bed together, Bob plucked up his courage and made an announcement:

'I ain't readin' no mo' books published b'fore my parents was born, an' – 'ceptin' fo' the Bible – I ain't readin' no book not written by an American. An' I gonna start choosin' my own books. You okay with this, Marsha?'

'When were your parents born?' Marsha asked sleepily.

'I ain't rightly sure, but I figure 1920.'

'Okay,' Marsha said. She then turned on her side and fell asleep. Bob could scarcely believe his luck; she'd given in so easily.

That night he started to fall in love with Marsha, and, the next day, reading for pleasure.

Bob wasn't a discerning reader, but he was voracious. He attached the same importance to the writings of the *National Enquirer* and *People Weekly* as he did to the novels of Ernest Hemingway and William Faulkner. He bought novels and serious non-fiction from bookstores, and quirk, trivia and gossip from supermarket checkouts. He also developed idiosyncratic habits. Possibly as a result of reading Tolstoy's epic, Bob would always check the number of pages in a book. If the count was more than 320, he would put the book back on its shelf and choose another. The only exception he made to this rule was for the Bible.

After twenty years of owning a copy, he opened Aunt Selena's gift and read it from cover to cover, from Genesis to Revelation, from *In* to *Amen*. It was, he believed, the culmination of everything he'd ever read: *War and Peace* and the *National Enquirer* rolled into one, and wondered why it was never sold at supermarket checkouts.

Marsha had given up painting abstracts long before she met Bob but, at heart, still yearned to be an artist. She decided therefore to try a different medium, and signed up for an evening course in screen printing. One afternoon, Bob returned to the house they now shared and found her old brushes, palettes and oil paints boxed up and set next to the garbage cans. He took them back into the house and waited for Marsha.

'You min' if I try my han' with these?' he asked.

'No, of course not, honey,' Marsha replied, 'but can you take them to the cabin and work there? I need to make room for a screen printing machine.' Bob agreed. The cabin was where Marsha also made him keep his growing collection of barbed wire.

Bob and Marsha's cabin was located in the remote and jagged landscape of Siskiyou County. Few people lived there, and the likelihood was greater of meeting a black bear or a mountain lion than another person. They would repair here together in the summer months when the climate was warm and dry, and Bob would go there alone in the winter when the snow lay heavy.

Bob carried no illusions that he had conventional artistic abilities. He could neither draw figures nor put landscapes in correct perspective. He did, however, have patience and a steady hand, traits that had made him a valuable and deadly sniper. Oil paint attracted him. He liked its thickness and texture, its malleability. He learned how to mix colours and add flecks to highlight and change an overall effect. On pieces of wood and later canvasses, he would draw thick bands of textured colours juxtaposed against each other, sometimes horizontal, sometimes diagonal and sometimes vertical.

It was the horizontal bands that sparked the idea of *The Barbed Wire Flag*.

Bob's interest in barbed wire stemmed from his days working for Morris in the field, scouting rural areas for churchyards and cemeteries. Although he'd known of the existence of barbed wire from his time in the army, he'd never once seen a barbed wire fence until the day a barb caught his pants and ripped open the flesh below. Once the pain had subsided he'd taken a closer look at the wire and become fascinated by its design. On subsequent field expeditions he noticed that the shape of the sharp-edged prongs varied enormously, and concluded that there was more than one signature in play. He decided to start collecting the wire, and later, after he'd started reading for pleasure, bought books on the subject and visited fairs and dealers to add to his collection.

It took Bob almost two working months over a six-month period to perfect the prototype of his Barbed Wire Flag. Once satisfied, he wrapped it in a thick woollen blanket and secured it carefully to the roof of his car. Back in Seattle he placed it on an easel in Marsha's studio and once again draped the blanket over it. He said nothing to Marsha about it when she returned from the bookstore, but after they'd eaten he took hold of her hand and led her into the studio.

'I got somethin' to show you, doll. Somethin' I been workin' on. Now close yo' eyes an' open 'em only when I says so.'

Marsha smiled and did as instructed.

'Okay, you can open 'em now.'

When Marsha saw Bob's creation, she was stunned into silence. The canvas before her was four feet by three feet in size and framed in thick weathered fence wood. It depicted the flag of the United States, its thirteen alternating red and white stripes painted in thick textured oil and separated by twelve strands of antique and rusted barbed wire (Brinkerhoff Face Clamp Barb, Bob would later explain to her). The rectangle, which would have housed the fifty stars, had been rebated by two inches to allow for the insertion of six vertical metal prison bars, and behind the bars was a grainy photograph of Bob that had been tinted blue and flecked with white.

'So, what you think, Marsha? I'm callin' it *The Barbed Wire Flag.*'

'I think it's the saddest, most beautiful thing I've ever seen,' she said quietly. 'Do you know what you've done?'

Bob looked puzzled. 'Made me a Barbed Wire Flag, doll. No mo', no less.'

Marsha wanted to take the piece to a gallery whose owner she knew, but Bob was wary of the idea. Too many people would see his face, and even though Fogerty was now dead he still nursed the paranoia of discovery. He told her that this Barbed Wire Flag was for them only, and that it would hang in the cabin. They could, however, make others, and she could help in their construction. The barred window, he suggested, could be filled with all kinds of icons – images that he could never draw but she could screen print.

Together they made a list of images they would display in the rebated window, and decided that each representation would be replicated fifty times to mirror the number and arrangement of the stars in the real American flag. Each concept would be limited to only ten editions, and each edition would use a different type of barbed wire.

The first image they decided upon was that of an American Indian. The Indians, Bob told Marsha, referred to barbed wire as the Devil's Rope, because it had excluded them from their traditional hunting lands.

'How do you know that?' Marsha asked.

'I read it in a book, doll,' he replied.

The second image was that of the buffalo, another native of America almost brought to extinction by its gung-ho settlement.

'How do you know this?' Marsha asked.

'I read it someplace. You oughta try readin' books yo'self some time,' he replied.

Later images included a black slave, an atomic mushroom cloud, Che Guevara, a helmeted West Virginian miner, a vulture, a drug death, and the McDonald's Arches. (Marsha also wanted to include images of bananas, soup cans and Brillo pads, but Bob vetoed these on the grounds that they were derivative. 'How do you know that?' Marsha challenged him. 'I've see'd 'em in books,' Bob replied. 'Books on yo' shelves!')

Marsha left Bob to decide which types of barbed wire they would use for the Flags. After looking through his collection, Bob settled on the Glidden Hanging Barb, the Glidden Large Square Strand, the Knickerbocker Applied Three Point Barb, the Merrill Four Point Twirl, the Kelly Thorny Common, the Hodge Spur Rowel on Large and Small Strands, the Cady Barbed Link, the Jayne and Hill Locked Staples and Wood Block, and the Brinkerhoff Opposed Lugs Lance Point.

They formed a limited company called Rainy Day Sneakers, to which all expenses were charged and all monies paid. It was decided that the artwork would be signed TT Hancock, and that Marsha would be the public face of both the company and the artwork; as always, Bob would remain in the background, in comfortable shadow.

Rainy Day Sneakers took off like a rocket and Marsha stopped working at the bookstore. After the initial launch of *The Barbed Wire Flags* in the bayside community of Sausalito, galleries vied with each other to represent Bob and Marsha's work. The Flags sold for thousands of dollars each. People waited patiently on lists and bought sight unseen. Bob and Marsha moved into a bigger house in Seattle and had the cabin extended. Life for both of them was good – and always for the better when Doc came to visit.

Although Marsha was educated to a high standard herself, she was surprised that Bob had any other friend so educated. Wrongly, she presumed that any friend of Bob's was more likely to be a graduate of the School of Hard Knocks than an actual university. That Bob's closest friend was also a general practitioner confused her even more.

Marsha hated visiting doctors, and the idea of a doctor visiting them slightly concerned her. Meeting Doc, however, had been a pleasant surprise. He didn't look like a doctor, didn't talk like a doctor and was completely unaware of himself. His history was with Bob, but he made a point of making her a part of their present. They grew comfortable around each other, and Marsha was pleased when Doc started to tease her the same way he teased Bob. She thought it a genuine pity that these two men in her life had been unable to spend more time of their own lives together.

Circumstances, however, had prevented this from happening, and for many years Doc and Bob's relationship was necessarily one of long distance. They had communicated solely by letter and phone, and met only after Fogerty – Bob's nemesis – had died. At first they rendezvoused in anonymous cities, but then, as their confidence grew, in their respective homes. It was during a visit to the Klamath Mountains retreat that Bob presented Doc with *The Barbed Wire Flag* that Nancy had admired. In the rebated rectangle were fifty identical images of a cadaver.

There had been one visit by Bob, however, of which Doc was still unaware: to the funerals of Beth and Esther. At the time of their deaths, Bob had been afraid of exposing either his grieving friend or himself to discovery, and had therefore felt unable to attend the service. He had, however, been there, and, as at his own funeral, in the background. He'd watched as the mourners filed into the church, the limousines arrive and Doc and his family step into view. He'd looked on helplessly as the two coffins were unloaded from the hearse and Doc, his father's arm around him, followed them into the church. His friend had looked a broken man. He'd wanted to run to him, hold him close and tell him it would be okay – but he didn't. He couldn't. Instead, he'd stayed where he was, silent and unmoving, his head bowed in prayer. Only after the coffins had been taken from the church to the crematorium did Bob take his own leave and head back to Seattle.

'Who's Nancy?' Marsha asked. 'I don't remember you ever mentioning her.'

Doc had phoned, suggesting he and Nancy pay them a visit.

'An ol' friend o' mine he dated back when he was at Duke. 'Bout tore him up when she left him, an' then, outta the blue she phones him. You'll like her, Marsha. Nancy wouldn' stand fo' any o' my shit neither! Ha!'

Deterioration

Doc and Nancy's trip to Seattle didn't take place. Shortly before its due date Doc caught pneumonia and, afterwards, suffered an endless series of complications. Simultaneously, Nancy's life also became more complicated. Areas of her brain progressively shrank, and the cells located there were ransacked. Slight memory loss became severe memory loss, and minor confusions, significant. Though faces and objects remained familiar, their names escaped her. She came to forget her address and phone number, lose track of where she put things and invariably find her car keys in the microwave oven. She drove not knowing why she was driving or where she'd intended driving to; lost her bearings easily and failed to recognise once familiar landmarks. Eventually, she stopped driving, sold the car and very soon forgot how to drive.

Money, in value and amount, now confused her. Shop assistants would help her count the dollars and cents she'd take from her purse, and with varying degrees of patience explain that prices had changed considerably since 1972. Nancy also began to confuse the hours of the day with the hours of the night, and would often phone Doc at four in the morning; every day of the week became a Sunday to her, the dead day of the week when nothing ever happens.

As the past grew in importance, recent events and the present became meaningless. In Nancy's altered state of mind, Ruby and her parents came back to life. She'd prepare meals for them and wonder why they never arrived to eat them; stand for hour after hour at the window or on the front porch waiting for their cars to turn into the driveway. Often, she'd look at herself in the mirror and wonder who the old woman staring back at her was; certainly not the young Nancy Travis she imagined herself to be.

Nancy's pride in her appearance evaporated. There came a time when she rarely combed her hair or brushed her teeth. Her dress sense and colour co-ordination disappeared, and on a cold winter's day she would as likely be clothed in a light summer's dress as a thick woollen sweater. Eventually she started to smell of urine, and so too did the house.

The stays Doc made with her became longer and more fraught: her restlessness, the way she anxiously clasped and unclasped her hands, her habit of pacing rooms, trying doorknobs and endlessly bending to pick imaginary pieces of lint from the carpet. She'd agitate easily and, on occasion, become aggressive; she'd shout at Doc, sometimes scream at him to take his goddamn hands off her! Towards the end of the period he visited her in Hershey – and while paying a visit to the bathroom – Nancy mistook him for a night-time prowler and hit him over the head with a baseball bat. Recovering in hospital the next day, fresh stitches in the back of his head, Doc reluctantly judged that their time to travel to Coffeeville was approaching.

By the time Doc celebrated his seventy-second birthday, he had already decided on a plan of action. Ideally, he would have preferred to have driven Nancy to Coffeeville, but his failing eyesight made such a long journey impossible. Although nervous of taking Nancy on any form of public transport, he'd decided they would fly from Harrisburg to Philadelphia and then take another flight to Memphis; there he would hire a car and drive the remaining distance. Within days of his birthday, however, he was forced to abandon such ideas and think again: Nancy had been admitted to the secure wing of a nursing home.

It transpired that Nancy had set out from her house one

evening and left the front door wide open. She'd passed through the streets of her own neighbourhood unnoticed, walked along East Caracas Avenue and down Para Avenue until she came to Hwy 422, one of the town's main arteries. Instead of turning left, which would have taken her to the centre of Hershey, she'd headed east in the direction of Lancaster and Reading. As she tramped unsteadily down the hard shoulder of the road and alongside the Spring Creek Golf Course, she'd been spotted by a passing police car. The cruiser pulled over and its driver climbed out, adjusting his hat and taking the precaution of unclasping his holster.

Immediately, he'd discerned Nancy's distress, but had been unable to calm her. Just as Nancy could make little sense of the world she now lived in, neither could the policeman make any sense of Nancy's: she didn't know where she was or where she lived, what day it was or what time of day it was. All she could tell him was that her name was Nancy Travis and that she was looking for her parents. The policeman had coaxed her into the back of his cruiser with the promise of helping her find them. Why he thought they'd be found in a police station, Nancy never fully understood, but together they searched for them there the rest of the evening.

As Nancy had no purse or form of identification on her, and the police could find no record of a Nancy Travis living in Hershey, she was detained at the station overnight. It was only after a neighbour phoned the following morning to report an open front door that her true identity became known. Her own doctor was on vacation at the time, and the practice administrator revealed to the police that her next of kin was listed as Brandon Travis, a resident of Clarksdale, Mississippi. (Nancy had always intended replacing Brandon's name with Doc's, but too late: Brandon was the person the police contacted.)

On hearing the news, and unaware he was no longer a beneficiary of Nancy's will, three like fruits lined up in Brandon's slot machine mind, and he started to imagine the dollar coins that would soon be tumbling his way. He told the police it would take him time to re-arrange his schedule and scrape together the necessary bus fare to Hershey, but that until he could get there, they should put his sister in a nursing home. He explained to them that although Nancy had money, he didn't want them putting her anywhere fancy.

'I'm glad he's not my next of kin,' the policeman who'd made the call to Brandon said to a colleague. He then checked her into the fanciest secure unit he could find.

Doc knew he had to think fast. Once a person got caught up in the care system, extrication was no easy matter; next-of-kin pulled the strings and well-meaning friends counted for nothing. He had to get her out of there, and quickly.

Fortuitously, on the same day he heard from Nancy's next-door neighbour, he also received a phone call from his godson, and a new plan started to shape in his mind.

The next day, he flew to Pennsylvania and went in search of Nancy. The neighbour who'd reported her missing to the police and her detention to Doc was helpful. A close friend of Nancy herself, she told Doc she knew the whereabouts of the Nursing Home but not its name. She drew a map and asked him to give Nancy her love. 'Tell her I'll be along to visit as soon as I can.' Doc thanked her and climbed back into his rental, declining the cup of coffee she'd offered. The directions were easy to follow and he drove there directly. 'God in Heaven!' he exclaimed out loud when he read the name of the retirement centre: *Oaklands!*

The Oaklands Retirement Community had been in existence for ten years, and was the creation of a syndicate of doctors motivated by profit. Their initial idea had been to provide independent living in a communal atmosphere for senior citizens who were lonely, frail or tired of doing chores. Necessarily, their intended clientele had also to be wealthy, as the rents charged for the one- and two-bedroom apartments in the community's three storey building were high and increased yearly.

The doctors' intention had been to keep fee-paying customers – or cash cows, as they occasionally referred to them – in the community for as long as possible – ideally, until the day they died. They found, however, that despite their best efforts to maintain the mental health of the people they cared for, they were fighting a losing battle against the waves of dementia that crashed on to the shores of old age and pounded their residents' brains into mush. They lost residents to Alzheimer's, to vascular dementia, to Fronto-temporal dementia, to Binswanger's disease and occasionally to dementia with Lewy bodies. The inevitable transfer of such valuable assets to outside specialist facilities threatened to undermine the community's business model, and it was then that the doctors decided to build and open their own dementia care amenity: The Assisted Living Community – or Secure Unit, as it came to be called.

The plan worked: not only did the new unit plug a potential hole in the community's finances, but actually boosted them by allowing the facility to tap into a new, lucrative and ever-expanding market – dementia care. In-house guests who succumbed to the disease were no longer transferred to outside institutions, but simply wheeled – with a minimum of fuss – from one community building to another. There, they joined patients from other retirement communities unable to provide a similar service.

Unlike the Retirement Community, where guests enjoyed freedom of movement and choice, residents in the Assisted Living Community were deprived of both. There was no sign over the door to the secure unit reading *Morituri Te Salutant*, but there might as well have been: like all such institutions, it became no more than a holding tank for death. Those who walked through its portals left only on a gurney and, while there, had little or no say in their own lives.

Nancy had been placed in the secure wing of the centre, accessed by a door code. Doc signed the visitor's register and followed the instructions given to him by the receptionist. 'It's easy to remember,' she'd said. 'Once you reach the door, punch in 1111 – it's the same code to get out.'

Nancy was standing by the door dressed in a green hospital gown, randomly pushing the buttons she hoped would release her back into the world. Upon seeing Doc, she flung her arms around him.

'Gene. Darling Gene. I thought I'd never see you again! Take me home with you, Gene. *Please*, Gene! Take me home with you.'

Doc stroked her hair. 'It's going to be fine Nancy, just fine, but let's go someplace we can talk.' Nancy led him to the bedroom she'd been given, and when the door closed behind them started to cry.

'Hey, what kind of greeting is this for an old friend? You're supposed to smile when you see me, not cry. Now dry those tears and give me a smile.'

Nancy calmed and gave Doc the biggest forced smile he'd ever seen. He couldn't help but laugh.

'A policeman arrested me, Gene, and I swear to God I hadn't done anything wrong. Why have they put me in prison? I haven't broken a law in my life!'

'It's not a prison, Nancy; it's a nursing home. There's been a big misunderstanding, but I'm going to sort it out. It might take a few days, so you'll have to be patient.'

'Can't you just tell them I didn't do anything and take me home with you? They'll listen to you, Gene: you're a doctor! Or at least, you said you were. You are a doctor, aren't you, Gene?'

'Yes, Nancy, I am, but listen to me. I can't take you with me today; it's just not possible. I promise you, though, the next time you see me will be the time we leave together. You'll never have to return here again. Now, how does that sound? Do you understand?'

Nancy nodded her head, seemingly understanding his words, but then said: 'Shall we go now, Gene?'

Doc explained the situation again, and afterwards Nancy asked him the same question. He held her to him and whispered: 'Nancy, my dear, dear Nancy.' In that moment, he wondered if he'd ever loved her more. He then opened the door, walked to the reception area and signed out.

Doc didn't drive straight to the airport, but instead to Nancy's neighbour's house. For emergencies, she held a duplicate key for Nancy's house and Doc borrowed it. He filled suitcases he found in the bedroom with some of Nancy's clothes, and then went to the medicine cabinet and took out all her prescribed tablets. He unlocked the safe Nancy had shown him in the hall closet and took out a shoe box filled with dollar bills. He then returned the key to the neighbour and drove to the airport.

He arrived home late that night, a new plan formulated in his head. The next day, he phoned Bob.

'Hey, Marsha, it's Gene. Bob there?'

'Sorry, Gene, I didn't quite catch that. Were you asking me how I was?'

'You know your welfare's always uppermost in my mind, Marsha; it's just that phone calls cost money.'

'What century are you living in, Gene? Phone calls are cheap! Now tell me, what are you up to?'

'Right now I'm trying to make a phone call to Bob, but there's some damned woman seems to think I want to talk to her instead. It's kind of urgent, Marsha.'

Marsha laughed and went in search of Bob. Doc looked at his watch as the minutes ticked by. Eventually, Bob's voice sounded.

'G-Man!'

'What the hell, Bob! I thought you'd fallen down a drain.'

'I was on the can, man, so I guess a part o' me's down the drain, but I came fast as I could. Marsha tells me it's a matter o' some urgency. What's ailin' you?'

'It's Nancy, Bob. She's got herself locked up in a nursing home and I need your help to get her out. How are you fixed – can Marsha spare you for a couple of weeks?'

'Sure she can. She could spare me fo' a coupla years, if you wan' the honest truth!' He laughed, and then became serious. 'Nancy real bad, now?'

'She's a fair way down the hill, but not bad enough to be locked up in a secure unit. I'm going to get her out of there and take her to Mississippi.'

'An' you wan' me to help spring her?'

'No, my godson's going to do that. What I need you to do is to source some drugs and find an unrented vehicle that can accommodate four, and then meet me in Hershey a week on Monday. Will you be able to do this? I'm presuming you still have your old contacts.'

'Time frame's a bit tight, Gene, but I'll be there. Drugs is no problem, but the vehicle might be mo' diff'cult. Let me get a pen...'

Doc read out the list of drugs, carefully spelling each one as Bob wrote them down, and then added nonchalantly: 'Oh and I'll need you to overnight me a handgun. It doesn't have to be anything fancy.'

'A gun! What you wanna gun fo', man?'

'I'm not planning on using it, but I have to be prepared for all exigencies: I've never held up a nursing home before.'

'You ain't never shot a gun b'fore neither, Gene. You as likely blow yo' damn foot off loadin' the thing. Guns ain't fo' foolin' with, man.'

'I know it, Bob, and I'll be careful. If it makes you any happier, I'll buy one of those *Dummies* books on how to load guns and shoot people. Now stop worrying, will you.'

There they left the conversation, and agreed to meet in the parking lot of the Stoverdale United Methodist Church, a week Monday.

3

Jack

Fog

Jack Guravitch searched for a bell but couldn't find one. He knocked on the door and waited: there was no reply. He knocked again, louder this time, and tried the handle. The door was unlocked. He pushed it open and walked into the house. Voices came from the direction of the living room and he moved towards them.

A man called Lou was telling a woman called Mary that he appreciated the efforts she'd made to find him a date for that evening's awards dinner – he really did! But why, he asked, had she fixed him up with a woman who was eighty-three years old? Jack smiled when he realised the voices were coming from the television and that he was listening to a re-run of the *Mary Tyler Moore Show*. It was like meeting up with old friends again.

Doc was asleep in an armchair snoring gently, a small rivulet of drool trickling from the left corner of his mouth. Jack decided to let him sleep, catch up on some of the rest he'd missed out on over the years. He walked quietly to the kitchen and took a beer from the fridge and a packet of Doritos from one of the cupboards. He prised the cap off with his teeth and returned to the living room just in time for the start of another episode of the *Mary Tyler Moore Show*: Ted was having an argument with Georgette, his long-time girlfriend. Jack sat down on the couch and rested his feet on the coffee table.

'Tell me, Jack, do you know of anyone who makes more noise eating a tortilla chip than you do?'

Part of a Doritos went down Jack's throat the wrong way and he started to cough violently. He reached for the beer and took a deep gulp. 'Jesus, Doc!' he spluttered, 'You almost killed me.'

Doc smiled at his godson. 'A few moments ago, I was riding a unicycle through the centre of Paris on pavements smooth as silk, and all of a sudden I hit gravel and start to fall. I wake up and see you sprawled on my couch crunching your way through a packet of Doritos. Do you suppose by any chance the two events are related?'

'The amount of drool leaking from your mouth, old man, you might just as easily have woken up thinking your bike had gone into the Seine. Now stand up and let me hug you,' Jack said. 'And another thing: why don't you have a bell on your door?'

Although Doc would have preferred to have simply shaken hands with Jack, he allowed himself to be hugged. It seemed to be the way of the world these days.

'I don't have a bell because bells remind me of churches, and churches remind me of death. I'm sure I've explained this to you before. Anyway, everyone's got a pair of knuckles, and it's not as if I'm deaf.'

'Hell, Doc, you were fast asleep with the television on and your door unlocked. Anyone could have walked in and burglarised the place, strangled you to death if they'd wanted to. You're lucky it was just me and all you're missing is one beer and a packet of tortilla chips. And, by the way, if you had any dips in your fridge I wouldn't have made so much noise eating them and you'd still be cycling through France.'

Doc went to the kitchen. 'You eaten?' he asked.

'I stopped at a diner a couple of hours back, thanks. Sorry I didn't get here sooner but there was a last-minute problem with the rental car – I'll take another beer, though.'

Doc got a beer for Jack and poured himself a glass of red wine. He took a selection of cheeses from the fridge and placed them and an unopened box of crackers on a large plate. He brought them to the coffee table and sat back in his armchair. His expression turned serious. 'So tell me, Jack: how are you doing? What's your situation now?'

'I'm a new man,' Jack replied, and then after a pause, and with slightly less bravado, added: 'Kind of.'

If Walter Guravitch hadn't moved his family to Doc's home town in 1948, then Doc would have never been Jack's godfather. And if Walter had shown no interest in fog, it is doubtful that Jack would have become another city's favourite weatherman.

If such a thing as a Guravitch family tree had existed, then Walter would have been listed as a first second-generation American. He was also the product of his grandparents' fervent belief in the virtues of assimilation, and consequently had little knowledge of either his religion or culture. (On reaching the United States both grandparents had taken a vow never to speak of the past again, but to live only in the present. Roots, they often said, weren't everything – unless, of course, they were vegetables.) Walter vaguely knew that Passover was celebrated in April and Yom Kippur in October, but would have struggled to explain the significance of either. He was similarly vague about the origins of his family. He thought, but wasn't sure, that the family had originated in the Moldovan part of Russia and immigrated to the United States to escape either Czarist pogroms or a succession of failed harvests.

Walter's father, now called George rather than Georg, had followed his own father into the family tailoring business on New York's Lower East Side, and it was presumed that Walter would similarly follow suit. Walter's interests, however, lay elsewhere. His real enthusiasm was art. In his spare time he would visit the city's art museums and look through the windows of galleries he could never afford to enter. He bought books and schooled himself. In time he became proficient in oils and later photography. His favourite school of painting was Impressionism and his favourite Impressionist, Monet. In particular, Walter admired the artist's depiction of fog. In his paintings of *Waterloo Bridge*, *Charing Cross Bridge* and the *Houses of Parliament,* Monet had captured the changing nature of light like no other artist before him. After seeing these paintings, Walter became as captivated by fog as, in later years, Nancy Skidmore would be imprisoned by it.

On the death of his parents Walter went in search of fog. He sold the family business and moved with his wife to the Monongahela Valley, where the river fogs, in Walter's mind, replicated the London of Monet's paintings. He and Hannah settled in Donora, and Walter opened the town's first photographic portrait studio. Unlike Hannah, he never noticed the brutality of their new surroundings. He had eyes and paintbrushes only for fog.

Walter painted canvas upon canvas of Donora and its locality. For some he would use only browns, greys and blacks to portray buildings and boats emerging from, or disappearing into, the unnatural cloud. Other times he would add bright splashes of colour to characterise the bizarre nature of fog when sun shone through its haze: mauves, oranges, yellows, pinks, blues and purples. These were Walter's favourite paintings. Occasionally one would sell, but never to a Donoran. Donorans didn't share his enthusiasm for fog. They lived with it because they had to. For them, fog had nuisance value but no artistic value. The last thing they wanted after a hard day's work was to return home and find a painting of fog on the wall waiting to greet them.

Walter's romance with fog, however, came to an abrupt end after the Death Fog struck Donora in the fall of 1948.

By nature fog is an innocent: romantic, mysterious, even beautiful, and no more sinister than a cloud. If, however, it mixes with the wrong crowd, tiny particles of soot or chemicals, for instance, then its character changes: Jekyll becomes Hyde and Dr Fog turns into the unpleasant Mr Smog. The arrival of heavy industry in the Monongahela River valley accordingly changed the complexion of fogs there.

By 1948, the economy of Donora was dominated by the American Steel & Wire Company and the Donora Zinc Works. Money pumped through the town's veins and smoke and other fumes belched into its environs. Pollution became an accepted way of life for the town's 13,500 inhabitants and, in their minds, a necessary trade-off. Consequently, when another fog enveloped the town on October 26, no one gave it a second thought, and the Halloween parade scheduled for that Friday evening went ahead as planned.

Overnight, however, the fog built, and when the high school football team took to the field the following afternoon, players lost sight of the ball and spectators lost sight of the players. That evening the town of Donora disappeared under a blanket of thick white odorous smoke. Donorans couldn't see to drive, couldn't even see the hands they placed in front of their faces. They found their way by touch, like blind people reading Braille maps.

Donora's world had been turned upside down by an unusually long temperature inversion. A mantle of warm air had trapped the cold layer beneath it and effectively placed a lid over the town. Pollution from coke plants and blast furnaces could no longer escape into the atmosphere and the town was transformed into a chemist's sweetshop, its shelves stacked with sulphur dioxides, carbon monoxides, fluorides and the heavy dusts from lead and cadmium. Air came to a standstill, and oxygen was sucked from the town.

The fog prowled the streets like a silent killer that night, creeping into houses through windows and under doors. House plants wilted and family pets died. The fog constricted the throats of the Donorans, tried to choke them and paralyse their respiratory systems; it gave them headaches that split their skulls in two, burned their eyes and made them vomit. During the four days it lingered, twenty people coughed and gasped their last, seven thousand were hospitalised and hundreds more left seriously damaged. It was only after rain started to fall on the fifth day that the fog eventually lifted.

That same day, the fog blinding Walter to its dangers also lifted, and for the first time he was able to link the early signs of his son's asthma to the area's pollution. Immediately, he left Donora and moved his family to a town far away, where the air was clear and the doctor was called Chaney. There, his eight-year-old son, Sydney, became the new best friend of a ten-year-old Doc.

Weather

Although his grandfather had never once tired of describing the beauty and dangers of fog to his grandson, in truth it was cloud in its pristine form that had drawn Jack to the subject of meteorology. He became transfixed by clouds, and by the time he entered high school was not only familiar with their ten basic genera, but also their species, varieties, accessory clouds and supplementary features.

He revealed to his friends the differences between layered stratus clouds, heaped cumulus clouds and curly-haired cirrus clouds, and warned them to expect rain whenever depressing nimbus clouds came into view. He pointed out jellyfish trails to them, twisted tousles, Father Christmas beards, comb-over hairstyle clouds, cloud fingers, dissipation trails, cigar-shaped fallstreak holes, horseshoe vortexes, sundogs and circumzenithal arcs.

It was no surprise, therefore, when Jack told his parents he intended to become a meteorologist. He took an undergraduate degree in geography and then embarked on a doctoral degree in meteorology. He acquired exemplary computational and mathematical skills and honed them to a fine point. That he was swayed from building forecasting models for a living was the consequence of the Donora Death Fog and an appearance on local television.

The city where Jack's university was located had a low-level smog problem caused by car fumes rather than heavy industry. The year 1998, however, was the fiftieth anniversary of the Donora Death Fog, and although Donora was in a different state and completely unknown to the city's population, the television station hoped to draw parallels with that disaster and, more importantly, fill five minutes of airtime. The researcher who contacted the university's meteorological department was given Jack's name as a person capable of talking about smog and its causes. When Jack let it be known that his grandfather had actually lived in Donora at the time of the Death Fog, he was immediately assigned to the project.

What impressed the television executives most when the segment aired wasn't Jack's knowledge of the subject under discussion, but his ease in front of the camera. They judged him a television natural, possessing all necessary attributes: he was handsome and photogenic, his teeth were white and strong, and he had a full head of hair. They offered him the position of weatherman on the evening news, and Jack accepted: the salary was more than generous, and the station's medical and dental plans were similarly unsparing.

It was another two months, however, before Jack was able to start his career in television. He himself had to finish writing and defending his dissertation, while the television station needed time to terminate the contract of the channel's existing weatherman, who had made the mistake of growing old and was now as bald as a turnip.

On his first day at the station, Jack was shown around by Ed Billings, the station's manager. Billings was an overweight bear of a man, whose chest and back hair sprouted from the inside of his shirt collar. He had a brusque, no-nonsense manner, and moved Jack efficiently from one person to the next.

Jack received a warm welcome. He was greeted with wall-to-wall smiles, an array of firm handshakes and several friendly slaps on the back. People congratulated him on joining the most successful and forward-thinking local television station in America, and advised him that, if he played his cards right, he might well be approached by one of the nationals.

Eventually, Billings left Jack in the hands of Human Resources and told him to meet him in reception at noon, when he'd introduce him to the anchors of the evening news – Phil Wonnacott and Mary Margaret Jennings. Jack filled in forms, watched health and safety videos and drank coffee until it was time for him to meet back with Billings.

'Phil, Mary Margaret, this is Jack. Go eat lunch and get acquainted,' Billings said. He then about turned and went back to his office.

Phil Wonnacott and Mary Margaret Jennings were both in

their thirties – Phil's later than Mary Margaret's. There was an ease about Phil not mirrored in the harder-edged Mary Margaret. Whereas Phil had achieved anchorman status, Mary Margaret was still only co-anchor, and while Phil was content to remain in local news as the big fish in a small pond, Mary Margaret longed for the national arena.

Phil was tanned with teeth the size of bleached tombstones. He had an athletic build and wore shorts and a polo shirt; all that was missing was a tennis racket. By contrast, Mary Margaret was as white as pure snow, as scared of the sun's ageing properties as she was any meal over four hundred calories. Her dark mascara-ed eyes were hidden behind large sunglasses; her lipstick was bright red; and her chemical blonde hair was tied back with a gold scrunchie.

Phil Wonnacott had worked as a reporter for several small California newspapers before moving into television. His credentials were those of a journalist, and he would often change for the better any copy handed him by the station's writers. His baritone voice brought gravitas to the more serious news stories of the day, and viewers felt safe in the knowledge that no harm would come to them while Phil Wonnacott was reading their news. Phil's first wife might have told them a different story: one of infidelities, blackened eyes and bruised ribs. As she still lived in Sacramento, however, no one heard her voice – certainly not Phil's second wife Bonnie, or their two daughters.

'You'd think Billings would do something about that body hair of his,' Mary Margaret said. 'I swear to God, Jack, I once saw him take off his shirt at a company picnic and he looked like he was wearing a mohair sweater. I'm surprised his wife doesn't say something to him.'

'His wife just left him,' Phil said.

'I didn't know that,' Mary Margaret said. 'Why didn't I know that?'

Phil shrugged his shoulders. 'Where do you want to eat, Jack? There's a good steak house around the corner if that sounds okay.'

'Fine with me,' Jack said, who was used to eating only sandwiches at lunchtime.

The three of them arrived at the restaurant and ordered lunch. While they waited for the food to arrive, Phil and Jack drank beers and Mary Margaret a glass of spritzer. 'So, what do you think of Billings?' she asked Jack.

'Businesslike,' Jack replied.

'He sure as hell doesn't do warm and friendly,' Phil smiled, 'but he's solid as a rock, Jack. If we ever have a problem, he's the one we turn to. Right, Mary Margaret?'

Mary Margaret nodded in agreement. 'He's a big pussycat really; his bark's a lot worse than his bite.' Jack glanced at Phil to see if he too had noticed Mary Margaret's mixed metaphor but, deciding that he hadn't, wisely made up his mind not to raise the matter.

Food was served and Jack and Phil cut into their steaks. Mary Margaret played with the salad she'd ordered, but only occasionally placed any of it in her mouth.

'So what experience of television do you have, Jack?' she asked.

'Just that segment I did for the station last year on photochemical smog,' Jack replied.

'Oh, I remember that,' Mary Margaret said. 'It was about that man called Donald, who got lost in the fog and died, wasn't it?'

'Not quite,' Jack said. 'It was about the town of *Donora;* but you're right, people did die.'

Phil looked up from his plate. 'Where is Donora?' he asked Jack.

'Pennsylvania. About twenty miles south of Pittsburgh.'

'Well, I'll be damned,' Phil said. 'For some reason, I'd got it into my head that it was in Sweden. I wonder why that is?'

'It's probably because it aired around the same time that Swedish guy tried out for weatherman,' Mary Margaret said. 'Do you remember him? Tall as a tree.'

'Oh yeah, now I do. Why on earth would we want to hire a Swede?'

'Why not a Swede?' Mary Margaret asked him.

Phil put down his fork and gave the matter his full attention.

'As you ask, I'll tell you, Mary Margaret. We all know what Germany was doing during World War II, but what the hell was

Sweden doing? Nothing, that's what! Just sitting on its butt waiting for the war to blow over. To tell you God's honest truth, I'd rather work with a German than a Swede any day of the week. You know where you are with Germans, and at least they've got backbones. Sometimes, I think the United States has more in common with Germany than with any other nation. And if you think about it, we're the only country since Germany that's ever had the balls to invade anyone... you any thoughts on the matter, Jack?'

Jack had: he thought Phil was completely gaga! Rather than say this, however, he picked up the conversation where Mary Margaret had left off. 'What Mary Margaret said about the Swede being tall? Did you know that Norwegians and Dutch are taller still, probably the tallest people in the world, in fact?'

'I have to confess I did *not* know that,' Phil said somewhat sarcastically. 'Any more nuggets you'd like to impart?'

'The Finns have the highest mathematical level,' Jack ventured.

'I can believe what you said about the Dutch,' Mary Margaret chipped in. 'I travelled there once and they're huge. At first, I thought it was an optical illusion, because we'd just come from Belgium and they're all like midgets there. But it wasn't. They're *seriously* tall. And the language! Have you ever had a Dutch person talk to you? It's awful, absolutely awful! The language sounds *awful* for a start but, worse still, when Dutch people talk, they spray your face with spit. I had to carry antiseptic wipes with me the whole time I was in the country. It was gross!'

'And what do you suppose the Dutch were doing during World War II?' Phil asked, determined to recapture the conversation.

'They were occupied,' Jack said.

'There's occupied and there's occupied,' Phil replied. 'Our GIs were *occupied*, trying to fight their way across Europe and liberate people. I don't call sitting around at home eating cheese and doing drugs being occupied. I despair, I really do. Sometimes I think we let the rest of the world ride roughshod over us. Someone at the station should be saying these things, but no one ever does. Too scared of their own shadows, if you ask me.'

It was difficult to tell if Phil and Mary Margaret were friends or merely colleagues. They chatted easily enough through lunch, but there seemed to be little warmth between them, certainly not the camaraderie they displayed on television the times Jack had watched them.

'Watch out for Mary Margaret,' Phil whispered to Jack as they left the restaurant. 'Don't let her sink those talons of hers into you.'

'Watch out for Phil,' Mary Margaret whispered to Jack as they reached the television station. 'Don't ever turn your back on him.'

Jack weighed these thoughts in his head until Billings collected him from reception.

'Wonnacott talk politics to you?' Billings asked.

'Kind of,' Jack said.

'Jeez! That guy never misses a beat. Keeps asking me if he can have a two-minute editorial slot at the end of every show, like Eric Sevareid used to have at CBS. We'd be off the air in no time if that happened. I told him, if he wants a chance to air his views, he should get a job as one of those radio nuts.'

When Billings had stopped talking, Jack asked him where he'd find the computers for his weather forecasts. The station manager looked at him incredulously.

'You don't have to worry about that, kid. We get the forecasts from the National Weather Service and a local private one. It's not as if there's a whole lot of weather to predict around here, anyway. It's either going to be hot or less hot; some days it'll rain but most days it won't. All you have to do is present the weather. Didn't they tell you that?'

'I honestly can't remember, Ed. I suppose I must have just assumed I was going to be doing the actual forecasting as well as the presenting. Seems like only half a job.'

'Yeah, but just think of how much money you'll be getting paid for only half a job. There'll be plenty of other things you'll be able to fill your time with... by the way, did they tell you we're calling you Jack Green?'

'No!' Jack said.

'It's a thing we do all the time. The important thing is to get you connected with the audience fast, and most of them around here will never be able to get their heads around the name

Guravitch, let alone spell it. Jack Green's easy for them to remember, and it's a strong name, too. You won't have to change your name in real life, and your checks will still be made out to Jack Guravitch. That's the main thing, eh, kid?' he said, slapping the back pocket where he kept his wallet. 'Now come on and let's start getting you trained up as a weather presenter. Your first broadcast will be a week from today.'

Jack interacted well with his colleagues at the station, and quickly secured his place in the hearts of viewers. Billboards advertised the new evening news line-up, and the smiling faces of Phil, Mary Margaret and Jack beamed down on the city; three happy friends offering their friendship to all who cared to raise their eyes. In reality, the three anchors of the evening news were never more than colleagues. They rarely socialised, each preferring to go their own separate ways after broadcasts: Jack to his friends at the university, Mary Margaret to her cat or favoured beau of the moment, and Phil — or so Jack presumed — to his wife and daughters.

That Phil didn't always return to his family after broadcasts became apparent after the news anchorman unexpectedly invited him out for a drink one evening. What Jack hadn't realised until too late was that the venue for this drink was a downtown singles' bar. They bought drinks and sat down at a table. They talked about the broadcast they'd just finished, a bit of station gossip and then, during a lull in conversation, Phil leaned toward Jack conspiratorially.

'Do you know what makes an attractive woman beautiful, Jack?'

There was only going to be one correct answer to this question, Jack realised, and that answer was already stored in Phil's head. 'Tell me,' he said.

'Low self-esteem,' Phil leered, and then laughed. 'It's God's gift to man. Now look at those two over there. They can't take their eyes off us. I tell you, of all the fringe benefits TV celebrity status bestows upon a man, none comes sweeter than this. Let's buy them a drink and play it by ear.'

Jack hated the idea. 'You're married Phil,' he said. 'What would your wife say if she knew what you were about to do?'

'What's marriage got to do with any of this? Sure, I'm married, and I love my wife. I'm not intending to marry either of those girls at the bar, and what my wife doesn't know isn't going to hurt her. This is normal man stuff, Jack, a bit of rest and recreation for the family breadwinner. Now are you coming over there with me or am I on my own?'

'I'm afraid you're on your own, Phil. I've just started seeing someone and I'm not about to screw it up.'

'Suit yourself. One day, though, you'll realise that life's too short for your kind of morals – *especially* in television. See you tomorrow, chump.'

Phil left Jack at the table and strolled nonchalantly towards the bar and the two waiting girls. Jack quickly emptied his glass and left. He'd lied to Phil. He had no girlfriend, but he sure as hell didn't want to find one in that desperate place.

The next day, Phil mentioned nothing of the evening to Jack, and neither did Jack ask him anything. It was as if the time they'd spent together had been airbrushed from both their lives. Fortunately, in case Phil ever did decide to ask him out for another drink, the weatherman met his imaginary girlfriend at a colloquium on two-winged flies.

Flies

The first day of the Diptera conference had been devoted to mosquitoes, the second day to sand and black flies, and the third day to midges. The conference organisers had invited Neil Murray, a leading authority on Scottish midges, to give the keynote speech on the final day. He'd been a controversial choice of speaker, but his standing in the fly community, and reputation as the wild man of Scottish entomology, ensured that the auditorium would be full to capacity when he strode on to the platform.

For the many delegates who had never seen Murray before, his actual physical appearance came as a huge disappointment. They had wrongly presumed that a Scottish wild man and authority on

Scottish midges would at least have looked and sounded *Scottish*. Though none would have admitted it, they had fully expected to see no less a character than Rob Roy climb on to the stage that Friday afternoon, dressed in a kilt, wearing a sporran and with a set of bagpipes carelessly thrown over his shoulder. Murray sported none of this apparel – didn't even throw his audience the sop of wearing a Harris Tweed jacket. Rather, he wore a quiet suit and, when he spoke, betrayed only the slightest hint of a Scottish accent. What he lacked in appearance, however, Murray more than made up for in presence: his enthusiasm for midges was unbridled, passionate, and covertly fortified with swigs from a flask containing fifteen-year-old single malt whisky.

Once the Scottish entomologist had settled at the podium, his performance commenced. He started by pacing the platform slowly and deliberately, but then quickened his tempo and became animated. Without warning he leapt from the platform, raced up the aisle on the right side of the hall, exited through the rear doors, and then rushed back into the auditorium down the left-side aisle before climbing back on to the platform. He did this several times during the next hour-and-a-half, while simultaneously haranguing his audience on the subject of midges. Sometimes he would come to an abrupt halt in front of, or next to a delegate, and lecture him or her on a one-to-one basis for an entire minute; other times he would simply stand there in silence and salute them.

Murray waved his arms to portray the midge's mandibles and maxillae piercing and then cutting deeper into the skin of its victim. He dramatically fell to the floor and lay on his back mimicking the same scissor-like cutting action with his legs, before suddenly rolling on to his side to avoid the imaginary blood spurting from a broken capillary vessel. To represent the midge's food canal, he curled the day's printed agenda sheet into a narrow tube, put it to his mouth and pretended to suck blood from a delegate's arm or head. He then mimicked the midge preventing its newly-sourced blood from clotting, by spitting mouthfuls of saliva into the air. The audience was left mesmerised, off-balance and, some of them, wet.

Murray told his captives that of all the world's midges, the fiercest lived in Scotland, and of the thirty-four varieties living there, the Highland Midge or *Culicoides impunctatus* was the most merciless. This midge, he told them, with something verging on pride, had probably caused more discomfort, misery and pain than any other midge in the history of mankind; in doing so it had also conserved the natural beauty of its habitat from the ravages of human activity. For this, he argued, the midge was owed a debt of gratitude, and he encouraged the delegates to rise from their seats and give the small fly three cheers. The delegates duly obliged.

Murray thanked his audience, told them he looked forward to meeting them individually at the reception that evening, and then sat down.

In attendance at the reception was a middle-ranking administrator from the Faculty of Sciences called Laura Yandell. She had no interest in flies. She was there as one of several women invited by the organisers to counter-balance the largely male complexion of the Diptera conference, and to bring a touch of glamour to the evening's proceedings.

Laura Yandell had the reputation of being able to talk to anyone and feign interest in anything. She bridged social and educational divides effortlessly, and laughed easily – if sometimes a little too soon. For this reason, she'd been introduced to Neil Murray and asked to keep him sober until it was time for the delegates to take their seats for dinner.

'I'm afraid I missed your address, Professor Murray, but I gather it was well received.'

'Yes, it went well enough, thanks, but bearing in mind the previous speaker was a Nicaraguan blabbering on about sand flies in his second tongue, then you have to figure the odds were stacked in my favour.'

Laura laughed and accused him of being too modest. 'Do you mind if I say something about the midge, Professor?' The Professor indicated he didn't. 'It's their biting that puts me off. Why do they have to bite people?'

Neil Murray's eyes lit up when he mistook Laura's inane and time-filling question as a sign of genuine interest.

'It's only the females that bite, Laura, and they don't simply bite for the fun of it: they do it for the sake of their unborn children. If their eggs don't get a blood-meal, their eggs die, and if that happened year after year, eventually so too would their species. It's the only way they know how to survive. And it's not as if they drain a person dry: the most they ever take is one ten-millionth of a litre of blood. I think we can spare them that, Laura, don't you? What's that small amount to a person with 5.6 litres sloshing around inside them? Drop in the ocean, my dear!'

'Put that way... but why do their bites cause so much swelling and itching? Are they poisonous or something?'

'No, they're not poisonous!' Murray laughed, 'It's just the... damn! That drinks waiter has ignored me again! It's as if he's doing it on purpose. Did you see that? If you catch his eye before I do, give me the heads up, will you, or just grab him. I can only drink so much of this grape piss without getting heartburn.'

'I will,' Laura lied, 'but you were just about to tell me something about how the midge isn't poisonous.'

'The midge *isn't* poisonous, Laura. It's the human body over-reacting to the bite that causes all the fuss. Imagine, if you will, what it would be like if the Department of Homeland Security upped the level of terrorist threat every time one of its cameras picked up a small boy dropping a piece of litter in the street? It's the exact same thing. A bit of harmless midge saliva...' At this point, Murray broke off his conversation and, with an indignant harrumph, went storming after the drinks waiter who had ignored him yet again.

Laura looked around the room. She knew it would only be a matter of time before someone else joined her, no doubt another man, but she didn't wait for this to happen. She'd recognised Jack Green standing diagonally across the room from her, and decided to introduce herself.

'Hi, I'm Laura Yandell,' she said as she approached. 'You may not remember me, but I knew you back in the days when you were Jack Guravitch.'

'Sure I remember you,' Jack smiled. Or at least, he remembered her hair.

Hair

If Jack's first interest in life was meteorology, a close second was hair – and also the fear of losing it.

This interest was his alone. It had no family roots – and this was also the source of his fear. Until Jack came along, no male Guravitch had ever given two hoots about how their hair looked, or whether in fact they had any. They had more important things on their plates – like what to put on them, for one – than to give a damn about what they had, or had not, on their pates.

It was difficult to pinpoint the exact time hair became important to Jack. As a child it wasn't, but some time during his teenage years it became critical. He grew unhappy with his father's use of the family clippers and insisted on visiting one of the town's barbers. As life progressed, Jack moved from barber to barber and from salon to salon, searching fruitlessly for the one person who could understand the idiosyncratic nature of his hair. He agonised over whether he should keep his hair parted on the left, move the parting to the middle or do away with a parting altogether. He worried whether to comb his hair backwards, forwards or allow it free rein. He wore it short and spiky for a time, medium length other times and sometimes long. Occasionally the style was dictated by the day, but mostly by his own whim.

On Saturdays he would visit drugstores and hairdressing salons in search of new shampoos, conditioners, gels, balms, mists and sprays that might have made it to market since his last visit. He read the list of ingredients printed on the sides of the plastic bottles with a magnifying glass but little understanding. He'd skim over the complicated names of the acids, chlorides, phosphates, proteins and sulphates, until he reached the more interesting names of the plants and flowers the manufacturer used; aloe, avocado, brazil nut, coconut, grapefruit, lavender, lemon, Californian meadowfoam, seeds of the African moringa tree, rosemary and wheat. Sometimes the manufacturer would identify the source of a particular ingredient, the Peruvian rainforest for instance, but most times didn't. For birthdays and Christmas, Jack's parents bought him hair care products he'd identified to them from such visits.

Jack looked upon hair as mankind's last frontier, and hair salons as the New American West. He believed that people could express themselves better through the medium of hair than they could any other part of their anatomy: conformity, rebellion, allegiance, individuality – the whole caboodle. Hair allowed a person to stand out from the crowd or merge seamlessly into it; it also afforded a person the opportunity to change their life without joining a wagon train. Jack's theory, however, only worked if a person had hair. For him, the loss of his hair would be tantamount to the loss of his very being, and a diagnosis of *androgenic alopecia*, the equivalent of a death sentence.

Consequently, Jack fretted about losing his hair, and from the age of eighteen checked regularly for signs of premature baldness. He would stand in front of a mirror and hold a second mirror to the back of his head, scrutinising the reflection for any change. Shortly before his twenty-first birthday, and after a particularly dissatisfying haircut, Jack found that however he brushed or combed his hair, the hair at the back of his head refused to lie down. Checking with the hand mirror, he was alarmed to see two small bald spots. The shock literally caused his legs to give way and he collapsed to the floor, cracking his forehead on the bathroom washbasin. He lay there for twenty minutes or so, simultaneously bleeding and collecting himself, and then walked unsteadily to Doc's house.

Doc opened the door and saw before him an ashen-faced Jack with dried blood on his forehead, and rivulets of the same down the side of his right cheek.

'What in God's name happened to you, Jack?' he asked.

'Doc, this is urgent! I need your medical opinion on something.'

Doc examined the back of Jack's head and then stepped to the front of the chair Jack was sitting on. 'No baldness I can see,' he said. 'The problem, if it is a problem, is that you have two crowns at the back of your head instead of one. It's not unusual, and certainly nothing to worry about.'

Jack was relieved and gave an audible sigh. He then took a photograph from his pocket and showed it to Doc.

'Who's this?' Doc asked.

'It's my mother's grandfather. I was wondering if it's possible to X-ray it and see what his hair's like underneath the hat.'

Doc laughed out loud. 'Of course it's not possible. It's a photograph, you damn fool, not an actual head. Why are you even bothered what's underneath it?'

'Because if I know how his hair is, then I'll pretty much know how mine will be when I get to his age. My mother can't ever remember seeing him without a hat, so X-raying the photograph was my last hope. You know that baldness for a man is inherited from the maternal grandfather, don't you?'

'It can be,' Doc replied. 'But even if your great-grandfather was bald, there's still only a fifty per cent chance of you inheriting the bald gene. Your parents are just as likely to influence any hair loss you might have – and they both have good heads of hair.'

Jack walked slowly back to his parents' house reassured, at least for the moment, that he wasn't going bald, but unable to rid himself of the nagging thought that one day he *would* go bald. It was a cross he bore alone; a monomania no one else appreciated. He was aware there were more pressing problems in the world – hunger, poverty, disease and war, to name but a few – but in his world none of them ever featured. He wondered if, in this respect, he was uniquely without social conscience or just like everyone else except for his honesty in admitting that he was self-centred. He did, however, take umbrage at his father's assertion that he was vain, and his constant admonition that there was only the finest of lines dividing an Adonis from a donut!

If Jack was overwhelmingly attracted to women with thick and lustrous hair, which he undoubtedly was, then the women attracted to Jack were more likely to be on medication or in therapy. Laura Yandell was one such woman. After five years of therapy, she now stood on her own two feet and, apart from an open-ended prescription for small yellow pills, faced the world alone.

In truth, Laura suffered from life no more than any other woman of her generation, and despite protestations to the contrary was no more complicated or crazy. Put simply, Laura Yandell was just another of the nation's spoilt children who looked upon therapy as a fashion accessory. Indeed, the only issue of any consequence that had arisen during the five years of therapy – and one that seemingly explained the estrangement from her parents – was that Laura was ashamed of her family's wealth; its origins, rather than its amount. Laura told the therapist that she would have preferred her family's fortunes to have come from the proceeds of slavery, rather than canned spaghetti.

It was the therapist who suggested Laura stop coming to see her. She led Laura to believe that her journey was complete and further therapy unnecessary. In truth, the therapist was sick to death of Laura's moaning and analysis-to-death of things that had little or no bearing on anyone's life, let alone her own. She had taken particular offence at Laura's assertion that the therapist was raping her; this after Laura had discovered that the words *therapist* and *the rapist* corresponded exactly.

'It must be more than a coincidence!' Laura had said to the therapist.

'It is,' the therapist had replied. 'It's Greek!'

The therapist wished Laura well, wrote her a prescription for the occasional 'difficult day' that might lie ahead, and then moved to Sedona.

Jack had been invited to the reception for the same reason Laura had – to bring colour to an otherwise dull evening. An alumnus of the university and now a local celebrity, he was introduced to the delegates as the city's favourite weatherman.

Jack took the hand that Laura proffered. He vaguely remembered her working as a secretary in the Geography Department after he'd moved to the Meteorology Department, but had never known her name. The memory of her long dark hair, however, with its thick and natural waves had stayed with him, and he was pleased when she introduced herself.

Jack and Laura chatted easily, and Laura laughed at the jokes Jack never told. He was aware, however, that the day wasn't one of his best, and started to worry that his breath had become stale. He asked Laura if she had a spare stick of gum and she answered that she did. She was about to remove the gum from her bag when the conference organiser took her by the arm and asked if he might have a quick word. She moved a short distance away, but left her opened purse in Jack's hands. 'Help yourself,' she told him.

Jack felt flattered to be allowed such an unsupervised search, something that only usually happened in a relationship. He found the gum and was about to take a piece when he caught sight of a box of Tic Tacs and opted instead for the breath candy. He clicked the mechanism twice and out popped two small mints. Having noticed their unfamiliar colour, Jack was prepared for a different Tic Tac flavour but, even so, was still surprised by their slightly metallic taste. He thought no more about it, however, and washed the taste from his mouth with a good rinse of the white wine he was drinking.

By the time Laura re-joined Jack, the delegates were already seating themselves for dinner. Laura explained that she had to sit next to Neil Murray at the organiser's table, but asked him if they could meet for dinner the following evening. Jack was more than okay with the idea.

By the end of the first course, Jack could barely keep his eyes open and, worse still, couldn't stop yawning. The yawns were cavernous, noisy and impossible to hide, and left other guests at the table with the impression that Jack found both them and their conversations boring and, worse still, was completely unconcerned that they know it. Between yawns, Jack tried to apologise, but eventually thought it best to excuse himself from the table, find a bathroom and splash cold water on his face. He was at a loss as to why he felt so tired.

The water, however, failed to refresh him, and the temptation to take a nap in one of the stalls proved too strong to resist. He slid the catch on the door, hung his jacket on its hook and sat down on the toilet seat. Within seconds he was fast asleep.

Jack was woken at nine-thirty the next morning by a cleaning janitor knocking on the stall door and threatening to call the police. The city's favourite weatherman had no idea where he was.

How the two of them laughed that evening!

Laura explained that the Tic Tac box contained prescription pills. Partly because of the container's dispensing mechanism, but largely to disguise the medication from other people, she kept the pills in the mint box. The effect of these pills on anyone not used to taking them was soporific, and as the manufacturers also warned that alcohol should be avoided when taken, their effect on Jack had consequently been even more marked.

Laura found it easy telling Jack these things, and wrongly recognised in him a strength she herself didn't possess. She told him her life story, the death of her parents in a car accident and her work in the Faculty of Sciences. Although she had a degree in business administration, she told Jack that her real passion was writing, and that one day she hoped to make a living from it. Already in love with her hair, Jack now fell in love with her voice and, more gradually, her entirety. He felt sorry for Laura, empathised with the cruel hand life had dealt her, and made it his business to throw a couple of aces her way. Jack Guravitch had been suckered.

Laura allowed Jack to read two of her short stories. *The Trail of a Snail* was about a private detective who liked plants, and *The Man who Broke the Internet* was about a man who played the fourth movement of Beethoven's Ninth Symphony on his computer keyboard and accidentally broke the internet. Although Jack liked the titles, he had no idea what the stories were about, or if they were supposed to have meaning. He did, however, think that Laura's style of writing was as good as anything that came out of the station's newsroom, and when a vacancy arose there suggested she apply for the position. Laura got the job and Ed Billings took a shine to her. Six months later he appointed her roving reporter: her articulation and good looks, Billings told everyone, were wasted in the copy room; it was time for her to get in front of the camera.

Laura and Jack moved in together shortly after Laura joined the network, and almost immediately things started to go wrong. Like most couples, they'd fallen in love listening only to the best tracks on the other's metaphorical life album; living together, however, they got to hear all the album tracks, and most of what they heard they didn't like.

Laura was the first to question their compatibility. She started to analyse their relationship in depth, and involve Jack in long and wearying discussions: was it right for her; was it right for him; or right for either of them? She'd dismantle their relationship like a car mechanic stripping down an engine, and place bits of him and pieces of her on a sheet of newspaper on the kitchen table. Some pieces she'd clean and others she'd discard. Each time the engine was taken apart and pieced back together again, fragments of machinery invariably remained on the table and the motor never ran as smoothly. It was only a matter of time before the engine stopped running altogether.

Conversation between the two of them also changed in nature. Once carefree and spontaneous, it now turned into pre-programmed chunks of dialogue that could have been found on the shelves of any convenience store, and spoken by anyone to anyone. Jive talk had become Java talk.

Even though Jack and Laura lived in the same house, they started to speak to each other long distance, and over a crackling line. They missed the occasional word, sometimes a whole sentence and rarely understood the other's meaning. 'You are so…' Jack had once started to say to Laura. He never got the chance to finish: Laura left the room under the impression that Jack had just called her an asshole.

'You're such a loser,' Laura once shouted after him as he left their apartment.

'Maybe I am,' Jack replied, 'but at least I'm at the top of my game!'

It was only after the door slammed shut behind him that the asinine nature of his reply struck home. Intending to puncture her soufflé, he'd unintentionally ended up icing her cake. That he was now thinking in mixed metaphors also caused him concern.

Laura started to spend time away from Jack. She insisted on going to an old school friend's wedding by herself, and spent weekends away from him looking after friends with cancer, or talking other friends through difficult relationship problems. Curiously, Jack realised he didn't care that Laura went away on her own, and was almost relieved to have these weekends to himself. It also registered that Laura's hair wasn't quite as thick as he'd once imagined it to be, but an illusion. Laura Yandell, he realised, had a big head.

It was while looking through a photograph album the two of them kept that Jack made the decision to call a day on their relationship. All the photographs, he noticed, showed him and Laura smiling, pulling silly faces, holding hands or with their arms around each other. They showed happy times, but, Jack realised, selective happy times. For obvious reasons, there were no photographs showing the bits in-between – the unhappy moments and the times they'd been miserable together – and Jack knew there were many more of these than the former.

Jack heard the door open and braced himself for the conversation he knew they would have to have. He looked up as Laura walked into the room. She threw her purse on the couch and then unexpectedly flung her arms around him. 'I'm pregnant, darling. You're going to be a daddy!'

The wedding was a small and low-key affair, close family and friends only. An unexpected pleasure for Jack was meeting Laura's dead parents for the first time. 'We're not taking her back,' Laura's mother whispered.

The Cuckold

If news of Laura's pregnancy had been a surprise to Laura, then it was certainly a shock to Jack, who in his junior year at college had contracted mumps. An unfortunate side effect of the virus had been to diminish the size of his testes, and although Jack had never been formally pronounced infertile, it was generally assumed that he'd be welcomed with open arms if he ever applied for membership of the sub-fertility club.

Even when Laura grew to the size of a house, the reality of becoming a parent never really hit home for Jack; fatherhood forever remained an abstract. He hoped that once the child was born the mantle of paternity would slip naturally over his shoulders – but it never did. Laura gave birth to a healthy boy and Jack felt nothing. He held the child in his arms and still felt nothing.

As Conrad grew, Jack found himself actually starting to dislike the child. One evening when Laura was working late, Jack sat in the den watching over Conrad and Laura's cat, Perseus. The room was silent. Conrad played with his toys on the floor and occasionally looked up at Jack and glared. Perseus, whom Jack believed to be responsible for most of the neighbourhood's knife crime, stared at him from another corner of the room. He looked from Conrad to Perseus and back to Conrad, trying to figure out which was the creepier and more sinister of the two. How could a father feel this way?

In truth, Laura had never given Jack any encouragement to feel anything different. She monopolised the child. It was she who'd chosen the name Conrad, she who'd fed him and her who'd insisted on changing his diapers. She took him with her wherever she went, and discouraged contact between him and his father. They had secret conversations that ended abruptly whenever Jack walked into the room. On the day of his fifth birthday, Conrad had even approached Jack and told him he would never speak to him again – even if he lived to be the age of twelve! Laura simply laughed.

Jack felt hopelessly trapped, not just in his marriage but also in his job. Weather forecasting had proved to be the *un*fulfilment of his professional life. Not only had the television executives failed to inform him that he'd only be presenting the weather and that his name would be changed to Jack Green, they had also forgotten to mention that as weatherman, he would also be expected to be the punch line for all the dumb jokes that came out of Phil and Mary Margaret's mouths. It was the same tired format employed by all local television stations in America – and probably around the world.

It was bad enough being the object of Phil and Mary Margaret's prosaic wisecracks, but Jack took especial umbrage at having to be the butt of Troy Robicheaux's ridicule. (Robicheaux was the station's sportscaster, and regarded by Jack as the most stupid person he'd ever met.) Jack, however, played the game: he forced smiles that caused his jaws to ache, and acted like a good ole boy having the time of his life with his best buds.

Ed Billings had also encouraged Jack to be a panellist on game shows, and guest on daytime cooking and lifestyle programmes. He was invariably introduced to the studio audiences as the city's favourite weatherman, which was code, Jack now knew, for the city's favourite fool. As Jack's popularity and bank balance grew, so too did his dignity fall into the toilet. By the time Laura announced she was pregnant, Jack had already reached breaking point and was on the verge of resigning. Laura's news, however, changed this, and job satisfaction once more took a backseat to money. It seemed that Jack would be weather-forecasting now until the day Conrad graduated from college.

The day Jack discovered Conrad wasn't his child, therefore, was one of the happiest days of his life.

The sequence of events that led to this realisation started with a daytime repeat of a popular medical drama, whose main character – unlike Doc – *was* a misanthrope. This television doctor derived satisfaction from curing patients of obscure ailments, but never any enjoyment. His only enjoyment was telling patients, or the families of patients, that they or the people they loved were about to die. He was an unhappy man who took heart from other people's pain and sadness. Oddly, the viewing public loved him.

Jack was home that day, eating lunch and reading through bank statements. He was only half listening to the programme until something he heard caught his interest: the doctor started to discuss cleft chins. The boy with the mysterious ailment, the television doctor told his fawning colleagues, couldn't possibly be the son of the man who claimed to be the child's father, because the son had a cleft chin and the supposed father didn't. 'Goddamn!' Jack exclaimed, 'Conrad's got a cleft chin!'

Conrad did indeed have a cleft chin, and a marked one at that. Jack had once joked to Laura that Conrad looked more like Kirk Douglas than he did either of them, and what had Laura said to him by way of reply? 'Don't be so fucking stupid, Jack!' At the time, he thought her response uncalled for but, thinking about it now, maybe understood it better. Laura didn't have a cleft chin and neither did he; Laura's parents didn't have cleft chins and neither did his. In fact the only person he knew with a cleft chin was… 'Goddamn!' Jack exclaimed for the second time: 'Phil Wonnacott's got a cleft chin!'

Jack put his unfinished sandwich to one side and went to get his laptop. He keyed in *cleft chins and paternity* and clicked the search button. Unsurprisingly, there was no shortage of information on the topic but, disappointingly for Jack, none of it as hard-and-fast as the declarations of the television doctor. A cleft chin, he read, was more likely to be inherited from a parent or grandparent than just happen – but it might also just happen. Jack decided, however, that probability was on the side of genetic determination – or certainly this is what he hoped – and started to look through the phone directory for the number of the private investigator Ed Billings had used at the time of his divorce. He spoke with a secretary and arranged to meet with the detective.

The detective's name was Tommy Terpstra, and his office was three floors above a Laundromat in the city's downtown district. Tommy was an ex-cop but looked more like an accountant. He had a slight build and a slight lisp, as if his tongue was too large for his mouth, and mannerisms that were overly exaggerated. He grasped Jack's hand and shook it firmly, indicating with a flowing gesture of his left arm that Jack should take a seat. 'How can I be of help, Jack?' he asked.

Jack spelled out his reasons for doubting that Conrad was his son. He started with the mumps and ended with the cleft chin. He then mentioned Phil Wonnacott's cleft chin and the weekends Laura had spent away from home in the months leading to her pregnancy. Terpstra listened intently and made notes with an old-fashioned lead pencil, heavily chewed at one end and now only half its original size. When Jack finished talking, Terpstra sat back in his chair and tapped the pencil against his cheek.

'Weirdest thing about cleft chins, Jack, is they get such a positive press. Men pay plastic surgeons good money to have them implanted. They think it makes their features look more chiselled, stronger, while all the time a cleft chin is a failure of nature. Both sides of the lower jawbone are supposed to fuse together – right here,' he said, tapping the pencil against the centre point of his chin, 'and when they don't, you get an indentation, a cleft. The only example I know of man glorifying a cock-up.

'Anyway, there's a sure way of finding out if you're right about this, and it's fast too. It'll save me a lot of legwork and you a lot of money.'

'DNA testing?' Jack asked. Terpstra nodded.

'What I need from you, Jack, are samples from you, Conrad and Wonnacott. You're easy enough. I'll take a swab from your cheek once you bring me samples from Conrad and Wonnacott. We'll get them sent off to the lab at the same time and we should have the results in three days. My advice is to get Conrad's toothbrush, but make sure you replace it with an identical one: no point in arousing any suspicions. Getting a sample from Wonnacott might be trickier, but I'm guessing you'll have access to his dressing room at the station. Strands of hair or a used razor would do the trick, a toothbrush would be ideal. You think you can do that?'

Jack took the samples to Terpstra two days later. Terpstra then swabbed the inside of Jack's cheek with a Q-Tip, and called a courier service to take the samples to the testing lab. Terpstra then took a bottle of bourbon and two glasses from a filing cabinet and poured two single measures. He handed one to Jack.

'You look like you need this,' he said. 'What will you do if Wonnacott does turn out to be Conrad's father?'

'I'll divorce Laura, for sure. Probably leave the station too. I'll tell you something, Tommy. For the first time in years I feel hopeful, like I'm on the verge of getting my own life back. Can you understand that?'

Labor Day weekend came and went. Jack spent it with Laura and Conrad, aware that this would be their last holiday together. He'd known for a week that Phil Wonnacott was Conrad's father, but had revealed nothing of this to Laura. He couldn't explain why.

The news that Wednesday evening was unusual only in that it was slower than usual, and therefore demanded more off-the-cuff filler from the presenters. After a studio discussion on anorexic pets and an interview with an eighty-four-year-old weightlifter, Phil introduced the final story of the evening. It was a longer than usual piece recorded by Mary Margaret earlier in the week, and dealt with the station's very lifeblood – grand tragedy on the local scale.

Jackie and Ferris Wheeler were the type of young couple that made people proud to be American. They lived in a gated community in a large six-bedroom house and had a five-year-old son called Skip. Ferris owned a small electronics company and Jackie stayed home looking after Skip and playing golf.

One Thursday afternoon, Jackie was standing on the teeing ground for the fourth hole waiting for her friend and golf partner, Kristy Birdsong, to complete her shot. Kristy sliced the ball and let out an expletive. Despite her headache, Jackie couldn't help smiling at her partner's reaction. She then carefully placed her own ball on the tee and looked to the distant green, where the flag flapped in the day's gentle breeze. She positioned her feet carefully, adjusted her grip, and swung back the golf club. Jackie hit the ball full and square, and then dropped to the ground dead as a doorknob. Unaware that it would never be hit by the same person again, the golf ball continued along its target line and dropped neatly into the cup on the fourth green.

Initial coverage of Jackie Wheeler's death focused on the bizarre nature of its circumstances and ran along the lines of: 'Dead Woman Hits Hole in One'. Mary Margaret, however, saw an opportunity to tell another story: the story of a young widower coming to terms with grief and struggling to raise a child on his own. Shortly after the funeral – and for what passed as a sensitive period of time at a news station – Mary Margaret arranged to interview Ferris.

The footage of Mary Margaret's film was accompanied by a suitably melancholic soundtrack designed to tug at the viewers' heart strings; it was also intended to show her and the station in a caring light. After the report had finished, the studio camera honed in on Phil and Mary Margaret's sad faces, magically capturing Mary Margaret dabbing a tear from her eye. There being a full three minutes of airtime left to fill, Mary Margaret and Phil embarked upon their inevitable chat about the story.

'That sure was a sad story, Mary Margaret. I know my heart goes out to Ferris and Skip, and I'm sure the hearts of all our viewers do, too. I know a round of applause is never suitable at a time like this, but I wish there was some kind of equivalent.'

'Right, Phil. I know exactly what you mean. The most poignant part of the story for me was listening to the way Ferris explained the situation to little Skip. While I was there, Skip asked his daddy where Mommy was, and Ferris had to explain to him again that Mommy was gone, that she was dead. And when Skip asked him to explain what 'dead' meant, Ferris put it in the sweetest of ways. He said: 'It means we've got to start cooking for ourselves, son.'

'Boy, that really says it all, Mary Margaret,' Phil said. '*We've got to start cooking for ourselves*. Hmmm.'

Mary Margaret agreed. 'And what's so peculiar about Jackie's death, Phil, is its symmetry. It starts with a stroke on the tee and ends with a hole in one on the green. It's so ironic.'

'I think you'll find you mean *iron*,' Phil corrected Mary Margaret, 'Probably a 3 iron is my guess. That's what my wife would have used for such a hole.'

When the glance Mary Margaret gave Phil looked as if it might kill him stone dead too, the producer of the show hastily told them to bring Jack into the conversation. Jack had been listening to their exchanges disbelievingly, and despite the seriousness of the piece couldn't help smiling. When the camera turned to him, he looked, somewhat inappropriately, like the happiest man on the planet.

Jack had filled time successfully on many an evening. He'd talked about tsunamis, the El Niño effect, global warming, blizzards and the differences between tornados and cyclones. What Jack really liked to talk about, however, was fog and clouds. That he rarely got a chance to do so became a running joke at the station. He would be told through his earpiece that there was time for him to talk about fog for two minutes, and after maybe getting four words into the subject then told by Phil they were out of time. Mary Margaret would laugh, and Jack would have to stand there grinning, pretending to enjoy the joke: 'You guys,' he would say shaking his head. 'Got me again!'

This time, however, there really was plenty of time left, and Mary Margaret fed him a great line. Could he explain to the viewers the difference between nimbostratus and cirrostratus cloud formations? Jack took the bait. He'd been speaking for barely twenty seconds before he started to hear titters of laughter from the studio floor. He looked at the monitor that showed the picture viewers at home would see on their TV screens, and there were Phil and Mary Margaret pretending to be fast asleep, bored out of their skulls by Jack's enthusiastic explanation. Jack stopped mid-sentence.

A fine line divides a person losing their senses from one coming to them, and the exact location of that line is open to interpretation. What many later described as Jack having a mental breakdown, Tommy Terpstra rightly construed as Jack regaining his mind.

'Fuck this!' he said. 'And fuck you, Phil! Thanks for fucking my fucking wife!'

He unclipped the microphone from his lapel and left the building, never to appear on television again.

A Changed Man

If not a new man, by the time Jack arrived at Doc's house there was no doubting that he was a changed man. His on-air resignation from both his job and family had been a cathartic and freeing experience, and emotions that had long been suppressed broke through to the surface and blessed him with an unprecedented clarity of vision. Although his initial words hadn't accurately reflected the wholesome nature of his reformation, *fuck this* did give a strong indication of the depth of change that had taken place. The days of behaving like a man whose confidence allowed him only to write in pencil were now behind him. In future, he would speak his mind, confront issues head on and, if necessary, upset people and not care.

When Jack walked off the news set, he kept walking. He didn't stop to gather any personal items from his office, but went straight to the elevator and punched the button for the lobby. He walked through the foyer, out of the building and kept walking. He had no intention of going home: he no longer had a home to go to. He tore off the station blazer he wore for broadcasts, shoved it into a garbage can and continued to walk. Ten blocks from the station he checked into a small but comfortable hotel and phoned Tommy Terpstra.

'Tommy, I need a divorce lawyer – a good one. Do you have any suggestions?'

Tommy had: his daughter, Tina. 'She's kin, Jack; I'm not about to hide that fact from you, but she's also damn good at what she does and her speciality's family law. What's more, she's a woman, and women are always better in cases like this – you ask Billings, if the two of you are still talking.'

Jack agreed to Terpstra's suggestion, and Terpstra arranged for Jack to meet his daughter the following day.

Tina Terpstra was a junior partner in a large legal firm located one block from the hotel where Jack was staying. Jack's appointment was for eleven o'clock, but he'd misjudged the time it would take for him to walk there and arrived early. He was shown to a seat in the reception area and served coffee. He had a dull headache and wished he'd eaten breakfast. He took in the surrounding decor and noted it was expensive and tasteful. He wondered how much the visit would cost him. Shortly after eleven, one of the receptionists asked him to follow her. She led him to an office at the very end of a long corridor, knocked on the door and entered. 'Jack Guravitch to see you, Tina,' she said, and then left.

Tina stood up from behind a large mahogany desk and extended her hand to Jack. Jack took it, surprised by its firmness, and then sat in the chair indicated. Tina wore a dark pin-striped trouser suit and, although looking to be about the same age as Jack, already had flecks of grey in her short hair. She wore little, if any, make-up, and Jack imagined that from a distance Tina could easily be mistaken for a man. He also noticed that she wore no wedding ring. In his newly-acquired state of mind, Jack came straight to the point.

'Are you gay?' he asked Tina.

(Jack had emerged from his epiphany with something resembling a mild form of Tourette's syndrome, and it took time for him to appreciate that freedom of speech wasn't a licence for tactless or graceless behaviour: it had its responsibilities. He had to learn to harness and finesse this new freedom, and recognise that remaining true to oneself didn't necessarily involve smashing another person over the head with a claw hammer. If he wanted to influence people with his words, which he now did, then people would have to feel comfortable around him; if they didn't, this newly discovered freedom would gain him little.)

'Yes. Is that a problem for you?' Tina asked.

'Not in the least, Tina. The thought just crossed my mind, so I thought I'd ask it.'

Tina looked at him, still dubious. 'I might not date men, Jack, but neither do I hate them. If I agree to represent you, then I'll be representing you and not your wife. I won't be taking it easy on her just because she's a woman, if that's what worries you. Do you understand this?'

Jack apologised for any misunderstanding he might have caused. Secretly, however, he couldn't help thinking that Tina was a tad sensitive for a dyke.

Tina questioned Jack carefully about the personal and financial aspects of the marriage: Laura, Conrad, and Phil Wonnacott; the house, savings accounts and pension arrangements. She ordered more coffee from reception and a snack for Jack, whose stomach was now rumbling uncontrollably. While Jack ate his cheese sandwich, Tina took two encyclopaedic-looking books from a shelf, studied them and made notes.

'Okay, Jack, these are your options,' she finally said. 'You can proceed with the divorce presuming Conrad is your child…'

'But he's not,' Jack interrupted.

'Hear me out,' Tina said. 'I'm just giving you your options. You can proceed with the divorce presuming Conrad *is* your child. This would be your quickest way of getting a divorce, and it would also allow you custodial and visitation rights if you so desired them. However, the downside of this is that once you legally acknowledge paternity of Conrad, you can never challenge paternity at a later date – even if you prove not to be the father – and you'll also have to pay child support.

'If, on the other hand, you decide to challenge your paternity of Conrad, then now's the time to do it. It's clear from the tests you've already had done that you're not Conrad's father, so we can confidently expect that any further tests will have the same outcome. And, if you're proved not to be the father, then you'll have no child support to pay, but in all likelihood you'll also lose all visitation rights *vis a vis* Conrad.

'I think I can guess your answer, Jack, but I need to hear it from you. What are you thinking?'

'Option two,' Jack said immediately. 'I'm not Conrad's father and I want this known. My obligation ends now. I'm not spending another cent on that ungrateful kid. Wonnacott will have to put his hand in his pocket for a change – and he's welcome to my visitation rights, too!

'I do have one question though, Tina. I've been shelling out for Conrad ever since he was born. I was tricked into doing this, essentially defrauded by Laura. Can I get my money back?'

'For the money you've spent on Conrad to date, you mean?'

'Exactly!'

'Hmmm. That's a difficult one. I can understand your point of view, Jack, but there's no legal precedent for this. From a lawyer's point of view it would be fun to try, but it could take years and cost you a fortune, and there's no guarantee we'd be successful.

'My best advice to you is that we stay with option two. You'll be free of paying any more money on Conrad's behalf, and the marital property as it stands now – home equity, retirement, bank accounts and stocks – will be divided fifty-fifty between you and Laura once the settlement's been finalised.'

Jack thought for a few moments. 'Okay, let's do it,' he finally said. 'I'm in town for the next week, but then I have to make a trip with my godfather and I don't know how long I'll be away.' He tore a sheet from a notebook he carried with him and started to write. 'This is my mobile number and this, my email address, Tina. You can reach me anytime on these.'

They shook hands – firmly.

Against all expectations, Laura agreed to the terms of the divorce as set out and presented to her attorney by Tina. She neither challenged the assertion that Jack wasn't Conrad's father nor quibbled over the suggested fifty-fifty division of assets. There was no apology.

Jack was untroubled by her silence: he was more than happy not to see her again; particularly happy never to see Conrad again.

Having made sure that neither Laura nor Conrad would be there, Jack visited the family house only once. He wasted little time, methodically moving from room to room and filling suitcases with clothes and items personal to himself: CDs, books, photographs, letters and documents. That night, he phoned Billings and asked if he could buy him a drink. Billings laughed.

They met the following evening in a bar close to Jack's hotel. Billings was in a surprisingly jovial mood and gave Jack a friendly punch on the arm. 'You made an old man happy, Green,' he said.

Billings told Jack bluntly that his broadcasting career was pretty much dead in the water, but congratulated him on ending it in such great style. For him, the ex-weatherman's outburst had been the unexpected apotheosis of what, until then, had been a dull and repetitive career in broadcasting. He recalled for Jack his silent joy at seeing the look of abject horror on Wonnacott's face after Jack had accused him of sleeping with his wife, and burst out laughing at the still-warm memory.

'Wonnacott's a pompous ass, Jack, and everyone at the station knows it. He's always had a predatory nature around women, and at ground level he's not getting a whole lot of sympathy – that's all going your way. At brass level, it's different. The station's got a family ethos, and as Wonnacott's their most valuable asset, they'll protect him by hanging you out to dry. There's a statement being prepared apologising for your outburst and explaining it in terms of a mental breakdown. You might want to know that even as we speak, the station's providing you with the best treatment available.'

'You mean beer?' Jack asked.

'That's about it,' Billings smiled. 'Publicly, they'll be saying Wonnacott's an innocent man who got caught in the crossfire. They'll also be saying that even though he's been wrongly maligned, Wonnacott forgives his old buddy the weatherman and wishes him a speedy recovery. What a guy, eh?

'Raise your glass, Jack, and let's make a toast: To you, Jack Green. May your pastures new be even greener!'

The two men clinked glasses. 'What are you going to do, by the way?' Billings asked.

'I'm thinking of becoming a hairdresser,' Jack replied.

The Plan

'So let me get this straight, Doc. We're going to spring an old girlfriend of yours from a nursing home and then get the hell out of Dodge?' Doc nodded. 'And she's half loco?' Doc nodded again. 'And I'm your wife.' Again, Doc nodded. 'Jeez!' Jack said.

Doc, however, was pleased with his plan, the logistics of which had fallen into place after he'd made one further trip to Hershey. That visit, he hadn't called on Nancy. He was aware of his promise that the next time they'd meet would be the time they'd leave together, and hadn't wanted to run the risk of distressing her further. Instead, he limited himself to driving around Hershey and its environs until he was satisfied with the route they would take and the place where they would rendezvous with Bob.

The plan was this. Rather than fly to Harrisburg, Jack would drive them to Hershey in his rental car. The evening before the planned abduction, the two of them would check into a motel close to the town, and the following morning Jack would become Doc's wife. Doc would take the wheel for the final leg of the journey – a short one, fortunately – and drive to the nursing home.

After parking the car, Doc would help Jack into a wheelchair and push him into the nursing home. He would sign them in as Doctor and Mrs Chaney and they would then go looking for Nancy; if she wasn't already in her room, they would find her and take her there. Jack would then take off the women's clothes he was wearing and Nancy would slip them on over hers. They'd wait in the room for a half hour or so and then leave. Nancy would climb into the wheelchair and Doc would wheel her to the car, stopping only to sign out at the reception desk. After a short interval of time, Jack would follow and drive them to a pre-arranged meeting place, where Bob – Doc's friend – would be waiting for them. Doc and Nancy would transfer to Bob's RV, and Jack would re-join them after dropping his rental car at Harrisburg airport. They would then leave Hershey, a town known for its chocolate, and drive to Coffeeville, a town not known for its coffee.

'So, what's wrong with her nose?' Jack asked. While Doc had been explaining the details of the plan, Jack had been staring at the portrait of Nancy that hung on the wall.

'Nothing,' Doc said. 'The artist got it wrong.'

'How come he got the fruit right, then? The apples and pears look real enough to eat.'

'I don't know,' Doc said exasperatedly. 'You'll see her soon enough.'

'Are the two of you getting it on?'

Doc looked at him incredulously. 'You're asking me if we're having *sex*?'

'Yes,' Jack said, not at all abashed by his question. 'I haven't upset you, have I?'

Unaware of the epiphany's after-effects on Jack, Doc had trouble understanding why his godson had asked him such a personally intrusive question.

'No, we're not having sex! In our twenties we had sex, but not now. Unless you grow old with a person, the chances are you're not likely to want to have sex with them after not seeing them for forty years. You know how your own body's changed in that time – and that's difficult enough to come to terms with – so why would you want to inflict it on someone else? And why would you want someone else to inflict their worn-out body on you?'

'In short, Jack, the answer's no. I'm glad Nancy's my friend these days, and I'm also glad there was once a time when we did have sex.'

Another question came to Jack's mind. 'Should I try and get inside Nancy's head before we go, Doc; choose clothes she'd wear?'

'You're not supposed to be Nancy, Jack: you're supposed to be *my* wife. Believe me; you don't want to get inside her head. There's no fun to be found there. Choose someone else if you have to choose anybody.'

'Okay, Mary Tyler Moore then. We'll buy clothes Mary would have bought.'

'Let's play it by ear. I doubt we have her budget.'

The first thing they bought was a wheelchair. They tried out several models, Jack sitting and Doc pushing, before deciding on a rigid rather than a folding chair: it had fewer moving parts and the joints were permanently welded; it was lighter and required less energy to push and, just as importantly, could be dismantled quickly.

Next, they bought make-up and went shopping for a wig and suitable clothes. It took Jack no time to decide on a wig, but the clothes took longer as he put himself inside Mary's head. They ended up buying a thick red polo-necked sweater; a pair of dark slacks – so Jack wouldn't have to shave his legs; some ladies' sneakers and white socks; and a large cashmere shawl. Doc was about to question the need for a shawl made out of cashmere when Jack raised his palm and gestured for him to stop: 'Mary's got class, Doc, and she's a doctor's wife now. This is the way it has to be. We've got to play it for real.'

The last stop was the bank. Jack remained in the car, while Doc went through the swing doors and emerged a good half hour later.

'I didn't see anyone coming out,' Jack said. 'How long was the line?'

'There wasn't a line,' Doc replied. 'I was the only customer.'

The next morning the two men prepared to leave for Hershey. They put the wheelchair and a suitcase filled with Nancy's clothes into the trunk of the car, and their own bags on the back seat. Doc told Jack to start the car while he made one last check of the house and set the alarm.

Jack looked at his watch. How long did it take a man in his seventies to check a house? He pushed a CD into the player and, in the moment of silence when the radio quieted, heard a sharp crack. He looked up and saw Doc hurrying down the drive with a gun in his hand. 'Jesus H. Christ!' he exclaimed.

Doc climbed into the car reeking of cordite and slammed the door behind him. 'Drive, Jack! Now!'

Jack put his foot down on the accelerator and the car sped away from the house. 'What the fuck did you just do, Doc? You didn't shoot Frisbee, did you?'

Doc turned to him and gave a wry smile. 'Just his dog,' he said, and then fell silent.

Men with Blue Eyes

The journey to Hershey was long but uneventful. Jack drove while Doc snoozed, lured into a fitful sleep by the motion of the car and the warmth of its interior. Occasionally, Jack took his eyes from the road and glanced at his passenger. Although the two men had spoken frequently since Sydney's death, this visit was the first time Jack had seen Doc since the funeral. The man sitting next to him was now looking old – older, in fact, than his actual years. Dark and permanent circles ringed the man's eyes, lines that had once creased his face had deepened into cracks and previously full cheeks had hollowed conspicuously, as if scooped out with a spoon. The picture of age surprised him, but what disquieted him more was the haggardly look that framed this picture. Not only did Doc look drawn when his guard was down, he looked haunted.

Jack knew better than to mention this observation to his godfather: from experience, he realised that any such conversation would be pointless. As a boy in his late teens, he'd once asked Doc if he was happy. He still remembered the withering look his godfather had given him. The glance had been only fleeting, but the question had hung in the air and never been answered; Doc had simply changed the subject. Jack had mentioned this episode to his father.

'I'm probably his closest friend, Jack, and even I wouldn't have asked him that,' Sydney had replied. 'He doesn't wear his heart on his sleeve. I don't think he can afford to. The only thing you'll ever find there are cufflinks and buttons. He's pretty much been that way ever since he returned from Maryland. The man has feelings, but he internalises them and never shares them. It's the way he is and so I respect that. But he doesn't do himself any favours.'

'Does he like me?' Jack asked. 'It's hard to tell, sometimes.'

His father had laughed. 'Sure he likes you, maybe even loves you, but never expect him to tell you this. Doc bonds with few people because most people he doesn't like, but once he does become your friend he's your friend for life and you'll always be able to depend on him. Why else do you think I asked him to be your godfather?'

Jack had been pleased with his father's reply. He liked Doc and, despite their age difference, had always looked upon him as a friend rather than an informal relation. As Jack matured, his friendship with Doc strengthened. When Jack was in town visiting his parents, the two of them would meet for meals, go for drinks, or simply hang out on Doc's back terrace. Jack was comfortable sharing his own thoughts and feelings with Doc and would openly discuss any problems he might be having. Doc would listen intently while his godson spoke, counsel any advice he might see fit to give, and respect any confidences Jack preferred his parents and others not to know. Doc, however, never reciprocated and Jack learned not to pry into his older friend's emotions. From what his father had said, it was clear that Doc wasn't a man who bled in public. Looking at him now, however, asleep as he was in the passenger seat of a rental car, it was clear that his godfather had been bleeding internally for most of his life.

'We almost there yet?'

Doc's voice startled Jack. 'I was beginning to think you'd died on me, old man,' he replied. 'We're getting close, so you might want to start wiping that drool off your chin. It's like you've got an artesian well pumping away inside your mouth.'

Doc pulled a handkerchief from his trouser pocket and rubbed his chin with it. 'It'll happen to you someday, kid. Age doesn't play favourites and it doesn't take prisoners, either: it inflicts its sorry ass on all of us. You won't escape. By the time you're sixty, your rhythmic walking pattern will have started to deteriorate, by the time you're seventy you'll have twenty per cent less bone, and by the time you're seventy-five you'll be shorter by two-and-a-half inches. Drooling's the least of it.'

'Well, aren't you the barrel of laughs? I'll tell you what, though…'

'Hey, you're passing it! This is the turn-off, Jack. Start signalling!'

Jack didn't have time to signal. He braked hard, turned the wheel to the right, but even so still clipped the grass verge on the passenger's side. Once the car had regained its equilibrium, Jack pointed out to Doc that this wasn't the exit for Hershey.

'I know it's not,' Doc replied. 'We're staying the night in Lebanon. We'll drive to Hershey in the morning. It'll only take thirty minutes.'

They found a small motel on the outskirts of the town close to US 422. Doc paid cash for two adjoining rooms accessible from the parking area and Jack drew the car up outside.

'I wouldn't have minded sharing, Doc. It would have saved you some money.'

'Nothing personal, but I can't sleep with someone else in the same room these days, let alone someone in the same bed. Don't ask me why, because I don't rightly know why. I'm guessing it's because I've spent too much time on my own.'

They unloaded the car, took what luggage they needed to their rooms and walked to a nearby diner. It was late, approaching closing time, and there were few other customers in the restaurant. They sat down in a booth and looked through the menus brought to them by a woman about Doc's age.

'I love this kind of food,' Doc said. 'If it was up to me, I'd choose a diner over a fancy restaurant any day of the week. Look at this: T-Bone Steaks, Sirloins, Grilled Pork Chops, Fried Country Ham Steak, Baked Western Ham Steak, Golden Fried Shrimp, Broiled Trout and Pan Fried Chicken. And the most expensive thing is only $15!

'You know the first thing I did when I retired from practice? I went to a burger bar and bought the biggest hamburger they had, and the biggest portion of French fries they served. The next day I went to a pizza restaurant, the day after that to a fried chicken restaurant, and so on. By the end of the week I was five pounds heavier.'

'Why did you do that?' Jack asked.

'Because I was no longer a doctor. I didn't have to lead by example anymore. All my professional life I'd been telling people to cut down on junk food, watch their cholesterol, eat more vegetables, eat more fruit, cut down on alcohol, do more exercise, and who'd have listened if the guy telling them that had been the size of a blimp? Retirement freed me, Jack. For the first time in years I felt like I could eat what I wanted and it was no one's damned business but mine. I'm like everyone else now. Once more a man of the people!'

The waitress arrived and interrupted Doc's flow. He ordered pork chops and mashed potatoes, while Jack chose the sirloin steak and French fries. They agreed to share a bowl of turnip greens as a gesture to healthy living, and cemented the gesture with two beers.

Jack finished his meal first and laid his knife and fork on the plate. He looked around the diner. They were the last of the customers and the waitress and cook were now sitting at the counter drinking coffee, no doubt waiting for them to leave.

'It's a good job only one of us here has blue eyes, Doc. The people of Lebanon get suspicious of men with blue eyes gathering together. In fact they hang them.'

'What are you talking about?'

'You've never heard of the Blue Eyed Six?'

'No,' Doc replied, 'Only the *Brown Eyed Girl* – a song from the sixties,' he added, when he saw Jack looking perplexed. 'Who were they?'

'Six men who took out an insurance policy on the life of a hobo. It was supposedly one of those win–win situations: they'd look after him while he was alive, feed and clothe him and the like, and then collect on the policy when he was dead. The only fly in the ointment was that within the year the guy *was* dead – supposedly fell off a plank and drowned in the creek. At first, his death was ruled an accident, but then the son-in-law of one of the six stepped forward and said that he'd seen the man being drowned. Even though only two of them were alleged to have carried out the killing, all six were charged with first degree murder. Reporters from all over the world came to cover the trial, and one of them noticed that all six defendants had piercing blue eyes – hence the Blue Eyed Six. Apparently, 1879 was a slow year for news.'

Ostensibly satisfied with his explanation, Jack ended the story there. Doc, however, was left hanging.

'So what happened? Were they found guilty?'

'Yes, and even though it came out in the trial that the son-in-law was a deserter from the army and had caught his wife having an affair with one of the accused, the jury still found them guilty. Five of them were hanged, and the sixth was given leave to appeal and then acquitted at his retrial on the very same evidence that had convicted his friends. Strange old world, eh?'

'How do you know all this?' Doc asked.

'There was a guy at the TV station who was a big Arthur Conan Doyle fan. Occasionally, we'd eat lunch together, and it came up in conversation that the Sherlock Holmes short story called *The Red-Headed League* was inspired by a trial in America. When I asked him what trial that was, he told me this story about the Blue Eyed Six. Never thought I'd ever be staying the night in the actual town, though. Remind me to send him a postcard of Lebanon in the morning, will you? He'll get a kick out of it.'

'No postcards,' Doc said. 'It's best no one knows you're here.' He then peeled off two twenty-dollar bills and put them on the table. 'Time to go, Jack. We've got a big day ahead of us tomorrow.'

Doc woke with a start, gasping for breath and covered in perspiration. He lay there exhausted; his stomach churning, his heart pounding. He looked at the clock on the bedside table and groaned when he saw the digits 04:30 glowing red in the dark of the room. He resigned himself to the fact there would be no more sleep for him that night, turned on the television and tuned it to a news channel.

At 7:30 am, he climbed out of bed more exhausted than when he'd climbed into it. He went into the bathroom and ran the shower, stood under it for a good fifteen minutes while he collected his thoughts, and then shaved and dressed. He walked over to the diner, drank three cups of coffee and ordered two large coffees and some sausage and biscuits to go. Again, he paid in cash: no trails.

It was 8:30 am when Doc knocked on Jack's door – three times, to be precise. Jack eventually opened the door looking dishevelled and still wearing the boxer shorts and T-shirt he'd slept in.

'What time is it, Doc?' he asked groggily.

'After 8:30,' Doc replied, looking at his watch. 'There's no rush but you need to start getting ready. Here's your breakfast,' he said, handing Jack the bag containing the coffee and biscuits. 'We need to leave at 10:00. I'll leave my door unlocked – knock on it when you're ready.' Jack nodded and Doc returned to his own room.

Doc was sitting on the can when Jack walked into the room. 'I'll be with you in a minute,' he shouted through the bathroom door. Jack sat down on the bed and waited for Doc to admire his transformation. He heard the toilet flush and then the sound of a tap running. Shortly, Doc walked into the room drying his hands on a small towel. When he saw Jack, his jaw dropped.

'Hell's teeth, son!' he exclaimed. 'You look like some over the hill hooker!'

'A hooker! How do you figure that? I think I look like one classy broad, even though I do say so myself.'

Doc said nothing, but spent the next ten minutes adjusting the amount of padding Jack had stuffed into his bra, toning down the eye shadow and lipstick, and adding more foundation to cover the shadow of his beard. He then stepped back and surveyed his handiwork.

'That's more like it,' he said. 'I can't see you getting any dates, but if you keep your head down and wear these sunglasses you'll serve the purpose. Now let's go.'

Doc loaded their belongings into the car, and when the coast was clear called for Jack – passenger side, he reminded him. He then took control of the car and accelerated out of the motel's grounds, narrowly missing two large ornamental pots. Jack looked across at him. 'You sure you're okay to drive?'

'Sure,' Doc answered. 'One eye's worse than the other, but I've still got some central vision left – for now, anyway. Fine details are a problem, but I can usually see cars in front of me – at least for the next thirty minutes, I can. Feel free to holler if it looks like I'm going to hit one.'

'Okay, Doc, but maybe you should slow down a bit. You're doing 70 mph. Did you know that?'

'No. I can't make out the dials. Dials come under the heading of *fine details*. Hope to God I can recognise Nancy when I see her.'

Despite Doc's erratic use of the accelerator pedal and questionable lane discipline, they made it safely to the nursing home. Doc parked the car in a quiet area away from the main entrance, rubbed his eyes and smiled at Jack. 'Okay, son, let's do it!'

Jack waited in the car while Doc lifted the wheelchair from the trunk, assembled it and wheeled it to the passenger side door. He made pretence of helping Jack into the chair and then pushed it slowly to the main entrance. He was relieved to find that the receptionist on duty wasn't the one who'd signed him in on his previous visit, and decided on the spot to use a pseudonym.

The receptionist was in conversation with an old man complaining about the fish tank in the foyer and seemed to welcome the interruption. Doc said his name was Homer Comer and that he and his wife Ruby were here to visit Nancy Skidmore in the secure unit. She smiled politely and asked him to sign the visitor's book, noting the time of arrival in the column next to his name. She then wrote four numbers on a post-it note and handed the piece of paper to Doc.

'This is the code you'll need to open the door, Mr Comer.'

Doc thanked her. He then turned the wheelchair in the direction of the secure unit and casually pushed it down the corridor. He looked at the piece of paper in his hand. He muttered something under his breath that Jack couldn't quite hear, and then punched the very same numbers into the keypad he'd punched on his previous visit: 1111. The door swung open.

The Fish Tank

In the beginning was the Word, and then the Word – all words – became meaningless.

The Nancy Skidmore who now resided in the secure unit of the Oaklands Retirement Center was a person who had travelled a long way from her true self. Lichens and mosses clung to her mind as they would an ancient gravestone and the door to her memory, destined as it was to be locked and bolted from the other side, was fast closing shut.

If Nancy's craziness had been a constant, a condition she was unaware of and accepted at face value, then life for her would have been easier, and certainly preferable to the life she now lived. There were times, however, when the fog enveloping her mind lifted and she found herself gazing into clear blue skies, conscious of what was happening to her and, more worryingly still, mindful of the inevitable fate awaiting her. It was then that she became anxious. Being crazy and *knowing* it was the scariest hell of all.

Nancy spent her days in the unit standing at its entrance and peering through the glass door into a world that was now denied her. For hours at a time she remained there unmoving, endlessly punching numbers into a keypad that would release the door from its latch and allow her escape. If, in the event, the door was opened from the other side by either attending staff or visitors, she would slip through the gap like greased lightning, only to be turned back with a gentle but firm hand and, often as not, escorted to the lounge area.

There, Nancy would pace the room's perimeter or sit restlessly in one of the high seat armchairs that lined its walls. She sat as far from other residents as possible and spoke to them no more than she had to. She never started conversations, seldom understood the meaning of things they said to her, and was unsettled by their mumblings and occasional screams. She didn't understand why she'd been placed with people who were so obviously wrong in the head, and couldn't for the life of her comprehend why she wasn't allowed to return home. Time and again she'd plead with nursing staff to let her go back to her own house, but she may as well have been speaking to a brick wall: all they did was smile at her, ignore her questions and treat her like a six-year-old child.

Nancy tried to remember how she'd got there, but remembering anything now was getting harder by the day. She vaguely remembered walking on the side of a road and being given a ride by a kindly policeman, but after that – nothing. She had a hazy recollection that someone was supposed to come get her, but wasn't sure who that someone was: was it her husband, her parents, Ruby, or that nice boy she used to date in college? She had no real idea, and no one ever came. She lost track of the days, was unsure if she'd been there one day or ten, and started to worry that she'd always be there. Consequently, the morning Doc walked into the lounge, a huge feeling of relief swept over her – even if he was pushing a wheelchair with what appeared to be the ugliest woman in the world sitting on its seat.

'Gene! Gene! I'm over here,' Nancy called. She raised herself from the chair she was sitting in and moved towards him as fast as her sixty-seven-year-old legs would allow. Doc put his arms around her and held her to him.

'You have to call me Homer, Nancy,' he whispered. 'It's important!'

'Why? Your name isn't…'

'You just do, Nancy,' he interrupted her. 'Now, where's your room?'

She took his hand and led him the short distance, glancing at the woman in the wheelchair. 'I thought you said your wife was dead, Gene,' she whispered. 'Have you been lying to me?'

Once inside the room, Doc closed the door and wedged it shut with a chair. He allowed Nancy to hug him one more time and then gently pushed her away. 'Do you remember me telling you that the next time you saw me we'd be leaving here together?' Nancy nodded. 'Well, today's the day. This is my godson, Jack, by the way. He's going to help us.'

Jack held out his gloved hand to Nancy. 'I'm pleased to meet you, Mrs Skidmore, and if I might say so, you're a lot better looking than your name might suggest – and certainly more attractive than the portrait Doc has of you.'

'What's he talking about, Gene?'

'He's just being friendly,' Doc replied, casting a glance in Jack's direction and silently imploring him not to complicate things. 'Okay, Nancy, now listen to me carefully. This is what we're going to do…'

While Doc talked, Jack took off the wig, sunglasses and clothes that masked his true identity and stood before Nancy as himself, wearing a pair of dark blue jeans and a crew-necked sweater.

'Who's this?' Nancy asked.

'I told you, Nancy, he's my godson. He's here to help us.' He then helped Nancy put the clothes Jack had just taken off over her own, and handed her the wig.

'I'm not wearing this!' Nancy said. 'That man's been wearing it and he might have nits.'

'Believe me, Nancy, the care Jack takes over his hair, he'd be the last person on earth to have head lice.'

'Actually, I did have them once,' Jack said. 'I got them from Conrad.'

'Who's Conrad?' Nancy demanded.

'He's my son; or rather the boy I *thought* was my son.'

'What's he talking about, Gene?'

Doc took Jack by the arm and led him towards the room's small bathroom. 'Excuse us a minute would you, Nancy?'

'What the hell are you doing, Jack?' he said. 'You're confusing her; can't you see that? Keep things simple and just agree with anything I say. Okay?'

'Okay... Sorry, Doc. Sometimes things just come out.'

'Yes, I've been noticing that.' Doc replied. The two men re-entered the room.

'I've checked his hair, Nancy, and it's fine. No nits!'

Reluctantly, Nancy pulled the wig over her own hair and Doc handed her the sunglasses. He looked at his watch. Twenty minutes had passed since they'd signed in. 'It's too soon to leave yet. We'll wait another ten minutes.'

'Are we going now?' Nancy asked.

'Soon, Nancy. Soon.'

Doc spent the remaining time searching the room for anything Nancy might need for the journey, patiently responding to her as she asked the same question over and over again: 'Are we going now, Gene? Are we going now, Gene? Are we going now, Gene?'

Doc looked at his watch again: thirty minutes had passed. He told Nancy to sit in the wheelchair and hooked the arms of the sunglasses over her ears. He then knelt down and placed his hands on either side of her face. 'Until we get outside, Nancy, you don't say a word – even if someone speaks to you. Do you understand?' She nodded. He kissed her on the cheek and then pushed the wheelchair out of the room.

Jack remained. He was to follow ten minutes later and, if challenged by anyone at reception, sign his name in the book against another visitor's name. He rinsed his face with cold water, dried with a hand towel he found hanging at the side of the basin and then checked himself in the mirror. What he saw alarmed him, for while the foundation and lipstick had washed off, the mascara had stubbornly remained and left him looking like a droog from *A Clockwork Orange*. He swore under his breath, and kicked himself for having mistakenly bought waterproof instead of non-waterproof mascara. The only course of action left was to walk with his head down and hope he didn't collide with anyone. He left Nancy's room and walked self-consciously to the door of the Secure Unit. No one stopped him, no one looked. He punched the code into the keypad and started down the long corridor to the foyer. 'So far, so good,' he thought.

It was then he heard the explosion of a gun being fired, followed quickly by the noise of glass breaking and voices screaming. 'Jesus, Doc!' he exclaimed, 'What the hell have you done now, you crazy old fool?' He ran the remaining distance with his head up.

William Hoopes was a retired policeman from Berks County, Pennsylvania, and a man used to getting his own way. As an officer of the law he'd been a stickler and never once cut slack for anyone, friend or foe. The law was the law and so too, to his way of thinking, were his prejudices. He'd been used to power his whole life and had enjoyed seeing the look of fear in people's eyes when he'd exerted it. He'd had few friends but believed himself to be widely respected. It therefore came as a surprise to him when, at the first high school reunion he attended after retiring, the other attendees booed him. Retirement, it seemed, had de-authorized him: what he'd presumed to be respect had, in fact, been fear all along.

What really annoyed him, however, was the constant jibing about whether he was going to run for President again, maybe get a few more votes this time. Damn his namesake! He wasn't even a relative of the Reading man they alluded to, and not even of his generation. And he certainly wasn't a Socialist! In his book, Darlington Hoopes had been nothing more than a troublemaker, and if it had been left to him in 1956 he would have gladly strung the presidential candidate from a lamppost. Although he took solace in the fact that the old lawyer had polled only 2,192 votes – a mere 363 more than a New Jersey pig farmer standing as an independent candidate – it rankled that people connected him to such a loser.

William Hoopes tired of the ridicule and decided to leave Berks County for a town where no one knew him. He walked into the kitchen one morning and told his wife they were selling the house and moving to a retirement community in Hershey. For a while, he fitted in well at Oaklands. He made new friends and joined in many of the activities, but then the fish tank began to trouble him.

The aquarium was located in the foyer. It was large and filled with a variety of tropical marine fish. It was an eye catcher for anyone visiting the Oaklands Retirement Community and radiated an air of calm. As a result, the lobby had become a popular area for residents to sit and while away their time. During lulls in conversation, their eyes would turn to the multicoloured fish swimming in the tank and, often as not, they would fall asleep. All, that is, except William Hoopes, who had to constantly excuse himself and use the bathroom. The sound of running water, he found, was far from conducive to a man with an enlarged prostate.

Hoopes mentioned this to receptionists on the desk, brought it up at meetings, and wrote letters to the owners of the centre. He told them he was a reasonable man and willing to compromise: he was happy for the aquarium to stay where it was, but wanted the water pump turned off during daylight hours. When it was pointed out to him that the fish would die if such a course of action was taken and that the aquarium was there to stay, the authoritarian streak in Hoopes reared its ugly head and the man who claimed to be reasonable morphed into a *fucking nightmare*, as the administrators now described him. If he and his wife hadn't occupied an expensive two-bedroom apartment in the complex, he would in all likelihood have been asked to leave.

It had been William Hoopes talking to the receptionist at the desk when Doc and Jack had arrived at Oaklands that morning. Unbeknownst to them, he'd been in the process of giving her an ultimatum: either she agreed to the removal of the aquarium from the foyer or he'd take matters into his own hands! The receptionist had made it clear – as she had done on many previous occasions – that the administration had no intention of removing the aquarium from the foyer and then, somewhat unprofessionally, had suggested that he tie a knot in his John Thomas. Hearing that, Hoopes had gone apoplectic and stormed out of the foyer.

Moments after Doc had wheeled Nancy out of Oaklands, Hoopes had charged back into the reception area brandishing a Colt Python revolver. 'Why don't you tie a knot in this,' he shouted at the receptionist. He'd then aimed the gun at the aquarium and fired a .357 Magnum bullet into it. The aquarium had immediately shattered and the enclosed water cascaded on to the floor. Homeless fish, gasping for breath, flapped among broken pieces of glass, and the receptionist ducked behind the desk in fear for her life. Some of the residents sitting in the foyer screamed, two women fainted and an old man clutched his heart.

Hoopes remained standing there, the realisation of what he'd done slowly sinking in. He released his grip on the revolver and the gun dropped to the floor. Staff came running from all directions, and in the ensuing pandemonium not one of them noticed the man with unusually dark eyes side-stepping the debris and exiting through the doors to a waiting car.

Friends Reunited

Jack drove, while Doc sat in the backseat of the car holding Nancy's hand. He looked at their reflections in the driver's mirror and smiled: 'Hey you two! No making out back there. I've just had the car valeted.'

'Just drive, Jack!' Doc snapped. 'And make sure you don't miss the turning.'

Jack pulled the car on to Governor Rd and headed west. He passed the Medical Center and turned left on to Bullfrog Valley Rd, and then took another left on to Wood Rd. At the intersection of Wood and Middletown Rd, he turned into the parking lot of the Stoverdale United Methodist Church, empty apart from a forty-foot bus that filled it. 'What the hell's that thing doing there?' Doc wondered out loud.

They'd arrived twenty minutes earlier than expected, and Doc worried that his well-laid plans were already starting to unravel. He'd chosen this particular location for its seclusion, to ensure that the rendezvous with Bob would go unnoticed; God only knew how many prying eyes were peering at them through the darkened windows of the bus.

He soon found out: four – two belonging to Bob, and two belonging to a small boy wearing a bicycle helmet. 'I'll be damned,' Doc said when he saw the two of them climb out of the bus.

'Remember him, Nancy?' he said. 'It's Bob, Bob Crenshaw! We used to ride buses with him back in the day. Looks like we'll be riding another one with him, now.'

'I remember Bob,' Nancy said, 'but this man's old. Bob wasn't old.'

'We're all old now, Nancy. He's grown ancient like the rest of us.'

'Oh my,' she said. 'Oh, my goodness. I thought he was dead.'

The two old men embraced each other and then Bob embraced Nancy. 'Hey, Nance. Beautiful as ever!'

'Oh shush, Bob. You're talking nonsense just like you always did.'

'I ain't talkin' 'bout you Nance – I talkin' 'bout me!' He laughed loudly and Nancy laughed too – the first time in a long time.

Jack and the small boy stood to the side, watching. Jack went up to the boy and introduced himself. 'Hi, I'm Jack. What's your name?'

'Eric, sir, Eric Gole.' They shook hands.

'You just stepped out of the shower?' Jack asked him.

'No, sir, my hands are always wet: they sweat a lot. What's wrong with your eyes?'

'It's a long story, Eric, but when I buy some stuff to get the black off, I'll take you with me and we can get something for your hands. I used to have the same problem when I was your age: I could have cultivated watercress on them!'

Jack was intrigued by the boy's ingenuousness. It was like

meeting a child who'd grown up on a Christmas tree farm. Why couldn't Conrad have been like him? He shuddered at the thought of his erstwhile progeny.

'Who's the kid?' Doc asked Bob. 'And what's he doing here?'

'I'll explain on the bus, Gene, but take my word on it, man, there a good reason fo' him bein' with us... Eric, c'mon over an' meet Gene an' Nancy.'

The luggage and wheelchair were transferred from the car to the larger vehicle, and then all but Jack climbed on to the bus. 'We'll follow you, Jack,' Doc told him. 'You're clear about what you have to do?' Jack nodded. 'And wear sunglasses, for God's sake: you look positively strange.'

They left Hershey behind, passed through Middletown – a municipality that had left its better days behind it – and headed towards the plumes of steam rising from the cooling towers of Three Mile Island. Bob pulled the bus into the car lot of a large pharmacy opposite Harrisburg International Airport, while Jack drove into the airport and dropped off the car at the rental agency. He then walked calmly through the short-term parking garage, crossed the airport road and climbed the railway embankment. Once certain no trains were approaching, he stepped over the tracks and carefully descended the other side of the embankment. He waited by the roadside until there was an opening in the traffic, and then crossed Highway 230 to the waiting bus.

'Give me a minute will you, Doc? I need to go to the pharmacy for some things. Eric, you want to come with me?'

They returned after a few minutes with mascara remover for Jack, and a pair of red washing-up gloves for Eric. 'Red was the only colour they had,' Jack explained to the others.

Bob turned the engine and pulled the bus out of the car park. Their journey to Coffeeville had begun.

They drove through Harrisburg, passed over the Susquehanna River and headed south on I81. They drove through rural Pennsylvania and crossed the Mason–Dixon Line into Maryland. As they approached the Potomac River, Bob slowed the bus and gave the gun he'd retrieved from Doc to Jack. 'Throw it, man. Far as you can.'

They entered the eastern panhandle of West Virginia and continued along the Shenandoah Valley into Virginia; the Blue Ridge Mountains visible to the east and the Appalachians to the west. Doc and Nancy sat together, and Eric sat with Jack. Bob hummed.

'Is there a bee in here?' Nancy asked.

'No. Bob's humming a tune to himself – what's the song, Bob?'

'There ain't no song.'

'Well, what are you humming, then?'

'I ain't hummin'.'

'And I'm not a doctor, either,' Doc said.

'No, you ain't. You retired.'

Doc smiled at Nancy. 'Hasn't changed, has he?'

Nancy returned his smile. 'No, he hasn't,' she laughed. 'Who is he?'

'It's Bob, Nancy. You remember him? We were at Duke together.'

'Oh, of course we were. Yes, I remember him now. He was that nigger friend of yours, wasn't he? The one we thought was selling drugs? You'll have to forgive me, Gene: I forget things all the time these days… where are we going, by the way?'

'We're driving to Coffeeville, Nancy.' He looked at her nervously, took her hand and squeezed it gently. The smile on Nancy's face froze. She squeezed his hand back and turned to face him.

'I understand,' she said. 'Thank you, Gene – thank you.' She kissed him on the cheek. 'There's no rush, though, is there? We can take our time?'

'Sure we can, Nancy. We'll make a holiday of it.'

Eric interrupted their conversation: 'Have you seen my gloves, Mrs Skidmore?'

'My, aren't those nice?' she said to him.

'They're a present from Jack. Shake my hand, Mrs Skidmore – go on, shake it.' Nancy took hold of Eric's hand and did as requested.

'You shake my hand, too, Doctor Chaney.' Doc did. 'What do you think?'

'I think Jack's a man of boundless generosity, Eric, and I like your handshake, too: firm and dry.' The beam on Eric's face grew bigger, and he made a move to shake Bob's hand.

'Probably best not to bother Bob while he's driving, Eric,' Doc advised. 'Besides, he's humming some tune or other and I don't want him to lose his place and have to start from the beginning again.'

'I already told you, man – I *ain't* hummin'. You prob'ly got tinnitus in yo' ears or somethin'. Anyways, you shouldn' go raggin' on the driver. My concentration goes – y'all go!'

They pulled into the next rest area, where Doc decided it would be safer if Nancy remained on the bus and out of sight. He and Bob would stay, while Jack – now his eyes were back to normal – would go with Eric to the vending machines. 'I'll be right outside having a cigarette,' he told Nancy.

Bob joined him. 'Give me one o' those, will you, Gene?'

'I thought you didn't smoke these days.'

'I don't as normal, 'specially roun' Marsha, but I have one ever' now an' then.' He shook a cigarette from the opened pack and lit it from the flame of Doc's lighter.

'I think we need to pull off the interstate and find somewhere quiet to spend the night,' Doc said. 'They'll have probably figured out that Nancy's missing by now, and even though they won't know how she got out or where she's heading, we'll still need to play it safe. You know this neck of the woods better than I do. Any ideas?'

Bob thought for a moment. 'Three Top Mountain ain't far from here. We could park up by the fire tower fo' the night. No one'll see us there.'

Doc liked the idea. He took one final draw on his cigarette and then ground it underfoot.

'Who's the kid, by the way? You said there was a good reason he was riding with us.'

4

Eric

Headaches

Eric Gole's parents were dead. This is what happened.

Eric's father, Daniel, looked upon life as perfect in every way except for one thing – he suffered from headaches, unordinary and severe. They came without warning and with no recognisable trigger. In a year he'd have seven such headaches, no more and no less and each headache would last for exactly seven days. No medication alleviated the pain or the accompanying nausea, and all Daniel could do was put life on hold. He would move into a spare bedroom, pull down the blinds, draw the curtains and take to his bed; for their duration he lived in a cocoon of darkness, unable to work and unable to eat. This he did with a matter-of-fact stoicism that impressed all who knew him.

Daniel's stoicism, however, didn't run to not worrying about the headaches or searching for a cure. It frustrated him that while other people enjoyed fifty-two-week years, he enjoyed only forty-five of them. He felt he forever had to run to make up for lost time, especially where work was concerned, and therefore felt guilty taking any but the shortest of holidays.

It was the pain, however, rather than his shorter working year that spurred Daniel to seek a cure. At first, he likened the pain to having a small man with a pneumatic drill tunnelling inside his head, but as he became more and more convinced that there was a natural disaster of mammoth proportion taking place there, his descriptions became more dramatic. Dependent on the news of the day, he'd variously describe his symptoms to doctors as a tsunami of pain or as a volcanic eruption of pain; other times it would be the searing pain of a wildfire or a seismic quake splitting his skull in two.

Despite the vividness of these descriptions, and the barrage of tests he underwent over a two-year period, the doctors were left mystified. They could find no discernible cause, and certainly no sign of the brain tumour Daniel had feared. Invariably, he was turned loose to his own devices with either a firm handshake or a consoling arm around the shoulder. It was at this point that Daniel turned to the church for help.

From birth, Daniel had been a believer; he believed in God the Father, God the Son and God the Holy Spirit, and, given half a chance, would have also believed in any uncles, aunts, cousins or other members of an extended family God chose to reveal. From an early age he'd believed that if more people in the world were like him, then the world itself would be a better place, and while privately of the opinion that he was one of those rare individuals already born again at the time of his actual physical birth, Daniel had the political acumen to recognise the necessity of renewing his commitment to Jesus as his personal saviour in a more public forum. This he chose to do after mastering calculus in his first year of college; something he felt could never have been achieved without divine intervention.

The church Daniel attended was a happy church full of animation, noise and drama; and a church where people were regularly slain in the Spirit by divine bolts of lightning emanating from the hands of The Reverend Pete, God's special emissary in Santa Cruz. In this church of pogoing Christians, Daniel stood out as a champion of religious expression. As hymns were played and prayers were said, he would either jump up and down or sway from side to side, his arms high in the air, the palms of his hands facing upward, and an inane smile on his face. If God's was a small voice of calm, as some people said, one could only wonder if it stood any real chance of being heard in this particular church. Even Eric was embarrassed by the behaviour of his father, associating his unembarrassed movements more with the antics of a circus than the House of God.

The church, however, was no more successful than the doctors in curing Daniel's headaches. The prayers of Daniel and the prayers of an entire congregation on his behalf went unanswered. A laying-on of hands similarly came to nothing, and the lightning bolts from the hands of The Reverend Pete proved an abject failure. Daniel was again turned loose to his own devices with either a firm handshake or a consoling arm around his shoulder. Reverend Pete suggested the headaches might have been sent by God as a test of his loyalty, much the same way He'd tested Abraham. 'As long as I'm not expected to sacrifice Eric in the Mojave Desert,' Daniel had said, slightly disconcerted by The Reverend Pete's remark.

At last, Daniel was thrown a life and, ultimately, death line, by a chance meeting he made at a symposium on carbon dating. Ironically, Daniel – who held the position of Associate Professor of Egyptology at Santa Cruz University – was there only reluctantly, having been delegated by his colleagues in the Archaeology Department during an absence.

On the afternoon of the symposium's first day, a man wearing green tweeds and a polka dot bow-tie climbed the short flight of stairs to the podium. Professor Mitchell Bennett was an unembarrassed creationist, and the paper he delivered to the assembled delegates contended that Carbon 14 not only challenged the widely held assumption that the earth was of an ancient age, but proved beyond doubt that the earth was little more than 6,000 years old. As Carbon 14 could only survive for 5,730 years, he argued, how could it possibly be found in rocks and fossils previously judged to be hundreds of millions years old? Moreover, laboratory tests he'd recently conducted on samples of coal and diamonds corroborated this thesis. On completion of the paper's delivery, Professor Bennett stood down from the podium to the sound of a throat clearing, and what he would later describe to sympathetic friends as a scientific silence of rapturous proportion.

During a coffee break on the second day of the conference, Daniel approached Bennett to congratulate him on his paper. He confided in Mitchell that he too was a creationist, but for reasons of self-preservation had not yet divulged this to his own colleagues at Santa Cruz University, and had therefore felt unable to applaud publicly. It was, however, his cough that Mitchell would have heard.

For no particular reason, other than the fact that all professional conversation between the two men had dried up, Daniel mentioned to Mitchell the problem of his recurring and unresolved headaches. Although Bennett had no comparable personal experience, he did know of an herbalist who had successfully treated a friend of his for rheumatoid arthritis; again, this after mainstream medical practice had drawn a blank. As luck would have it, the herbalist, whose name was Arthur Annandale, lived in Santa Cruz.

Arthur Annandale was a man in his early sixties. He had a slim frame, a bald head, kindly eyes that swam happily behind thick spectacle lenses, and hammer toes. He listened intently as Daniel described his headaches and the various tests doctors had run. It was the time sequence of the headaches that captured Annandale's attention: seven headaches a year, each lasting precisely seven days. He questioned Daniel carefully on this particular point and, when confident that no other time sequences were involved, excused himself and went through a door to his laboratory. The clomping noise Annandale made when he walked drew Daniel's attention to his feet. He was surprised to see Arthur wearing what appeared to be either a pair of large hoofs or two small boxes.

Arthur returned to the consultation room after an elapse of some fifteen minutes holding two brown bottles. He told Daniel he was confident he could help him. The medicines, he explained, wouldn't work immediately, but over a period of time would shorten the length of the headaches and eventually eradicate them altogether. One bottle (marked Bottle 1) contained a liquid mixture of herbs that Daniel was instructed to take orally at the onset of each headache: an initial dosage of ten millilitres followed by subsequent doses of five millilitres every six hours until the headache was gone. The liquid in the second bottle (marked Bottle 2) was to be used for preparing a poultice that Daniel should place over his forehead; Annandale emphasised that no more than two poultices in any one twenty-four-hour period should be applied. Both bottles should be stored in a refrigerator and the contents thrown away three months after opening; the bottles, however, should be returned to the herbalist's office for reuse. Daniel was then instructed to make another appointment after the end of his next headache which, Annandale assured him, would surely come.

The expected headache arrived within two weeks of the consultation, its onset announced by the familiar optical zigzagging and blurring of vision. Daniel drank his medicine, prepared a poultice and climbed into bed; blinds down and curtains drawn. His wife, Sarah, ministered the dosages over the following days and was about to pour another five millilitres draught at the start of the seventh and final day of the headache when Daniel walked carefully into the kitchen and announced that the headache had gone! The duration of each subsequent headache shortened, sometimes by as much as a full day, as on this first occasion, but more often by a half day. Within eighteen months, and after ten consultations, the headaches had disappeared altogether, and Daniel was placed on a defensive regimen of one five millilitres dosage of Bottle 1 every two months.

The British Israelites

Daniel and Arthur Annandale struck up a friendship. It wasn't purely feelings of gratitude that drew Daniel to Arthur's company – he genuinely liked the man. Similarly, it wasn't just a genuine liking for Daniel that drew Arthur to him, or encouraged him to share with Daniel his long-held personal conviction that the leprosy germ was located in the pieces of black found at both ends of a banana. More importantly, Arthur recognised in Daniel a person who had been sent to him by God for a reason, and that reason was to further the cause of British Israelism.

Arthur deemed the time right to share the ideas of British Israelism with Daniel and intimate the role he believed God intended for him to play, shortly after he noticed Daniel biting off the end of a banana and depositing it in a waste receptacle. He started by lending Daniel a handful of carefully chosen books, well-thumbed hardbacks published early in the previous century with titles such as *A People No One Knew, Our Descent from Israel, Israel and Orthodoxy, Empire in Solution,* and *The United States and British Commonwealth in Prophecy.*

In a variety of formats and with varying degrees of emphasis, the books told the same story: that the peoples of Great Britain and the United States were the lineal descendants of the House of Israel.

The Kingdom of Israel had originally comprised twelve tribes, and in its entire history had only three kings: Saul, David and Solomon. When Solomon died, the ten northern tribes rebelled and established a kingdom of their own: the House of Israel, or the Ten Tribes. These tribes were taken into captivity by King Sargon II of Assyria, and on release moved to the Black Sea area of Scythia and intermarried with people already living there. Subsequently, they lost their Hebrew identity and passed into obscurity: the Ten *Lost* Tribes of Israel.

It had always been God's intention that these tribes would one day live in their own safe haven – a group of islands located north-west of Jerusalem – and from there dominate the world. Over the centuries and millennia that followed, God led the Ten Tribes from Scythia through Europe to the British Isles. They arrived variously as Cymry, Angles, Danes, Saxons, Normans, Walloons, Scots, Irish, Celts, and Gaels. All that remained was for the Davidic kingship (retained by the House of Judah or the Two Tribes) to be transplanted to these same islands.

After the Two Tribes were themselves captured and taken to Babylon, the surviving member of the Davidic line, a young girl called Tea Tephni, escaped to Northern Ireland. She was accompanied there by Jeremiah, who brought with him the oblong stone used by Jacob as a pillow. The Stone of Destiny came to symbolise the direct descension of the royal house of Great Britain from the royal house of King David, and all British monarchs were crowned on it.

Great Britain grew in prosperity and power, and its reach spread out across the Old World and into the New. Britons founded and settled colonies in North America, and these colonies grew and matured into the United States of America. As God had foreordained, this one-time daughter of Great Britain and lineal descendant of the House of Israel became the greatest and wealthiest single nation in earth's history – and also home to Arthur Annandale.

Daniel read the first book with little more than cursory interest, as much curious as to why the history of the House of Israel was littered with the names of so many champagne bottles as to its actual migration to the British Isles. (He couldn't help but remember that a Jeroboam was four times the size of a regular bottle of the sparkling wine, a Rehoboam six times the size and a Nebuchadnezzar, a whopping twenty times the size.) Daniel also noted that the books Arthur had loaned him were all seventy to eighty years old; if the message they contained was as important as Arthur indicated, why weren't the publications more recent? But here he caught himself and remembered that the Bible itself was more than two thousand years old! And there was also the fact that it had been Arthur who'd given them him to read: the man who'd cured his headaches when medical science had failed. If Arthur had been right about his headaches, then he was as likely right about this.

In this new frame of mind Daniel read on, and increasingly found himself drawn to the message of the books. He finished the last page of the final book and felt the Spirit move him. He placed the book carefully on the table, fell to his knees and proclaimed himself a British Israelite.

The conversion happened in the early hours of a Thursday morning, barely a week after Daniel had first taken receipt of the books. He retired to the family bed, careful not to wake Sarah, but too excited to sleep more than fitfully. He looked forward to the day breaking and the opportunity to phone Arthur. At breakfast the next morning he said nothing of his new-found beliefs to Sarah, and called Arthur only after he'd reached his campus office.

Rather than the restaurant-cum-coffee house where the two men usually met, Arthur invited Daniel to meet him at his home that evening: a large two-storey house in one of the town's wealthier suburbs. The first thing to strike any first-time visitor to the Annandale household was the number of books that lined the lounge and hallway walls: history books on Assyria, Babylonia, Britain, Egypt, Israel and the United States; books on astronomy, ethnology, gematria, genealogy, hieroglyphics, linguistics, numerology and philology; books on Christianity, Judaism and Islam; books on archaeology, particularly relating to the Pyramids and Stonehenge; books on the Greek, Hebraic and Latin languages; and, naturally enough, books on herbalism, herbs, medicine and pharmacy.

The second thing to strike a first-time visitor to the house was the neat row of handmade hooves-cum-boxes that were Arthur's shoes. Arthur was sockless this particular evening and wearing open-toed sandals. Daniel could see his hammer toes clearly, and noted there were only four toes on Arthur's left foot. Daniel tried hard not to stare at the deformity, but it proved difficult, especially after Arthur's dog started to lick the feet of his master. He did, however, make a mental note not to mention them. No one was more surprised than Daniel, therefore, when, once comfortably seated in an armchair, the first words out of his mouth were: 'You have an impressive collection of toes, Arthur.'

A look of abject horror crossed Daniel's face as he stammered his apologies. He explained to Arthur he'd meant to say books, and had no idea why his words had become so mangled; instantly regretting his use of the word *mangle*.

Arthur came to his rescue and even apologised for wearing sandals rather than his usual shoes. He explained that the muscle imbalance was the result of flat feet, aggravated by wearing shoes as a child that hadn't fit properly. Unfortunately, by the time his parents had noticed and taken him to a chiropodist, the toes had become fixed in their hammer settings.

'And would you believe it, Daniel; it's one thing herbs can't cure!

'But you're right about the books,' he continued. 'They are a good collection. Fortunately, my wife is understanding. She doesn't like having to dust them, but she does appreciate their importance.'

They settled into two facing armchairs separated by a glass-topped table on which sat a pot of coffee and a plate of cookies. Daniel started to speak enthusiastically about the books Arthur had loaned him; how at first he'd started to read them with a detached interest, but then recognised their truths. He wanted to know more, much more. How, for instance, had Arthur come to British Israelism, and why had he never heard of it before? Also, why had Arthur decided to share the ideas of British Israelism with him?

The smile on Arthur's face said it all. This was the reaction from Daniel he'd been praying for.

'My father believed in it, Daniel,' he said. 'In fact, most of the books in this room belonged to him. For me it was a natural progression. A person can read the Bible and be forgiven for thinking that God turned his back on the world two thousand years ago, but this is just nonsense. God didn't stop being God and lose interest in the people He'd chosen to bring about His rule on earth. The Ten Tribes didn't disappear, and I also think it's apparently clear that they're not living in Israel today. The House of Judah lives in Israel. It was the House of Judah that crucified Jesus and chose not to believe – not the Ten Tribes.

'It's no secret that the Ten Tribes have had their shortcomings. They turned away from God, but also came back to Him and, more importantly, accepted that Jesus was His son and the living Christ. And it's also important to remember that the Ten Tribes aren't Jews. They never were. They're us now: you, me, the United States and Great Britain. *We* are the chosen people, Daniel, and consequently we have great responsibility placed upon our shoulders.

'When we first met, I knew it was no coincidence. It was the time frequency of your headaches that alerted me. Seven in a year, each one lasting no more than seven days.

'What I've come to learn over the years is that no number in the Bible is ever used without good reason. Each number means something different. The number three, for example, is associated with completeness or resurrection: Jonah spent three days and nights inside the belly of a whale; Peter denied Christ three times after His arrest; Christ was buried in a tomb for three days before He was resurrected; and Paul, after his conversion on the road to Damascus, was blinded for three days.

'It's the same for other numbers. Forty is always used to denote testing or temptation: Jesus spent forty days and nights in the wilderness after he was baptised by John, and after His resurrection spent another forty days on earth before ascending to Heaven. And don't forget that when the Israelis escaped from their captivity in Egypt, they wandered in the wilderness for forty years.'

On a numerical roll, Arthur continued to explain the meaning of other numbers. Twelve was the number of governmental perfection; thirty related to blood; and thirteen denoted apostasy and disintegration. At long last, Arthur got to the number he'd first mentioned – the number seven.

'Even today, Daniel, the number seven is considered a lucky number. It's used in the Bible to signify spiritual perfection and completeness. God created the seven-day week, remember, the perfect unit of time. And did you know that Jesus cast seven demons out of Mary Magdalene when he first met her?

'So when you came to me with all those number sevens in your life, I couldn't help but be curious, especially when you were born in July, the seventh month of the year. I knew then that you'd been sent to me for a purpose, and if I'd been left with any doubts then your name was the clincher – Daniel, Daniel Gole.'

Arthur explained that the name Gole originated in the north-west of France, where the tribe of Reuben had settled. It was not so much his last name, however, as his first: Daniel. In the migration of the Ten Tribes across Europe, the tribe of Dan had played an elemental role and left its mark on many of the names in use today: Danmark (Denmark), Swedan (Sweden), Londan (London), Danzig and the Danube. More importantly, it was the early Danite settlers in Northern Ireland who had prepared the ground for the transplantation of the House of David to the British Isles and been there to welcome Tea Tephni.

Daniel chipped in here, and said that he'd been struck by other names: the similarities for example between Jute and Jew, and Saxons and Saac's sons. The latter, he presumed, related to Isaac.

'You're right, Daniel,' Arthur said. 'But don't think that any of this is coincidence. It's not! Did you know, for instance, that Gael, as in Gaelic, means the Nation of God in Hebrew, and that there's a great similarity between ancient Cornish and the Hebrew language? And the word British is derived from two Hebrew words: Bryth meaning covenant, and ish meaning man. Covenant Man!' he exclaimed: 'The inheritors of the covenant God first made with Abraham!

'And it just doesn't stop there: it goes on and on, never ending. When St Paul went to Britain, he met with Druids and found similarities between their beliefs and Christianity; he also considered that the rites and ceremonies they practised were descended from the Jews. And Joseph of Arimathea, he went to Britain too. Soon after the crucifixion he went there with Jesus' mother and took with him some sacred relics, the most famous of which was the Holy Grail.'

Daniel sat in his chair mesmerised by the facts that rolled effortlessly from Arthur's tongue, and felt flattered that Arthur had chosen to impart this information to him. But he had one question that interested him more than any other: 'Why me Arthur? Why do you think God sent me to you?'

Arthur smiled at Daniel as a father would to a son. 'You came to me because you had headaches; if you hadn't had these headaches, it's doubtful we'd have met. But God gave you those headaches just so that we would meet. He planned it this way. He wanted me to talk to you because He has a role for you. But before I tell you what that role is, I'd like you to read one more book.'

He then handed Daniel a slim brown hardback entitled *The Great Pyramid – Its Construction, Symbolism and Chronology.*

The Great Pyramid

Daniel was familiar with the Great Pyramid at Giza. It was a characteristic example of Old Kingdom architecture, built as a tomb for the Pharaoh Khufu and completed in 2560 BC. More than 480 feet high and containing more than two million limestone blocks, each block weighing two and a half tons, it was thought to have taken 100,000 men twenty years to complete, and was now the only surviving Wonder of the Ancient World.

What Daniel read in the book Arthur had given him consequently came as a surprise. The opening sentence stated categorically that the Great Pyramid was *not* built as a tomb for royal burial. Rather than being a sarcophagus, the coffer in the King's Chamber was merely a lidless stone box intended to be no more than a measure of capacity – four British quarters of wheat, to be exact.

Furthermore, although the Great Pyramid had been erected in Egypt, it was not of Egyptian origin: the involvement of Pharaoh Khufu and his subjects had been purely logistical – to supply the necessary labour force. The pyramid had, in fact, been built by members of another civilisation altogether, a nation of builders called Barats or Brits, whose symbol was the year circle. This circle had a circumference of 3,652.42 inches and was unknown to Egyptians; in later years, however, it would reappear as the mathematical basis for the construction of Stonehenge. Neither were the other units of measurement employed in the construction of the pyramid native to Egypt: the polar inch (almost identical to the Anglo-Saxon inch), and the Hebrew or sacred cubit (twenty-five Anglo-Saxon inches).

If the pyramid hadn't been built as a tomb to house a dead Pharaoh and hadn't been built by Egyptians, then why had it been built? To the author of the book the answer was obvious: it had been built under divine inspiration for the purposes of prophetic chronology. He had no doubts that this pyramid was the very same *sign and witness unto the Lord in the land of Egypt* described in the Book of Isaiah. That the pyramid was of a divine nature also explained the suppression of paganism in Egypt during the time of its building, and why the pyramid itself was totally free of hieroglyphics and pictures.

The key to deciphering this prophetic chronology, the author continued, was in understanding its geometrical design and measurements. The internal construction of the Great Pyramid was unique. No other pyramid contained similar passages and chambers, and it could therefore be assumed that the chronologic record was enclosed within them, and that major events in mankind's history were defined by structural changes.

On completion of the book, Daniel summarised its key arguments in a journal: (1) The Great Pyramid was built more than 4,500 years ago; (2) It enshrined the message that Christ was the Saviour and Deliverer of mankind, and detailed the circumstances of His return; and (3) The pyramid provided a record of mankind from Adam through Biblical times to present day Great Britain and the United States – the countries where God's chosen people now resided.

Three days after finishing the book, Daniel returned to Arthur's house. Arthur had invited two other people: Donald Baker, a Baptist minister, and Ted Snellgrove, a property developer. All were interested in hearing Daniel's thoughts on the book, and any questions he might have.

'I was quite overwhelmed,' Daniel told them, 'and I fully appreciate the author's arguments. I do, however, have a couple of questions. The first has to do with the scales of measurement used: I don't understand why the scale suddenly jumps from one pyramid inch representing a solar year to the same inch representing just one month.'

'That's from the Gallery onward, and after the crucifixion of Jesus, right?' Snellgrove said. Daniel nodded. 'The design of the pyramid,' Snellgrove continued, 'was intended to give greater detail to modern times, because the pyramid's message is specifically addressed to modern times – to the British peoples in particular. No one before then was supposed to decipher the pyramid.'

'That answers my first question then,' Daniel said, 'but why does the chronology stop in 1953? I think I found this the most perplexing.'

'August 20, 1953, to be precise,' Arthur said. 'The same day, coincidentally, that the USSR announced it had successfully tested a hydrogen bomb.'

'We presumed that this was the date responsibility would be taken from the hands of mankind and vested solely in God's,' Snellgrove said. 'The actual terminal point of the pyramid's chronology, however, is 2001, and like many people we believed that this year would be the start of Christ's millennial reign on earth. I don't have to tell you that it wasn't, and so the fact that the Great Pyramid is silent from that year onward is an oddity.'

Baker now stepped up to the plate. 'There's consensus building, Daniel, that we're missing something because there *is* something missing. We now think that the Great Pyramid was never intended to tell the full story, and that there's a missing piece of the jigsaw somewhere else, possibly another structure.

'We've every reason to believe it will be found in Egypt, but we're not, in all honesty, sure just what it is we're looking for. We've had money to finance a search for some time, but until tonight, never the person to lead it. We now believe that we have that person in you Daniel: you're an archaeologist, an Egyptologist, a Christian man in all senses of the word, and now a British Israelite. We could never have found anyone more suited to the task.'

What Baker said was true: Daniel did have the necessary credentials. What he hadn't said but intimated, however, was that the Egyptian authorities would never give permission to an organisation like the British Israelites to mount an expedition. It was understandable that they would be unsympathetic to claims that their greatest tourist attraction had been built by Israelis under the guidance of God for the benefit of the USA and Great Britain, and had in fact nothing to do with Egypt whatsoever.

By evening's end, it had been agreed that Daniel would lead an expedition to look for the missing sections of chronology and prophecy. They ended with a prayer and asked God to bless their venture, and Daniel, in particular.

Five years passed before the expedition was under way. Daniel's researches led him to believe that the missing messages might be located in a recently discovered pyramid eight kilometres north of Giza at Abu Rawash. This area of Egypt had previously been kept out of bounds by the military authorities and had never become a part of the tourist trail. Egyptologists generally considered it to be the tomb of the lost fourth dynasty Pharaoh Djedefre, a son of Khufu. In its day it would have been an impressive structure, and as it stood on a mountain overlooking the plain of Giza would have also been fractionally higher than the Great Pyramid. There was now very little of the pyramid left, its pre-cut stone slabs having been plundered and reused by the Romans, but there was a surviving shaft that ran deep into the mountain, and Daniel surmised they would find other passages leading from it. The expedition, he decided, would start here.

Throughout this time, Daniel was enthusiastically supported by his wife. If Sarah's character had a flaw, it was that she lacked all critical faculty when it came to her husband. Any she might have once had now slept with the fishes and her loyalty to Daniel was consequently unquestioning. Therefore, when Daniel became interested in British Israelism, so did she; when he became interested in the Great Pyramid, she did too; and when Daniel decided to take Arthur's offer of leading an expedition to Egypt, she agreed to go with him. This kind of love is dangerous. It led to both their deaths.

It was decided that Eric would stay with the Annandales during the month his mother would be travelling with Daniel. On hearing the news, Eric swallowed hard. Although Arthur and Alice Annandale had become close friends with his parents, he himself had never warmed to them and found both slightly strange. If they themselves didn't smell like old people, then their house with its old and depressing furniture did. He also found conversation with Arthur difficult and suspected Arthur had similar difficulty talking to him. Concerning these new arrangements, the words *sensible* and *best* had come to his parents' minds. To Eric's, came the words *Gosh dang!*

Daniel and Sarah flew to Egypt and were met at Cairo's international airport by an administrative assistant from the Egyptology Department of the American University. Rather than driving them to the small bungalow they were expecting, he took them to the Mena House Oberoi Hotel: Arthur had gifted them two weeks here, in the belief that a period of comfortable acclimation would be essential for them both. In the note they were handed at the registration desk, Arthur had written: 'It's a beautiful hotel but don't trust the ice cubes!' The hotel was palatial and its gardens beautiful. Even so, Sarah couldn't help feeling slightly disappointed that the view from their room was blocked by a pyramid – the Great Pyramid, in fact.

For the first few days, Daniel and Sarah became tourists. They stood in line with nationalities from around the world and entered the Great Pyramid; they walked around the Sphinx, took trips into the desert, rode camels and spent a whole day inside the archaeological museum in Cairo. On the fifth day, Daniel left Sarah by the pool and went to meet the foreman of the crew he'd hired. Together they drove to Abu Rawash and decided the areas to be cleared of rubble. The foreman's name was Walid El Baradei and he told Daniel to call him Wally. Wally estimated it would take his crew six days to prepare the site for the first exploratory dig.

The last barrow-load of rubble was removed from the site late Friday morning – Daniel's tenth day in Egypt. It was arranged that everyone would take the rest of the day off and return the following Monday.

That afternoon, Daniel returned to the site with Sarah. He wanted her to experience the intense spiritual quiet of the site before the dig started, and to pray with him for the success of their undertaking. He also wanted a photograph of them standing there together, and so positioned his camera on a tripod facing out toward the Giza plain. He then delayed the timer by a minute.

What overcame Daniel next is difficult to say. Perhaps it was the heat of the day or the emotion of being surrounded by so much sand; possibly it was the spiritual tranquillity of the location or the enormity of the discovery he was on the verge of making; or maybe it was simply plain and old-fashioned love for Sarah. Whatever the prime motivating force might have been, all now combined to send Daniel into a pogo frenzy of veneration, which Sarah quickly joined in.

Chanting the name of Jesus in unison, their arms outstretched and their palms facing upward, they jumped up and down together. 'Jee-sus, Jee-sus,' they chanted. Up and down, up and down they jumped. The seconds ticked away as the camera readied itself. 'Jee-sus, Jee-sus,' they chanted. Up and down, up and down they jumped.

And then, a split second before the camera clicked, there was an almost indiscernible cracking noise caused by the splintering of centuries old timber hidden beneath the surface of the flattened rubble on which Daniel and Sarah danced. Moments later the ground gave way, the camera's shutter clicked, and the Goles plunged down a deep, pitch-black shaft. Their bodies ricocheted against its walls and against each other before coming to an abrupt halt on the shaft's floor. And there they stayed. There had been one long *po* but no corresponding *go*, and no more mention of Jesus.

As a sepulchral resting place, the old pyramid once more came into its own.

News of Daniel and Sarah's deaths reached Arthur several days after the event. It came as a double blow: on a personal level he'd lost dear friends, and on a professional level any chance of discovering the missing chronology of God's voice in the near future – and possibly even in his lifetime. He felt remorse but surprisingly no guilt. 'Mysterious Ways' came readily to his mind, and clung to its walls like an analgesic.

Eric was given the news of his parents' death early that evening. After school, Eric had developed the habit of either staying behind for extra activities or spending time at the house of a friend; anything that would delay his return to the Annandale house, its museum-like character and its curator-like keepers. He looked forward to the day his mother would return from Egypt and he could once more regain his old life. He missed his house and his bedroom; having his own television and playing his own music; but above all he missed his mother's cooking. Mrs Annandale's was plain bad.

When Eric returned to the Annandales' house, Arthur asked him to step into his office. There was something about Mr Annandale's manner that led Eric to believe that something was wrong, and he braced himself. Eric sat down in an armchair while Arthur remained standing, his back to Eric and looking out of the window on to the garden. Arthur Annandale was a man used to confronting situations behind a person's back, and was uncomfortable imparting bad news face to face.

'It looks like the roses are going to excel this year, Eric,' Arthur started by saying. 'I'm just sorry your mother and father won't be here to see them. I know your mother was particularly fond of roses, her favourite flower in fact.'

'What do you mean?' Eric asked. 'Why won't they be here to see them?'

'Because they're dead, Eric: as dead and dried up as the herbs on those shelves there. I wish it were different, son, I really do. I wish I could tell you everything's going to be okay, but it isn't. You're an orphan now, and once the funeral's over we need to start making plans about what to do with you. But there's time for that: we don't need to think of that now. What we need to keep in mind at this moment is that your Mom and Dad died in God's service doing God's work. They died martyrs, Eric, and if you have to go, there's no better way. I honestly wish it could have been me.'

He turned to Eric and continued: 'You, I and Mrs Annandale have to get on with our lives now, and I think we should make a start by eating the liver and onions Mrs Annandale has cooked especially for us this evening. What do you say we do that, Eric? Shall we do that?'

Eric looked at him in stony disbelief. All he could say was: 'I don't like liver, Mr Annandale.'

As Eric lay in bed that night, he replayed in his mind everything Arthur had eventually told him: how his parents had discovered a shaft by accident, had then fallen down that shaft to their deaths, and that he was now an orphan – but not to worry as things would work out fine and he'd be well looked after. His parents had joined other martyrs who'd died in the Bible and would now be sitting with them at God's feet, swapping stories and telling jokes. If the Bible were still being written today, his parents would have a chapter all to themselves.

It was at this point that Eric became curious about the people who'd died in the Bible and were now his parents' friends. He already knew a lot of the stories in the Bible from attending church and going to Sunday school, but had never read the Bible and didn't know who Arthur was specifically referring to. It became strangely important to him that he find out more about these dead people and, furthermore, write down their names. He determined there and then to read the Bible from cover to cover.

He would count the dead.

The Eye of the Storm

The intervening period between news of a death and ceremonies for the dead is a strange time, very similar to living in the eye of a storm. Unfortunately for Eric, there was nothing for him to do during this hiatus, and he stayed in his room in a state of suspended animation, insensible and disbelieving.

It was Arthur who took control. He appointed a funeral director and took care of all arrangements, from the repatriation of Daniel and Sarah's bodies to the choice of funeral plots. He talked with The Reverend Pete, who announced the deaths to his congregation, and then contacted the head of the archaeology department, who in turn announced the news to faculty. He himself contacted Snellgrove, Baker and other members of the British Israelite fraternity who had met and known Daniel and Sarah.

As far as Eric knew, his parents had no living close relatives. His grandparents were dead, neither of his parents had siblings, and the only relatives he'd ever met had been introduced to him as second cousins twice removed. To Arthur, the relationship Eric described seemed more akin to the mathematical puzzles he'd been set as a child than to any blood relationship he could readily understand, but he contacted them nonetheless. The address he found for the Lawrences in Daniel's address book had them living in New York City. Eight days later, and one day before the funeral, Eric received a letter from Jeff Lawrence with a return address of the Lyon Mt Correctional Facility.

My Dear Eric,

The news of your parents' death came as a shock. I can only imagine how difficult it must be for you to make sense of such a totally unanticipated and unnecessary departure, and how wrenching it must be for you. I don't know what happens when you die – I never had the certainties of your Dad – but I do know that your parents will always be a part of you. As difficult as it is for you now, you must learn to be grateful that you knew and loved each other, and I hope that as time goes by your sadness will be relieved by your own fond memories of them. When I've had friends or family die, there's always been a regret that I didn't keep in touch with them more. Stupidly and wrongly, I just assumed they'd always be there. It seems to be human nature that only absence reveals the importance of a person.

If the letter had ended there, it would have been a good letter, but Jeff had continued. Abandoning the cogency of his first paragraph, he started to ramble and left the reader with the distinct impression that if two people hadn't written this letter to Eric, then Jeff Lawrence was probably psychologically unhinged. He talked about slippers and suede shoes, the Book of Leviticus, hunchbacks and men with crushed testicles, and then described the events leading to his incarceration.

You might notice from the notepaper that I'm in prison at the moment, Eric, so won't be able to come to the funeral. A couple of years back, life for us Lawrences started to fall apart. Susan left home to follow her dreams, which evidently didn't include finishing college, and then Mrs Lawrence and I started to drift apart, especially after she told me she never wanted to see me again. I don't think it was anything in particular I'd done, but she made it clear that I irritated the hell out of her and generally got on her nerves, and The Magic Boy *litigation was the last straw. 'Well, what about me?' I asked. 'Do you think it's been easy living with you?' But she never did answer because she was already walking out of the door with her suitcase packed and, as it turned out, my car keys. And that's pretty much why I'm locked up here now.*

One night, I got stinking drunk, Eric. It was late. I couldn't get a ride from anyone in the bar because I was the last guy there, and I couldn't find a taxi for love nor money. And then, as I was passing this car, I noticed its keys were in the trunk and, hey presto, the train to Lyon Mt Correctional Facility started to chug. I got charged with DWI, Grand Theft Auto and resisting arrest, though the resisting arrest bit was bullshit! All I said to the cop who stopped me was fuck off*, and that was just out of frustration rather than anything personal. If you'd have been followed by a car with its headlights on full beam for three miles while you were trying to drive a stick shift, you'd have probably reacted the same way yourself. And the car was only a Toyota Camry for God's sake, not as if it was anything special!*

Anyway, I got one year behind bars, though this place is mainly fencing because we're all considered low risk. I don't get many visitors, so if you ever find yourself in the neighborhood...

Good luck with the funeral, kid, and I hope that someday we'll meet again. Stay strong, little man!

Your father used to end his letters with 'Yours in Christ'. I wish I could do the same. In the meantime,

Yours in Prison,   Jeff

Eric remembered the Lawrences' visit to his parents' house as a short but exciting period in his life, and vividly recalled the circumstances of their departure.

It was the Lawrences' annual vacation. They'd flown from New York to San Francisco and hired a car at the airport and driven down to Santa Cruz. The last time Daniel and Sarah had seen them was at their own wedding, and that was fifteen years ago. They'd occasionally talked on the phone and exchanged Christmas cards, but that was about all. Being a Christian, and therefore theoretically oblivious to the cost of any kind action on his part or perceived slights of others toward him, Daniel still couldn't shake the feeling that he'd sent a lot more cards their way than he'd got back. He also remembered Jeff getting drunk and a bit rowdy at their wedding. Nevertheless, the Lawrences were the nearest thing to family they had. It would only be for a week, and they'd promised to bring along an extra concert ticket for Eric.

The concert the Lawrences planned to attend was scheduled to take place in San Francisco, and the artist none other than the world famous Paul McCartney. During non-Christian moments of doubting others, it crossed Daniel's mind that Jeff and his family were probably using his home as a convenient and cheap hotel, but as quickly as the thought came he tried as quickly to dismiss it. After the concert, Jeff and his family would drive to Los Angeles, where Jeff had some business matters to attend to.

For the first three days of the visit all went well. Eric liked Jeff. He was unlike his father's other friends, and wasn't serious like his father. He joked a lot, particularly at his father's expense. He liked it that Jeff addressed his father as Chuckles and kept telling him to lighten up. On one occasion, he'd burst out laughing – much to his father's annoyance – when, after his father had explained his interest in the Great Pyramid, Jeff had responded by saying he doubted a revelation from God could be arrived at by stretching a 'goddamn measuring tape along a pyramid corridor.'

Daniel had changed the topic of conversation at that point: 'So what are you up to these days, Jeff?' he asked.

'Still pitching, Daniel, still pitching.'

'Like in baseball?' Eric asked.

'No, kid, I pitch ideas to television studios and publishing companies. I'm hoping to get some interest from one of the studios in Los Angeles next week. I can't write worth a damn but I do get these ideas. You ever heard of *The Dwarf Detective*?'

'No,' Eric replied. 'Who is he?'

'Well, he's this detective who's a dwarf and specialises in high-altitude cases,' Jeff said, now unusually serious.

'I don't understand,' Eric said.

'It's simple really. He's a dwarf with a head the size of a watermelon, but he's bright as a button. He's got this kind of computer-type mind that can make connections most other detectives can't. He's good at ground level – on the mean streets so to speak – but he really comes into his own at high altitudes, like the Himalayas or the Andes, because he's small and compact and never gets altitude sickness like most of the other detectives, who are all taller. So he gets to travel to some great locations and this is what the studios like. One of the cable networks in New York picked it up and it's already achieved cult status, especially among the little people.'

'And tell Daniel just what you got paid for it,' Jeff's wife, Anna, said. Her manner was disparaging, and his Aunt Anna didn't strike Eric as being the supportive wife his own mother was.

'Okay, it was only $5,000, but if other networks take it up, the money will start pouring in,' Jeff said.

'What are you going to pitch in Los Angeles?' Sarah asked.

'Thanks for asking, Sarah. If I'm honest, I think this is my best idea yet. Provisionally, I'm calling it *The Magic Boy* series. I'm setting this one in England. It's about an orphaned boy called Barry Cotter who lives out in the country with a brutish foster family. He discovers he's got these magic powers after he finds an old trigonometric point on the moor close to where he lives. If he walks around it three times, he gets transported to this other world full of wizards and witches, and it's a real good versus evil story. I'm thinking this one is for the film studios rather than TV.'

'But Dad,' Susan laughed, 'you've just described the *Harry Potter* books!'

'Who's *Harry Potter*?' Jeff asked.

'Oh come on, Dad, everyone's heard of Harry Potter!'

(This was the birth point of the *Magic Boy* litigation that Jeff had alluded to in his letter to Eric. He became convinced that a publishing company or TV studio he'd mentioned his idea to had stolen it and developed it with some woman called JK Rowling, though he couldn't be certain that he hadn't also mentioned the idea to some random person he'd met in a bar and struck up a conversation with. The resulting litigation cost him his savings and his marriage, which at this time already appeared to be on shaky ground.)

What Eric remembered most about the visit was Susan. At the time of the visit, Eric had been eight and Susan seventeen. As far as Eric was concerned, Susan was the most beautiful girl he'd ever seen; she smelled of patchouli oil and wore clothes which adhered to the minimalist principle of covering as little of her body as possible while still remaining legal. What Eric also liked about her was that she talked to him as an equal and not some small kid; he had no doubts that, when he was old enough, they would get married.

They went everywhere together: to the beach, to the amusement park and to the movies; they sat in diners and talked endlessly, Eric oblivious to the furtive looks that came Susan's way from older boys and men. In fact they did everything together except the drugs, which sensibly, Susan decided to do by herself.

It was the drug taking that caused the Lawrence family's expulsion from the Gole house. The drug in question was plain and simple marijuana. Maybe Daniel might have excused this as a teenage aberration had Susan not substituted two pages of the Gole family Bible after running out of rolling papers. To Daniel, this act was sacrilegious and there was no room for compromise. Jeff's mitigating argument that the pages had only been torn from the Book of Leviticus was to Daniel completely irrelevant.

When the Lawrences left the next morning and checked into a hotel, Eric was heartbroken. It was only after Sarah pleaded with his father that Daniel relented, and allowed Eric to accompany the Lawrences to the Paul McCartney concert.

The only time Susan's name was ever mentioned in the house again was two years later. Eric had walked into the living room and overheard his parents mentioning her name and holding a letter from Jeff.

'How is she?' Eric asked.

'Difficult to tell.' replied his father. 'According to Jeff, she's dropped out of college and become a Polish dancer.' This wasn't what Jeff had actually written, but Daniel had presumed he'd made a grammatical mistake and unilaterally corrected 'pole' to Polish, though he did wonder why Susan had become attracted to Eastern European folk dancing. He'd also thought, however, that other than steroids, these Eastern Europeans wouldn't tolerate any drug use on her part, so maybe it was good news after all.

On the day of the funeral, Eric woke early and pulled back the curtains. Fog had rolled in from the sea during the night and still lingered. By the end of the day, all physical evidence of his parents' existence would have disappeared into another hole, the second hole in a matter of weeks; there his mother and father would lie next to each other for eternity. Eric would remain on the surface.

It still hadn't been decided what would happen to Eric. Arthur Annandale and his wife, although happy to take care of Eric for a couple of weeks, were in no position to either adopt or foster him if it meant that Eric would actually have to live with them. Arthur knew he had trouble connecting with children, but explained the impossibility of such a situation by intimating Mrs Annandale's nervous disposition and weak heart as the real reasons.

The Lawrence family, the only identifiable relatives, had apparently imploded. Jeff and his wife were divorced and Jeff was now in prison. Arthur had read the letter Jeff had written and come to the quick conclusion that, mentally, Jeff's train had left its tracks.

Money, however, would never be an issue for Eric: his parents had both taken out hefty life insurance policies; Daniel's pension from the university would pay out another lump sum; and the house was now mortgage free. As both Daniel and Sarah had been only children, they had also inherited their parents' assets, and consequently their savings and share portfolios were substantial. Eric was told these monies would be placed in trust until his twenty-fifth birthday; meanwhile a monthly allowance would be forthcoming and all costs of schooling and college paid for.

It was arranged that his father's attorney would become his legal guardian, and that Eric would go to boarding school in San Francisco. On holidays, he would be welcome to visit with the Annandales or stay with The Reverend Pete and his family. What Eric really wanted to do, however, was find Susan and live with her. He determined that, as soon after the funeral as possible, he would head to the correctional facility where Jeff was incarcerated and find out from him where she was.

Considering that Daniel and Sarah had few close friends, the turnout at the funeral was big. The bizarre nature of their deaths had captured the interest and imagination of the local media, and Eric, the orphaned son, was the icing on the ultimate human interest cake story. The closed caskets lay side by side at the front of the church, and Eric sat in the front pew between Arthur and the mother of one of his friends. The arms placed around him brought warmth to his shoulders in the air-conditioned church, but little comfort. The music was sad, The Reverend Pete's eulogy even sadder, and poor Eric just cried and cried, desperately alone; the leftover of what had once been a family.

Standing at the graveside, and aware of his father's penchant for sand, Eric threw two handfuls on to the coffins. As The Reverend Pete intoned the final prayers, the last of Eric's tears spilled from his eyes and rolled down his young crumpled face.

Returning to his room at the Annandale house, Eric found an envelope containing photographs on his bed. The photographs had been developed from film found inside Daniel's camera at the Abu Rawash site, and forwarded to Eric by Wally. There were photographs of the hotel his parents had stayed in; photographs of Cairo; photographs of the Great Pyramid, the Sphinx and other pyramids; photographs of the desert and his parents riding camels; photographs of the Abu Rawash site and...

Eric shuddered. At the very bottom of the six-by-four print he held in his hand were the two heads of his parents, looks of surprised wonder on their faces. Above their heads – and the unintended subject of the photograph – a vast ocean of blue, blue sky.

Slow, but not Deaf

Talbot Academy was a small traditional school committed to Christ-centred education. Its teachings were based on the principles and values of the Bible, and its pupils were expected to live lives of character and faith. It also promoted the love of freedom and loyalty to the United States by enforcing a strict dress code and discouraging slovenliness. What had escaped the notice of those now responsible for Eric's education, however, was that Talbot Academy was a school for the deaf and operated in a signing environment.

Talbot Academy had been one of three Christian boarding schools shortlisted by Arthur Annandale in conjunction with The Reverend Pete; while both men had known the school by its Christian reputation, neither had been aware of its special-needs association. They handed the list to William Strey, Eric's legal guardian, and allowed him to make the final decision.

Strey conducted no research of his own into the three schools, and chose Talbot simply because Talbot was the maiden name of his wife. He handed the paperwork for Eric's fall enrolment to Elizabeth Mills, a newly-appointed legal secretary. She was conscious that Talbot Academy was a school for the deaf but, never having met Eric, had no reason to believe that the Gole boy wasn't deaf.

It had been originally agreed that Arthur Annandale and his wife would drive Eric to the academy, but all plans were cancelled after Alice was rushed to hospital with stomach pains. The Reverend Pete was out of town and Strey tied up in court. It therefore fell to Elizabeth to take Eric to San Francisco.

At the Academy, he was greeted by Mrs Isabelle Armitage, a portly woman in her mid-fifties who wore flat-heeled shoes and no make-up. She spoke to Eric in a strange and unusually loud voice, simultaneously gesturing with her hands.

'HELLO, ERIC. WELCOME TO TALBOT ACADEMY. I

HOPE YOUR STAY WITH US WILL BE A HAPPY ONE.'

Eric thanked her and said he felt sure that it would be.

'YOUR LIP-READING IS EXCELLENT, ERIC, AND SO TOO IS YOUR DICTION. BUT YOU'LL HAVE TO USE SIGN LANGUAGE WITH MOST OF THE STUDENTS HERE.'

Eric had no idea what she meant by this, but gave her a thumbs up to show willing. In return, Mrs Armitage gave him a thumbs up and smiled broadly. After ten minutes of stilted conversation, there was a knock on the door and a boy about Eric's age came into the room.

'ERIC, I'D LIKE YOU TO MEET CRAIG. CRAIG WILL HELP YOU SETTLE IN.'

Craig piloted Eric to a hall of residence two buildings distant from the administrative block, and came to a halt outside a door on its first floor. Eric understood from Craig that this would be his room during his stay at Talbot College but, in truth, that was all he did understand: the sounds emanating from Craig's mouth were generally unintelligible, and he presumed that his guide's presence on campus was to fulfil a required quota for government funding. He smiled kindly at Craig, who responded with more of the same curious hand signs Mrs Armitage had made. Eric gave him a thumbs up identical to the one he'd given the Principal and Craig then left, a look of puzzlement on his face.

Classes at Talbot Academy didn't start for a further two days, and Eric spent most of that time either in his room or in the school's cafeteria. Craig had seemingly decided his duty of care to Eric had been fulfilled, and signed to his friends that the new boy was quiet and said very little.

'ALL I GOT OUT OF HIM WAS A THUMBS UP!' he shrugged. 'IT WAS LIKE GETTING BLOOD OUT OF A STONE. I THINK HE MIGHT BE HERE ON ONE OF THOSE QUOTA DEALS.'

The first day of classes arrived, and Eric took a seat towards the back of the classroom. As his new teacher started to speak, Eric found himself straining to catch the words. He raised his hand and asked if he might relocate to a desk nearer the front.

'WHY?' Mr Dexter asked.

'I can't hear you, sir. I'm not deaf or anything, but I'm having problems with your accent.'

'NONE OF US HERE IS DEAF…' Mr Dexter looked down at the register, 'ERIC. WE DON'T USE THAT WORD ANYMORE. THESE DAYS WE REFER TO OURSELVES AS HEARING IMPAIRED. CAN'T YOU SEE MY SIGNING FROM THERE? YOU'RE NOT BLIND AS WELL ARE YOU – SORRY, I MEAN VISUALLY IMPAIRED?'

'No, sir. I'm not blind or hearing impaired. I'm normal.'

There was a small gasp in the room when the teacher signed Eric's words to the rest of the class. The school prided itself on engendering a positive deaf identity among its students, and the word *normal* was at all costs avoided.

Mr Dexter temporarily halted proceedings and took Eric to Mrs Armitage's office.

'HE SAYS HE'S NOT HEARING IMPAIRED, MRS ARMITAGE.'

'OF COURSE YOU'RE HEARING IMPAIRED, ERIC. WHY ELSE WOULD YOUR PARENTS HAVE SENT YOU TO A DEAF SCHOOL?'

'My parents are dead, Mrs Armitage. I think my guardian's made a mistake.'

Mrs Armitage looked puzzled. She opened Eric's file and found a contact number. William Strey answered the phone and confirmed that a dreadful mistake had indeed been made. Eric was a little slow, he admitted, but he certainly wasn't deaf.

'WHAT DO YOU MEAN BY THAT, MR STREY? ARE YOU SAYING THAT BEING SLOW AND HEARING IMPAIRED ARE THE SAME THINGS, OR MAYBE YOU'RE SAYING THAT BEING DEAF IS *WORSE* THAN BEING SLOW?'

Strey apologised for his careless choice of words and asked if he might call her back in the afternoon.

Eric was as unhappy with his guardian's use of words as Mrs Armitage had been. Who was William Strey to call him *a little slow*? How could anyone with a solid C average ever be considered slow?

Eric and Mr Dexter returned to the classroom and, after explaining Eric's plight to the rest of the class, Dexter suggested they spend a moment in silent prayer. The students looked pityingly at Eric and then bowed their heads. In that moment, no one prayed harder than normal Eric.

After Mrs Armitage's phone call, Strey made phone calls of his own, but was unable to find an opening for Eric at any other boarding school; all places had long since been filled and there would be no vacancies until spring. As Eric currently had board and lodging at Talbot Academy, Strey arranged with Mrs Armitage for him to spend the remainder of the fall semester there. Mrs Armitage, however, made a stipulation: Eric was to take a crash course in American Sign Language. Strey had readily agreed – the boy was once more out of his hair.

The arrangement, however, mattered little to Eric. He'd never intended remaining in school for more than a few weeks, whichever school had been chosen for him. His aim had always been to abscond and go looking for Susan, and with this objective in mind, he had already written a letter to Jeff. While he waited for a reply, he learned what he could from the classes he attended, and struggled with the sign language that threatened his exemplary C average. In his spare time he continued to read the Bible and compile a list of its dead.

By the time Eric had enrolled at Talbot College, he'd already read the Books of Genesis, Exodus and Leviticus. They hadn't been the easiest of reads, and it had proved more difficult than expected to make an accurate tabulation of those who died. He drew up lists of dead who were named, dead who were specified in number but unnamed, and dead who were both unnamed and unspecified in number.

Of the 3,614 specified dead, only nine had names: Abel, murdered by his brother Cain in a fit of jealousy; Mrs Lot, turned by God into a pillar of salt for disobedience; Shecham and his father Hamor, killed by Jacob for the former's defilement of his daughter Dinah; Er, one of Jacob's sons, killed by God for wickedness; Onan, Er's brother, killed by God for spilling his seed on the ground; King Amalek, killed by Joshua; and Nadab and Abihu, the sons of the chief priest Aaron, burnt to a crisp by God for getting an offering ceremony wrong.

In the category of Almost Named But Not Quite were two men killed by Lamech, a descendant of Cain, for either wounding or striking him; the Pharaoh of Egypt's chief baker hanged by order of the Pharaoh; several people who fell into bitumen pits; an Egyptian killed by Moses for beating a Hebrew slave; a man of mixed Israeli and Egyptian parentage killed by the Israelis for blasphemy; six hundred Egyptian charioteers drowned in the Red Sea while pursuing the fleeing Israelis; and three thousand Israelis killed by the sons of Levi for building and worshipping a golden calf while Moses was up a mountain talking to God.

And then came the non-specified numbers: the cities of Sodom and Gomorrah; the male inhabitants of the city ruled by King Hamor; the people ruled by King Amalek; the world at the time of Noah destroyed by a flood; amorphous battle casualties; Egyptians killed by hailstones sent by God; Egyptian first-borns killed by a plague sent by God; and more of Pharaoh's army of horsemen and charioteers, drowned in the Red Sea while trying to recapture their old slaves.

And then Jeff's letter arrived, short but to the point. He said he'd very much welcome a visit from Eric and that he was now back in contact with Susan. He warned him, however, not to contact the prison authorities for an official visiting permit as, being a minor, he would be refused unless accompanied by an adult. Rather, he should just turn up at the gate and ask for Big Guy, a prison guard who was now his friend. He ended by saying he would shelve his plans for escape until after Eric visited, and looked forward to seeing him again. He signed off as he'd signed off his previous letter: *Yours in Prison, Jeff.*

The problem Eric now faced was how to actually get to Lyon Mt Correctional Facility. It was a distance of some three and a half thousand miles from San Francisco, and a bus journey of at least three and a half days. Affording the $250 for the journey wasn't an issue for Eric, but being under the age of fifteen was:

bus company regulations barred him from travelling unaccompanied on any journey lasting more than five daylight hours. He was also a young-looking thirteen-year-old, and would have easier passed for eleven than fifteen. The only thing for him to do was the one thing his parents had always warned him not to do: accept rides from strangers.

Eric was aware his absence from school would be noticed, and calculated he'd require at least two days start before the alarm was raised. He therefore gave the school three weeks' notice that he would be returning home one weekend to attend a church memorial service for his parents, and asked for, and received, permission to leave school at the end of that Friday's morning classes. He told this lie only reluctantly, and hoped that both God and his parents would forgive him its telling.

On the day of his planned departure, Eric was collected from school by taxi and dropped off near Union Square; from there he walked to the Greyhound bus station on Mission Street and bought a one-way ticket to Sacramento. In the Sacramento bus station he bought a ticket to Roseville, a community located at the outskirts of the Sacramento metropolitan area and close to Interstate 80 and, from there, walked the remaining distance to where Route 65 joined the interstate. He then took up position on the hard shoulder.

Eric slipped the rucksack from his back, placed it on the ground and then unstrapped the white bicycle helmet he'd taken to wearing, and tied it to one of the bag's straps. He knelt on the asphalt, closed his eyes and placed his hands together. He prayed that God would watch over him and keep him safe, lead him to Susan and back to a life of happiness. It seemed to Eric that God had answered his prayer when a two-hundred-and-eighty-pound angel with a belly the size of a pregnancy in its ninth month called out to him. The angel's name was Red Dunbar and he drove a truck.

The Kindness of Strangers

Eric's eyes were still shut tight when the long-nosed eighteen-wheeler hissed to a halt. He opened them the same moment the passenger door swung open, and a large crew-cut head peered out.

'Where you goin' to, kid?'

'Plattsburgh, New York, sir,' Eric replied.

'Okay, climb in. Quick as you can, I'm not supposed to stop here!'

Eric took hold of his rucksack and threw it into the cab.

The driver took his first good look at Eric and was surprised by the boy's youth.

'How old are you, kid?' he asked. 'Eleven?'

'No sir, I'm thirteen. I just look young for my age. My name's Eric Gole.'

'My name's Red – Red Dunbar. Tell me, kid, how come someone young as you is out here on his own? Do your parents know where you are – and why are you heading to New York?'

Eric told Red Dunbar the truth. All of it: the death of his parents, his placement in a school for the deaf and his search for the only family he had left – Jeff in prison and Susan somewhere not in prison.

'Crappen dap!' Red exclaimed. (It was one of only three expressions of surprise he ever used: crappen dappen and, if time permitted, crappen dappen doo-dah being the other two.)

Red Dunbar was fifty-four. He'd been born in 1956 and lived in Yuba City with the woman he'd married thirty-three years previously, and who'd borne him two children: a son who also drove trucks, and a daughter who drove him to distraction. Red had driven trucks the whole of his working life, first for others and now for himself. He'd bought his first truck in 1999 and ever since had been self-employed and a paid-up member of the Owner-Operator Independent Drivers Association.

Eric's story touched Red, and he could at least identify with one part of it: he too had lost his parents at a young age. He remembered clearly the day he'd returned home from a friend's house to find a police car waiting outside his house and neighbours milling around in the yard. A young policewoman had broken the news that his parents and younger sister had been killed in a car accident; she told him their deaths had been immediate, that they hadn't suffered.

Red had been fifteen at the time, and the suffering his parents had escaped now fell on him like a ton of bricks. He was placed in foster care for three years with a family that fed and clothed him, but showed little affection. He turned eighteen and left their house for good, never to return; he still believed them to be people who fostered for money rather than reasons of altruism. If, at the time, there had been the remotest possibility of him finding the loving relations Eric now searched for, then Red was sure he'd have made the same journey and, if necessary, *walked* the three and half thousand miles to find them.

'You eaten yet, kid?'

'I ate breakfast and some toffees on the bus. Are you hungry?'

'I will be soon. What do you say we stop at the next pickle park and get us some dinner?'

'I like the idea, Mr Dunbar, but I've never really liked pickles. If there's nothing there I like, can I just buy some chocolate?'

'Pickle Park's a rest area, kid,' Red laughed. 'It serves all kinds of food. By the time we get you to Chicago, you'll have meat on your bones. I can promise you that much.'

Twenty minutes later, Red and Eric were sitting at a table in the truckers' section of a diner, their plates piled high with food. Red had ordered an all-day breakfast with a side order of pancakes for himself and a chicken platter for Eric.

'You going to finish that, kid?' he asked Eric, when he saw the boy starting to struggle.

'I don't think I can, sir. I'm about as full as I've ever been.'

'Mind if I take over?'

Eric handed his plate to Red, and Red handed his empty plate to Eric. It was as clean as a whistle and showed no evidence that food had ever been placed on it. (Red wasn't two hundred and eighty pounds for nothing, and neither had his belly appeared overnight.)

A couple of truckers came to the table and greeted Red. 'This kid teaching you how to drive, Red?' one of the men joked.

'I'm getting old, Pete,' Red replied, 'I need all the help I can get these days. Who better than my own grandson? Eric, this is Pete, and the guy next to him, by the looks of things, is an escaped convict.'

The man next to Pete laughed and held out his hand to Eric. 'I'm Dave,' he said. 'Don't take no notice of your Granddaddy, son, he's getting forgetful in his old age. It was me who taught him all he knows!' He turned to Red and asked him what he was hauling.

'More prunes, Dave. The people of Chicago have gotten themselves blocked up again. Sometimes I think I may as well be driving for the Red Cross as the California Sunshine Corporation.'

At last, the men went their different ways: Pete and Dave to the food counter, and Red and Eric back to the truck. As they walked, Red told Eric it was safer all round if people thought he was his grandson.

Eric agreed. 'Do you want me to call you granddad, Mr Dunbar?'

'Only if people are around. Otherwise call me Red – that's my given name.'

'Okay, Red. How much money do I owe you for my meal?'

'Not a cent, kid! While you're travelling with me you're my guest. But thanks for asking. Not many people do that nowadays.'

It took more than three days for them to reach Chicago. The number of hours Red could drive in a day was limited by law to no more than eleven in any fourteen hour period, and had to be followed by ten consecutive hours of rest. Nights he would sleep in the purpose-built compartment attached to the cab, while Eric slept on the seat, covered by a blanket. They washed and showered in facilities provided by the rest areas, and ate their breakfasts and dinners there too; for lunch they ate sandwiches and chips bought from the rest areas and drank Dr Pepper.

They traversed the Sierra Nevada Mountains of California and the Continental Divide in Wyoming. They journeyed through the barren deserts of northern Nevada and the salt flats of Utah, the Great Plains of Nebraska and the rolling hills of Iowa. They crossed the Missouri and Mississippi Rivers, and passed from Pacific Time to Mountain Time, from Mountain Time to Central Time. All the while they chatted.

'I love this country,' Red told Eric. 'I don't always agree with its politics, and there's been more than one President I wouldn't have opened my door to if he'd been stood there knocking, but I love the country. It's beautiful, kid, and I never get tired of driving through it – hearing it, smelling it. And I think most of the people who live in it are good people and kind-hearted. I wouldn't want to live anywhere else. I've never once left its borders and I don't ever intend to.'

'I like sport but I'm not much good at it,' Eric told Red. 'I can't catch all the balls thrown to me, especially if they're thrown hard, but I do try. I'm usually the last to be chosen when it comes to picking teams, but I don't mind as long as I get to play. What I don't like though is the way people shout at me when I miss a catch or mis-hit the ball. I don't understand why winning's so important and losing's so bad.'

'It's people with tattoos and pieces of metal stuck in their faces I despair of most,' Red told Eric. 'I don't know why they do it or why they think it makes them look more attractive, either. And it's not just young kids who don't know any better, it's old people who do. I see men in their sixties with diamond studs in their ears and women of the same age with lumps of metal in their noses, tattoos of dolphins on their shoulders and barbed wire round the tops of their arms. It turns me right off.'

'My hands sweat a lot,' Eric told Red. 'They never used to, but they're wet all the time now, especially when I'm around girls. I never used to feel uncomfortable around girls but I do now. I never know what to say to them. My Dad said it was natural and a stage all boys go through. Do you think he was right, Red? Why would I have this problem when none of my friends has?'

'It's truckers who are the backbone of this country,' Red told Eric. 'And it burns me up when I hear the FBI telling everyone we're a bunch of serial killers. If you listen to them, we're responsible for hundreds of unsolved deaths: fallen women, stranded motorists, hitchhikers; you name them and we're supposed to have killed them. They say we drive mobile crime scenes! That's what they call our trucks these days. Can you believe that? I tell you, if I ever got into a jam, it's a trucker I'd want in my corner and not some suited-up college kid who thinks he knows all there is to know about the world. Burns me up big time!'

'Do you miss your parents?' Eric asked Red.

'Sure I do. Not like I did when they first died. It hurt even to think about them then, but it got easier.' Red turned to look at Eric. 'Time *does* heal, kid. You've probably heard it a thousand times from a thousand different people, and the chances are you didn't believe one of them, did you? But it's true. Take it from me, one who's been there and one who knows.

'You'll have your own family one day, kid, and believe me you'll appreciate it all the more for having lost your own. Mark my words: you'll make a better husband and a better father than most other men your age.'

The moisture from Eric's hands magically disappeared and found its way to his eyes. He bit his lip and in a voice that trembled said: 'I, I hope so.'

'Let it out, kid, let it out,' Red said gently. 'There's no shame in crying, no shame at all.'

As Chicago approached and their time together neared its end, Red got busy on the CB: who was heading towards New York or into Canada, who knew of someone who was? Each time they pulled into a rest area, he left Eric at a table and went to speak to truckers he knew and truckers he didn't, asking them the same questions. He eventually struck gold and came back to the table with a triumphant look on his face.

'Got you a ride with a gal, kid,' he beamed. 'We're meeting her at the South Holland Service Plaza and she'll get you to Albany. She'll also make sure you pick up a ride from there to Plattsburgh. You're almost there, kid. Another two days and you'll be talking to your Uncle Jeff.'

Sure enough, the woman, called Lily Gomez, was waiting for them when they arrived at the South Holland Plaza. She was standing by the entrance to the restaurant drinking coffee from a cardboard cup. She gave Red a hug and shook Eric by the hand.

'I don't mean to hurry you, Red, but I need to start rolling. Larry Hicks is going to meet us in Albany and I don't want to keep him waiting. He'll take Eric the rest of the way.'

'Crappen dappen!' Red said. 'I thought old Larry was dead! I haven't seen hide nor hair of him for ten years at least. Tell him I owe him one, will you?'

He then turned to Eric and handed him a piece of paper. 'It's got my home address and telephone number on it, and also my mobile number. I want to hear from you once you've found Susan, and anytime you're in Yuba City, you call in. Got it? Now come and give old Red a big hug, kid.'

Eric did, and as Red had suspected, the boy burst into tears. What did surprise him, however, were the tears he felt running down his own cheeks. 'God speed, Eric,' he spoke softly in the boy's ear. 'He'll look after you. And if you get yourself in a jam you can't get out of, don't go to the FBI! Come to me!'

Red waited in the parking area while Eric settled himself in Lily's truck, and stood there waving as the truck pulled away and headed for the exit and Interstate 90. He then took a handkerchief from his jeans pocket and gave his nose a mighty blow.

Lily was in her early thirties. She had an olive-coloured complexion lightly pitted with acne scars, and hair and eyebrows the colour of coal. When she rolled up her shirt sleeves, a tattoo of a truck came into view on her left forearm, encased in a heart with an arrow running through it. Eric wondered if Red knew about this.

Lily occasionally turned to Eric and smiled, but was otherwise taciturn. She didn't like small talk at the best of times, and even though she had two children of her own, disliked small talk with small people in particular.

The truck passed silently into Eastern Time and through the states of Indiana, Ohio and Pennsylvania. Lily and Eric ate dinner at a rest area near Cleveland and Lily paid with money given to her by Red. They spent the night close to Buffalo, Lily in her sleeping compartment and Eric again on the seat. The following morning they rose early.

They arrived in Albany mid-morning and Larry Hicks was there to meet them. He looked like a man who didn't have much waiting time left in him, and Eric guessed his age to be about one hundred and five. Lily must have also appreciated the limited amount of time Larry now had left on earth as she simply shook his hand, introduced Eric and left. 'Call Red once you've dropped the boy off,' she called over her shoulder to Larry.

Larry was in fact only in his early sixties, but had lived a life full enough to have satisfied three people. His thin face was webbed with broken veins and crevassed by deep lines. Most of his teeth were missing, and the stubble above his lip was the colour of nicotine. He had a voice that rasped and spoke with the speed of an express train. Most of the time Eric had no idea what Larry was talking about, and the chances were good that neither did Larry.

The journey to Plattsburgh took them two and a half hours and Larry then insisted on driving Eric the extra fifteen miles to the town of Dannemora, where Lyon Mt Correctional Facility was located. They arrived outside its gates at two in the afternoon.

Eric thanked Larry for all his help and reminded him to call Red. 'Sure thing,' Larry replied, and a mile down the road promptly forgot.

The Hair in the Plughole

Eric went into a reception room to the side of the gate and asked the man standing behind the counter for Big Guy. The man folded his newspaper and peered down at him over half-moon glasses.

'And who should I say is asking for him, young man? His big brother?'

'No, sir. Tell him Eric Gole has arrived. I think he'll know who I am.'

The man left through a door to the rear of the counter and told Eric to wait. Almost five minutes passed before the door opened again but, unusually, no one appeared to pass through it. Eric became curious and had just started to peer over the counter when a small man jumped on to the stool and scared him half to death.

'I'm Big Guy,' the man said. 'Follow me.'

Big Guy was a three-foot-six-inch dwarf. He had a large angular head and a bulging brow; his arms were short, his fingers even smaller and his little legs were bowed at the knees. He walked with difficulty and in pain. Everything about Big Guy was disproportionate, including his heart, which, according to Jeff – who they'd found sitting at a picnic table – was the size of the moon.

'I don't think I'd have made it in here without Big Guy,' he told Eric.

Big Guy laughed when he heard Jeff say this. 'Man alive, Lawrence, if you can't make it in a holiday camp like this, God help you if they ever send you to a real prison. You have it made here. Look at yourself: you've got a coffee in one hand and a fat cigar in the other. What kind of torture is that? The most you ever have to do is pick up litter from roadsides or repair little league fields. Anyone can make it here. All I've done is given you paper and pencils.'

'You've given me more than that and you know it, Big Guy. You've given me inspiration!'

He turned to Eric. 'Big Guy was a huge fan of *The Dwarf Detective*, and once he knew it was me who'd created it, suggested we try writing something together. So that's what we've been doing, and I think we've come up with something big, something that could well prove to be a defining moment in the history of cinema. Do you want to hear about it?' Eric nodded that he did.

'We've come up with this great idea for a film. It's about a man who's been wrongly imprisoned for killing his wife, and he's been sentenced to life without parole. He's a loner and stands up for himself, won't take shit from anybody. He gets beaten up but he never snitches. He spends time in the prison hospital and time in solitary, but he never gives in; he's indomitable.

'And then he makes friends with this other prisoner, a black guy who gets things smuggled in from the outside for other prisoners. He asks him to get him a small rock hammer, supposedly for carving pieces of stone, but really he's planning to use it to tunnel out of the prison, even though it's going to take him years.

'In the meantime, he's also started working for the prison governor, doing his accounts and shit like that, and the governor's crooked as they come. When he escapes, he takes all these bogus bank account numbers with him – accounts the governor's been using to squirrel money away in – and cleans them all out and then sends all the evidence he has against the governor to a newspaper, and the governor's arrested and everyone in the prison cheers. And he's a rich man now, so he goes down to Mexico and lives a life of ease – it is Mexico we're thinking of, isn't it? Yeah, thought it was. He'll probably build boats down there.

'But he never forgets his old friend, and tells him that if he ever gets paroled he's got to go to this place where he'll find a tin full of money buried under a stone, and he's got to use it to follow him down to Mexico and become partners with him in the boat business. And the last shot of the film will be the two of them walking towards each other on the beach, and I swear to God, Eric, there won't be a dry eye in the house when the lights come on.

'And we're not just pitching the idea, either. We're going to insist we're in it. We're figuring I'll play the part of the guy who escapes, and Big Guy the part of the fixer. So what do you think, Eric, brilliant or what?'

Eric replied falteringly. 'I think it is brilliant, Uncle Jeff, but doesn't it remind you a bit of *The Shawshank Redemption*?'

'What's that?' his uncle asked.

'It was a film with Tim Robbins and Morgan Freeman in it. They were prisoners too.'

'You ever heard of this film, Big Guy?'

'It's a waste of money me even going to the movies, Lawrence. Someone sits in front of me and the damn screen disappears. So no, I've never seen this film, or any other film for that matter.'

'Me neither,' Jeff said. 'I can't see there being another film quite like this one, Eric.'

Eric told Jeff of his journey to Dannemora, and the help given to him by Red, Lily and Larry. He told him of his guardians in Santa Cruz and the school in San Francisco, his reasons for running away and his search for Susan.

'If it wasn't for being locked up in here, Eric, I'd be glad to take care of you myself. We're family, and there's nothing more important. We're here to look after each other, and I know if anything had happened to me your daddy would have taken care of Susan...' He paused for a moment, as if remembering something.

'That time we came to visit you in Santa Cruz. You remember it? I've always felt bad about it: the hurt and the scarring it might have caused...'

Eric interrupted him. 'That was all sorted, Uncle Jeff. My dad was annoyed at Susan for tearing up his Bible, but he forgave her.'

Jeff looked at Eric mystified. 'I'm not talking about your dad's Bible, Eric. I'm talking about taking you to the Paul McCartney concert!'

'It was never my idea to go to that concert. It was Mrs Lawrence, your Aunt Anna, who wanted to go. We were having problems at the time and I thought if I just agreed with her, it might help smooth things over. I should've saved my money. We got home and she started comparing me to the fucker – and you don't need to be an Einstein to figure out who came off worse.

'I told her she'd do better comparing Paul McCartney to my old man: he was nearer his age than I was, and she shouldn't get fooled into thinking he wasn't by some stupid dye job. You want Paul McCartney I said to her, you go get him. Best of luck to you too, sweetheart. Go break a fucking leg, lose one if you have to, makes no difference to me.

'Anyway, we arranged to buy tickets and Mrs Lawrence insisted

I get one for you. She thought you'd be company for Susan and told me I was being neurotic when I said a concert like that might damage you. Susan's one thing, I said to her, Eric's another.

'Susan was old enough to make up her own mind. She'd always been a *Beatles* fan, and the way she saw it, Paul McCartney in concert was the closest she'd ever get to seeing the *Beatles* in concert. I tried talking sense into her, but she wouldn't listen. I couldn't get her to appreciate that there's a chasmic difference between the next best thing and plain residue.

'You know when you wash your hair, Eric, and some of it always gets stuck in the plughole? Well that's how it was for me at that concert. I sure as hell didn't imagine I was listening to the *Beatles* that night, and I'm not sure I even saw Paul McCartney. All I remember is that every time I looked at the stage, I saw a plughole full of dyed hennaed hair!'

McCartney, he explained to Eric, had written some of his favourite *Beatles* songs and *Hey Jude* still remained his all-time pick. The last great song McCartney had written was *Maybe I'm Amazed* and, after that, he'd started a slalom run to hell, a descent presaged by *The Long and Winding Road* and confirmed by *Ebony and Ivory* and the *Frog Chorus*. The restraining influence of the *Beatles* had gone, and so too had any semblance of quality control. His music now was fit only for elevators and supermarkets.

'It's a damn tragedy, Eric, and if I ever met the guy I'd give him a good shake. I'd get hold of those fat cheeks of his, give them a good squeeze, and then slap him. And it's not just what the music's become; it's what he's become – a smug little bastard who tries too hard to be cool and pretends he's just a normal guy. Well, God help the person who ever treats him like he's just another normal guy: he'd be out of the door sitting with his ass in a puddle before he even knew what had happened.

'And he talks such grandiose shit these days, too. I saw him interviewed on television soon after 9/11, and he was saying how he was going to do something for the people of New York and the rest of the country; raise their spirits and make them feel good about life again. So what does he do? He records a song called

Freedom. You ever heard the lyrics? They must have taken him all of three minutes to write – and the music? Maybe two!

'Well, I'll tell you this for free, Eric: the song didn't make *me* feel any less crap about life! I didn't think: "Okay, we've lost a couple of towers, but at least we've got a new Paul McCartney song out of the tragedy." And you know where the song did best? Fucking Rumania!

'I tell you, I laughed silly when one of his tour buses got stolen. You hear him afterwards? Talking about how there was a lot of love in that bus and how he hoped the love would rub off on to the people who'd taken it. Well tell me, how the fuck would he know how much love there was in that bus? You ever think he ever stepped foot in it? No chance: it's limousines and private jets for Saint Paul.'

'But why were you worried the concert might damage me, Uncle Jeff?' Eric asked. 'I enjoyed the concert.'

'Because it was family entertainment!' Jeff said. 'We may as well have taken you to a recording of the *Sonny & Cher Show*. Music's meant to divide families not bring them together. Kids and parents shouldn't be listening to the same music: they should hate each other's music, and not even think about rubbing shoulders with each other in the same audience. And there was no audience worse than the one we became a part of that night! Middle-aged parents and grandparents behaving like eighteen-year-olds; old women moving suggestively and old men pulling strange faces and playing air guitars. I tell you, Eric, there's nothing more embarrassing than a bunch of old fuckers pretending to be young again.

'And tell me this, what kind of a brainless twat takes a six-foot sign to a concert with them? How the hell are the people sitting behind supposed to see? There was one in front of us until I tore it from them. And do you know what it said? *God Bless John, George and Linda.* I ask you, can you imagine either John or George turning up to that concert? More likely they were turning in their graves!

'Big Guy's got an interesting theory about their deaths. Tell Eric what you think, Big Guy.'

He looked around to make sure they were still alone, and then spoke conspiratorially. 'I think McCartney had them killed,' he said. 'He was the first to leave the *Beatles* and I think he resented that, felt he'd been pushed out of his own creation. I think he was right in thinking this too, and I think along the same lines as your uncle in thinking that it was *The Long and Winding Road* that prompted the others to throw him out. I think ...'

'That's the seventh time you've used the word *think*, Big Man. I've told you before: if you want to be a successful writer, you have to start broadening your vocabulary.'

'I'm not *writing* to Eric, Lawrence, I'm *talking* to him. This is how I talk. This is how other people talk. Now butt out!' He turned his attention back to Eric. 'McCartney wanted people to think of him when they thought of the *Beatles*. He wanted to tour the world and play *Beatles* music without being inconvenienced by two other people doing the same thing. Imagine what it would have been like if John and George had rolled into the same city and played concerts on the same night he was playing. It would have been commercial suicide and a popularity contest he might well have lost. He couldn't afford to take the chance.

'So what does he do? He recruits two crazies, one in the US and one in the UK, and probably promises them free tickets to his concerts for life. You've got to bear in mind that there *are* people crazy enough to accept such offers. One crazy succeeded and the other failed, but even the failed attempt resulted in Harrison becoming a recluse; it probably contributed to his early death too. So when we think of the *Beatles* now, who do we think of? That's right, Paul McCartney! I'm working on getting proof but it's proving difficult and, in the meantime, I'd prefer it if you didn't mention this to anybody. I can't afford law suits on my salary.'

'What about Ringo? Why hasn't anyone killed him?' Eric asked.

Both Jeff and Big Guy burst out laughing.

'Why would anyone want to kill Ringo?' Big Guy answered. 'He's no threat to anyone! Besides, if all the Beatles *but* McCartney were killed, there'd be too many questions to answer, too many coincidences to square.'

'I can buy into that, Big Man,' Jeff said.

Jeff's ready and enthusiastic support for such a preposterous notion would have set alarm bells ringing in the minds of most rational people, but in Big Guy's case, a man in the process of writing the *Shawshank Redemption*, they never made a sound.

'I don't mean to rush you guys,' Big Guy said, 'but you've got thirty minutes before I go off duty and The Blimp comes on. He'll blow a gasket if he finds Eric here, and that means trouble for all of us.'

'How come time slips by quickly when you're enjoying yourself, and the rest of the time, when you want it to pass quickly, it just strolls around like a three-legged tortoise on Quaaludes?' Jeff asked.

'I don't know,' Eric said. 'Do you think we should talk about Susan now, where I'll find her?'

'Hershey, Pennsylvania,' Jeff replied.

Chocolate

The last Eric had heard of Susan was when news reached the Gole family that she'd dropped out of college and started dancing with a Polish folk troupe. Jeff smiled at Daniel's misunderstanding of the situation, and clarified it for Eric. He told him that Susan had left college to pursue a more alternative career; rather than climb the conventional greasy pole to success, his daughter had decided to slide down one for a living!

'If I'm honest, Eric, I'd have to say I disagreed with her decision. I don't mind going to those clubs once in a while, but like any father, I sure as hell don't want to turn up and find my own daughter dancing there. It's hypocritical I know, but that's how life is and that's the way I am.

'Susan knew I was on shaky ground and she didn't hold back from telling me. She said there was nothing wrong with such entertainment, that the body was a thing of beauty and shouldn't be hidden from view. She argued that if people were more open about their bodies, there'd be less crime of a sexual nature in the world, and that what she was doing was neither sordid nor pornographic.

'I knew she was right, but I wasn't about to tell her so. I know I can be headstrong and obdurate at times, but so too can Susan. She went her own way after that argument and we lost touch. And then out of nowhere, she turns up here at the correctional facility!'

A rapprochement had taken place between them in the grounds of the prison, close to the picnic table where they now sat. During the time of their separation, the father's indignation had mellowed and the daughter's naive idealism quietened.

Susan had been a popular dancer in the clubs where she entertained and had made good money. Unsavoury elements, however, had now started to encroach upon her innocent world, and many of the once well-managed venues had become lax and undisciplined. Many of the newer dancers openly used drugs, and managements now subordinated the artistry of the pole to the fatuity of the lap. Susan had always refused to perform such dances, and consequently employment opportunities for her had become scarcer. She did, however, have new ideas of her own, and these ideas incorporated chocolate.

The three loves of Susan's life were her body, dancing and chocolate, and it had always been her dream to blend all three into one artistic performance. The brainwave rolled to shore in Galveston while Susan was walking along its beach. It was the height of the city's hot summer and temperatures were in the high nineties. She was with a friend, who was extolling the virtues of blue M&Ms and their power to help paralyzed rats walk again. She placed two on Susan's hand and told her to eat them. 'Better than fish oils,' she'd said.

It wasn't so much the colour of the M&M's that intrigued Susan as the fact that they didn't melt. 'It's a pity they don't make milk chocolate that doesn't melt in your hand,' Susan had said to her.

'Oh, but they do,' her friend had said. 'They've been making it since the forties. Tastes like shit, too.'

'You ever heard of the Desert Bar?'

Eric shook his head.

'It was a chocolate bar developed by Hershey that could withstand temperatures of 140 degrees. It was made for the soldiers fighting in the Gulf, but the company made too much and there were stocks left over after the war ended. They packaged the excess bars in desert-camouflage wrappers and marketed them as chocolate novelties. I bought one, and it tasted like wax – the only damn chocolate bar I've ever had to chew!

'Anyway, there's supposed to be stock of this chocolate in Hershey somewhere, and Susan's gone looking for it. She arranged to meet a guy called Finkel. I tried calling him one time to find out how Susan was doing, but he's not listed in the phone book. I've got his address though, or leastways, the address Susan gave me. She passed this way about three months back and I can't say for sure she'll still be in Hershey, but you could start by talking to this guy Finkel.'

Jeff pulled some crumpled pieces of paper from his pocket, smoothed them on the picnic table and examined each one. 'Here it is!' he said, 'Fred Finkel, Gravel Road, Hershey.'

'Time to make a move,' Big Guy said. 'We need to get Eric out of here. I can take him into Dannemora and he can get a bus from there.'

The two distant relatives said their goodbyes. Jeff thanked Eric for dropping by and told him to give Susan his love. 'You find her, she'll take care of you,' he said. 'She's a good girl.'

Eric kissed him on the cheek and followed Big Guy to a parked car. Big Guy unlocked it and told Eric to climb in. 'I'll be back in ten minutes, Eric,' he said, and true to his word he was. He returned dressed in civilian clothes, and fired the engine of the specially adapted car. A child's booster seat enabled him to see through the windscreen, and large blocks of wood attached to the pedals allowed him to accelerate and brake. He drove slowly and with great care, checking the mirrors every five seconds. They were overtaken by every car and truck heading in the same direction, and though they arrived at the bus station in one piece, they also arrived there too late for Eric to catch his intended bus.

'Still, better to arrive ten minutes late in one life than ten years early in the next,' Big Guy said cheerfully.

Eric would have gladly settled for the happier medium of arriving on time, but was in no position to say so. He was, however, both grateful and relieved when Big Guy offered to take him to a rest area on the interstate. 'You seem to have luck hitch-hiking, Eric. Maybe your luck's still in.'

It was dusk and a cold rain had started to fall. Big Guy gave Eric his umbrella, told him to take care of himself and then drove off.

Eric looked around the rest area. There were few cars there and only one vehicle with a light on. The bus looked vaguely familiar, and Eric decided to approach it.

Bob sat at the wheel reading a manual, something he should have done in Montreal. He was unsure of the vehicle's controls and even less sure of its legal pedigree. The accompanying registration papers, however, had been professionally forged and he didn't doubt they would pass inspection; crossing the border from Canada had been a breeze.

He played with the controls, turned every switch and pressed every button until he was happy he understood them. He then turned the ignition key and was about to pull away, when there was a sudden knock on the window.

'Goddamn!' Bob yelled.

If the knock hadn't scared him sufficiently, the sight of what he took to be an alien peering through the window certainly did, and as the side door slowly opened, his body tensed. Bob breathed a sigh of relief when the shape of a small white boy came into view wearing a strangely shaped bicycle helmet.

'Excuse me bothering you, sir,' the boy said, 'but is there any chance you could give me a ride?'

'Jesus, kid, you almos' give me a heart attack! I thought you was one o' them aliens. What you doin' out here?'

'Visiting my uncle, sir. There's no bus till morning and I need to get to Hershey.'

'Couldn' yo' uncle give you a ride?'

'He's in prison, sir. The one back there off the road.' He pointed with his free hand, the one not holding what Bob took to be a girl's umbrella.

'Okay, kid, climb in.'

Eric climbed in and fastened his safety belt. He then held out his hand to Bob and introduced himself: 'My name's Eric Gole, sir. What's yours?'

'Otis Sistrunk,' Bob said, 'Call me Otis.' He then put the vehicle into drive and steered toward the exit.

Fred Finkel's Living Room

'She was the most beautiful girl I'd ever seen,' Finkel said. 'No one would have turned her down. I was lucky to be blessed with brains when I was born, but I didn't do too well in the looks department. It never used to bother me until I met Susan, but then I started to wonder how life might have been if I had been handsome and met someone like her thirty years ago. I don't mind telling you, it unsettled me. Don't go getting me wrong, there was no funny business between the two of us, but when she left it was like my heart had been broken in two. Strange thing that, isn't it?'

Bob and Eric were sitting side by side on a small couch in Fred Finkel's living room, drinking cups of tea. It was Sunday afternoon and their second visit to Finkel's house. Although they'd arrived in Hershey on the Saturday, Finkel had been out of town visiting his sister.

The man who'd opened the door to them had the appearance of a wire coat hanger on edge. He was in his late sixties, about five foot six and thin as a rake. His head was particularly narrow – more like a side profile than a full face – and gave the impression of a man who'd been delivered from his mother's womb by a doctor who'd pressed on the forceps too hard.

'Sorry to disturb you like this, Mr Finkel, but our understandin' o' the matter is that you an acquaintance o' Susan Lawrence. Susan's a cousin o' this young man here, an' he tryin' to locate her. We was wonderin' if you can help us.'

At the mention of Susan's name an immediate change came over Fred Finkel: his guard dropped and a tremulous smile jerked uneasily across his face. He held out a surprisingly firm hand and invited them into the house.

'I was just making a cup of tea,' he said. 'Would you care to join me?' Finkel disappeared into the kitchen and left Bob and Eric alone in what passed for a living room.

'What's tea like, Otis?' Eric whispered. 'I've never drunk it before.'

'Tastes good,' Bob said. 'Jus' diff'rent is all.'

The curtains in the living room were old and made from a heavy velvet material. They were drawn shut to prevent any natural light from seeping into the parlour's cheerless interior, which was illuminated by a sole standing light. There was no television, no radio and no CD player, and the walls – apart from a small round mirror – were completely bare. There were only three ornaments in the room and these sat on the mantel over the fireplace: an old glass candy jar filled with buttons, a black wooden elephant sat on its haunches with a clothes brush sticking out of its hollowed head, and a small rosewood tea chest.

Finkel came back into the room holding a tray. He placed it carefully on one of the tables.

'I've brought milk just in case,' he said, 'but I think you'll find the tea tastes better if you just squeeze lemon into it. One more piece of advice: it's wisest to sweeten the tea only *after* you've tasted it.' He then poured three cups. 'I don't know whether you've drunk Lapsang souchong before, but it's special.'

Bob squeezed the lemon into his cup and took a taste. 'Mmmm, this good, Mr Finkel. It's got a kinda smoky taste to it, don't it?'

'Exactly so!' Finkel replied.

'I notice you got an ol' tea chest on the shelf, there. You keep tea in that, too?'

'No, Mr Sistrunk, I keep my caul in there.'

'Coal? How you fit coal in there, Mr Finkel? Looks too small.'

'Not coal, Mr Sistrunk. Caul! It's a veil of skin that covers the face of some children when they're born – rather like a mask. It's rare that it happens, but not that rare – Napoleon Bonaparte had one, for example.

'In Eastern Europe, they believed that a child born with a caul over its face would grow up to be a werewolf, but in our culture it's always been interpreted as an omen of good luck. Legend has it that the bearer of a caul never drowns, and sailors in particular are still prepared to pay large sums of money for them. It's nonsense, I know, but harmless nonsense.

'Having said that, my mother made me promise never to throw it away. She believed that if the caul wasn't buried – or burnt – with me when I died, then my soul would never rest in peace, and like all mothers she wanted the best for me. So that's what will happen when I die, and in the meantime it stays locked away in the tea chest there.'

Bob was fascinated by Finkel's story, Eric rather less so.

'I hope I'm not interrupting, Mr Finkel – and that story of yours about coal was very interesting – but can you tell me about my cousin Susan?'

'Of course I can, young man,' Finkel said. He put down his cup, closed his eyes and then appeared to fall asleep.

Eric looked at Bob uneasily, and was about to prod the man when Finkel suddenly burst into life.

'I was up at the plant and got a call from the post room to say they'd taken receipt of a letter addressed to *The Person who invented The Desert Bar*, and wanted to know if they should forward it to me. I wasn't the inventor as such, but I was probably the last member of the original project team still working at the factory, and so I said yes. It was an unusual letter, handwritten in purple ink with big hearts over the 'i's and 'j's, and flamboyant loops on all the upper and lower sticks. To tell you the truth, I thought it had been written by a child, and because I was in the middle of something else I didn't read it immediately. I stuck it in my pocket and only remembered about it after I got home.

'The writer of the letter introduced herself as Susan Lawrence and described herself as an artist who was interested in doing something with chocolate that didn't melt in the hand. She wanted to know if she could come to Hershey, perhaps buy me dinner and pick my brains. I was intrigued and wrote back to her the next day saying I'd be happy to help. I think if she'd said at the time that she was an exotic dancer, I probably wouldn't have done so; but I didn't know that then and, when I did know, it no longer mattered to me.

'I didn't hear anything back, and then, about two weeks later, there was a knock on my door and a young lady standing there telling me she'd come to take me to dinner. My twitches started up and I couldn't think of anything to say, and that's when she leaned across and kissed me on the cheek – right here,' he said, pointing to his left cheek. "Come on, pull yourself together, Mr Finkel," she said. "I'm Susan: the person who wrote to you about the Desert Bars."'

'I'd just opened a can of sardines when she'd arrived and washed some tomatoes, but I just forgot all about them and followed her to the car meek as a lost lamb. It wasn't until I got home again that I realised I'd never even shut the door behind me: it was still wide open, believe it or not.

'She took me to the Fire Alley Restaurant down on Cocoa Avenue, looked at me and said: "Mr Finkel, what you need is a steak! You look like you're about to waste away," and so that's what I ordered. People in the restaurant kept looking over at us, probably wondering what a good-looking girl like her was doing with a decrepit old man like me, and I tell you, it felt great. She was a tactile person and when she talked she kept touching me, and every time she did, it was like a jolt of electricity shooting through my body.

'She told me right off that she was a dancer rather than a fine artist, but a *fine* dancer. She smiled when she said that. I'd never seen a smile as beautiful as hers and I just smiled right back. She said she wanted to incorporate chocolate into her act in a *tasteful* way – and she smiled again when she said it, and I smiled right back at her. I think that's when I fell in love.

'Anyway, she explained how she wanted to cover her body with chocolate that didn't melt when it was applied, and would then only melt slowly. She told me it was for "human installation art purposes" and wanted to know if the Desert Bar would be appropriate. I told her I didn't know a thing about human installation art, but that I did know a thing or two about chocolate, and that yes, it would be possible – but the chocolate they used for the Desert Bar would first have to be modified. It was simply too solid to spread over a human body, too intractable, and the window between melting and re-solidification was too short a time for the chocolate to be applied to a person's body without burning the skin.

'"So, what can we do?" she asked me, and I told her we'd have to add more cocoa butter to the mix. I explained to her that I couldn't be sure how much cocoa butter would have to be added without doing a few experiments, but that I'd be able to do these tests in my own kitchen. I said if she came back in a couple of weeks, I'd probably have something ready for her. But she'd have none of that. She said she wanted to stay in Hershey and help me – in fact, she was insistent on it – and the next day, we got down to work.'

There had been no problem locating the chocolate that formed the basis of the Desert Bar, but it had taken a few days for the necessary paperwork to clear and for the blocks to be released into the hands of its maker. Finkel had been right in thinking the whole process would take no more than two weeks. Working nights and at weekends, using conventional cooking pans and a microwave oven, Finkel and Susan made chocolate mixes with varying amounts of cocoa butter until the right consistency was finally achieved and the chocolate spread easily and evenly over Susan's arm, hardening without cracking. Although pleased with the final outcome, Finkel was also crestfallen by its success: he knew Susan would soon leave and no longer be a part of his life.

'Two days after we'd finished making enough batches to keep her going for a while, we loaded up her car and she headed off to Nashville. That's where she thought she'd try out her new act first. I got a postcard from her soon after she arrived, but I haven't heard anything since. The day she left she gave me a hug – the first hug I've ever had from a woman, except for my mother and sister. There are times when I close my eyes that I can still smell her perfume. Odd that, isn't it?'

He pulled the card from his jacket pocket and showed it to them. The card ended with *Lots of love, Susan* and, underneath her name, a line of kisses. Bob knew it would be in Finkel's possession until the day he died, and would be either buried or burnt with him along with his caul. There was, however, an address on the card: 2010 Honey Pot Estate, Nashville, and Bob copied it down.

'We 'preciate the time you given us, Mr Finkel, an' we 'preciate the help you given Susan, too. I'm sure she holds you close to her heart.'

'You think so?' Finkel asked, excitedly. 'Really think so?'

'I do,' Bob said. 'Ain't that the truth, Eric?' Bob prompted his companion to agree by nudging him in the ribs.

'Yes sir, Mr Finkel. The truth!'

'Some kinda heartbreaker, this cousin o' yo's, ain't she,' Bob said, after they'd returned to the bus.

'I don't think she means to be,' Eric said.

'I'm sure she don't, but she sure left po' ol' Fred in the doldrums.'

'Did you like him?' Eric asked.

'I didn't dislike him,' Bob replied. 'The ol' guy's lonely, an' until yo' cousin came 'long he prob'ly never even knowed it. Prob'ly never been in love b'fore, neither. Lived his whole life in the dark an' then yo' Susan comes along an' turns the light on. He'll get reacquainted with his self eventu'ly but, 'til he does, he ain't gonna be enjoyin' life too much. Hard to dislike someone you feel sorry for.'

'He made me nervous,' Eric said.

'Ever'thing makes you nervous, son. That's why you wander roun' with a damn-fool cycle helmet on yo' head when you don't even have yo'self a bike to ride.'

Eric fell silent for a moment. 'Is it okay if I stay with you another night and then leave in the morning?'

Bob could never have lived with himself if he'd let the boy go off by himself. Eric had been lucky so far, but no man's luck ran forever. Something bad could happen to the boy, and he didn't want that on his conscience – there were too many deaths sitting there already. Gene, he knew, would grumble because it was in his nature to do so, but he'd mellow; Bob knew – if most others didn't – that the man had a soft centre.

There was, however, another and more calculated reason for

taking Eric along: the boy knew the tour bus's provenance! Bob knew in his heart that Eric would never knowingly compromise him, but in his head worried that the boy might well let slip that he'd been given a ride in a tour bus that had once belonged to Paul McCartney. The last thing Bob wanted was the attention of the law.

The first inkling Bob had that the tour bus he was driving was the same tour bus stolen from Paul McCartney five years previously, was when Eric showed him how to disconnect the endless music droning from the speakers. Ever since he'd picked up the bus in Montreal, all he'd been able to listen to was Paul McCartney, and he was now more than tired of it. Eric told him that the music was coming from an iPod connected to the sound system from inside his armrest. Bob had no idea that the armrest even opened but, when he raised its lid, sure enough he found an iPod there. He immediately unplugged it, opened the passenger side window and hurled the annoying device on to the roadside.

The second inkling came when Eric asked to use the toilet. He was about to give the boy directions when Eric told him he knew where it was.

'How you know all this? You been on this bus b'fore or somethin'?'

'I think I have,' Eric replied. 'If it wasn't this bus, then it was one just like it. Me and Susan got invited onboard when we went to a concert in San Francisco. I'll know for sure once it stops.'

Once the bus stopped, Eric led him to the bunks in the sleeping area. He told Bob that if this was the same bus, then under the top mattress of the three-tiered bunks on the right would be a small heart drawn in purple ink. Inside the heart would be Susan's initials. Bob climbed up and, sure enough, once he pulled back the mattress he saw a small faded heart with letters inside it: SL = PM.

'Well, I'll be damned,' Bob said. 'So there is. I'm fig'rin' the *new* owners who bought this bus never even see'd it.' (He emphasised the word *new* to give Eric the impression that the tour bus had been bought legally.)

'The new owners won't mind me being on the bus, will they?' Eric asked.

'I doubt it, but I wouldn' go mentionin' it to nobody. Bes' keep this a secret – yo's an' mine. No point causin' any trouble for Susan.'

Eric had readily agreed.

Part Two

LOCATIONS

5

Two Mountains and a Plateau

Missing Persons

Brandon Travis walked into Oaklands just as William Hoopes was being led from it in handcuffs. Signs warned that the floor was wet, and a member of the janitorial staff was in the process of removing what looked to have once been an aquarium. He slowed his pace and walked carefully to the reception desk.

'What's been going on here?' he asked.

'Nothing to speak of,' the receptionist replied innocently. 'There's been a small misunderstanding, but it's all sorted now. How can I help?'

'My name's Brandon Travis. I'm here to see my sister, Nancy Skidmore. She's locked up here, someplace.'

The receptionist typed the name into the computer. 'She's in the Assisted Living Community wing, Mr Travis. If you sign your name in the visitor's book, I'll give you directions.'

Brandon signed his name, noted the time, and then walked down the corridor leading to the Secure Unit.

The receptionist turned to a nurse who'd been standing close by. 'My God, did you smell that man? I doubt he's been near a bar of soap in weeks!'

Ten minutes later, Brandon returned to the desk huffing and puffing.

'She's not there,' he shouted. 'She's gone!'

'Sir, please don't raise your voice – there's been enough

excitement for one day. Now what do you mean *she's not there*? Where else would she be?'

'How the hell would I know? I've only just got here! All I know is that she's not in her room. She's not in any of the other loonies' rooms either, and she's not in the communal area. You work here – you go figure where else she'd be.'

The receptionist asked Brandon to take a seat while she made some calls. She did this not out of any consideration for the missing patient's brother, but for herself: his aroma was truly foul! She phoned the head nurse in the Secure Unit to confirm Brandon's story and then called Howard Franks, the day manager of the nursing home. 'We have a situation, Mr Franks.'

Franks listened carefully, replaced the phone in its cradle, and then rested his head in his hands. 'Un-fucking-believable!' he eventually said.

Howard Franks was having a bad day, the worst he could remember in more than thirty years of healthcare administration: first the shooting and now a missing client. Word was bound to get out, and word getting out would be bad for business. The top priority for Franks was always the bottom line – dollars and cents, profit and loss. Unless the situation was contained, Oaklands would be facing an expensive lawsuit. He took a deep breath, left the safety of his office and went to meet the irate Brandon Travis.

'Mr Travis? I'm Howard Franks, day manager of the nursing home. I gather Nancy's gone missing.'

Brandon rose from the chair he was sitting in to take Franks' outstretched hand, but lost his footing on the slippery floor and fell back heavily into the chair. 'Let me give you a hand there,' Franks said, automatically sweeping the foyer with his eyes for signs warning that the floor was wet. They were still there, thank God, so no lawsuit to be feared from Travis on this score. He led the overweight man to his office and phoned for coffee.

'Have you had a long journey, Mr Travis?'

'I have,' Brandon answered. 'I've come from Clarksdale, Mississippi, and travelled here by bus. It took two days! Two days of waiting in bus stations with vagrants and riding with trailer trash. Do you think I enjoyed that?

'I did it for my sister, Mr Franks; did it out of love for her. I don't have much in my life these days – certainly not money – but I've always had Nancy. But now I don't even have her because you've gone and fucking lost her – and, God dammit, you were being paid good money to look after her. I want an explanation, Mr Franks, and I'll also want recompense for the mental anguish I'm now experiencing. Do I make myself clear?'

Franks got the message loud and clear – after all, it was a money message. 'There was an incident here this morning, Mr Travis, and it's possible that in the confusion Nancy might have slipped out of Oaklands unnoticed – but she won't have gotten far. I feel confident she'll be back in her own bed by nightfall.' Brandon looked at him sceptically.

'There is one thing. It might just be a coincidence, Mr Travis, but this morning your sister was visited by some other relatives: Homer and Ruby Comer. Do you know them?'

'I know them,' Brandon said surprised, 'but unless they came to haunt her, I don't know what they'd be doing here.'

'Why do you say that, Mr Travis?'

'Because they've both been dead thirty years, Mr Franks!'

The day manager arranged for a taxi to take Brandon and his small rucksack to a nearby hotel, while he called the police and enquiries were made into the true identities of Homer and Ruby Comer. It would take the police a few days to pinpoint Eugene Chaney III as a person of interest. According to the visitor's log, a man named E Chaney had previously visited Nancy at the nursing home, but had left no address. It took time for them to equate the name in the register with that of Dr Eugene Chaney III, and it was only after it was established that Chaney himself was missing from his home address – a dead dog in his wake – that the pieces started to fall into place.

If Pennsylvania had a new missing persons' case to contend with, California had an older one – and this pertained to Eric Gole. After Eric hadn't returned to school by Monday lunchtime, Mrs Armitage had phoned his guardian. William Strey had been unaware that Eric had even been home for the weekend, and was totally ignorant of any memorial service for his parents. He made calls – to Arthur Annandale and The Reverend Pete – and then called Mrs Armitage back: there had been no memorial service and neither had anyone seen Eric. 'Do you think he's run away?' he asked.

'IT'S RATHER LOOKING THAT WAY, MR STREY. I THINK I SHOULD CALL THE POLICE.'

Strey always had to strain to understand anything Mrs Armitage said on the phone and misheard her: 'Who's the *priest*,' he asked. 'What's he got to do with anything?'

'NOT PRIEST, MR STREY, *POLICE*.'

Strey still had to think about the difference between the two words she pronounced, but eventually understood. 'Of course, Mrs Armitage: a sensible idea. Keep me informed will you, and please give them my details. This is worrying. The boy doesn't know it, but he's worth a small fortune. I just hope to God he hasn't been kidnapped.' Mrs Armitage shuddered at the thought, and phoned the San Francisco police department even more concerned.

The detective assigned to the case was John Cooper, and his experience told him that Eric had run away rather than been kidnapped – as Strey had suggested. He arranged a meeting of all interested parties to be held at Talbot Academy on the Wednesday evening. In attendance were Mrs Armitage, William Strey, Arthur Annandale and The Reverend Pete.

'It's clear to me that Eric planned his disappearance and planned it carefully,' he told them. 'He gave the school three weeks' notice he'd be away for the weekend, and also concocted a clever reason for his absence – a memorial service for his parents. Straightaway, that gave him a three-day jump on anyone wanting to follow him. The questions we have to answer are two. One: why did he want to run away; and two: where did he plan to go? First, however, can someone please explain to me why a boy with normal hearing was placed in a school for the deaf? This particular aspect of the case puzzles me.'

Strey and Armitage explained the unusual circumstances that

had led to Eric's initial enrolment and continued presence at Talbot Academy. 'Do you think he was happy here?' Cooper asked them, 'Because I don't.' They avoided the detective's gaze, but admitted that he probably wasn't.

'Okay, then,' Cooper continued. 'We know that Eric was unhappy. He'd been recently orphaned and then stuck in a school for the deaf, where he appears to have had no close friends. Am I right in thinking this, Mrs Armitage?' Mrs Armitage nodded. 'So, he decides to run away and, if I'm honest, I can't say that I blame the boy. But where does he go? Do any of you know of any friends or relatives Eric might have?'

'He has a distant uncle in New York,' Annandale said, 'but he's a ne'er-do-well and I'd be surprised if Eric had gone looking for him.'

'What do you mean by *ne'er-do-well*, Mr Annandale?' Cooper asked.

'A good-for-nothing, an idler,' Annandale answered.

'I know what the damn word means! What I want to know is *why* you describe him this way.'

'Well, Detective Cooper, he couldn't come to Eric's parents' funeral because he was in prison at the time, and the letter he wrote Eric was just plain strange, ungodly almost.'

'Do you remember his name?'

Annandale checked his notes. 'His name's Jeff Lawrence and the return address on the envelope was the Lyon Mt Correctional Facility.' Cooper made a note of this.

'We need to send out a description of Eric. I'll need a recent photograph, but what are his distinguishing features, things that might help people recognise him?'

'He's thirteen but looks nearer ten,' Strey said. 'And his hands are unusually wet.'

Cooper paused from taking notes and looked at Strey. 'Do you honestly believe he'll be travelling around the country shaking hands with people? Do you think he's on a book tour or something?'

Strey shrugged. 'I was just trying to be helpful, Detective Cooper. I don't think there's any call for sarcasm.'

'IT MIGHT BE WORTH MENTIONING THAT HE MAY BE MASQUERADING AS A HEARING-IMPAIRED PERSON,' Mrs Armitage said.

'I'll write down deaf for that,' Cooper said. 'No disrespect intended, Mrs Armitage, but if I write down hearing impaired, Joe Public's going to be looking for some kid with no ears. I'm afraid you always have to cater to the lowest common denominator when you write descriptions like this.'

Despite Cooper's energy and determination, the investigation into Eric's disappearance ground to a halt. Although the taxi driver remembered dropping Eric off near Union Square, and ticket clerks in San Francisco and Sacramento remembered selling one-way tickets to a boy matching Eric's description, the trail petered out in Roseville. The uncle that Annandale had mentioned told police sent to question him that he hadn't seen Eric since taking him to a Paul McCartney concert five years ago, and the prison's visiting log appeared to confirm this.

Seated at his desk that Monday afternoon, Cooper surmised that the boy could be anywhere. That Eric was about to approach Three Top Mountain with another runaway five times his age, never even crossed his mind.

The Fire Tower

Doc was about to light another cigarette when he saw Jack and Eric returning. He placed it carefully back in the pack and climbed on to the bus.

'There was a poster of Eric at the entrance to the services building,' Jack said. 'It's not the greatest of likenesses and the boy's not happy with it.'

'It makes me look stupid!' Eric protested.

'Jesus!' Doc said. 'It's not for your school yearbook, Eric! Thank God it is a poor likeness. Did anyone take an interest in him?'

'No. Most people just walk past those things, and his cycle helmet disguises his features. To be on the safe side, though, I think we should buy some hair dye – that white-blonde hair of his is too distinctive. I didn't know he was a runaway, did you?'

'Not until a few minutes ago,' Doc said.

They exited the interstate at US 11 and headed east towards the small town of Edinburg. There they left the highway and climbed into the George Washington National Forest. The road wound through dense woodland, its curves tight. They turned off on to a minor road and then on to an even more minor road. The hard surface turned to gravel, the gradients became steeper and the bends sharper.

'Are you sure about this, Bob?' Doc asked. 'These roads don't seem suited for a vehicle this size.'

'Sure I sure. Jus' gotta take care, is all. Make us a few three-point turns here an' there. It'll be worth it, man. You see if it ain't.'

Doc looked at the milometer on the bus and then at his watch. They'd travelled only twenty-two miles since leaving the interstate, and it had taken them close to an hour-and-a-half. 'How much further, is it?' he asked.

''Bout a mile,' Bob replied. He was right, but it would be another thirty minutes before he drew the bus to a halt and applied the handbrake.

'How do you know about this fire tower?' Jack asked him.

'Stumbled on it. I lived in these parts fo' a while, an' me an' a frien' used to ride out in the country when we got the chance.'

'What exactly did you ride out on?' Doc asked.

'A motorcycle,' Bob said, hurriedly climbing out of the bus. Doc stared after him, a look of disbelief on his face.

It was decided that Doc and Nancy would sleep in the bottom bunks of the bus's two-tier compartments. These beds had the advantage of greater headroom over the three-tier coffin bunks and would, Doc argued, lessen the likelihood of Nancy getting claustrophobia. At Eric's request, it was agreed that he would sleep in the bunk Susan had written her initials on at the top of one of the three tiers; Jack would sleep two bunks below him and Bob would take the bunk opposite Jack.

Once these arrangements had been settled, Bob took two large pizzas from the fridge and mixed a salad of greens and tomatoes with a dressing of oil and vinegar. Doc excused himself, and used the time to examine the medicines Bob had procured: pills and capsules of all shapes, sizes and colours, small phials of clear liquids and syringes. He read the leaflets carefully; made notes in a pad he carried with him and figured out a regimen he hoped would keep Nancy on an even keel. He then re-joined the group in the larger lounge, closest to the kitchen.

'Soun's like a piece o' work, yo' wife,' Bob said. 'Why you stay with her fo' so long, man? I'da hightailed it.'

'The boy,' Jack answered. 'Even though the two of us weren't exactly buddies, I thought maybe one day we would be. You know, father and son going fishing together – that kind of thing.'

'Did it happen?'

'No. It never happened because Laura didn't want it to happen. She went out of her way to keep us distant. There was maybe one time when I thought I was getting through to Conrad and then, out of nowhere, he gets this postcard from his dead hamster.'

'What you talkin' 'bout, man? How can a dead hamster write a pos'card?'

'Because Laura wrote it for him!'

'You need to explain it from the beginnin', Jack. I'm lost, an' I suspec' ever'one else is, too. You know what he's talkin' 'bout, Gene?' Doc indicated he didn't.

'Conrad had this hamster,' Jack began, 'and he called it Bingo. He'd had it for about six months when it died, and you might guess that I was the only one in the house when it happened.

'Laura and Conrad were out of town that weekend, visiting some friend of hers who was supposedly feeling lonely. I didn't want the hamster smelling up the house and I didn't want Conrad seeing it dead, either, so I did what anyone would have done. I wrapped it in bubble wrap and put it in the next door's garbage can.'

'Why the neighbour's?' Doc asked.

'Because if I'd put it in ours, Conrad would have gone rummaging for it and probably tried to give it the kiss of life. God knows what kind of disease he might have caught.

'So they get back and I tell them what's happened, and they

both break down in tears as if a person had died! I tell you, if it had been me that had died, they probably wouldn't have batted an eyelid and just got on with their lives. And what's more, they both looked at me as if I'd killed Bingo!

'Three weeks later, Conrad gets this postcard and I can still remember it word for word:

Dear Conrad: This is Bingo writing to you. Although
I'm dead now, I wanted you to know that I enjoyed living
with you and your mother. I didn't like your father though,
and he was the one that killed me. All the best, Bingo.

'That's just plain mean,' Nancy said, who had somehow managed to follow Jack's story. 'Accusing you of killing the boy's pet. That's awful.'

'Exactly!' Jack said. 'She had no way of knowing.'

'So, you did kill it? I thought you said you didn't.' Bob said.

'Only indirectly,' Jack replied.

'Jeez!'

'Don't you start, Doc. Hell, you just killed a dog, for God's sakes!'

'Mercy killing,' Doc said quickly, when he saw that all eyes had moved to him. 'So, what happened, Jack?' The eyes, as Doc had hoped, returned to Jack.

'You don't know what it was like living in that house. No one does. When it was just Laura and me, it was pretty much level-pegging. But then Conrad comes along and the pecking order changes: first Laura, then Conrad, then me. And then Laura buys a cat and the pecking order changes again: first, Laura, then Conrad, then Perseus and then me. That was bad enough, but then Conrad got Bingo and I slipped another rung down the ladder, and I was damned if I was going to play second fiddle to a hamster!

'The weekend they were away, I opened the door to Bingo's cage and then the front door of the house. I figured he'd shuffle his fat ass out of the house and find himself a new home somewhere else. But he didn't. Instead he toddled off into the kitchen and climbed into the clothes dryer where I'd just put a pair of sneakers I'd washed – probably mistook it for a larger version of the wheel he had in his cage. Believe me, I had no idea he was in there, and any noise he might have made was drowned by the tumbling of the sneakers.'

'This ain't gonna end well, is it?' Bob smiled.

'No,' Jack said. 'My sneakers got completely messed up. I had to throw them away.'

'I think Bob was referring to the hamster,' Doc said.

'Do we have to do this, Jack?' Eric asked. The meal had ended and Jack was applying black dye to Eric's hair.

'You're a man on the run, Eric, and we have to take precautions. If someone recognised you and stopped you from finding Susan, how would you feel then? Now keep still and keep your eyes closed.'

'But what if it stays this colour?'

'It won't. Your hair will grow back its normal shade. You've got good hair, too: thick and strong. I might borrow it sometime.'

Eric smiled. 'You say silly things, Jack. You can't borrow someone else's hair.'

Jack took a towel and wrapped it around Eric's head. They went to the lounge and sat next to each other on one of the couches.

'Did you like being a weatherman, Jack?' Eric asked.

'I like weather, but I didn't enjoy being a weatherman. Weathermen are always made out to be clowns.'

'Clowns scare me,' Eric said. 'I'm going to be a postman when I grow up.'

'Why a postman?'

'Because I'd bring people happiness every day: birthday cards and Christmas cards, letters from friends and presents.'

Eric had seemingly no concept of the rest of the mail he'd be delivering, Jack thought: utility bills, traffic fines, court summonses, tax demands, divorce papers and unwanted junk mail. 'Sounds good,' he said. 'Maybe I'll become a postman, too. I've nothing else planned. Maybe we could become postmen together.'

Eric smiled.

'Keep an eye on Nancy, will you, Jack? If she wakes up, tell her I've gone for a walk with Bob. I'll be back soon.'

Doc and Bob left the bus and climbed the metal stairs of the fire tower. The views had long since disappeared, but the distant lights and stars above made the ascent worthwhile.

'Pity we didn' get here while it was light, Gene – views is special. You cain't see nothin' now, but the Shenandoah Valley's down there, an' also the seven bends o' the North Fork River. You can see the Appalachians an' the Blue Ridge Mountains, too.'

'Maybe we'll get a chance in the morning,' Doc said. 'How's Marsha, by the way? She okay with you being here?'

'She fine 'bout it. Next time you visit though, she gonna sit you down an' give you lessons on telephone manners. Ev'dently, yo's ain't up to much.'

Doc smiled. 'Did you tell her what we were doing?'

'Kept it vague, man. Tol' her we was jus' helpin' out an ol' friend. No need fo' her to worry.'

The common denominator in Doc and Bob's early friendship had been Nancy, but Nancy was now an insoluble puzzle and the conversation turned to her. 'Still looks good, don't she?' Bob said. 'Hard to b'lieve, she ain't right.'

Doc nodded. 'It's the wiring inside her head that's the problem. It's shot to pieces. She knows this – or at least she used to – and that's why she wants to go back to Mississippi.'

'Hell, man, her head's gotta be messed up if she wan's to go back there. Las' place I'd wanna spend my final days.'

'She's got good memories of growing up there, and it's where her family's buried. She wants to be buried with them.'

'How long you think she got, Gene? How long b'fore she dies?'

Doc shrugged. 'There's no way of telling, but I'm guessing not long.'

'How you know that, man? Looks like she got a good few years yet. An' what you gonna do – jus' stay with her till she goes? People gonna be lookin' fo' you – you ever thought o' that?'

Doc shrugged.

'You ain't tellin' me somethin', Gene. There's somethin' you ain't sayin.'

Doc looked away. 'There's nothing to tell, Bob. Nancy wants to die in Mississippi.'

'It makes no sense, Gene. How you gonna hide yo'selves away an' not be foun'. They'll catch up with you, man, an' when they do they'll take her back to the home an' you to jail.'

'That won't happen, Bob. Nancy doesn't want it.'

'Square with me, Gene. What the two o' you plannin'?'

'Okay, Bob. But you can't tell Jack and you don't talk to Nancy about it. Agreed?'

Bob nodded.

'Nancy's been scared of Alzheimer's her whole life – it's been running in her family for generations. Back when we were at Duke, she asked me if I'd bring her life to an end if she ever inherited it – before the real shit kicked in. I promised her then that I would, and another time five years ago when she asked me again. I don't have a choice in the matter.'

Bob was taken aback. 'Sure you got a choice, man. An' you a doctor, Gene: you ain't suppose' to do things like this: you took the Oath!'

'You just reminded me earlier today that I wasn't a doctor, that I'd retired. Remember? I'm not acting as a doctor, Bob; I'm acting as her friend. Do you honestly think I'm happy about this?'

'But it's killin', Gene, an' killin's wrong!'

Doc turned to Bob, suddenly annoyed. 'How many people have you killed in your life, Bob? People who in all probability wanted to live? Nancy doesn't want to live, for Christ's sake!'

'That ain't fair, Gene, an' you knows it.'

Immediately, Doc regretted his words and apologised. 'I'm sorry, Bob. I didn't mean that. It's just that this isn't something I enjoy talking about – or thinking about for that matter.

'But let me ask you this. If you were on the battlefield and a friend of yours was mortally wounded, what would you do? Would you leave him to bleed out in agony or would you put him out of his misery – especially if he asked you to?'

'That ain't the same thing, Gene. This diff'rent.'

'But it isn't, Bob! It's exactly the same. All that's different is the time line. It will take Nancy something like five years to bleed out, and throughout that time she's going to be in the worst kind of agony you can imagine!'

'All I know, Gene, is that if Marsha aksed me the same thing, I'd say no. I'd stay with her, be there fo' her, but I wouldn' kill her. How could I? She the love o' my life.'

'You'd do it because she *was* the love of your life,' Doc said quietly.

Neither of them spoke for a while.

'So, you goin' through with it once we get to Coffeeville?'

Gene's shoulders slumped. The conversation was exhausting him. 'I wish I knew, Bob – I really wish I knew. I probably won't know for sure until we get there. It's what Nancy wants – or at least what she wanted when she was still Nancy – but is it something I want? No, it isn't. Is it something I can do? I really don't know.'

'I ain't gonna say no more on the matter, Gene, but when the time comes I hope you make the right decision: right fo' Nancy, but right fo' you, too. Nancy should never o' laid somethin' like this on you. Ain't right.'

They fell silent, lost in their own thoughts, staring at the flickering lights far below them.

'There is one thing, Bob,' Doc said eventually. 'Nancy wants this trip to be like a holiday. I can think of things to do in Nashville and Memphis, but I don't know of anything to do between here and there. Can you suggest anything?'

Bob thought for a while. 'Walton's Mountain ain't far from here, an'…'

'There *is* such a place?'

'Sure there is: over in Schuyler. An' there's Crawford, o' course. I got a packet fo' an' ol' friend o' mine still livin' there, so we got to go through there anyways. It's a nice place an' Nance'll like it. We could stay a couple days or so, if you like.'

'Who's the friend?'

'A guy called Merritt Crow. I stayed with him fo' a time when I got back from Cuba. You'll like him.'

Doc looked at him. 'Is there something about the packet you're not telling me?'

'No more 'n what you ain't tellin' me,' Bob smiled. 'I'll level with you though, Gene: it's marijuana. I guess we all got reasons not to be caught!'

Doc smiled. 'Okay, Walton's Mountain first and then we'll run some drugs into Crawford. Sounds like a plan.'

Eric was already in his bunk reading the Bible when they returned to the bus. He'd now completed the Books of Numbers, Deuteronomy, Joshua, Judges, Ruth and I Samuel, and the body count had risen by a further 356,825.

'Where's Eric got to?' Doc asked. 'And who's this dark handsome stranger sleeping in his bunk?'

'It's me, Doctor Gene!' Eric said excitedly. 'Jack dyed my hair. It looks good, doesn't it?'

'It does, Eric. Maybe tomorrow we can persuade Jack to dye your eyebrows too. You might want to take those gloves off, by the way. It'll give your hands a chance to breathe overnight.'

'Will do, Doctor Gene,' Eric answered.

Nancy and Jack sat facing each other in the lounge area, neither one speaking. 'Gene, thank goodness you've come back!' Nancy said, agitated. 'That man's been trying to kill me. He said he was going to put me in the washing machine!'

'I was only joking,' Jack said. 'Besides, there isn't a washing machine.'

'Jesus, Jack!' Doc said.

He went to a top cupboard in the kitchen and took two pills from a container. He filled a glass with water and gave it to Nancy. 'These will make you sleep well tonight, Nancy.'

She swallowed them one at a time, eyeing Doc suspiciously. 'You're not trying to kill me, are you?'

'Of course not,' he replied evenly.

He handed her a towel and the wash bag he'd packed, and brought her a nightgown to change into. He waited while she used the bathroom, and then led her to her bunk.

Eric was the last one to turn out his light. It was at night, in the quiet of his own bed, that he always felt most alone; remembered his parents and sometimes cried. He still found it hard to believe he'd never see them again, that they were gone from his life forever. For weeks after the funeral he'd fantasised that his parents were still alive and victims of a giant misunderstanding. Maybe Mr Annandale had identified the wrong bodies and mistaken two hideously deformed strangers for his mother and father. Maybe his parents were still in Egypt, lost in the desert and sheltering in the tent of a friendly Bedouin who lived by himself in the middle of a sand dune and didn't have a telephone. Maybe they'd lost their memories and joined a travelling circus and were training as trapeze artists. Maybe they'd been kidnapped by abductors who couldn't read or write and didn't know how to send a ransom note. Maybe, even, they'd converted to Islam and were now too embarrassed to return home and face disappointing Mr Annandale and The Reverend Pete.

But for all the maybes that passed through his head, the day eventually came when a single sad and definite truth lodged there: his parents were dead, now and for all time. Once he accepted this reality, he realised that he had to start looking to himself but, to be on the safe side, also decided to place his small frame in the hands of a loving God. If God was alert to the plights of tiny sparrows and lost sheep, then Eric was certain He'd bust a gut to help an orphan boy find his only cousin. Secure in this knowledge and insulated by his own naivety, he'd journeyed safely and without fear through a world inhabited by murderers, child molesters, muggers and kidnappers, and found only kindness and good turns. (If God wasn't looking out for Eric, then he was certainly having his fair share of good luck!)

He lay there thinking, counted his blessings, and wondered if Doc was like a modern-day Moses leading them to a Promised Land, and if he should amend his personal prayer list.

Every night, for as long as he could remember, Eric had recited the Lord's Prayer, and followed it with a short prayer his mother had taught him:

> *God bless Mummy, Daddy,*
> *Grandmas and Grandpas,*
> *Uncles, Aunts,*

Cousins and Everybody.
Please make Eric a good boy,
Amen

This night he made up his mind to refine the prayer. He'd never met his grandparents but decided to leave them on the list anyway. He had but one uncle, one cousin and, since Jeff's divorce, no aunts; he therefore decided to start blessing Jeff and Susan by name. He also decided to include the names of the people who'd helped him since the deaths of his parents: Red Dunbar, Lily Gomez, Larry Hicks and Big Guy; Otis Sistrunk, Doctor Gene, Mrs Skidmore and Jack. (Arthur and Alice Annandale, The Reverend Pete and Walter Strey, he felt, were covered by the general description *everybody.*) It pleased him that his new world was becoming populated.

He tried out his new prayer and liked it:

God bless Mummy, Daddy,
Grandmas and Grandpas,
Uncle Jeff and Cousin Susan,
Red Dunbar and Lily Gomez,
Larry Hicks and Big Guy,
Otis Sistrunk and Doctor Gene,
Mrs Skidmore, Jack,
and Everybody.
Please make Eric a good boy,
Amen

Leaving Three Top Mountain

A cold front had moved into the area overnight, lowering the temperature and shrouding the mountain in mist. It was now raining heavily, and pools of water had formed on the uneven surface of the road. Nancy had slept peacefully, but the change in weather appeared to depress her. Doc helped her dress and took her to the bathroom.

Bob was already in the kitchen, toasting bread and making coffee. He'd set a carton of orange juice on the counter and placed cups, bowls and packets of cereal on the table. 'How she doin', Gene?'

'To tell you the truth, I don't know. She slept well enough, but now she seems preoccupied, a bit otherworldly. I'm hoping she'll come to once she's properly woken up.'

They were joined by Jack and then Eric.

'Everyone sleep okay?' Doc asked. It seemed everyone had – apart from himself, that is. Nancy's voice came from the bathroom; Doc braced himself as the door opened and she came storming out.

'Did you buy this toilet paper, Arnold?' she challenged Doc. 'You're a cheapskate! Do you know that? My finger went straight through it. Why on earth did I ever marry you?'

Doc made a move towards her. 'Don't touch me! Take your goddamn hands away from me!' He stopped in his tracks. Eric hid behind Jack, but Bob pretended nothing untoward was happening: 'You wan' cereal or toast, Nance?'

'Toast please, Bob,' Nancy answered, and then sat in the lounge as if butter wouldn't melt in her mouth. 'Where's Gene?' she asked. 'Shouldn't he be getting up?' Doc volunteered to go find him, waited in the sleeping area for a couple of minutes and then wandered nonchalantly back into the kitchen. 'Morning, Nancy,' he said. 'Morning, everyone.'

'About time too, Gene,' Nancy said. 'We're about to eat breakfast!'

After the breakfast plates had been cleared, they prepared to leave the mountain.

'How are you going to turn the bus around?' Doc asked Bob.

'I ain't. I'm gonna follow the road down the other side o' the hill.'

'Have you been down there before?'

'No, but I'm guessin' it ain't no diff'rent from the road we jus' drove up.'

Bob started the engine, and carefully edged the bus down the single track dirt road that cut its way through the mountain. It was steeper than yesterday's road and took longer to navigate. Bob managed to get the bus around the first two curves, but came to an abrupt halt at the next turn – a hairpin.

'Hmmm. This ain't lookin' good, Gene. I could maybe get us roun' this one, but I'm wonderin' how many more o' these bends there is. Las' thing we need is to get the bus stuck. I think we need to send out a scoutin' party.'

'Hey Jack, can you walk down the road a distance and see what it's like down there?' Doc asked.

'Can I go with Jack, Doctor Gene?' Eric asked. 'I've got an umbrella.'

'Okay with me,' Jack said. 'Open the door, Bob.'

Bob opened the door and Jack walked straight into the hillside – a mere two inches from the opening – and bounced back into the bus. 'I guess I won't be leaving through this exit,' he said. 'Open the back door, will you?'

The problem of leaving the bus through the rear door was the polar opposite of trying to leave through the front door. Although there was nothing to prevent Jack from exiting the vehicle, neither was there any ground for him to rest his feet on: while the bus's wheels remained on the road, its body overhung a void. 'I'm going to need some help back here, Bob,' Jack shouted.

Bob joined him, and stood at the door scratching his head. 'I'll have to lower you,' he said. 'Take my hand.' Jack took it, and while Bob slowly lowered him, his feet searched for the hillside. 'Okay, Bob, I'm there. You can let go now.' Bob let go and Jack slithered down the slope to the road below.

Jack walked for a half mile before turning back. He disturbed a couple of white-tailed deer and a red-tailed hawk, but what he saw of the road told him it wouldn't be possible for the bus to descend any further. He climbed back to the rear entrance where Bob was waiting. 'Too many switchbacks, Bob. You'll never get the bus round them.'

There was no alternative but to reverse the bus up the road and back to where they'd started out. It wouldn't be easy.

'I need a point man front o' bus an' one at back,' Bob said. 'I'll lower you firs', Jack, an' then you, Gene.'

Jack found his footing and then waited for Doc to be lowered.

'Man, Gene, you mus' weigh the same as a damn elephan',' Bob gasped. 'Get ready to catch him, Jack, I cain't hol' him much longer.' He suddenly lost his grip and the weight of Doc sent both him and Jack sprawling down the hillside. 'You okay?' Bob shouted after them.

'I don't know about that,' Jack said, 'but we're alive – and Doc's going on a diet once we get back on the bus!'

'Jesus, I'm too old for these shenanigans,' Doc complained. 'Look at my pants!'

'You take the front and I'll take the back, Doc. You want a hand getting there?'

'No, I can manage. Why the hell did Bob have to drive down a road like this? We'll look well if the bus gets stuck.'

After they were both in position, Bob put the bus into reverse and slowly applied the accelerator. The front wheels skidded, eventually gripped, and the bus moved steadily backwards until Jack shouted out. 'You're going into the side of the hill, Bob!'

Bob let the bus slide forward, and then mistakenly applied the accelerator and sent Doc scurrying.

'Dammit, Bob, you almost killed me!' Doc shouted.

Bob broke into a smile, adjusted the turn of the wheel and reversed again.

Ever more mindful of the clay wall Bob had almost driven into, Jack completely forgot about the drop at the other side of the track, and before he'd noticed what was happening the nearside rear wheels slipped over the edge and the bus lurched.

'Holy shit!' Bob yelled, and immediately pressed the accelerator pedal to the floor. The bus juddered for a few seconds and then shot forward, hitting the hillside hard and sending Doc again running for cover.

Jack moved to the front of the bus to talk strategy with Doc and Bob. 'Do you think we should get help?' he suggested.

'We're not in a position to get help!' Doc retorted. 'We've got a kidnap and a runaway on board. And the bus is stolen!'

'I didn't know that,' Jack said.

'Neither did I till yesterday!'

'Don't go blamin' me – it was all I could get hol' of at such short notice! Anyway, it ain't as if the vehicle's hot. Bus was stole five years ago.' Bob said. 'No one'll be lookin' fo' it now.'

'Is there anything else either one of you thinks I should know?' Jack asked.

'I got drugs fo' a friend o' mine, but that's 'bout it.'

'Jesus Christ!' Jack exclaimed. 'If we ever get off this damn mountain, I'm going to dye *my* hair!'

Eventually they managed to get the bus back up the track, but it took them more than two hours of edging backwards, then forwards and then backwards again; sometimes moving a few feet and sometimes only inches. Surprisingly, the bus suffered only minor scratches and two small dents.

Back at the fire tower, Doc and Jack remained outside the bus while Bob executed a one-hundred-and-two-point manoeuvre – Eric counted each turn of the wheel. Eventually the bus was turned around, but another hour had now passed.

Nancy, who had slept through the excitement, woke up as Doc re-entered the lounge, his clothes wet and his pants covered in mud. 'What time is it, Gene?' she asked.

'Just gone noon,' Doc answered.

'How long have I been asleep?'

'About three hours, give or take.'

'And where are we now?'

'About two feet from where we were when you fell asleep!' Doc sighed.

The bus slowly retraced its steps to the interstate. 'You think they mighta mentioned some place that the road ain't suitable fo' vehicles like this,' Bob grumbled.

'They did,' Eric said. 'We passed a sign yesterday. It said: "WARNING – No Access to Trailers, Motor Homes and RVs".'

'Come to think, I did see a warnin' sign,' Bob said thoughtfully. 'Musta missed that bit.'

It took them a further two hours to reach the interstate, and they then continued their journey south. 'We can get us a late lunch in Staunton,' Bob said. 'I know a real good diner there.'

For the next sixty miles, Doc and Nancy snoozed. Jack went to the front of the bus and chatted with Bob, while Eric finished reading I Kings and updated his notebook: another 306,393 dead.

They arrived in Staunton and entered the diner. As Doc looked through the menu, he realised he was in his dream restaurant and saliva started to trickle from the corner of his mouth. He looked at his watch. 'Be ready to order when the waitress gets here,' he said. 'It's past two already and we need to get to Walton's Mountain before it closes. What time did you say it closed, Bob?'

''Bout six, I think.'

'Here she comes. I'll order for you, Nancy.'

Doc ordered first: meat loaf, mushroom gravy and green lima beans for him; pan fried chicken, mashed potatoes and green beans for Nancy – and a plate of corn bread for all to share. Bob opted for fried clams, turnip greens and pickled beets, while Jack picked out the pork ribs, yams and baked tomatoes.

'What are you going to eat, Eric?' Doc prompted him.

'I'll have the same as Jack,' Eric replied.

When the food had been eaten, Doc called the waitress back to the booth and everyone, except Nancy, ordered slices of pie: coconut cream, pecan, lemon and cherry.

Bob noticed Eric staring at the young waitress. 'You ol' hound dog, Eric. You checkin' out the waitress?' Eric turned as red as the washing-up gloves he was wearing and immediately denied it.

'Nothin' to be ashamed o', boy. She pretty as a picture. If I was fifty years younger, I'd be thinkin' o' movin' to Staunton an' eatin' all my meals here. Ha!'

While the others ate their pie, Nancy kept staring at a man sitting at the counter. He was wearing a light-coloured suit and appeared to be in his late fifties. 'Gene, I think that's my father,' she whispered. 'Why doesn't he come over?'

'Your father's dead, Nancy,' Doc said gently. 'It's probably just someone who reminds you of him.'

'My father's *not* dead, Gene. I know he never liked you, but there's no need for you to say such mean things about him. It's him! I wouldn't make a mistake like that.'

'Look at him, Nancy. He's younger than you are. How can he be your father?'

'You're being silly. He's not younger than I am. How old do you think I am?'

'You're four years younger than me, Nancy. You're just about to turn sixty-eight.' Nancy stared at him. Doc opened her purse, took out a small mirror and handed it to her. Nancy looked at the reflection. 'Oh my, Gene. I'm old. When did I get old like this?'

'When you weren't looking, Nancy. The same way we all did.'

'My parents are dead, then?'

'I'm afraid so, yes. My parents are dead, too, Nancy. So are Bob's and Jack's. And Eric's parents are also dead. We're all orphans here, Nancy. We have to take care of each other now.'

Afraid of how Nancy might react, he signalled for the waitress to bring the check. Nancy sat quietly, but still glanced at the man sitting at the counter.

'What yo' name, chil'?' Bob asked the waitress when she brought them the check.

'The same name that's on my badge,' she smiled.

'He doesn't read signs too well,' Jack said. 'You might just want to tell him and get it overed with.'

'Camille,' the girl answered.

'That a pretty name. I'm Otis, an' I wanna introduce you to a friend o' mine – this here is Eric.' Eric looked at her petrified, but Camille was kind and smiled at him.

'It's a pleasure to meet you, Eric,' she said, taking his hand and shaking it. 'I like your gloves.'

Eric's voice got stuck somewhere deep in his throat and he was unable to utter a single word.

'Your name's not Otis,' Nancy said. 'You shouldn't tell lies like that. The next thing you'll be saying is that you're white!'

'Okay, let's make a move,' Doc said quickly. 'Bob's got another mountain to drive up – and you know how long it takes him.'

He paid the bill in notes and left Camille a generous tip. As they left the diner, Nancy escaped from his arm and stepped towards the man sitting at the counter. When she got within range, she swung her bag and hit him hard on the back. In no uncertain terms she told him never to pretend to be her father again. 'It isn't funny!'

Doc took Nancy's arm and guided her firmly away from the man and towards the door. 'I'm sorry about that,' he turned and said to the man.

'Don't apologise to him, Gene,' Nancy snapped. 'That man's pure evil!'

The door closed shut behind them and the man at the counter was left wondering what the hell had just happened.

They headed east on Highway 250. 'This is a pretty town,' Nancy said, as the bus rolled through Waynesboro. 'I wonder who lives here.'

'My guess would be the people of Waynesboro,' Jack said.

They climbed into the Blue Ridge Mountains, heading first south on Highway 6 and then east. They passed vineyards at Cardinal Point and the first traces of kudzu. The area was still overwhelmingly wooded and the leaves were now starting to turn: splashes of red, orange, yellow and purple. They finished their journey on country roads and arrived at Walton's Mountain shortly after five. There were no visible lights and the car park was empty.

'Looks a bit quiet,' Doc said. 'Are you sure it's open?'

Bob climbed out of the bus and walked across the uneven surface of the car park to the entrance of an unprepossessing brick building. There was a notice board there with the opening hours printed on it: 10 am-4 pm.

'Damn, if it ain't shut,' Bob called.

'Try the door, Otis,' Eric called back. 'The Waltons never used to lock their door at night.'

Bob laughed at the boy's naivety, but turned the door's handle anyway. 'Well, I'll be…' he said.

The door opened.

J. PAUL HENDERSON

Walton's Mountain

The Waltons was a television series that aired 1972–81. In hour-long episodes, it told the story of an extended family living in the Blue Ridge Mountains of Virginia during the years of the Great Depression. The key to the series was young John Boy Walton, an aspiring writer, and his was the voice that introduced each week's episode – albeit, the voice of a grown-up John Boy now living in New York and recollecting his mountain days from the vantage point of an air-conditioned skyscraper. The times portrayed in the series were simpler and less complicated than the years of its broadcast, and the storyline of each episode was invariably positive: friends and neighbours pulling together to overcome personal and economic hardships. Every instalment ended with the Waltons tucked up in bed and saying goodnight to each other: 'Goodnight, John Boy; goodnight, Mary Ellen; goodnight, Jason; goodnight, Erin; goodnight…'

The programme became a ratings success, and television audiences found themselves longing to return to this bygone age of community. They coveted its certainty, and sought to recapture the time when God had been feared, values been traditional and families close-knit and loving. They hungered for the days when everyone had known and talked to each other and loneliness was only a word, and dreamt of finding a time warp, of climbing into it and travelling back to the time of *The Waltons*. They would turn their backs on the materialism and convenience of their present, and take with them only the barest of necessities, the one thing they still considered essential – nuclear weapons!

The utopian times they imagined, however, were distant, long-gone and destined never to return. That they were illusory and made of celluloid mattered little to the millions of viewers who watched the programme. For them, these times *had* existed, and each week they lost themselves in the lives and struggles of the people who lived on Walton's Mountain, and conveniently forgot that the actor playing Grandpa Walton had, at one time, been a member of the Communist Party.

Doc stood in the car park with his hands on his hips taking in their new surroundings. 'You're sure this is Walton's Mountain? It looks nothing like it.'

'It ain't the *actual* mountain, no,' Bob said. 'This is Walton's Mountain *Museum*. There's a diff'rence, but it's close you gonna get – realer 'n the real thing, anyways.' Doc waited for an explanation.

'The real thing's a sham, Gene – an' the mountain, too. House an' rest of it's in California, back o' Warner Bros Studios. This here,' he said, pointing to the brick building in front of them, 'is where Earl Hamner went to school. Schuyler's where he growed up an' he's the one what wrote *The Waltons*. It's his story, man. He's the real John Boy!'

'How do you know all this?'

'I read trash magazines. Buy 'em at the supermarket.'

Eric and Nancy joined them, Eric holding on to Nancy's hand. 'I said the door would be unlocked, Otis,' Eric said proudly. 'Did you hear me tell him, Doctor Gene?'

'I did, Eric. Now, where's Jack got to?'

'He's combing his hair.'

Doc rolled his eyes. He was about to go and get him when he saw his godson step from the bus pulling strands of hair from a comb and looking wistful.

'Come on, Jack! We haven't got all day.'

'The day's already gone, Doc. We've got the whole damn night to tour this place.'

They walked carefully into the old schoolhouse where Bob was searching the walls with the beam of a small torch. 'What are you looking for?' Doc asked.

'A light switch. How else we gonna see this place?'

He located a long row of switches and tested each one until satisfied with the degree of illumination. 'Man, I shoulda worked in the theatre fo' a livin': I gotta gift fo' this.'

They found themselves standing in a large school hall, empty but for a few tables. The old classrooms leading from it had been converted into replicas of rooms featured in the series: John Boy's bedroom, the Waltons' kitchen and living rooms, Ike Godsey's store and the Baldwin Sisters' recipe room.

They wandered from room to room, at first as a group and then in ones and twos. They walked into John Boy's bedroom and saw a writing table; moved on to Ike Godsey's store and saw an old crank telephone; entered the Waltons' living room and saw a radio, and in their kitchen, an ironing board. Finally, they went into the Baldwin Sisters' room and saw a sour mash whiskey still.

'Well, weren't that somethin'?' Bob laughed.

'Not really,' Jack replied. 'It looks like kids did it. I mean, we're not talking professionalism here, are we? More like enthusiastic amateurs. How much do they charge for this?'

'Seven bucks,' Bob said.

'I liked it,' Eric said enthusiastically. 'I saw John Boy's spectacles, his fountain pen *and* his typewriter. He used to write all the time – did you know that?'

'Sure, I knew it,' Jack said. 'Who could forget Mr Goody Two Shoes? I used to get tired of my parents telling me I should be more like him. The best day of my life was when he left the show.'

Doc joined them, slightly breathless. 'Have any of you seen Nancy?'

'I thought she was with you,' Jack answered.

'She was, but I lost her when she went to the restroom.'

'She musta gone back to one o' the rooms then, Gene. She ain't passed us by.'

Doc went in search of Nancy and found her rummaging through Ike Godsey's store, stuffing T-shirts, coffee mugs and fridge magnets into a plastic bag. 'We'll take these for the children, Gene. They'll be sorry to have missed this.'

'What children?'

Nancy looked at him as if he was being purposely obtuse. 'The children at Milton Hershey, of course! What other children would I be talking about? I teach there – or have you forgotten?'

'We can't take these things, Nancy. There's no one to pay.'

'You don't have to pay for them, silly. They're free. We're meant to take them.' The expression on Nancy's face became fixed, and she pulled the bag away from Doc, well out of his reach.

'Okay, Nancy, but we need to leave. The others are waiting for us.'

Nancy quickly helped herself to some postcards and then followed Doc into the main hall.

'Watch Nancy for a minute, will you, Bob?' Doc asked.

He then returned to Ike Godsey's store, peeled off five twenty dollar bills and placed them on the counter. He figured there was no need to add larceny to the list of charges they already faced.

They ate pizza again that evening, and after the meal had finished, Doc loosened the belt of his pants. He went to the sleeping area for the box where he kept Nancy's medicines. Eric and Nancy were chatting happily there, and Eric was now wearing a T-shirt Nancy had given him. It was mauve with a drawing of the Walton's house on the front (the one in California), and underneath it the inscription: *Good night Mama …'night Daddy … good night John Boy*. Nancy was telling Eric about the children in her class and Doc left just as Eric asked her if any of them had been deaf.

Doc still wasn't sure if the dosages he was prescribing Nancy were correct, or if the combinations he'd decided upon complemented or worked against each other. He'd noticed that her mood swings were sudden and unpredictable and that she agitated easily. This was certainly the nature of the disease, but even so, he should have been able to control it better. He sat down in the lounge and started to review the information accompanying the pills, amending his notes and recalculating dosages.

Seemingly apropos of nothing, Jack asked Doc what he thought of the name Zebulon, and if he'd had a son would he have ever considered calling him by that name.

'Why do you ask that?'

'Just curious. Why did you call your daughter Esther?'

'Beth came up with the name. She liked the sound of it – and I liked it too. Why?'

'Because there are times when I wish my parents had come up with something a bit more imaginative than Jack: it's a bit ordinary, isn't it?'

'You are ordinary. It suits you just fine. And if you think about

293

it, it could have been a lot worse: your dad was called Sydney and your grandfather was called Walter. The day they were born, they both sounded like they were eighty years old. You got off easy, kid. If you changed your name to Zebulon Guravitch, anyone seeing it written down would think you were a hundred and ten, never mind eighty. If I were you, I'd stick with Jack.'

'Yeah, I guess you're right. I must admit though, I do like the sound of Zebulon. You don't know what the name means, do you?'

'No, but Bob probably will. He seems to know all kinds of junk these days. Hey Bob, what's the derivation of Zebulon?'

'He was one o' Jacob's sons. Name means *intercourse*.'

'Maybe not Zebulon, then?' Jack concluded.

Doc drew the conversation to a close. 'Time to turn in, gentlemen. We need to be up early tomorrow morning and be ready to leave before anyone arrives. I'll use the bathroom first and get Nancy ready for bed.'

After the lights in the bus had been extinguished and they were lying in their beds preparing for sleep, a small voice rang out:

'Goodnight, Mrs Skidmore... goodnight, Doctor Gene... goodnight, Otis... goodnight, Jack.'

'Goodnight, Eric,' Doc said. 'Now, go to sleep.'

In the morning, Eric was gone.

Way Down Yonder

Bob was the first to notice Eric's absence. 'Where's Bible Boy at?' he asked, once everyone was dressed and in the kitchen.

'He's probably still in bed,' Jack replied. 'I'll go get him.'

Eric, however, wasn't in his bed or anywhere else on the bus. 'Where the hell's the boy got to?' Doc asked.

'I'll check outside,' Jack said. 'Maybe he's gone for a walk.'

Jack stood in the car park and listened. He called Eric's name but there was no response. He walked across the gravel to the museum and tried the door. It was locked. He looked around and saw an empty house across the road and below it a gift shop. He went to them and tried both doors but they too were locked. He called out Eric's name again, his voice travelling through the silence like wire through a slab of cheese.

'There's no sign of him, Doc,' Jack said, now slightly alarmed. 'You don't think he's run off, do you?'

'Why would he do that, and where would he go? We're in the middle of nowhere here, and his rucksack's still on the bus. He's got to be somewhere close. Did you try the museum? He might have gone back in there for a last look.'

'The door's locked. He can't be in there.'

'I was last out an' I didn' lock it,' Bob said. 'Left it jus' like we found it. Soun's like he gone back in an' the door's locked shut behind him. I'll come take a look with you.'

Jack and Bob circled the building, knocking on windows and shouting Eric's name. Still, there was no response.

'It's getting light and there'll be people driving by soon,' Jack said. 'Can't you break in or something?'

'Why you aks me that? A black man able to break in buildin's a white man cain't?'

'I didn't mean it that way, Bob. It's just that, well, you're more resourceful than we are.'

'An' how you figure that?'

'You found the light switch!' Jack said, somewhat unconvincingly.

They circled the building again and checked for any open windows. They found one at the rear, a high restroom window slightly proud of its frame. 'Do you think you'll be able to climb through it, Bob?'

'Hell no, I cain't fit through that! This a job fo' a skinny white boy.'

'I'm thinner than you are, but I'm not skinny. I'm not sure I could squeeze through it.'

'You the neares' thing we got, so stop yappin' an' climb on my shoulders.'

Bob squatted to allow Jack to clamber on to his shoulders and then slowly rose. Jack pushed at the window and it opened. He called out Eric's name again, but there was still no reply. He put his arms through the opening and then his head, slowly manoeuvring his body forward. His feet left Bob's shoulders and he continued wriggling until his hips caught.

'I'm stuck, Bob!' he yelled. 'You'll have to push me!'

'I cain't even reach you, man. You sure you stuck?'

'Of course I'm stuck! Do something for Christ's sake, will you! I'm in danger of losing my manhood.'

'I'll go get Gene,' Bob said, smiling.

Despite the seriousness of the situation and the increasing likelihood of having to leave Eric behind, Doc burst out laughing when he saw Jack's legs sticking through the window.

'This isn't funny!' Jack shouted.

'How's your hair, Jack? Is that okay?'

'Fuck off, Doc! Maybe you could do something useful and help Bob get me out of here before people start to arrive.'

'Boy's right, Gene. We need to get movin'. Climb on my shoulders an' then try an' ease him through the hole.'

Bob squatted again, but this time rose with much greater difficulty. 'Hell, Gene,' he gasped. 'Fo' a live man, you a dead muthafuckin' weight. Why you let yo'self get like this?'

Bob's legs started to wobble and Doc swayed dangerously. He grabbed on to Jack's legs to stop himself from toppling and Jack yelled. Doc apologised, but even now couldn't stop chuckling. He eased and pushed Jack's hips until they were free from the grasp of the frame, and his godson shot through the window. There was thump, followed by a loud groan.

'You okay, Jack?' Doc asked, for the first time concerned.

'What do you think? I've just fallen six feet on to a tiled floor!'

'He's okay,' Doc said, turning to Bob and smiling again. 'Bob and I will go back to the bus, Jack. We'll see you there.'

'But what if Eric isn't in here? What do we do then?'

'Let's have that conversation once we know. Now start looking!'

It was eerily quiet inside. Jack left the restroom and checked rooms as he came to them. Finally, and with relief, he found Eric sleeping soundly in John Boy's bed. There was a strange, almost serene look on the boy's face, but when Jack shook his shoulder and spoke his name, a look of acute pain crossed over it and Eric's body convulsed.

'Hey, Eric, wake up, kid. You're having a nightmare. We thought we'd lost you, little man.'

Eric's eyes opened and his body jerked upright. He was breathing heavily, palpitating and looked terrified. He scrambled out of the bed and rushed past Jack. 'What the hell was all that about?' Jack wondered. He straightened the sheets, tucked them into the bed and then smoothed the bedspread. Once he was sure all traces of Eric had been removed, he left the room, let himself out of the museum and returned to the bus.

'What's wrong with Eric?' Doc asked.

'I think he's had a nightmare,' Jack replied. 'Why?'

'He just dashed straight past everyone and into the bathroom. He's still in there.'

Jack knocked on the bathroom door. 'You okay in there, Eric? Need any help?' He thought he heard the sound of sobbing, but then Eric answered.

'I'm alright, Jack. I'll be out soon.'

'Okay, but watch your balance: the bus is about to set off. I'll leave your breakfast on the table and you can join us up front when you're ready.'

Bob was already sitting at the wheel, but Doc and Nancy were still in the rear lounge. 'Is he going to be alright by himself?' Nancy asked.

'I think so,' Jack replied. 'He just needs time to get over his dream.'

'I wonder what he was dreaming about.' Nancy mused. 'You should know, Gene. You're his father.'

'He's not my son, Nancy.'

'Is he my son, then?' Nancy asked.

'No, he's an orphan, Nancy. We're his friends. We're helping him find his cousin – she's going to look after him.'

'The poor boy,' she said. 'It must be awful not to have parents. I'll be glad when I see mine again. This time, I'm not leaving them.'

Bob started the bus. 'I think that track yonder might be a short cut to the main road. Might give it a try.'

'Just go back the way you came,' Doc said. 'We don't need a repeat of yesterday's performance.'

'You the boss man, Gene. Jus' tryin' to save you some gas money, is all.'

Bob drove the bus slowly down the deserted road and back in the direction of Highway 6. They'd decided to head west, connect with I151 and follow Skyline Drive along the crest of the Blue Ridge Mountains. There was little traffic, and little movement in the houses they passed. It was 6:45 am and the morning was overcast.

Eric joined them in the front lounge. He was unusually quiet and sat reading the Bible. Doc couldn't be sure from where he sat, but it appeared that Eric was reading the Book of Genesis again – the same verses over and over. He caught Eric's eye and smiled at him: 'You didn't lose count, did you?'

Eric was about to say something when his voice caught and he started to sob uncontrollably. Tears poured from his eyes and dripped from his cheeks on to his Walton's Mountain T-shirt. His small body quivered, and when he attempted to catch his breath he made strange, high-pitched braying noises. Jack went to Eric's side and pulled the boy towards him. 'It's okay, Eric. It's okay.' He waited for the emotion to drain, and once he'd felt the boy's body go limp in his arms, took hold of his red washing-up-gloved hand and led him to the rear lounge. Five minutes went by and then Jack returned by himself.

'He thinks he's dying and wants to talk to you, Doc. My guess is it's a New Orleans matter.'

When Doc joined the practice in Maryland, he entered a world of code and euphemism. The practice had been led by Paul Hargrove, a doctor in his early sixties, a native of the town and a man both traditional and obdurate in his views. He insisted that junior doctors follow his own dress code and wear dark suits, white shirts and bow ties. He was equally adamant that they have a smile on their face and a shine on their shoes (preferably black) at all times. 'The community looks up to us,' he admonished. 'We should neither disappoint nor offend them!' He warned them against public crapulence (a sackable offence), and encouraged them to attend church every Sunday – preferably the Episcopalian service.

When it came to examinations of patients below the waist, Hargrove was particularly stiff-necked: he wanted no mention of either penises or vaginas. Although he allowed for the fact that these were *bona fide* medical terms, he was emphatic in his belief that both caused offence and distress to patients. The only expression he would permit them to use was *Down Below*. He contended, however, that at heart he was a tolerant man, and would be willing to review the situation if any doctor were able to coin an equally anodyne representation of the subject matter at hand – or rather – down below. He doubted, however, that this was a possibility.

Doc had been one of two junior doctors in the practice. He found the whole idea of using the description *Down Below* ridiculous, but from a position of powerlessness proceeded to use the phrase and gave the matter little more thought. The other junior doctor, however, made it his mission in life to find an expression of equal blandness, and eventually proved successful. His first suggestion, that they use the term *South of the Border*, was rejected by Hargrove on the grounds that it was too Mexican. It was then he came up with the phrase *Way down Yonder*.

It was taken from *Way down Yonder in New Orleans*, a song written in the early nineteen-twenties and recorded by various artists. Freddy Cannon's version was the most recent, but the recording familiar to the doctor was Louis Armstrong's. He was listening to the album at home one evening and sat bolt upright when he heard the lyric:

> *Way down yonder in New Orleans*
> *in the land of dreamy scenes*
> *there's a Garden of Eden… you know what I mean*

Garden of Eden was the first phrase to resonate, but was quickly dismissed: Hargrove would have judged it too suggestive. But *Way down Yonder*, he believed, was in with a strong chance. He brought it up at the following day's practice meeting and Hargrove considered it carefully – longer than he usually considered such suggestions. Eventually, he shook his head. 'It's too black, too rural,' he said. 'But, repeat the first line again, will you?' The junior doctor did.

'What about *New Orleans*? Why don't we refer to *Down Below* as *New Orleans*?' Hargrove suggested. 'It's a city with a good reputation, it's in the south of the United States rather than Mexico, and they serve good food there, too. I like the idea!'

The junior doctor winked at Doc, and Doc smiled back. That night, they went to a local bar and celebrated the junior doctor's triumph.

Only once did the maxim cause confusion and then only after Doc had retired from practice. At the time he'd been walking through a department store and been accosted by a middle-aged woman. Her face was familiar, but he wasn't sure why.

'Hi, Doctor Chaney, how are you?' she'd said. 'I'm Gwen Collins. I used to be a patient of yours.'

'So you did, Gwen. I'm well thank you, and how are you?'

'There's been a terrible disaster in New Orleans, Dr Chaney!'

'I'm afraid you'll have to see your new doctor about that, Gwen – I'm retired these days. Good luck to you.' And with that, he'd walked briskly away. It was only after he'd returned home and listened to CNN that he realised she'd been talking about Hurricane Katrina.

Doc walked to the rear of the bus where Eric was sitting. The boy was calmer now but still visibly upset. He sat beside him and, in a practised bedside manner, asked Eric what was troubling him. His style was both sympathetic and disarming; worthy of first place in any medical death bed competition, and it therefore surprised him when Eric burst into tears again.

Eric had been woken during the night by the sounds of Doc and Bob snoring. He was on the verge of falling back to sleep again when Nancy had started to make strange whimpering noises, and Jack to talk in his sleep: 'Tell it to my ex-wife, buddy... You try telling her... Fuck Bingo... Heavy downpours tomorrow, folks: don't forget your umbrellas.' The noises disquieted him and made him think of the empty bed in John Boy's room. Careful not to disturb Jack, he'd climbed down from the bunk, quietly put on his sneakers and walked the short distance to the brick schoolhouse. Once there, he'd made his way to John Boy's room and climbed into bed. Within minutes he was fast asleep.

He told Doc he'd been dreaming, but remained tight-lipped as to the exact nature of his dream. All he would say was that his thing down there – pointing to his pecker – had grown in size and, as he awoke, sticky stuff had started to spurt from it. He knew from the accompanying sensation that something bad had happened, that he'd done wrong and would now probably die.

Doc smiled at Eric. 'You needn't worry yourself about this, young man. It's all part of growing up: it happens to everybody. It's happened to me, it's happened to Bob and it's happened to Jack. What you had was a wet dream. They just happen. But tell me, why do you think something bad happened?'

'It felt too good to be right,' Eric said. 'And in the Bible it says that God kills people for this. He killed a man called Onan.'

'I don't know much about Onan, Eric; but Bob, Jack and I are all still alive: He hasn't killed us. You mustn't worry and get yourself upset over something as unimportant as this. You haven't done anything wrong and believe me, it *will* happen again. Like it or not, it's going to be a part of your life from now on.'

Eric went to the bathroom to wash his face and Doc returned to the others. Jack looked at him expectantly.

'You're Jewish, Jack: what do you know about Onan?'

'Why would I know any more about onions than the next person, just because I'm Jewish? It's a vegetable and it's used for cooking. What more is there to know?'

'Not onions, you dimwit – Onan! He was a vegetable of the Biblical variety and God cooked him. *Now* does his name ring a bell?'

'I've never heard of him. You know my family was never practising. I'm not sure we even had a Torah in the house, let alone a Bible.'

Doc turned to Bob: 'Hey, Bob. Do you know anything about Onan?'

'Know all 'bout the man. People think he was a masturbator but he weren't: he was a birth control man. Used to withdraw his John Thomas b'fore he came, an' that's why his seed splashed on the ground. It mo' likely Eric thinks he did somethin' ungodly 'cos he left a stain in John Boy's bed. Ha!'

'The boy's growing up, Jack,' Doc said. 'He needs to know the facts of life. You're closest to him in age and the two of you seem to be hitting it off. I think he'd be more comfortable hearing them from you than he would from either me or Bob. How about it?'

'Jesus, Doc! Do I have to? I've never done anything like this before in my life, and to tell you the truth, I'm not sure I even know all the facts.'

'You know enough – and I'm counting on you. Do it now, will you? He's in the back lounge and the occasion seems right.'

Jack grimaced, but got to his feet and walked slowly to the rear of the bus. Forty minutes later the two of them returned, Jack as red as a beetroot and Eric as white as a sheet.

'Don't even ask!' Jack said to Doc. He sat down and folded his arms. Eric sat beside him and opened the Bible. Doc was relieved to see him reading II Kings.

An Aura of Fake and the Smell of Horseshit

The fog thickened, and any views they might have enjoyed from the ridge were effectively blanketed. They decided to turn off Skyline Drive and head back to the interstate. It was a good decision: there were checkpoints on the road ahead, and if Bob had troubled himself to read the signs, he would have known that their vehicle had no actual right being on the road.

They descended the steep side of the mountain and followed a route that took them through Augusta and Rockbridge counties and past the small communities of Steeles Tavern and Vesuvius. They rejoined the interstate close to Buena Vista and followed it south, merging seamlessly into a stream of trucks and buses heading in the same direction. The tour bus, Doc was pleased to note, blended right in.

The interstate was a world unto itself, dotted with visitors' centres, rest areas and exit developments more thriving than the towns they served. Like old-fashioned barkers standing outside a club, unremitting billboards touted for custom and tempted motorists to leave the interstate and spend money at nearby attractions. Towns proclaimed themselves to be the birth, residency or burial place of past presidents, generals and other notables: Woodrow Wilson, Robert E Lee and Stonewall Jackson among them. They left the I81 at Christiansburg, where Davy Crockett had once worked in a hatter's shop, and headed towards the small town of Crawford. Or, at least – it used to be small.

'Man, this place has growed,' Bob said. 'Used to be way smaller 'n this.'

'How long has it been since you were here?' Jack asked.

'Forty years – maybe more.'

'And you're *surprised* it's changed?'

'Surprised it's bigger, yeah. If anythin', I thought it woulda been smaller.'

'It's still not big though, is it?' Doc said.

'Maybe not to you, but it sure ain't the same.'

Bob pulled into Merritt's driveway and parked at the rear of the house. Taking a slip of paper from his pocket, he punched the numbers written there into his cell phone. 'We arrived an' parked up, Merritt. You wan' us to wait here fo' you?' He then hung up.

'Did you just leave him a message?' Doc asked.

'Didn't need to. I was talkin' to the man.'

'That was a conversation?' Jack asked, somewhat incredulous. 'How long has it been since you've seen him?'

''Bout forty years, but we talk an' stuff. He don't like usin' phones.'

'So what's the plan? Do we wait here?'

'Yeah: he says he'll be right over. Jus' needs to lock up.'

Crawford had changed. The town's population had maybe quadrupled in size since Bob had lived there, and Merritt's house

– which had been on the outskirts – was now almost at its centre. Developers and realtors were in the ascendant, and old downtown buildings had either been gentrified or torn down and replaced by newer structures in the style of *fucking twee*. In the name of progress, the old era had been pushed to one side and superseded by a fake New Age of organic foods, complementary medicines, low carbon footprints and a contrived spirit of togetherness. The past had been re-written, and all traces of hippy drug culture erased from the town's history as ruthlessly as images of disgraced Politburo members in the time of Stalin had been wiped from official photographs.

Although by any standards the town was still small, it now gave the impression of a town flexing its muscles, a town preparing itself for bigger and better things. A powerful PR machine promoted the area's natural beauty, its music and its art. It encouraged people to visit the town, stay overnight in one of the many bed-and-breakfast establishments, eat in its restaurants and sample its wineries. It organised beer and wine festivals; orchestrated markets that sold gourmet, health and organic foods; and arranged activities that exemplified the area's commitment to rural living: how to make apple butter, how to dry fruits and vegetables, how to husk corn.

The dumping ground for all such information was the town's Chamber of Commerce, a small shop front located on Main Street and staffed by volunteers and part-time employees on minimum wage. Merritt Crow belonged to the latter category and had few qualms about leaving the office thirty minutes early. He stuck a notice to the inside of the glass door apologising for any inconvenience, grabbed his cane and set off in the direction of home. It was only a short walk and took less than ten minutes. He stopped at the entrance to his driveway and looked down. 'Goddamn son-of-a-bitch!' he muttered, and then walked to the rear of the house.

'Goddamn, Merritt! You look like a muthafuckin' elephant! What happened to yo' ears, man?' Bob exclaimed.

'Is that any way to greet an old friend, T-Bone? Now come here and give this man a hug!'

Jack's explanation of the facts of life was still fresh in Eric's mind, and on seeing the two men embrace he turned to his older friend. 'Are they happy?' he mouthed quietly.

'I should think so,' Jack said. 'From what Bob said, they haven't seen each other for forty years.'

'No, I mean… are they happy men, those men who…?'

It suddenly dawned on Jack what Eric was talking about. 'The word's *gay*, Eric, not *happy,* and no, they're not gay, not a chance of it. It's okay for men to hug each other. It's the other stuff…'

'I see your conversation with Eric went well,' Doc said.

'At least I *had* the conversation!' Jack responded. 'I didn't hear you volunteering.'

'Hey! Come an' meet Merritt Crow,' Bob called to them. 'An' don't go mentionin' his ears, neither – man appears to be sensitive 'bout 'em.'

Merritt smiled and asked them to follow him to the front of the house. Eric couldn't take his eyes off the man's ears and from a safe distance again whispered to Jack. 'Have you seen the size of his ears?'

'Yeah,' Jack whispered back. 'They look like ping-pong paddles, don't they?'

Merritt's ears were the same size they'd always been. When Bob had known him, Merritt's hair had been long and covered his ears. Bob had only ever seen their tips and had been completely unaware of the giant icebergs lurking below.

'Why we not usin' the back door?' Bob asked.

'I want to show you something,' Merritt explained. 'Get your opinion on it.'

He stopped at the entrance to the drive at the same spot where he'd hesitated only a few minutes earlier. 'Look at this shit, will you?'

The six of them gathered around a large pile of excrement and stood there like mourners at an open grave.

'Why we standin' here lookin' at a pile o' horseshit, Merritt? This a new touris' 'traction or somethin'?'

'Every day a guy rides by my house with a towel on his head, and every day his horse takes a dump here. The one time I saw it happen, I grabbed hold of the horse's reins and gave the man a piece of my mind, asked him what the hell he thought he was doing. I told him he should carry a shovel with him, stick the shit in his saddle bags and take it home with him. If he'd been walking a dog he'd have had to have done that, and that horse of his drops the equivalent of two months' dog shit at a time!'

'Who's the man an' what the towel 'bout? He an Arab?'

'No, his name's Spencer Havercroft. He's one of the realtors in town and a vain son-of-a-bitch. Every morning he washes his hair, wraps it in a towel and rides into town to get it blow-dried and waved at one of the salons. They shape it into something like a surfing wave that's just about to break – a bit like that guy in *Hawaii Five-O*.'

'Jack Lord,' Nancy said absent-mindedly. 'I don't remember him riding a horse, though.'

'Maybe he rode seahorses, Mrs Skidmore,' Eric suggested helpfully.

Merritt looked confused for a second, but continued. 'He's a tightwad, too. All his money and he still washes his own hair to save himself a few bucks at the salon…

'Anyway, he won't apologise and he won't change his ways. He told me I should pay him for his horse's trouble; how horseshit's a valuable commodity these days and I should put it on my roses. I asked him if he saw any roses in my garden. He said he didn't, but then told me I should go and buy some and brighten the place up. He said my house was letting the whole town down, disgracing the community. "If you ever decide to sell it," he said, "let me know and I'll send in the bulldozers." I told him he could fuck off, and then the horse reared and knocked me over. That's how I sprained my damned ankle,' he said, pointing to the bone with his cane.

'Anyway, I've got a councillor coming round tomorrow and I'm going to take the matter up with her… shall we go inside?'

Entering Merritt's house, for Bob, was like entering a time capsule: the room was smaller than he remembered, but otherwise absolutely nothing appeared to have changed. A guilty thought crossed his mind: Merritt's living room was little different from Fred Finkel's.

'Surprised?' Merritt asked, noticing the expression on Bob's face.

'Kinda,' Bob said, 'I thought it mighta changed some.'

Merritt smiled at him. 'Oh but it has, T-Bone. The house has been completely reconfigured. The room we're standing in now is for show. It's where I receive unwanted callers, and this is where I'll receive the council woman tomorrow – even though it's me that's asked her here. Remember that door there?' He pointed with his stick to a door on the far wall.

'Sure I remem'er. Leads into the backyard.'

'Not anymore,' Merritt replied.

He opened the door and revealed to his guests a large open-planned living space. Its style was modern and its furnishings expensive: large couches, comfortable armchairs, metal framed tables with glass tops, polished oak floorboards and oriental rugs. Two life-sized crow sculptures stared down on the room from roosts close to the ceiling, one carved from bog oak and the other assembled from pieces of felt, leather and metal, and a large ceramic hippopotamus stared languidly from a corner position.

To one side of the room was a kitchen area with a tiled floor, granite worktops and state-of-the-art appliances, and leading from it – and back into the original building – a hallway with doors to three bedrooms and a marble-floored bathroom.

'It's Italian,' Merritt said when he saw them admiring the bathroom floor. 'Cost a small fortune but worth every cent. Laid it myself.'

'Okay if we take a shower, Merritt? None of us has showered fo' two days, an' though I b'lieve my own scent to be a thing o' natural beauty, I ain't so sure 'bout Gene an' the others.'

'Sure, it's okay. And take any clothes you need laundering into the utility room. Decide amongst yourselves who's going to sleep in the bedrooms and who'll take the couches. I'll go get some towels.'

It was decided that Doc and Nancy would sleep in one of the two available bedrooms, Bob in the other, and that Jack and Eric would remain on the bus.

'Y'all go ahead,' Bob said. 'I'm gonna talk to Merritt an' find out what he done to my damn house while I been away – and, more to the point, how the hell he paid fo' it all.'

Merritt grasped the opportunity to explain the new spatial arrangements with both hands: it had been a labour of love that had taken him more than twenty years to complete. 'I had some help in the early days, but once the structural work was completed, I pretty much did it on my own. It took a while, but I enjoyed doing it and it kept me occupied.'

After Bob had left Crawford for Seattle, Merritt had set up a small building services company and found work easy to come by. He'd built extensions, made renovations, installed bathrooms and kitchens, repaired roofs and painted houses. His rates had been reasonable and his reputation had grown by word of mouth. He'd made a good living. His needs had been few and he lived frugally; the money he saved he invested in his own property, never once stinting on the quality of materials used and never cutting corners. The only thing Merritt wished for now was that the house was located elsewhere – some place other than Crawford.

'You done good, Merritt, 'specially fo' a man who don't look strong enough to lift a hammer. I fixed up an ol' cabin in the Klamath Mountains, but it ain't near as well finished as this. If I'da knowed you was this good, I'da hired you myself.'

Doc walked into the room. 'That's an excellent shower you have there, Merritt – blew the cobwebs right off. The bathroom's free now, Bob, if you want to get cleaned up.'

Bob went to the bus for his wash bag and then to the bathroom. The sound of his voice carried over the noise of the water: *Drove into Crawford, I got them Crawford blues, Drove into Crawford...* 'Quite a tunesmith, isn't he?' Doc said to Merritt.

'It's a damn sight more melodic than his humming,' Merritt laughed. 'He just about drove me crazy with that buzzing noise of his when he lived here.'

'And I'll bet he always denied he was humming, right?'

'Always did,' Merritt said. 'Beats me how he ended up with a good-looking girl like Marsha. I'm figuring she's deaf or something.'

Doc laughed. 'I appreciate you putting us up, Merritt. I don't know if Bob's told you, but Nancy's not doing too good. She has dementia, so her behaviour's a bit unpredictable. Don't take any notice if she says mean things to you: she won't intend them.'

'There's nothing to thank me for, Gene: I'm glad of the company. And don't go worrying about Nancy, either. I've had a couple of friends go down the same hill she's going down, so I know the drill.'

'I wish I did,' Doc replied solemnly. 'I'm still trying to figure out her medication but, touch wood, I think we're heading in the right direction. She's had a good day today... can we take you out to dinner tonight, by the way?'

'No need, Gene. I've got a ham baking in the oven and you'll be my guests this evening. Maybe tomorrow night.'

'It's a deal,' Doc said.

'What's a deal?' Jack asked. He and Eric had just entered the room.

'Life,' Doc replied.

Alex with a Kiss

After the others had retired for the night, Bob and Merritt poured the remaining wine into their glasses and moved into the living room.

'You got the marijuana?' Merritt asked.

'Yeah, medicinal quality, too: courtesy o' the state government of Oregon. But how come you cain't get it here no mo'? Used to be easier 'n gettin' a carton o' milk.'

'The place has changed, T-Bone,' Merritt bemoaned. 'It used to be a frontier town but not anymore. It's all law-abiding now, cleaner than Caesar's wife. A bunch of new people moved in and took over. They know about the town's past, but they don't want anything to do with it. They've eradicated everything that made it special. Said it was bad for business, bad for the town's image and the community's future.

'Community's the big word 'round here these days. I hate that fucking word! We're supposed to care for each other and be able to put a name to every face we see. In our day, everyone used to keep to themselves and mind their own business, and that's the way I liked it. No one pried, asked you for your life story or your five-year plan. People had secrets to keep, pasts they'd rather forget and they figured that other people did too. Now it's all gone topsy-turvy, and we're expected to tell everyone our business and spill our goddamned guts to complete strangers.

'These days the place is chock full of do-gooders and busybodies, doing their own kind of good and interfering in peoples' lives without a person's say-so. If I was younger, I'd move, but it's too late for that so I guess I'll just have to die here and hope to God I inconvenience them – not that any of them here believes in death. They seem to think that perfumed candles and a bunch of wrist bands will keep them going for ever. Fucking idiots, the lot of 'em!'

'Man alive!' Bob said. 'An' all I was thinkin' was it bigger.'

'It's bigger, too,' Merritt said. 'Once was I could just reverse into the road and not worry about colliding with a passing car. Nowadays I've got to look before I back out of the drive. I tell you though, I'm sorely tempted to wait for that Spencer guy and just slam my damn car into his horse – plead senility or deafness or something. If I did do that though, you can bet your bottom dollar they'd have me in a nursing home before either of us could blink. My disappearance would be just another part of the beautification process.'

'That's what they did with Nancy,' Bob said. 'An' all she did was leave her house door open an' go fo' a walk. You kill a horse an' they'll more 'n likely strap you in a chair an' shoot bolts o' 'lectricity through yo' body. You don't wanna go endin' yo' journey that way. Ha!'

'I hate that fucking word, too' Merritt said.

'What word?'

'Journey! I hate it almost as much as I hate the word community, or when some numskull mother refers to her daughter as her best friend. Every last one of these sapheads has been on a damned journey. They cross the road and they think they've been on a journey; they see some guy whittling a piece of wood on his porch and that's another journey; and they pass some old crone taking a dog for a walk and they describe that as a journey, too. You and me, T-Bone, we've been on journeys; these people just rattle around inside their own empty heads and go nowhere.'

Nancy slept well that night and woke refreshed. Doc's sleep, however, had been more fitful than usual. The last time he'd slept with a woman had been the night he'd slept with Beth, and the following day she'd been killed. He hadn't been able to relax. It wasn't that he believed any woman he slept with would die the next day, but he found himself forever looking over at Nancy and checking on her. Every time she moved or made a whimpering noise, he worried she would wake up and wonder who the hell he was, what he was doing in the same bed as her and start screaming.

Over breakfast, Merritt broached the subject of rum buns. 'I don't suppose any of you knows how to make them?'

'I know how to make them,' Nancy said. 'They're easy as pie.'

'You do? I don't suppose you'd make some while you're here, would you, Nancy?'

'I'll be glad to, Granddad,' Nancy replied. 'Let me take a look through your cupboards and see what ingredients you have and what you're missing, and Gene and I will go to the store and buy what's necessary. Is that alright with you, Gene?'

'Sure. It'll give us a chance to see the town. How do you know how to make these buns? I've never even heard of them.'

'Arnold grew up in Washington DC,' Nancy replied. 'He loved rum buns.'

Doc took hold of Nancy's arm and they walked the short distance to the town's centre. The day had yet to warm up and the temperature still hovered in the low forties. The sun looked more like a lozenge with the goodness sucked out of it than a potential source of heat. Nancy's nose had started to turn red, but she was smiling. 'What a beautiful day this is,' she said to him. 'It reminds me of Mississippi.'

The streets of the town were dominated by studios that sold

ceramics, jewellery, lutes, stained glass, textiles and wood carvings; and galleries that exhibited the work of local artists: acrylics, charcoals, oils, pastels and watercolours. Interspersed were coffee shops, bookshops, fabric stores and a large country store selling food and clothing.

Doc and Nancy looked around several of the galleries and studios but didn't buy anything – what point would there have been at their time of life? They stepped into a small restaurant and ordered coffee and cake.

'I'm enjoying today, Gene. I like this town. Did Bob used to drive buses here, too?'

'Not that I'm aware of. I don't think they have buses.'

'After all the unpleasantness the three of us went through, I wonder why he decided to become a bus driver. I don't think I ever went on a bus again.'

'You remember the trip?' Doc asked.

'It's not something you easily forget, Gene. I've never been as embarrassed as when that driver came to look at our tickets and we didn't have any. Do you remember how he made us get off the bus and then set it on fire?'

Doc often found it easier to go with the flow than correct Nancy's memories. They did no harm. He did, however, miss the time when he'd felt free to tease her and make jokes at her expense. But there was a mountain between now and then and, for him, these were only half conversations. He was as much an onlooker as an interested party.

'Did you ever tell your parents about the bus ride?' Nancy asked.

'Sure I did, didn't you?'

'I'm not sure. I think my father was sympathetic to buses, but he never felt free to express his opinions publicly. I don't think many people in Mississippi did, either. And, of course, Arnold hated them. He was concerned by the amount of gas they guzzled and said they were bad for the environment. That man! He was always concerned about resources.'

'Do you think Arnold ever thought that perhaps you were the most precious resource in the world, Nancy?'

'What a sweet thing to say, Gene. I really don't know.'

'Well you are, and never forget that. Now let's go to the store and buy those ingredients. You have some baking to do.'

They were the only customers in the country store. Doc took out the piece of paper Nancy had written on and read through the list with difficulty. They were looking for raisins, cinnamon, icing sugar, nutmeg and a bottle of Myers's Rum – Jamaican dark rum blended from nine other rums. Nancy had insisted on this brand.

They found what they were looking for and took them to the old-fashioned check-out. 'Make sure this time that you pay for these items, Gene,' Nancy said. 'We're not on Walton's Mountain now!' She looked at the two women behind the counter and gave them a conspiratorial wink, as if to say: *Men! What can you do with them?* The women laughed and fell into conversation with Nancy. Doc, meanwhile, counted out the money and placed it on the counter.

'What do you think of our bear, Nancy?' one of the women asked her. 'It's the town's mascot.'

'It's the most beautiful bear I've ever seen,' Nancy said. 'I wish it were mine.'

Doc looked at the bear and wondered if it was the same bear Nancy was looking at. What beauty could there possibly be in a cheap-looking black bear dressed in a Crawford T-shirt and holding a Crawford pennant in its paw? At best, it belonged in a fairground: a prize for some young sap trying to impress his girlfriend.

The two women had fallen in love with Nancy: in their book, there was no person more lovable than a mild-mannered senior citizen as dumb and undemanding as they were. As Nancy walked towards the door, however, her demeanour changed, and all sweetness and light disappeared. She turned to the two smiling women and called out to them: 'Someone should set fire to that bear,' she said. 'It's as ugly as sin! And don't expect me to shop here again! Come on, Gene,' she commanded. 'We have rum buns to make.'

Doc shrugged his shoulders and gave the women an

apologetic smile, as if to say: '*I'm just a man. What can I do?*'

It was just after eleven thirty when Councillor Alexx Calhoun knocked on the door. 'Hi, Merritt,' she said breezily, walking into the old lounge. 'My oh my, what did this room do to upset you?'

'I didn't ask you here to discuss my living room, Alexx. It's Spencer Havercroft that pisses me off, not the room. This is a friend of mine, by the way.'

'Hi, Merritt's friend! My name's Alexx. Alexx with two Xs.'

'T-Bone Tribble,' Bob replied, holding out his hand. 'Two Ts, three Bs.'

'Alexx is from Portland,' Merritt said. 'She moved here two years ago.'

'Portland, Maine, or the main Portland?' Bob asked.

'Portland, Oregon,' Alexx said hesitantly. 'I only had one X to my name then, though.'

Alexx was an overly cheerful birdlike creature closing in on sixty. When she'd been fifty-five, a man called Mike Calhoun had walked into the bar where she spent her evenings and stumbled into her life. Mike had been on vacation with his wife and son visiting her brother and his family. They'd been there only two days when his wife informed him that she wanted a divorce: she was tired of Crawford and tired of him. In particular, she was tired of him sharing their private lives with everyone else living in Crawford. 'If I want people to know I haven't had an orgasm in fifteen years,' she'd said, 'then I'll tell them myself. I don't need you to tell them for me!'

'Honey, I had...'

'Forget it, Mike. It's over!'

'It came right out of the blue,' Mike said to Alexx. 'I had no idea she felt that way.'

Alexx had gone to the bar to buy a round of drinks when Mike had struck up the conversation. He'd been sitting on a stool next to where she was standing, and had just started to pour out his troubles. Alexx had delivered the drinks to her friends, returned to the bar and then sat on the stool next to Mike. She had remained there for the rest of the evening, while Mike told her of

Crawford and the beauty of the Blue Ridge Mountains. 'You should visit,' he said.

A year later she did. After meeting in the bar, she and Mike emailed every day and talked on the phone every other day. Alexx fell in love with Mike and, after visiting the town, also fell in love with Crawford. It was then that she added another X to her name – a kiss for Mike, a kiss for Crawford and a kiss to the world. She went back to Portland, handed in her notice and a month later returned to Crawford and moved in with Mike Calhoun. Two years after arriving in the town, she ran for office and was elected to the council. Shortly thereafter, she received a phone call from Merritt Crow, who wanted to discuss the matter of horseshit with her.

'There's nothing I can do about this, Merritt. There's no ordinance that covers it.'

'Then tell me why there's an ordinance covering dog shit,' Merritt replied.

'Because there are more of them,' Alexx replied. 'They're domestic pets and they live among us.'

'What's a horse then – a wild animal?'

Alexx thought for a moment. 'Not a wild animal – I'd say it was more of a trained animal.'

'Then why can't Havercroft train it not to take a dump outside my house every morning? It strikes me he's trained it to do just the opposite!'

'Oh, I'm sure he hasn't, Merritt. I know Spencer, and he's not that kind of person. It's coincidence, that's all it can be. What I'll do though is have a quiet word with him and tell him of your concerns.'

'He already knows about my concerns, Alexx. He just doesn't care about them! He's more worried about the paint on my house than he is me.'

'Hmmm. Well, as a matter of fact, Merritt, your house has been mentioned by a few people. It is a bit of an eyesore, isn't it? I'm sure if you gave it a lick of paint, Spencer would look upon it as a gesture of goodwill and maybe do something about his horse. It's worth a try, don't you think?'

Merritt sat there grinding his teeth and Bob started to hum.

Alexx's discomfort was spared, however, when Jack and Eric walked into the room. 'I'm going to take Eric into town and buy him some undershorts and T-shirts,' Jack announced.

Alexx stood up and held out her hand. 'Hi, I'm Alexx – two Xs. The second X is a kiss.'

To avoid any awkward questions, Bob saw fit to introduce Jack and Eric as uncle and nephew. Alexx insisted they sit and join them for a while, determined to bring the conversation about Spencer Havercroft's horse to an end.

'You'll love this town,' she told them. 'I came here as a visitor and loved it so much I decided to stay. And I'm so glad I did. For the first time in my life I feel a part of something truly special. The people here are so friendly and there's always lots to do. Last Sunday lunchtime, for instance, my partner Mike and I were invited to a neighbour's house…'

'Is Mike a cowboy?' Eric asked.

'Why do you ask that?' Alexx smiled.

'You said he was your partner – like in cowboy movies.'

Alexx chortled. 'No, Eric, he's not a cowboy. He's just the most special person in my life, honey – he's my life partner.'

Eric was left none the wiser but allowed Alexx to continue her story. 'Anyway, like I was saying, Mike and I were invited to a neighbour's house for Sunday lunch, and it was the most delicious meal you could have imagined. And afterwards, we were sitting talking when five deer come into the yard and started to eat the grass. It was so magical. Have you ever seen deer eat grass, Eric?' Eric said he hadn't.

'I have an idea,' Alexx said to Merritt. 'Why don't I walk into town with Jack and Eric, show them the new museum and take them to a really unusual house owned by a friend of mine?' Merritt had no objections. 'And about that problem of yours, Merritt; I promise I'll look into it. Give me a day or so and I'll get back to you. And don't forget the open mic tonight. Mike's counting on you being there.'

She was about to leave when she remembered something else. 'I don't suppose you'd like to make a contribution to the animal refuge, would you?'

'You suppose right,' Merritt said.

'Shame on you, Merritt. You don't have anything against charity, do you?' she teased.

'I have nothing against charity, Alexx,' Merritt said matter-of-factly. 'I just don't like the idea of giving money to it.' He then brought the conversation to an end by shutting the door on her.

Bob looked at Merritt. 'That's an hour o' my life I ain't never gettin' back.'

'Tell me about it,' Merritt said.

'So, how long are you staying in Crawford?' Alexx asked.

'We're leaving tomorrow morning,' Jack replied. 'Heading for Nashville.'

'If it's music you're after, you'd do better staying here in Crawford,' Alexx chuckled. 'We've got all kinds: bluegrass, blues, Celtic jam, folk, gospel, mountain, smooth jazz, traditional string band and even world music. You name it; we've got it! It's a pity you can't stay till the weekend.'

'Did you know that you list things alphabetically?' Jack asked. 'The types of music you just mentioned: you listed them all in alphabetical order.'

'It's the only way I can remember things,' Alexx laughed. 'The town's growing and the number of tourists coming here is increasing every year. The day's going to come when Crawford needs its own tour guide, and I'm aiming to be that person. I've been practising my socks off for months, but you're the first person to have ever sussed me – you bad man.'

'Jack's not bad, Ms Alexx,' Eric said, alarmed that she might think this. 'He bought me these gloves.'

'Oh honey, of course he's not! And your gloves are just lovely. It's just a figure of speech. I was teasing Jack. I'd never say anything to hurt another person – I'm too giving for that. That's why I want to be a tour guide: to give back to the town a small fraction of what it's given me, and also to help the people who come to visit.

'Do you know the first words I ever spoke as a child?' Alexx asked them. Both Jack and Eric confessed they didn't. '*I want to help people*. Can you believe that? My mother swears on the Bible that it's true – and you know something? I believe her.

'But listen to me blathering on like this. I want to hear about you two. What are you going to be doing in Nashville?'

'We're going to visit Eric's cousin,' Jack said. 'She moved there recently and Eric hasn't seen her for a while.'

'That'll be nice for you, Eric,' Alexx said. 'What does she do there? She's not a famous singer, is she?'

'No,' Eric replied. 'She works in chocolate.'

'Ooh, chocolate,' Alexx gasped. 'I go bananas for chocolate! It's my one weakness. It's the only thing that stopped me from becoming a nun.'

Jack raised an eyebrow at that statement, but refused to ask for an explanation: he wanted to deflect the conversation from the personal to the mundane. He particularly didn't want Alexx asking Eric any more questions – there was no telling what the boy might say in reply. His small friend, he had to confess, hadn't been born yesterday, but that very morning!

'This house that belongs to your friend, Alexx? Why is it unusual?'

'You'll soon see. It's right across the street there.'

From the front, the house she pointed to looked like any other house: one storey and wooden. It's only distinguishing feature was a totem pole stuck in the lawn.

'I wonder how Jimmy will be dressed today.' Alexx said. 'He's got all kinds of outfits: a Confederate outfit, a cowboy outfit, a Davy Crockett outfit, a General Custer outfit and an Indian outfit.' (Again, the listing was alphabetical.) She knocked on the door. 'Hi, Jimmy, are you in there? It's Alexx; I've brought some visitors to see you.'

The Missing Ear

'It was really interesting, Mrs Skidmore,' Eric said. 'We went to this house with dead animals in it and Jack started sneezing. Mr Jimmy had paintings of wild animals in his backyard as well, and he said he was going to build an African village in it. And then Ms

Alexx took us to a museum which wasn't as interesting, and Jack said it was full of nothing and that he was older than most of the things in it. And then we went to a store and Jack bought me some underwear, another pair of washing-up gloves, a pair of jeans and a shirt. He said I had to look smart when I meet Susan.'

'Who's Susan, dear?' Nancy asked him.

'She's my cousin, Mrs Skidmore. Me and Jack are going to look for her when we get to Nashville.'

'That sounds nice. Do your parents know where you are?'

Eric's excitement waned at the mention of his parents and he became serious. 'I think they do. They're both dead now, but Reverend Pete said they'd always be looking down on me and checking that I was alright.' (Eric was hoping that his parents had been taking a nap when he'd had his accident in John Boy's bed: he wouldn't have wanted them seeing that.)

'I'm sure they are, Eric,' Nancy said. 'And they'll be very proud of you, too. Now if you don't mind I'm going to lie down for a moment. I went for a walk with Arnold this morning and he just about wore me out. If you see him, will you tell him where I've gone?'

Eric was puzzled. He didn't know who or where Arnold was, but Doc was sitting on the couch right next to her, and he'd been the one to go for a walk with her. Sometimes, all the names confused him: some people called Doc, Gene; some people called Otis, Bob, and Merritt called Otis, T-Bone.

Nancy left the room and Doc started to tell them of the walk they'd taken that morning, and how Nancy had wanted to set fire to the bear in the country store. Bob and Merritt laughed; Jack didn't.

'We're not making fun of Nancy, Jack,' Doc said. 'The only way you can get through some things in life is by seeing their funny sides – and you don't see that too often with Nancy.'

'Sorry, Doc, I wasn't judging you. I was thinking of something else.'

'How was your time with Alexx? Was she a good tour guide?' Merritt asked.

'She laughs too much,' Jack said. 'I'm suspicious of people who laugh as easily as she does. They want to be liked but they don't want you to know them, and so they use laughter as a deflector – like flak. I reckon I could have spent a whole week in her company and still not known her.'

'You're probably right,' Merritt said. 'People know where she's from and what she did for a living, but no more than that. The irony of it is that she's living with Mike Calhoun, and he's the most open person in town. People call him Open Mike because he doesn't draw a line at telling people his personal information. He's too honest for his own good, and there are times when I think he even drives Alexx to distraction.

'I bumped into them on the street one time and the three of us fell into conversation. I asked Mike how his son was doing and he hummed and hawed for a moment, and was just about to tell me when Alexx jumped into the conversation and said he was doing fine, just working through a few behavioural problems. I figured I'd just been given notice that this topic of conversation was off-limits, when Open Mike pipes up and tells me his son keeps stabbing people! You should have seen the look she gave him. And then she stepped in to try and retrieve the situation: "He's getting help though, isn't he Mike? He's enrolled in a good programme?" And Mike just says: "Yeah, he's been sent to Folsom Prison for two years." I couldn't help but smile at that.

'For all her laughter, I don't think Alexx has a sense of humour – not one that amounts to much, anyway; and she's too blinkered to pick up on nuances and double meanings. You know how she makes a big deal of spelling her name with two Xs? Well, in the election, she had these posters made up which read: *Put your X next to Alexx's name and make her Triple X*, and then had to withdraw them.' Merritt started to laugh. 'She had people thinking she was going to make Crawford a part of the adult entertainment industry and star in the movies herself. Who the hell would have voted for her if they thought they'd have to see her buck naked?'

There was a beeping noise. 'That'll be the dryer,' Merritt said. 'That was the last load, so you might want to retrieve your clothes and start folding them away. I'll start making dinner. I hope to

God I can get that naked image of Alexx out of my head before we eat.'

'You sure we can't take you out to dinner?' Doc asked.

'Thanks, Gene, but there's no time. After we've eaten Nancy's going to show me how to make rum buns, and besides, it's open mic tonight so the restaurants will be shutting early. You should go to it, by the way. I can look after Nancy and Eric.'

'Let me think about it,' Doc said.

Nancy lay on the bed thinking, awakened by voices from another room. There was a fluttery feeling in her stomach and she looked around the room anxiously, trying hard to anchor herself to the surroundings. It wasn't her own room, she knew that, and this wasn't the bed she shared with Arnold. For an awful moment she thought she was back in the nursing home, but then remembered being taken from there by two men, one of whom she'd known. But what was *his* name? A bus also came to mind and a dead black man who drove it for a living. But why did he eat with them, sleep in the same room as them? Niggers didn't do that.

And then she remembered: she was at her grandfather's house and she'd gone there to bake for him. A wave of relief swept over her, but just as quickly dissolved. What was she going to bake for him and what day was it? What time was it and what was the year? How old was she: was she a child or had she grown up? And where were her parents; where was Ruby? She never went anywhere without Ruby; why wasn't Ruby in the room with her?

She thought she could smell the wet loam of the cotton fields and hear the familiar noises of Oaklands – Dora clattering pans in the kitchen and Ezra's deep voice. Was it a school day or was it the weekend?

The door opened and Gene walked in. Once more the anchor took its unsteady hold on the ocean's floor. 'How are you doing, old girl?' he asked.

Nancy tried to smile but started to cry. 'Is it always going to be like this, Gene? Will it ever get any better?'

Doc took her in his arms and tried to console her. Afterwards he thought he should have lied to her, told her it was all going to work out fine. 'No, Nancy. I wish it wasn't so, but it's always going to be like this. But I'll always be with you and we'll get through it together. Now dry those tears.'

He knew he should have acted sooner, taken Nancy to Coffeeville months ago and been truer to his word. It was what Nancy had asked him to do, and that he hadn't done so was down to his own selfishness: he hadn't wanted to lose her again – however imperfect she might be. She now hovered on the brink of being lost to herself and to all those around her; it was what she'd always dreaded, and he couldn't help but feel he'd failed her.

He got a tissue and brought it to her. Nancy sat up and moved her legs off the bed and dabbed at her eyes. Doc picked up her hairbrush and ran it through her flattened hair, and then stepped back to take a good look at her. 'Good as new,' he said. He then popped a couple of pills from their securing foil. 'Take these, Nancy: they'll make you feel better; get rid of those butterflies.' Nancy put them in her mouth and washed them down with water from a bedside glass.

'Everything's so muddled, Gene. Sometimes I think my parents are alive and other times I'm not sure. Are they alive? Is that why we're going to Coffeeville?'

'Your parents were good people, Nancy, but they've left us now. A part of them lives on in you – and that's the way it should be – but it would be selfish and cruel of us to expect them to be alive still. You'll bump into their memories in Coffeeville though, and that's something to look forward to. Even though you won't see them, they'll be close by.'

'You won't ever leave me, will you, Gene? You'll always stay with me?'

'Always, Nancy – wherever you go, I'll go.'

'You're a good person, Gene. What did I do to deserve you? I hope someday you'll be rewarded.'

'I'm not sure about either of those things, Nancy, but you can reward me now with a smile.'

Nancy obliged and then took hold of his hand and walked with him to the dining table. 'Just like old times,' Doc thought to himself, remembering the evenings they'd walked down the stairs at Oaklands together.

'It's lasagne,' Merritt announced, in case it wasn't obvious from the food's appearance. 'Pass your plates and then help yourselves to salad.'

'Don't give Nancy a big piece,' Doc said. 'Her appetite's not up to much these days.'

'Too late, Gene, but she's welcome to leave anything she can't eat – I won't be offended. If *you* leave food on your plate though, I might well be.'

It was halfway through the meal when Eric started to whisper to Jack. 'No whispering at the table, young man,' Nancy scolded. 'It's bad manners!'

'Sorry, Mrs Skidmore.'

'What did you say, anyway?' Jack asked him. 'I didn't catch it.' Eric mumbled something while keeping his eyes firmly on the table. 'I didn't catch that, either,' Jack said. 'You'll have to speak up.'

'One of Mr Crow's ears is missing,' Eric said in a loud voice.

Merritt's hand immediately went to the side of his head. 'Nobody move! I'll explain later.' Nobody did move: they were stunned into immobility. Nancy was the first to speak.

'Oh my God, Gene, the man's got leprosy!'

'Nonsense, Nancy. Crawford might have horseshit on its streets, but I doubt it has an outbreak of leprosy. Let's wait for Merritt to explain.'

Nancy wasn't so easily convinced and spat the food in her mouth on to the table. Doc used his napkin to wipe it up, while Merritt crawled around on his hands and knees looking for his ear.

'Got it!' he exclaimed from the kitchen. 'All the steam must have weakened the glue. Excuse me a minute, will you?' He then disappeared into the bathroom and emerged a few minutes later with two ears. 'I'm sorry about that,' he said. 'It happens sometimes, but fortunately not too often. I'll explain...' He picked up his fork and ate while he spoke, unwilling for the food on his plate to go cold.

'Do you remember the last words you said to me when you left Crawford, T-Bone?'

'Who's T-Bone?' Nancy asked.

'Otis,' Eric said.

'Bob,' Doc clarified.

'My las' words?' Bob asked. 'How I suppose' to remem'er what I said forty years ago? I'm guessin' I said somethin' like *goodbye.*'

'Your last words were *Get that lump on your neck seen to* and I should have listened to you. At the time I thought it was a sebaceous cyst, but it turned out to be Hodgkin's disease, and by the time it was diagnosed the cancer had spread to my ear. The chemo got rid of the cancer but they had to amputate my ear. They made me a new one out of rubber. I take it off at nights and stick it back on with theatrical glue in the morning. Nowadays they do things differently, put in a titanium implant and attach the ear to it, but I can't be bothered going through another operation at my age. Rubber and glue does for me.'

'Why didn't you say somethin', man? You shoulda said.'

'Why? What good would it have done? I wasn't going to die and you had your own life to sort out. Cancer's a conversation stopper, and I didn't want people phoning me up the whole time and fumbling for words.'

'Is that what the packet's all 'bout?' Bob asked.

'In a way. If I ever need to have chemo again – and the chances are that I will – then it comes in handy: counteracts some of the side effects. Chemo's brutal, man. It works, but it takes a lot of the good life out of you at the same time.'

'Thank goodness it was only cancer,' Nancy said, picking up her fork again. 'I thought you had leprosy.'

'I already told you, Nancy,' Doc said. 'You can't get leprosy in this country.'

'You can if you eat the ends of bananas,' Eric said. 'My daddy told me so, and Mr Annandale told him.'

Open Mike's Open Mic

Jack decided to stay and play Monopoly with Eric, and Doc and Bob went to the town's open mic event by themselves. The event was held in one of Crawford's larger bars close to the country store, and by the time Doc and Bob arrived there the room was already starting to fill. They sat down at a table and ordered beers from a waitress. Alexx was sitting at a table close by and waved to Bob when she saw him. Open Mike stood at the far end of the room, tapping the microphone with a ballpoint pen and checking that the sound system was in good working order.

Mike Calhoun – or Open Mike as people called him – had left school at the age of eighteen and gone to work at the town's one and only gas station. He'd had no interest in going to college and, if he had gone, would have had little idea of what to study. His one interest in life was gasoline, and from an early age he had been intent on forging a career in petrol pump attendancy.

After twenty years of pumping gas, Mike unexpectedly inherited the gas station from its owner, and welcomed this new responsibility. He painted the outside of the station, white-walled the curbs surrounding the pumps, hung baskets of flowers and hoisted an American flag. He placed a bench by the door to encourage people to sit for a while – customers and non-customers – and started to stock soft drinks, confectionery and cigarettes. He didn't have the capital to upgrade the pumps or the underground tanks, but he ensured they remained in good working condition. With time, the gas station became fashionably retro in appearance, and Mike contributed to the old-fashioned feel by continuing to give a full service: he put gas into the tank of every car that rolled on to its forecourt, checked oil levels and washed windscreens.

When he was thirty-nine, Mike married a girl he'd been dating on-and-off since the age of sixteen. Her name was Josie. It took twenty-three years and Mike's inheritance of the gas station for her to fall in love with him, but only three months of marriage to fall right back out again. In truth, Mike had always been her fall-back position, someone she was prepared to settle for if no better offers came her way. No better offers did, and when the alarm bell on her biological clock started to ring, and it looked as if Mike might have prospects after all, she agreed to marry him.

Josie conceived almost immediately and, thereafter, had no further use for Mike. The smell of gasoline that permeated his pores began to irritate her, and she resented his refusal to shower when he came home from work. Mike insisted that one shower a day was sufficient for any person, and that two would only deplete the natural oils in his body. 'Suit yourself,' Josie had said to him one day; 'but if you ever go up like a torch when I light a cigarette, I don't want anyone blaming me!' The marriage ended in Portland, the same day Mike met Alexx.

Mike Calhoun had lived and breathed gasoline fumes his entire adult life, and it was thought by some that the fumes had addled his brain – why else would anyone tell everyone his confidential business? Whatever the reason, Mike was a man who navel-gazed into his soul on a daily basis and usually came up with a medical condition, which he would then share with all and sundry. From the verruca on his foot to the lichen planus on his tongue, from the polyps in his urethra to the sebaceous growths on his torso, the whole town was intimate with Mike's intermittent medical problems. Most would avoid getting entangled in such conversations and simply say: 'Sorry to hear that Mike. Hope it clears up soon.'

There were a few, however, who would gladly discuss these ailments with him, and share ailments of their own. The man he'd told about his jock itch, for instance, had commented that if that was the sum total of his worries, then he was a lucky man indeed; he personally had the seven-year itch and that was far worse. It was the wrong thing to have told Mike. When the man's wife came to fuel her car the following week, Mike asked her how her husband's seven-year itch was coming along. 'It's just about to come to an end,' she'd said abruptly, and then driven off with the gas nozzle still attached to the car.

Despite such unintentional indiscretions, Open Mike was a popular man in town. People felt safe and comfortable around him, as they would any person they felt superior to, and when it came to finding someone to host a proposed open mic event, his was the name mentioned by most. He had a nice sounding voice, a relaxed and easy manner and, moreover, an interest in poetry – or at least words that rhymed. Mike liked words, wrote them down and then listed other words that were similar sounding. Two words, however, continued to confound him: orange and silver; he could find no words that rhymed with either.

Mike could never write poetry, but he admired those people who did, and eventually came to appreciate even poetry that didn't rhyme. He was happy to accept the position of emcee and under his tutelage the open mic for writers and poets became a popular monthly event.

The theme of the open mic that evening was poetry of fifty words or fewer.

'Hi folks and welcome. It's good to see so many of you here tonight, and I can guarantee you that you won't go home disappointed. We've got a great line-up, but before we get things started there are a couple of notices.

'There's a new exhibition of paintings by Evelyn Tate opening at the Brick Factory next week, and let me tell you these things are works of beauty – especially when you consider that Evelyn's arthritis means she can't hold a brush anymore and has to paint with her knuckles.

'Second one is to alert you to the fact that Dave Palmer's coming to town this weekend and he'll be playing right here on Saturday night. Dave believes that only innovation and self-expression can ensure the survival of traditional American music, and to this end he'll be playing many of his favourite nineteenth century banjo pieces on a moog synthesiser. Something to look forward to, I think.

'On a personal note, you might remember me mentioning to some of you that I'd been noticing traces of blood in my morning stools and was concerned that I might have bowel cancer. Well I'm glad to say that I haven't, and all the tests came back clear. It seems my haemorrhoids were playing up and I should have been using the ointment on a more regular basis.'

A big cheer came from the floor and Mike smiled. 'Okay

everyone, I appreciate the sentiment, but it's time to simmer down and bring on our first reader. First up, we've got Chuck Harrison and his poem's entitled *Caroline*. There was a murmur of apprehension in the audience as Chuck took to the small stage: he and his wife, Caroline, had recently divorced, and Caroline was sitting in the room with her new beau.

> *You use people, you used me*
> *you use the dead, your family*
> *You take from strangers, you take from friends*
> *you take from women, you take from men*
> *You need Valium, you need drink*
> *you need guidance, you need a shrink*
> *You think in mono, you talk shit*
> *you're all ass, you're all tit*

The uncomfortable silence at the poem's end was broken by Caroline. 'That's fifty-four words, Chuck. Never could get things right, could you?' There was a muffle of repressed laughter and Mike hurried to take the microphone from Chuck.

'Bad luck, Chuck,' he said. 'I'm afraid that disqualifies you on this occasion, but keep the poems coming.' Chuck walked off the stage and made for the exit. 'Bitch!' he said to Caroline as he brushed past her.

Mike looked at his notes and then called Cheryl Nelson to the platform. Cheryl was an active member of the local church and had just celebrated her twenty-second birthday. Her poem was entitled *Things Go Better with Coca-Cola*

> *Christ in the ruins of our love*
> *of possessions and concessions*
> *to ourselves*
> *Smile down at the wounds in your flesh*
> *and muse:*
> *would things have gone better*
> *without Coca-Cola?*

Again, the audience applauded. 'That's a deep one, Cheryl,' Mike said. 'I think you've given us all something to think about there!'

Doc drained his glass and gestured for the waitress to bring refills.

Meanwhile, Mike was introducing Kurt Wolfe, an artist who'd recently returned from a year in Nepal after suffering a nervous breakdown. 'Kurt's going to read two poems tonight. I know this is unusual, but they're both very short and it would be a waste of time me sitting down if he just read the one. Kurt tells me that Nepal taught him the virtues of minimalism, so let's see what he's got in store for us tonight.'

Kurt stepped to the microphone, closed his eyes and remained silent for a minute. He then opened his eyes and started to shout:

KATHMANDU
DOGMANDON'T

There was a momentary silence while the audience waited for Kurt to continue. When he didn't, and it became apparent that the poem had ended, they broke into polite, if puzzled, applause.

'Thank you. Thank you very much,' Kurt said. 'You've given me a lot. The second poem I want to read is called *Punctuated Free Love*. It came to me while I was visiting the source of the Bagmati River close to Bagdwaar. There was a dead goat in the water.'

Comma sutra
Period missed
Pause pregnant

Mike had never heard such balderdash and neither had most of the other people in the room. It seemed that Nepal had done Kurt no good at all. 'Thanks, thanks Kurt,' he stammered. 'Let's hear it for Kurt, everybody; it's good to have him home.' In turn, Kurt thanked Mike and kissed him on both cheeks.

'We'll take a short break,' Mike announced, slightly nonplussed. 'Stretch your legs, use the bathrooms and order more drinks. We'll be starting back in fifteen minutes.'

'How 'bout we get us a cigarette, Gene?' Bob suggested, and the two of them left their table and joined the one other person in Crawford who still smoked. 'This is a hoot, man. Glad we come?'

'I am. It's a pity Jack didn't come with us. He'd have enjoyed this – and for all the wrong reasons, too.'

'I hated po'try at school; al'ays thought that it was drug addicts or gays what wrote it. I don't think that now, though. After tonight, I know buffoons can write it, too. Ha!'

A woman came to the door and announced they were ready to start. While Bob bought more beer, Doc sat at the table casting furtive glances in Caroline's direction.

'You twice her age, man,' Bob said when he returned to the table. 'You should be 'shamed o' yo'self.'

Doc ignored him, thankful that Open Mike had taken to the platform again. Another fifteen poems were read that evening, but only Alexx's resonated with Doc and Bob.

Alexx told the audience that her poem had been written as a tribute to Mike – the love of her life, and a man who still made her weak at the knees.

> *Oh my love, you're so lovely*
> *and I my love am so ugly*
> *In your presence I feel small*
> *my nerves cause me to feel sick*
> *I want to vomit*
> *all over your carpet*

A tear came to Mike's eye when he heard the poem and the two of them embraced. The room erupted into cheers and wolf whistles, fortunately sufficient in decibel to hide the roars of laughter coming from Doc and Bob.

'Place smells good!' Bob said. 'I'm fig'rin' you got yo' rum buns made.'

Merritt smiled. 'Nancy did good, Gene. Best damn rum buns I've tasted.'

'I'm glad to hear it, Merritt. How was Nancy?'

'She was fine. Turns out we both have a common interest in memory loss, but a total recall of growing up in the 1950s. We spent the evening down memory lane and had us a ball.'

'Where is she now?'

'She's getting ready to turn in.' On hearing that, Doc excused himself and went to check on her.

'So where's my rum bun? You saved me one, right?' Bob asked.

Merritt looked uncomfortable at the question and didn't answer immediately. 'We ate them all,' Eric said. 'Mrs Skidmore said they had to be eaten fresh or not at all.'

'Sorry,' Merritt said. 'I was going to save you one, but they were just too damned good.'

'How many Nancy make?' Bob asked.

'Ten,' Eric said.

'An' the four o' you ate all ten of 'em! I cain't believe it.'

'Merritt ate five,' Eric said. 'Jack and I had two each, and Mrs Skidmore had one.'

'Five! Goddamn, Merritt, I hope you get indigestion tonight!'

'I beat Jack,' Eric said. 'I beat him at Monopoly and then we played Snap and I beat him at that, too. Do you want to play a game, Otis?'

'Not at this hour. Time we was all turnin' in. Got us an early start in the mornin'.'

'Good call, Bob. He cheats like you wouldn't believe. If my name was Esau, he'd have my birthright by now. We should start calling him Jacob.'

Eric cleared the board from the table and put it back in the cupboard. He and Jack then said their goodnights and returned to the bus.

'We never said goodnight to Mrs Skidmore and Doctor Gene,' Eric said.

'We'll say it to them when we see them in the morning, Jacob.'

'And stop calling me Jacob – Esau!' As Jack could remember, it was the first joke Eric had made. He smiled.

It was another cold morning, but at least the day had started dry. Jack and Eric went into the house and joined the others for breakfast. Merritt had made pancakes and fried some bacon. He poured coffee into their cups and then sat down at the table with them.

'I'm expectin' you sometime in the New Year, Merritt, an' I ain't wantin' to hear no excuses. Chamber o' Commerce ain't gonna' miss you fo' a couple o' weeks an' the change'll do you good. Get you away from all that horseshit. I'm bettin' once you ain't here, Spencer's horse'll get itself all constipated an' there'll be nothin' for you to shovel once you get back.'

'I will, T-Bone. I promise. My ankle will have mended by then.'

'I'll pick you up at the airport; we'll stay a few days in Seattle an' then head to the mountain cabin. Might well put you to work there.'

Doc said nothing. He envied the plans they were making, the futures they could look forward to.

'Can I have Mrs Skidmore's other pancake?' Eric asked.

'Sure,' Doc said. 'It doesn't look like she'll be eating it.'

'I can make some more,' Merritt said. They thanked him but declined his offer. It was time to make tracks.

'If you'da offered me a rum bun, I'da said yes, Merritt, but I keep forgettin' you ate 'em all.'

'I guess this is as good a time to go as any,' Doc smiled. 'I'll go pack.'

'We're packed aren't we, Jack?' Eric said.

'We never unpacked. Did you pick up your washed clothes?'

'No one picked up their clothes,' Merritt said. 'I put them in the bus – front lounge. You'll need to sort them.'

Doc carried his and Nancy's bags into the lounge and waited there while Bob finished using the bathroom.

'He's taking a long time in there, isn't he?' Jack asked. 'How long does it take him to do a dump?'

'I'm sure I don't know, and I'm sure it's something that Nancy doesn't want to know either. Sometimes…' He shook his head.

'Man alive, I got to get me mo' reg'lar,' Bob said, when he joined them. 'That was like givin' birth to a baby!'

As they left the house, Bob turned to Merritt. 'One mo' thing, Merritt.'

'What's that, T-Bone?' Merritt asked.

'Get that lump on your neck seen to!'

Merritt's hand reflexively touched the long scar there. 'What lump?' he asked anxiously.

'Yo' damned head, man! Ha!'

6

Nashville

Missed Deaths and Dreams

'I'm tellin' you, Francis Nash were an extortioner. They named the city after a corrup' court official,' Bob said. 'You ain't heard o' the Regulator Wars?'

No one had, but sat quietly while Bob explained the episode to them: the rich and powerful of North Carolina beating up on the poor and powerless of North Carolina in the late eighteenth century.

'But then Francis gets his self killed in the War o' Independence an' becomes a war hero. You know why? Cos elites honour their own, that's why! Ordinary folks not good enough to be war heroes. You ask 'em the names o' common folk what got 'emselves killed in battle and you ain't never gonna get an answer. They the invisible ones. Disappear from hist'ry like ink in the damn rain, man. Not Francis, though. Ole Francis gets towns, counties an' schools named after him, an' Nashville, Tennessee's jus' one of 'em. How's that for a piece of shit?'

'He wasn't a nice man, was he?' Eric said. 'Would you have been a Regulator if you'd been alive in those days, Doctor Gene? Doctor Gene!'

Doc was miles away, and Eric's question caught him off guard. He'd dreamt of Sydney that night and the vision had unsettled him. Sydney had been alive again, reprieved from eternity for a short while and doing handstands in the backyard of his house, talking excitedly with neighbours and laughing. Doc couldn't remember if they'd had a conversation or not and woke with a hollow feeling. He missed Sydney and regretted not being with him when he died. Doc had been present for the deaths of many of his patients, but never for those of people who'd mattered to him: Beth, Esther, Sydney, his parents.

The death of his mother troubled him the most. He'd visited his parents' house the day she died but had spent the time with his father. He'd looked into his mother's room but hadn't entered; neither had he spoken to her, sat with her or held her hand, and – most shameful of all – not even kissed her goodbye when he left the house. He'd persuaded himself it was an act of kindness not to disturb her, but who had he been kidding? He knew he'd been sparing himself, not his mother; safeguarding himself from the unsettling spectacle of life draining from her body.

His mother had died alone. He remembered visiting her body at the funeral home, her waxen effigy clothed in Sunday's best; kissing her on the forehead and being surprised by the coldness of her skin; whispering he loved her, before realising that his mother was long gone and unable to hear his words. He swore he would never make the same mistake with his father – but he did, and his father also died alone.

Doc had visited him on the day of his death, too; dropping off a prescription and cooking his lunch. His father had come down with a bug and was suffering from diarrhoea, but his condition – in Doc's opinion – wasn't serious, and certainly not life threatening. What he'd failed to take into account was that his father had lost the will to live.

He'd stayed for a while, but his father had been a reluctant conversationalist. Eventually, he took his leave and promised to return the following day and check on his progress; if his condition worsened, his father was to call him immediately. In the event his father had phoned, but only to ask his son to bring a newspaper with him when he came to the house. All had seemed well.

Doc had phoned his father the following morning but there'd

been no answer. This wasn't unusual: his father had grown into the habit of ignoring the phone when it suited him, and rarely checked the answering machine for messages. Doc made several more calls and still there'd been no answer. His concern, at first pettifogging, started to grow, and once the morning's surgery had ended he'd driven immediately to his father's house.

The door had been locked and he used his own key to gain entry. Immediately he'd sensed something was wrong. He called out his father's name but there'd been no answer; the downstairs rooms were empty and the lights were on. He remembered taking a deep breath and preparing himself for the worst, climbing the stairs and finding his father lying face down on the bathroom floor, dried faeces on his pants and shoes. He'd rolled the old man gently on to his back and straightaway known he was dead.

He'd phoned for an ambulance, and then sat quietly while the medics examined the body and pronounced his father officially dead. He'd answered the questions of a policeman who'd arrived in their tow, and waited while he satisfied himself that all was well and nothing untoward. He'd then phoned the funeral home. Two sombrely-dressed men arrived and manoeuvred his father's body into a thick plastic bag. He'd watched as they struggled with the zip fastener, and observed his father disappearing from view as the two sets of teeth slowly interlocked. It was the last time he'd seen his father: he decided against viewing his body at the funeral home.

'I just find it strange we didn't talk,' Doc said.

'What I find strange is that my father was doing handstands when he couldn't even do a push-up,' Jack said. 'I wouldn't read too much into it, Doc. Some dreams aren't meant to be understood. Mine are more straightforward. I dream about Laura and losing my hair. I can understand those.'

'I've heard of people dreaming about losing their teeth, but never their hair,' Doc smiled. 'You must be one hell of a special person, Jack.'

'You know how long a person dreams fo' in his life?' Bob asked, averting his eyes from the road.

'I'll have a guess if you promise not to turn around again,' Doc said. 'The last thing we need is for you to rear-end someone.'

'I can talk an' drive, Gene. T-Bone Tribble's a multitaskin' Renaissance man, or ain't you noticed?'

'Six months?' Jack guessed.

'Not even close! Mo' like six years, is what. You figure it this way: a person spends a third of his life sleepin', an' ever' time he sleeps he dreams fo' 'bout two hours. All adds up, man. Six whole years, an' most of us cain't even remem'er what we was dreamin' 'bout! 'Mazed you even dream, Gene, 'mount you snore.'

'Why? Does one preclude the other?'

'Sure it do. Dreamin' an' snorin' ain't compatible – even I cain't multitask 'em. You get recurrin' dreams, Gene?'

'One,' Doc said. 'I dream I'm in outer space, sitting in the back of a dump truck and looking down on the earth. It's night-time and the planet's lit up and looking pretty as a picture. Then the bed of the truck starts to rise and I start sliding down it. There's nothing I can hold on to that will save me from falling into the blackness and I keep on sliding… and that's when I wake up.'

'Soun's like an anxiety dream, Gene. Fallin's a classic – jus' like teeth. You ever dream 'bout gravy? I get that one all the time. Scares me to death, too.'

'How can gravy scare you to death?' Doc asked.

'Jus' does. I'm sittin' in a restaurant, an' a waiter spills gravy down my neck, though I don't feel it at the time. Once the meal's overed with, I go outside an' it's then I feel it. I put my han' there an' it comes back covered in gravy, an' then when I put my han' there again, it comes back covered in blood an' my damn head falls off!

'You notice how I al'ays sits in a booth or with my back to a wall when I go any place to eat? That's why I does it. I figure it some kinda warnin'. Laugh all you wan', Jack. Dreamin' 'bout yo' hair fallin' out's nothin' compared with dreamin' yo' head falls off.'

'My dreams are always good,' Eric said.

'That's because you're a young man who's led a good life,' Doc said. 'Get to our age and you'll be going to bed with a conscience

– and that's another story altogether. Enjoy your dreams while you can, son.'

'Hey, Gene: you ever dream o' me?' Bob asked.

'Why?'

''Cos I charge a royalty fee o' ten bucks an appearance. Figure out how much you owe me, an' then deduct $20. I only dreamed o' you twice, an' you weren't that interessin' in either one of 'em!'

The Bible According to Otis Sistrunk

Jack went to the rear lounge to remove pieces of gravel stuck in the soles of his sneakers, and picked up the first implement to hand. He was focusing on the job when Nancy walked in and sat down opposite. She stared at him.

'Hi, Nancy,' Jack said. 'How are you today?'

For a while she said nothing and just stared. 'Who *are* you?' she asked eventually.

'I'm Jack, Nancy. Doc's godson. I helped rescue you from the nursing home, remember?'

Nancy eyed him suspiciously. 'It was Gene and his wife who took me from there.'

'That was me, Nancy. I was dressed in women's clothing. Think about it: if it was Doc's wife who helped rescue you, where is she now? I don't see her on the bus.'

'She died,' Nancy said, showing no emotion. 'She asked me to look after him. Are you going to stab me with that?'

'Why would I want to do that? Besides, it's a letter opener, not a knife.'

'It makes no difference. If you jabbed me with it, I'd still bleed like a stuck pig.'

Jack was taken aback and, unsure of what to say next, said nothing.

'Do you ever worry someone might stab you with it?' Nancy continued.

'No, now let's change the subject. What are you looking forward to in Nashville?'

Nancy said nothing and continued to stare.

Doc entered the lounge. 'What's going on?' he asked.

'I honestly don't know, Doc. I think Nancy's trying to stare me to death.'

'Careful, Gene: he's got a knife!' Nancy said.

'Letter opener,' Jack corrected.

In the hope that a period of rest would help, Doc suggested that he and Nancy go to the sleeping compartment. He looked at his watch: another six hours before they reached Nashville. The journey would be hardest on Bob, the only person in the group capable of driving the bus – even though his licence was a fake. Bob, however, was nothing if not resilient, and as long as no one spilt gravy down his neck, Doc was confident they'd arrive in Nashville safely.

He'd decided they should now stick to the planned route and make no more detours. Although he doubted the potential for any pursuer from the nursing home to be hot on their heels, or for that matter even knowing in which direction their heels were travelling, the conspicuous nature of the bus still troubled him. The interstate, he believed, was a place of safety, and so too would Nashville be, where tour buses, he imagined, would be two a penny. Doc had also made up his mind that he and Nancy would stay in a hotel for the next two nights: it would be a treat for both of them. He asked Bob to book them into the Union Hotel and admired the man's carefulness when, after having made the call, he threw away the SIM card.

Jack remained in the rear lounge, disconcerted by his conversation with Nancy, while Eric sat up front with Bob and asked him about the Bible.

'Do you believe in God, Otis?'

'I b'lieve in God, Eric, but I ain't sure I b'lieve in the Bible. To my way o' thinkin', it's easier to b'lieve in God if you *don't* read the Bible…' He then elaborated.

God was a one off. Although He'd created man in His own image, He himself didn't have a body, and was neither male nor female. He'd always existed and He always would; God was incomparable, simultaneously everywhere and capable of anything. He was fair-minded and compassionate: he punished the wicked, rewarded the good and forgave sins. God had chosen to reveal Himself to the Jewish people and then come to an agreement with them: in return for total obedience, He would take good care of them.

There had never been a shortage of gods in the ancient world: they existed for every day of the week and for every occasion. All were attributed with mysterious powers that distinguished them from mortals, but in conduct their behaviour was little better than that of modern day celebrities. The God of the Jews was a radical departure from anything that had gone before: for a start there was only one of Him, and He behaved like a gentleman. He was also ethical and innately good. But then the Jews subverted Him, buried Him in their own humanity, and this, Bob claimed, was the God who appeared in the Old Testament.

'Scaries' muthafucker to walk the earth,' Bob said, before quickly apologising for his language. 'If you'da seen the man comin' towards you on the street, you'da crossed over quick as you could or ducked into a doorway. No tellin' what kinda mood the man mighta been in. Difficult to b'lieve Him and Jesus was even related, never min' father an' son.'

The mercurial thug who roamed the pages of the Old Testament was indeed scary. He was acquainted with vengeance and retribution, but seemingly unaware of kindliness, forgiveness and compassion. His language was one of violence. He threatened – and often delivered – cruel and horrible punishments: death by sword, famine, fire, evil beasts and pestilences that rotted flesh, eyes and tongues. 'It woulda been safer fo' ever'one if they'da jus' locked Him up in a prison some place,' Bob said.

The Bible was littered with examples of His petty and vindictive nature – traits more human than divine. He opened and closed wombs at will, made wives leprous for a week and tormented people with evil spirits and tumours. He killed people for getting ceremonies wrong, touching the Ark by accident, picking up sticks on the wrong day and eating in the wrong place.

'You'll know all this from yo' own readin' o' the Bible, Eric, but you ain't got to take no note. This ain't God: it people sayin' it

God to make sense o' somethin' that makes no sense. Old Testament defaces God, makes Him out to be a real son-of-a-bitch an' gives people too many reasons not to b'lieve in Him. They ever make a film o' the Old Testament, they'd give it one o' them X certif'cates. Too much weird stuff goin' on.'

Apart from His aversion to dwarves, hunchbacks and the handicapped in general, and His refusal to allow them to play a full role in society, God had other intolerances. Some made sense: who could disagree with His pronouncements that misleading a blind man on the road was wrong, or that bowel motions should be made in holes outside the perimeter of a camp rather than within it? There were others, however, that were plain draconian: stubborn and rebellious sons, adulterers, and women who pretended to be virgins when they married could be stoned to death. And pity the poor woman who intervened in a fight to protect her husband from the attack of another man and made the mistake of grabbing the assailant by his private parts: her hand would be amputated!

'You know the bes' place to meet a wife in those days? At a well,' Bob said. 'Wells was like Starbucks. Jus' hope the water tasted better 'n the coffee. You wan' good coffee, you gotta go to Cuba.'

'Have you been to Cuba?' Eric asked.

'Nah,' Bob lied. 'Numskull governmen' won't let us. Jus' what I hear, is all.'

Eric was now more confused about the Bible than before the conversation had started. It was difficult to tell if Otis believed in God or not. He decided to ask again: 'You do believe in God though, don't you?'

'Sure I b'lieve in God,' Bob replied. 'I b'lieve in Him, but not the Old Testament version o' Him. Ol' Testament's a hist'ry o' the Jewish people, not the hist'ry o' God, but the two's been blended an' it's this what gives God a bad name. Makes mo' sense once you get to the New Testament – that's when they chop God into three, an' me an' my brothers get to eat barbecue!'

Eric started to look even more doubtful.

Doc joined them just as Eric was proclaiming his belief in Jesus. 'I'm going to stick to Christianism, Otis.'

'Christianism?' Doc said. 'Is that the grammatical equivalent of Islamity?'

'Don't go messin' with the boy, Gene. I jus' been sayin' nice things 'bout you.'

'I'm just joking, Eric. When you get a chance though, ask Jack about Buddha. When he was about your age, he was under the impression that Buddhism was the friendliest religion in the whole wide world, but could never find a book on it. Saphead thought it was Buddyism.' He then sat down and allowed Bob and Eric to continue their conversation.

'So how far you got countin' the dead?' Bob asked.

'I've finished II Kings and counted another 205,353 bodies, and now I'm reading Chronicles,' Eric replied.

'That's mop-up territ'ry then, fillin' in the gaps o' what's gone b'fore. You can miss out Psalms, Proverbs, Ecclesiastes an' the Song o' Solomon, 'cos there ain't no deaths in them, an' they don't make a whole buncha sense, neither. Solomon was too wise fo' his own good, if you aks me.'

It had started to shower and Bob turned the wipers to the intermittent setting. Jack drifted into the lounge and sat down next to Eric. 'How you doing, kid?'

'I'm okay, Jack. Otis has been telling me about the Bible, and Doctor Gene said I should ask you about Buddha.'

'He was a fat guy, just like Doc,' Jack said.

Nancy joined them, rested and smiling. 'How are you, Jack?' she asked.

Jack eyed her suspiciously. 'I'm fine thank you,' he said cautiously. 'How are you?'

'Very well thank you, Jack.' She then turned to Doc. 'He's a nice young man, isn't he, Gene?'

'The best!' Doc said with feeling.

The Protestant Vatican

The bus rolled through Tennessee at a steady 70 mph. Interstate 81 turned into Interstate 40, Eastern Standard Time changed to Central, and intermittent showers developed into constant and heavy rain. The road climbed through cragged hillsides, disappeared into low cloud and then descended towards Nashville. Billboards appeared bearing messages from God: *All I Know Is Everything; Don't Make Me Come Down There; Evolution Is A Fairytale For Grown-Ups; What Part Of Thou Shalt Not Didn't You Understand?*

They shouldn't have been surprised by the black and white announcements. When the bus had crossed the Potomac River and entered the state of West Virginia, it had also entered the socially conservative and evangelically Protestant Bible Belt. Here, the church was at the heart of every community, and Moral Majorities and Christian Coalitions railed against the practices of abortion, homosexuality and the teaching of evolution. The area approximated to the old slave states and, paradoxically, boasted the nation's highest divorce, murder and teenage pregnancy rates.

If Nashville wasn't its buckle, then it was only a notch away. The city boasted more than seven hundred churches and was headquarters to the world's two largest Baptist denominations – the Southern Baptist Convention and the National Baptist Convention, USA. It was also the home of the United Methodist Church, the National Association of Free Will Baptists, a host of Christian publishing companies – including the world's largest producer of Bibles – and Gideon's International.

'You know who Gideon was?' Bob asked.

Apart from Eric, no one did. 'He was a Judge,' Eric said. 'He killed 120,004 Midianites.'

'He's the one! Anyone know what his name means?'

Not even Eric knew the answer to this question, but Jack hazarded a guess: 'Killer?'

'Means Feller – as in a man who cuts down trees. To my way o' thinkin' his name's 'propriate. You know how many Bibles them folks has handed out? 1.5 billion! Think how many trees was chopped down to make that much paper. They hand 'em out willy-nilly an' in diff'rent coloured covers, too: desert camouflage fo' military people, dark blue fo' people workin' in law enforcement an' so on. Ever' damn motel you check into's got one, an' you know anyone who's ever read it? 'Course you don't.

Guy ain't gonna go to his room an' start debatin' with his self whether to read Gideon's Bible or turn on the porn channel. He goes straight to the movie. Al'ays!'

'Hey Bob, remember Eric's with us, will you?' Doc said.

'Sorry, kid,' Bob said. 'Keep fo'gettin' you ain't a growed man.'

'Jack, why don't you and Eric make sandwiches for us?'

Jack and Eric went to the kitchen and Jack returned. 'Where did you put the groceries we bought in Crawford, Doc?'

'I thought you brought them on the bus. Did you bring them onboard, Bob?'

'No, guess we musta left 'em at Merritt's.'

They pulled into the next rest area, and Jack and Eric went in search of food.

'Make sure Eric wears his helmet, Jack, and just to be on the safe side give him my glasses to wear. And tell him not to talk to anyone!'

Jack and Eric climbed out of the bus. Doc's glasses disguised Eric's appearance well but effectively blinded him. He walked falteringly, as if the asphalt under his feet was criss-crossed with deep crevasses. Jack took hold of his hand. 'I'll let you know when we get to a step,' he reassured him.

They got provisions from the vending machines and then went to the restroom.

'Thinking about it, we should have probably used the restroom first,' Jack said. 'I need to use a stall. How about you?'

'I just want to pee.'

'Okay, I'll hold the bag while you pee, and then you take charge of it.'

Eric doddered uncertainly to the washbasin and unzipped his pants.

'Hey!' Jack called. 'The urinal's the other way!'

He took hold of Eric's arm and steered him to the urinal. 'It might be better if you take Doc's glasses off while you pee: you don't want to get your jeans all wet.' He waited the short time it took Eric to empty his bladder and then directed him to the door, instructing him to wait outside the restroom. 'And remember –

don't talk to anyone!' He then entered the stall.

Everything was a blur for Eric. He could vaguely make out shapes, but had no idea what the shapes were. Some of them spoke: ''Excuse me kid, you're blocking the door; hey kid, move out of the way; bozo, move to the side, will you?' Intimidated by the voices, he gradually moved from the doorway of the male restroom to the doorway of the female restroom. There, other voices similarly urged him to move on. By the time Jack exited the restroom, Eric was standing in the foyer talking to two policemen.

The police had seen Eric inching his way erratically through the lobby and become suspicious. One of them returned to the door and pulled off a poster he'd noticed.

'You think this could be the missing deaf kid, Lou?'

'Don't know, Murray. Let's find out.'

They took hold of Eric's arm, steered him to the side of the lobby and started to ask questions. 'Are you Eric Gole, kid, and are you deaf?' Eric said nothing. 'Are you Eric Gole and are you pretending to be deaf?' Again, Eric said nothing. 'What's your name? Where are your parents? Are you an orphan? Where do you live? Are you a runaway?' To all these questions, Eric made no reply.

'I think we should take him to the station, Lou. If he's not the runaway, then he's obviously someone who needs help. Does he strike you as being a bit simple?'

The police were about to haul Eric away when Jack came bounding into the lobby. His initial panic at seeing Eric in the hands of the police had subsided and been replaced by a practised nonchalance honed in the television studio.

'Hey, Con! What's going on?' he asked jovially. 'You haven't mugged anyone, have you?' Eric recognised Jack's voice and also the name Con. Jack had told him his son's name was Con.

'No, dad, and these men are trying to interfere with me. They've been calling me simple!'

'You his father?' one of the policemen asked.

'Yes. My name's Jack Guravitch and this is my son Conrad.' He took out his billfold and showed them his driving licence and a photograph of him, Laura and Conrad that he still carried with him. Conrad and Eric bore a passing resemblance.

The policeman looked at the photograph and then at Eric. 'How old is Con?' he asked.

'Nine,' Jack answered.

'Is there a reason why he refused to answer our questions?'

'I always tell him not to talk to strangers, and he wouldn't have recognised you as policemen because of his eyes. He's just got some new lenses and he's not used to them yet. Let him see your glasses, Con.'

Eric handed his glasses to the policeman who looked through them. 'Mother of God!' he exclaimed, and quickly handed them back to Eric.

'Do you mind if we ask Con to take off his helmet?'

'Not at all! Take off your helmet, Con.'

Eric did. 'It's not him,' the policeman holding the poster said. 'This kid's got blonde hair and it says here he's thirteen. No way is this kid thirteen.'

The other policeman was no longer looking at Eric. He was staring at Jack.

'Are you that weatherman?'

'I used to be a weatherman,' Jack said, slightly alarmed. 'Why do you ask?'

The policeman broke into a big smile. 'Goddamn, Murray, this is the guy who stuck it to the man! Told him to fuck off on primetime television!'

'How do you know that?' Jack asked, now intrigued.

'You're on YouTube!' he said. 'Let me shake you by the hand, Mr Guravitch. You said what a lot of us want to say, but daren't. Hey, Murray, take a photograph of me and Jack together will you? You don't mind, do you, Mr Guravitch?'

'No, not in the least,' Jack replied.

'You got video on that phone of yours, Murray? Good. Do me a favour, Mr Guravitch, and tell me to fuck off, will you? Say *fuck you, Lou, and fuck you, too, Murray!*'

Jack obliged.

The policemen thanked him, apologised for detaining Con

unnecessarily and again shook his hand. 'You've just made my day, man,' Lou said. 'Wait till I tell my wife.' The policemen then went to the restroom and Jack and Eric hurried to the bus.

'You've been a long time,' Doc said. 'What kept you?'

'We got stopped by the police, Doctor Gene, and Jack told them to fuck off. When my Uncle Jeff told them to do that they arrested him, but they just thanked Jack and shook his hand.'

Jack put mayonnaise on the bread, sliced a tomato and added bologna. He handed one of the sandwiches to Eric and poured two glasses of Coke.

'I bet your mom made better sandwiches than these, didn't she?'

'Yes, she did. My mom baked her own bread, too.'

'That's good. My mom just bought it from the store. She never baked, but she was a good cook.'

'My mom baked all the time. She made cakes and different kinds of cookies. My friends came to the house just to eat them.'

'Did you have many friends?'

'I had two: Gregory Thompson and Matthew Scott,' Eric said. 'We went to the same school. They weren't popular and never got invited to parties either, so we just went around to each other's houses. Greg's mom was nice, and she sat next to me at my parents' funeral.'

'Two friends are enough for any person,' Jack said. 'Two good friends – that's all you need in life. Do they know you ran away?'

'No, I didn't tell anyone. I didn't want anyone to try and stop me. Do you think we'll find Susan, Jack?'

'We'll give it our best shot, Eric. Bob's got the name and address of the person she went to see in Nashville, so we'll start by looking there. It will be like an adventure.'

Eric smiled. 'You'll like her, Jack. I promise you, you will.'

'I'm sure I will. Tell me, Eric, what was the church you attended like? What was The Reverend Pete like and did he do healings?'

'The Reverend Pete was nice,' Eric said. 'He never managed to cure my father's headaches – because God wanted Mr Annandale to do that – but he cured a man of catarrh once, and a girl who had pimples on her forehead.'

'If I find the right church service, would you like to go to church tomorrow night? I'm thinking of giving it a try.'

'You bet, Jack!'

And so the seeds of a memorable debacle were sown.

The Nashville skyline came into view. They'd been travelling close to nine hours and no one was more pleased to see it than Bob. 'There she is,' he said. 'Home sweet home!'

'Have you been here before?' Jack asked.

'Me an' Marsha came fo' a visit once – she wanted to experience the Grand Ole Opry fo' some reason I'll never understan'. If you plannin' on payin' a visit yo'selfs, you can count me out. One time was a time too many.'

'What's the big building?' Eric asked.

'AT&T Building on Commerce Street. Talles' buildin' in the whole o' Tennessee.'

'If Nancy and Doc are staying in a hotel, where are we staying?' Jack asked.

'I thought we'd park over in Music Valley an' stay close to Opryland. There'll be plenty o' buses like ours parked there, an' there's bars an' restaurants, too. We'll have us a boys' night out – jus' the three of us.'

Bob edged the bus through the rush hour traffic and eventually pulled into a parking area adjacent to the Union Hotel. 'You an' Nance all set, Gene?'

'Yes, all set. What are the plans for tomorrow? I was thinking of taking Nancy to Vanderbilt University in the morning and strolling around the campus. Do you want to meet up for lunch somewhere?'

'We can meet at the Loveless,' Bob said. 'You an' Nance get a taxi there an' we'll do the same: I ain't drivin' the bus roun' Nashville. The Loveless is close to where the guy who knows Susan lives, so once they've eaten Jack an' Eric can drive on out there.'

Gene and Nancy left the bus and walked through the doors of

the hotel, a large overnight bag slung over Doc's shoulder. Bob waited while Jack bought a copy of the local newspaper, and then reclaimed his place in the traffic and headed towards Music Valley.

'When I get home I ain't drivin' fo' a month!' Bob said. 'Marsha can take the wheel fo' a change, an' if she cain't, then I'll take taxis.'

'How many more miles before we reach Coffeeville?' Jack asked.

'Journey's back's broken, but I'm guessin' we got another three hun'red miles or so. We musta covered close to nine hun'red since we left Hershey. How many days we been on the road?'

Jack had to think. He always lost track of time when he travelled, and this trip was no different. 'About a week? Does that sound right?'

'Five days,' Eric said. 'We left Hershey on Monday and it's Friday today.'

'Well I'll be damned,' Jack said. 'It feels like I've known you guys forever.'

'Yeah,' Bob agreed. 'Spendin' time with some people really drags. Ha!'

They walked from the parking area and found a restaurant serving burgers. It was noisy inside and the atmosphere was friendly. Bob asked for, and was directed to, a wall table. He sat down with his back to the wall and beamed at his two companions: 'No point takin' chances.'

They ordered cheese burgers and fries from the waitress, a couple of beers for Bob and Jack, and a Coke for Eric. Jack poured the Budweiser into his frosted glass and waited for the foam to settle. Bob was reminded of Che and Fidel, and smiled to himself.

The food arrived and both Bob and Jack poured tomato ketchup over their fries. Jack offered the bottle to Eric, but he declined to take it. 'My mom said that people who use ketchup have been brought up eating poorly cooked food. She said they'd probably poured it over their food to make it taste better and never got out of the habit.'

'So much for our upbringings then, Bob,' Jack said.

As they ate, Jack listened to the music. 'Have you ever wondered why lyrics always capture the distress of life rather than its joy?'

'I ain't never thought about it, but now I do, I think you right. Why you think that is?'

'Probably because there's no market for happiness,' Jack said. 'The news is never happy. People like to be happy themselves, but they don't want to hear about other people's happiness. It seems to be a fact of life – though I doubt you'll ever get anyone admitting it.'

'Man, you been ridin' with Gene too long!' Bob said.

'Hymns are happy,' Eric said.

'That reminds me, Eric. There was a big advertisement in *The Tennessean* for a special service tomorrow night. I think it will suit us.'

'What the two o' you plannin'?' Bob asked.

'We're going to church tomorrow night,' Eric said.

Opals and Cigarette Butts

The Union Hotel was a former railway station built in the style of Richardson-Romanesque. The walls of the huge lobby stretched upwards until they reached a sixty-five-foot barrel-vaulted ceiling crowned with a Luminous Prism stained glass roof. The exposed floors were marble and tiled, the sitting areas carpeted, and the walls highlighted with old polished wood and plaster reliefs.

Doc walked up to the reception desk, glanced at the old railroad signs and timetables adorning its walls, and made himself known. He asked for a twin-bedded room well away from the railroad tracks: even though the hotel was no longer a station, the lines running alongside it were still heavily used. He paid in cash and checked in as Dr & Mrs Eugene Chaney.

After the cramped conditions of the tour bus, the spacious and comfortable bedroom was a welcome relief. While Nancy showered, Doc unpacked the overnight bag and arranged their belongings. He laid out some fresh clothes for Nancy and waited while she finished up in the bathroom. Ten minutes later they were sitting in the restaurant.

'You choose for me, Gene. I don't want to read all the writing.'

Neither did Doc: 'Steak okay for you?' Nancy nodded. 'How about an appetiser? Would you like an appetiser?' Nancy said no, but that she might have a dessert. 'Let's get some wine, Nancy. I can't remember the last time I had a glass. Red okay with you?'

'It's a pity Bob couldn't have joined us here,' Nancy said. 'I suppose they don't allow niggers to eat here, do they?'

'You use that word again, Nancy, and you'll get us thrown out. I keep telling you we're living in different times now. Things have changed for the better, and in a very small way you and I helped change them. Remember the bus we rode?'

'The bus we're in now?'

The bus situation confused Nancy and Doc should have known better than to introduce the subject. For parts of the day Nancy managed to cling to the present, but her fingers would then slip and she'd hurtle back to the past – just as she had done now. Since boarding the bus in Hershey, she'd suggested on several occasions that they stop at a rest area or a diner they happened to pass, and sit with Bob at the lunch counter and demand service. 'It's wrong that they're segregated, Gene. There's no point us being on the bus if we don't try and do something about it. What would they say if we returned to Duke and told them we hadn't done anything? They wouldn't be happy!'

Doc changed the subject. He'd noticed a ring on Nancy's finger that hadn't been there before. He could have sworn it was a ring he'd bought her: an iridescent precious white opal set in eighteen-carat gold. He could still recall the jeweller who'd sold it to him, a man who'd sounded more like a physicist than a sales assistant.

He'd chosen the ring for simple reasons: the opal had been Nancy's birthstone.

'Where did the ring come from, Nancy?' he asked her.

'It was in my toilet bag,' Nancy said. 'I must have put it there for safe keeping.'

'Is that the opal ring I bought you?'

Nancy looked at the ring and thought for a while. 'I don't think so, Gene. I've had it for years.'

'It's pretty. The Aborigines tell a story of God visiting the earth and bringing a message of peace. He descends on a rainbow and the stones where his feet touch the ground start to sparkle and eventually turn into opals.'

'Oh, Gene, that's just the prettiest story. Is it true?'

'It's true if you want it to be – just like all things.'

Nancy's attention was taken by two small children sitting at the far end of the restaurant with their parents.

'Aren't they cuties, Gene?'

'Who?'

'The children sitting at the table over there.'

'I'll have to take your word on that, Nancy. They look a bit blurred from where I'm sitting.'

'Do you think we should try for a family?'

Doc spluttered. 'A bit late for that, don't you think? How would a couple of old fogeys like us manage to bring up a young family? Besides, you spent your whole life around children. I thought you'd have had enough of them.'

'Did I? What was I doing?'

'You were a teacher, Nancy. A good one, too.'

'Well I never. All this time I've been thinking I lived on a farm. What a lovely surprise to know that.'

While he was rinsing his mouth with water, it suddenly dawned on Doc that Nancy's birthday must be close. Although he knew the date of her birthday, he had no idea of the day's date. He leaned across to an adjacent table, pardoned his interruption and asked the couple sitting there. It was the young woman who replied. She smiled and told him it was October 26.

'Goddamn, Nancy, it's your birthday today! How about that? This calls for a toast!'

He lifted the bottle of wine from the table and found it empty. Nancy had had only one glass, so he presumed that unless the couple at the next table had been helping themselves to the wine while his back was turned, he'd drunk the remainder himself.

'How about a glass of champagne, Nancy?'

'I won't, thank you. But I will have an orange juice. Will you join me?'

He called the waiter to the table and ordered an orange juice for Nancy and a large Maker's Mark for himself. 'I'm not toasting you with orange juice, Nancy. This is a celebration!'

The drinks arrived and Doc lifted his glass. 'Happy birthday, old girl,' he said and, without further thinking, added: 'Many more of them!' The stupidity of the remark dawned on him even as he said it.

She smiled and clinked glasses. 'I hope to goodness there aren't many more of them, Gene. I don't think I could cope.' Her voice was dreamlike but her stare clear.

Doc couldn't hold her gaze and looked away. He drained his glass and beckoned the waiter.

Doc woke with a headache. He climbed out of bed and took some aspirin. Nancy was still asleep. She had a look of determined concentration on her face, and clenched the bed linen with her fists. He showered, dressed and then gently roused her.

'Who the fuck are you?' she demanded. 'Gene! Gene, where are you? There's a strange man in the room!'

It was the start of another day.

They ate a light breakfast in the restaurant and then took a taxi to Vanderbilt. The university had grown since Nancy had studied there, but the old campus remained the same – lots of trees, old red brick buildings and green space. The university was named for Cornelius Vanderbilt, a late nineteenth-century shipping and railroad magnate. He donated the money for its construction but died without ever setting foot on the campus.

'Does this bring back any memories?' Doc asked.

'I think so,' Nancy replied. 'Is this where you and I met?'

'No, that was Duke. You came here after you dumped me.'

'This is all news to me, Gene. I don't remember that ever happening. Why did I dump you?'

'Because you had less sense then than you do now,' Doc teased.

'Well, I'm sorry. How long have you been holding this grudge?

You should have said something sooner... Gene, oh look Gene: there's one of those things with a fluffy tail!'

'So there is,' Doc said. 'There are squirrels everywhere.'

They walked slowly around the campus, occasionally stopping in front of a building Nancy recognised, and then continuing.

'Let's sit down for a while, Gene,' Nancy said eventually. 'My legs are starting to feel tired.' She sat down in the middle of a flight of steps just as a lecture in the building came to an end.

'Okay, but let's move to the side, Nancy. We're going to get trampled underfoot if we stay here.'

They moved to the side, and Nancy suddenly became concerned. 'I wasn't supposed to be in that lecture, was I? You haven't kept me talking and made me miss class?'

'No, you have no lectures today – or tomorrow, for that matter. Now stop worrying.'

'What about exams?' Nancy asked even more anxiously. 'Have I got exams this week? I haven't done any revision!'

'No lectures and no exams,' Doc assured her but, for the peace of her mind, thought it would be better if they moved away from the throng. 'Let's go and keep the Commodore company, sit with him for a while,' he suggested.

He took Nancy's hand and they strolled to where Cornelius Vanderbilt surveyed the world from the top of a pedestal. They sat on the grass, near its base. The sun was warming and Doc lit a cigarette.

'I think you're forgetting your manners, Gene. Aren't you going to offer me one?'

'You don't smoke, Nancy.'

'Of course I do! I've always smoked.'

Doc saw no harm in giving her one. He lit the cigarette for her, and then watched while she coughed a couple of times and then stubbed it out on the grass. 'That's the last cigarette I'm having, Gene. I'm never smoking again! I think it might be an idea if you stopped, too. You smoke all the time.'

'This is my first today, Nancy, and apart from your conversation, smoking's the only pleasure in life I have left.'

'Well, make sure you blow the smoke away from me then, and

don't blow it in the face of that man standing up there. I'm sure he doesn't want to get cancer, either!'

Doc moved slightly away from both Nancy and the Commodore and tried to enjoy what remained of his cigarette. He stubbed it out and placed it on the ground next to Nancy's aborted cigarette.

'Don't leave them there, Gene!' Nancy chided. 'We don't want the squirrels getting hooked on nicotine. They have a hard enough life as it is.'

Doc laughed. 'Squirrels have it made, Nancy. They live on Easy Street.'

He lay back on the grass and Nancy lay down beside him. 'Let's take a nap,' she said. Doc closed his eyes and was about to fall asleep when Nancy nudged him hard in the ribs.

'Don't fall asleep, Gene. I want to talk to you!'

Doc propped himself up on one elbow and looked at her. 'What do you want to talk about?'

'You'll never take me back to that place, will you? The place where they made me watch television all day.'

'The nursing home? Of course I won't!'

Nancy was relieved. 'They made me sit with crazy people there, Gene. Did I tell you that? I think they thought I was someone else and didn't really know who I was. Do people know who you are?'

'Sure they do, Nancy. How could anyone forget Eugene Chaney III?'

In truth, apart from the people he travelled with, he doubted anyone knew who he really was. His one regret in life was allowing himself to become a caricature of what others presumed him to be, rather than the person he knew himself to be. It was assumed that he didn't like people, preferred his own company and was a man without feelings. Rather than admit they were wrong, he'd lived up to their expectations.

'Sometimes I forget who you are, but that's allowed, isn't it? I can't be expected to remember everything these days, can I?'

Doc sat bolt upright and looked at his watch. 'I almost forgot, Nancy. We're supposed to meet Bob and the others for lunch at the Loveless Cafe at noon. I hear they have the best pecan pie in the whole of the United States, too – and I'm not about to miss a meal!'

'If I'm honest, Gene, I think you could afford to miss quite a few meals,' Nancy said. 'Now, don't forget to pick up the cigarette butts!'

Warren Kuykendahl's Special Cups

When Jack and Eric climbed out of the taxi, Warren Kuykendahl was waiting for them in his front yard. He held out his hand: 'Y'all are very welcome,' he said. 'Any friend of Susan is a friend of mine.'

Jack took Warren's hand and then Eric held out his own hand. 'What's wrong with your hand, son?' Warren asked, as he gingerly took hold of the proffered washing-up glove.

'Nothing, sir. I just like wearing gloves,' Eric replied. 'They keep my hands dry, and Jack bought them for me.'

'I'm afraid I have absolutely no idea how to pronounce your last name, Mister... er... um...' Jack said.

'It's Kuykendahl: *Kike* as in Jew, *en* as in Nigger, an' *darl* as in darlin' – Kuykendahl.'

The Kuykendahl family had moved to America in the middle of the seventeenth century and settled in the Dutch colony of New Netherland. No sooner had they unpacked their clogs and planted tulips in their front garden, however, than the colony was seized by the British and they were forced to look for new beginnings elsewhere. They migrated southward, staying long enough in Pennsylvania to fight against their old enemy in the War of Independence, and then upped sticks and moved again. Eventually they arrived in Tennessee and settled in the small town of Pulaski. Everything was fine until the outbreak of the Civil War when, once again, the Kuykendahls found themselves on the losing side of an argument.

Instead of following in the family tradition of moving to pastures new when things got rough, Peter Kuykendahl decided to remain in Pulaski and stay pissed-off there. On the Christmas

Eve of 1865, he left the house and went for a drink with six of his veteran friends, who were equally pissed-off with life. He returned home that night a little the worse for wear, and told his wife that he and his friends had just formed a new organisation. 'The Ku Klux What?' his wife had asked.

Having judged the new world order of equality not to their liking, Peter and his friends decided to do something about it – but only at night and only under the cover of anonymity. They masked and robed themselves in old bed sheets, climbed on horses and set about making the lives of Republicans, carpetbaggers, scalawags and blacks as miserable as possible. In their attempt to restore white supremacy and decency to the region, and prevent former slaves from exercising their newly-acquired civil rights, Peter and his friends burned houses, maimed and killed people.

Warren was intensely proud of his ancestor, and the bigotry that had motivated Peter continued to burn brightly in his own DNA. Although the strict Calvinism of his youth had, in mid years, given way to Calvin Kleins, his deep suspicion of international Jewry and foreigners remained.

'Tell me Jack: your name – Guravitch. Is that a Jew name?'

'Yes,' Jack replied, slightly surprised by the question. 'My ancestors came from Moldova.'

'Moldova?' Warren mused. 'That used to be communist, didn't it?'

'I'm not sure,' Jack replied truthfully. 'My family lost interest in the country decades ago.'

'Hey, Lola,' Warren called to his wife. 'Make some coffee will you, darlin', an' serve it in the special cups.'

The special cups he'd asked Lola for were mugs he reserved for uncertain visitors and trades people. Despite their claiming friendship with Susan, Jack and Eric – in Warren's mind – fell into the former category: Jack for his Jewishness and Eric for his washing-up gloves.

'Eric's Susan's cousin, Warren,' Jack began. 'He was orphaned recently and he's trying to find her. I'm helping him. We understand from a man in Hershey that Susan came this way.'

'I'm sure sorry to hear that, young fellah. Sure sorry. Let's go to the livin' room an' continue the conversation there, shall we?'

Warren led the way to a room that couldn't have been more different from Fred Finkel's – yet little the better for being so. It was fully carpeted in thick white shag and crowded with expensive couches, garish objets d'art and all manner of audiovisual technologies. It was a room where the Little House on the Prairie had met and fallen in love with the International House of Pancakes on Main St, and given birth to an amusement arcade of ostentation and lurid colours.

'This is a very nice room,' Jack lied. 'Very comfortable.'

'I have Lola to thank for that,' Warren said with pride. 'She's got a real flair for design.'

'Was Lola born poor?' Jack asked.

'Why do you ask that?' Warren asked.

'I honestly have no idea,' Jack lied again, shaking his head in puzzlement.

He was saved from any further questioning by Lola herself, who entered the room with a tray of coffees, and wearing a rhinestone leisure suit and a cowboy hat with a large feather stuck in its band.

'Jack,' Warren whispered, 'I don't feel comfortable talkin' about Susan with Eric in the room. I'm gonna ask Lola to take care of the boy, okay?' Jack nodded. 'Hey, Lola, why don't you take Eric an' show him the grounds while me an' Jack have a grown-ups conversation.'

'Sure, honey. Come on, Eric. Let's get out from under the men's feet and do something fun?'

Eric turned to Jack. 'What about Susan, Jack?'

'Don't worry, son. I'm gonna tell Jack all about her, an' then he can tell you.' He waited until they left the room.

'Susan was here,' Warren said, 'but she moved on – went to Memphis. She stayed with us for a couple of nights an' then rented an apartment. Lola took an immediate likin' to her. My wife's got great instincts when it comes to people, Jack, and she knew right away that Susan was in a class of her own – and she is. Compared to other girls in this line of work, she's the bottle of

Downy an' they're just leadin' fabric softeners. Bein' a good friend of hers, you'll know this yourself.'

'Actually, I've never met Susan. I'm just helping Eric find her.'

'Well, when you do meet her, you're in for a treat. Susan'll take your breath away, that's for sure. She's a bright girl, personable too; but she also has this amazin' natural beauty that's hard to put a finger on. Closest I can get is to say that makin' her acquaintance is like cubin' an oxymoron and gettin' gravy out of it.' Jack's brow furrowed momentarily.

'Off an' on, Susan worked for me over a period of years. She travelled around quite a bit in that time, an' told me that of all the clubs she'd danced in, mine was the best. That's why she came to me once she'd decided to add chocolate to her act: she knew I'd be the one person to appreciate it. Unfortunate thing though, was that since last seein' her I'd sold the club – sold it to a lawyer who converted the place into offices – and...' At this point Warren's voice faltered, and Jack wondered if his host was going to cry. 'It damn near broke my heart, Jack. Selling WK's was like burying a child.'

'What made you do it, then?' Jack asked.

'The Metro Council is what!' Warren said. 'People on it started gettin' all prissy; got this bee in their bonnet the size of a damned B52 bomber that Nashville didn't need any adult venues. They started makin' life as difficult as possible for me an' people like me. If I'd run a bad club I could have understood it, but I didn't: WK's did things by the book. We never violated liquor laws, never had disturbances that warranted a visit by the police, an' we didn't make noise. We were a respectable business dealin' in beauty an' dreams. That's all we did an' that's what we told 'em. We'd have done better tap dancin' on a shag carpet for all the impact we had on 'em. They started treatin' us like common criminals, law breakers. Still burns me up when I think about it! What goddamn right did they have to go rulin' we were an unpleasant smell stinkin' up the city?'

'Did they close you down?' Jack asked.

'No, I'm not sure they could have done that. They closed down some other places for violations of existin' ordinances – an' those clubs probably deserved to be closed down – but for clubs like ours they had to play sneaky. They passed new ordinances bannin' complete nudity an' makin' it a requirement for dancers an' patrons to keep three feet apart from each other an' not touch. An' then they went and prohibited alcohol on the premises! I tell you, Jack, it ruined the whole ambience of the place. Customers were made to feel like social pariahs, an' needless to say they stopped comin'. In the end I just said to hell with it all, an' sold the place.'

'But if the club was gone, why did Susan stay and rent an apartment? Why didn't she just leave?'

'Because I had other irons in the fire, Jack. I wasn't about to wait for old age to come an' pay me a visit, so I came up with an idea. Maybe the club was gone, but that didn't mean to say the entertainment had to stop: we could take it to the customers' houses – to their own living rooms.

'We called them Gentlemen's Soirees. Clients would call an' tell me what nights they were plannin' a get-together, an' I'd arrange the dancers. It worked well: the dancers made a livin', an' the customers got to enjoy themselves without havin' to worry about the police turnin' up an' askin' for their names an' addresses. I thought Susan would fit right into this business model, but I hadn't allowed for the chocolate.'

'Is this the chocolate she brought with her from Hershey?'

'Yeah, that's the stuff. It was supposed to be slow meltin', but it turned out not to melt at all – not in the early try-outs, anyway. Simple ideas are often the best, but not if you get them from simple people – an' that's what I thought this Finkel fellow was. You know the sayin' that if you get an ear shot off an' move to Texas, the only people you're likely to meet are Texans an' ear specialists? Well, to my way of thinkin', this was such a case in point.'

Jack had never heard of the saying, doubted that such a saying even existed and certainly had no idea what it meant.

'I'd take Susan to a client's house an' she'd go and prepare herself in the bathroom, smear her body with chocolate an' then come out. The idea was that she'd stand there motionless, let the chocolate melt an' then lick it off and slowly reveal her body to the people in the room. Trouble was though, the chocolate didn't melt – an' if she moved, it cracked. Customers had no idea what to make of it; didn't know if they was supposed to help lick it off or what. An' of course, that's what they weren't supposed to do. Susan never allowed anyone to touch her with their hands, so she sure as hell wasn't going to have people lickin' her body with their damned tongues!

'"It's just a glitch, Warren," she told me: "I just need time to get the mixture right." And because it was Susan, I listened to her. Anyone else, I'd have wished them good luck and bid them sayonara. Eventually, however, she did get a mix that worked.

'Susan always wanted to stand motionless, but for a crowd of onlookers that's just plain borin' – may as well be lookin' at a hat stand. Great events in history are usually the product of boredom, Jack, but you can't say that about cabaret. It took a lot of coaxin', but eventually Susan agreed to dance an', once she did, the chocolate melted a treat. Only problem was it melted too good. She couldn't keep up with it, an' had never before considered that lickin' so much chocolate at one time might make her feel sick.

'The end result was that the chocolate pooled on the carpet she was standin' on an' then, to cap it all, she went an' threw up. You can imagine how that smelled in a hot room. It was plain awful, an' other people started gaggin', too. You might guess I had to waive the fee for that night's performance, an' once I'd finished paying all the cleaning bills I was out of pocket an' in danger of losin' good customers.

'We tried it one more time, an' this occasion we had Susan standin' on some thick sheets o' polythene. To tell you the truth it was a bit of a mood killer, but we went ahead with it anyway. Rather than lickin' the chocolate off an' riskin' Susan getting ill all over again, we decided it would be better if she just wiped it from her body with her hands, an' for a while it went well an' people appeared to be enjoyin' the performance. But then a couple of guys who'd been drinkin' more than they should have been, stepped out of the audience an' decided to give her a helping hand.

'She slapped one of 'em hard, an' then punched the other fellah with her fist an' damn near broke his nose. There was blood all over the place. Now that kinda commotion's one thing that ain't good for business, Jack, and word got round. I had customers callin' up an' stipulatin' they didn't want the Chocolate Woman on no account, an' that's when I had to reluctantly call it a day.'

'You don't know where we'll find her in Memphis, do you?' Jack asked.

'She said she was gonna stay with a friend of hers an' think things through. Think about what she was gonna do with her life. I think even she realised this new art form of hers – Still Life Stripping, as she called it – wasn't goin' no place.'

'Do you happen to know her friend's name, an address or a telephone number that might be helpful?'

'Her friend's called Darla Thomas. She used to be a dancer, too, at one time. My understandin' is that she's some kind of manager at the Peabody these days. That's a hotel in the downtown. You might want to start your inquiries there.'

They caught up with Eric and Lola in the back garden – another display cabinet for the Kuykendahls' considerable wealth. Anything of value that could withstand the elements and be considered an object of prestige was carefully positioned for the benefit of neighbours and visitors: four luxury cars, two trucks, a speedboat, an oversized barbecue pit and grill, and a sit-on lawnmower. Eric and Lola were sitting on the edge of the swimming pool with their feet dangling in the water, Lola sipping from a tumbler filled with gin and tonic and absent-mindedly rattling the ice cubes.

It was difficult to know if Lola was drunk or not; more difficult to believe that any person not drunk would have dressed in the clothes she wore.

'Eric's the most sorrowful child I've ever met, Warren!' Lola said, and then fixed her eyes on Jack, as if somehow Eric's condition was his fault. 'It's your responsibility to make sure that this only child doesn't grow up to be an only adult, you hear?'

'Don't worry, Mrs Kuykendahl, I'll take care of him,' Jack said.

'You make sure you do. Children are the greatest of God's gifts and time spent with them is the most precious time of all. You remember that! Warren and I have two of the most darlin' children you could ever hope to meet, and we love them to bits, don't we, Warren?' Warren nodded.

'Where are they now?' Jack asked.

Lola slipped an ice cube from her mouth and let it drop into the glass. 'We sent them away to boarding school,' she said, without missing a beat.

'Did you find out where Susan is?' Eric leapt up to ask.

'She's in Memphis, staying with a friend. We'll find her there.'

'But what if we don't?'

'We will. I give you my word on it.'

It was time for them to leave, and Jack thanked Warren for his help and Lola for the coffee in the special cups. He then asked Warren if he'd call them a taxi.

'I can do better than that, gentlemen: I'll drive you there myself. There's some business I need to take care of downtown, an' you know what they say: death brings freedom but no extra television channels.'

Jack and Eric looked at each other.

Warren dropped them outside the Union Hotel. To the best of his knowledge, it was the first time he'd had a Jew in his car. Jack was a nice enough fellow, and he wondered if it was time for him to re-evaluate his prejudices. He decided it wasn't: it would be easier to have the car valeted.

The Revival – Aztec Two Step Style

They found Doc and the others taking coffee in the lobby. 'Any luck?' Doc asked.

'Yes and no,' Jack replied. 'She was here, but she moved to Memphis a couple of weeks ago. Warren was pretty sure she'd still be there.'

'Kind of elusive, this cousin o' yo's, ain't she?' Bob said to Eric.

'Jack says we'll find her and I believe him,' Eric replied. 'Do you know where the toilets are?'

'Over yonder,' Bob indicated. 'Is this gonna be the big day?'

'I hope so,' Eric said.

'What do you mean his big day? Is he getting married? You never told me anything about this, Gene. You're forever keeping secrets from me. I don't even have a hat to wear,' Nancy said.

'He ain't gettin' married, Nance,' Bob laughed. 'He's blocked up, is all. Got his'self constipated.'

'Well, that's a relief,' Nancy said. 'I thought he was a bit young to be getting married. And what would his parents have said?'

'What happens if we don't find Susan in Memphis, Jack? Nice as the boy is, he can't stay with us forever.'

'I've thought about that, Doc, and if we still haven't found her by the time we get to Coffeeville, I'll stick with him and make sure he gets home safely; try and explain things to the people there. I think I'd already decided on this, but what clinched it was something Lola Kuykendahl said. She told me Eric was an only child in danger of growing up to be an only adult. He's not the most confident of kids, and reading between the lines of what he's told me, I think the other kids at school picked on him; made fun of his naivety and the fact that he doesn't look his age. It's not much fun being ridiculed – and who's there to stick up for him now his parents are gone and his guardians are so caring they ship him off to a deaf school? Besides, I enjoy spending time with the boy. It's a whole lot more fun hanging out with Eric than it ever was with my own family, and if you think about it I'm as closely related to Eric as I ever was to Conrad!'

Eric returned at that moment. 'Any joy?' Jack asked.

'No, I pooped a few times but nothing came out. Do you think I should see a doctor?'

'There's one sitting right there,' Jack said, pointing to Doc. 'What do you think, Doc?'

'Take him for a Mexican meal. It'll blow it right out of him.'

'Is that what you used to tell your patients?' Jack asked him.

'No – but it's what I wanted to tell them! Believe me, it'll work, and all it will cost is the price of a meal you'd have had to buy anyway.'

'Shall we all go for one?' Eric asked.

'I'm afraid we can't, Eric. When Bob told me you and Jack were going to church tonight, I went ahead and booked a table for me, Nancy and Bob in the hotel's dining room. Nancy's hoping to desegregate the restaurant this evening, aren't you, dear?'

'Yes, I am. And if they refuse to serve Bob, we're all walking out!' Nancy said firmly. 'Right, Gene?'

'Right, Nancy. We could meet up for a drink afterwards, though. We were planning to go to a place where they play music. What time does your service finish?'

'I don't know,' Jack said. 'It starts at six-thirty, so I'm figuring about eight. I'll have to borrow a phone from you though, Bob – to call a taxi after it ends.'

Bob took a phone from his pocket and inserted a new SIM card. He handed it to Jack.

'Thanks. What's the name of the place you're going to?'

'I can't remember the name of it, but you can't miss it. It's a honky-tonk on the McGavock Pike, right across from the Opryland Hotel. We'll be there by eight-thirty at the latest. Any problems, give Bob a call.'

Jack went to the front desk and got the name of a nearby Mexican restaurant. He returned to where the others were sitting. 'Come on, Eric – let's go and kick-start those bowels of yours.'

The Happy Sombrero was an inappropriately named Tex-Mex restaurant within easy walking distance of the hotel. Sombre Sombrero would have been a better designation, as the taqueria was anything but happy. It was apparent to any customer who ate in the restaurant that, on a sliding scale of enjoyment, the waiters and waitresses viewed their jobs as ranking somewhere close to a near-death experience; something to be done until something better came along.

Despite having grown up in California, Eric knew nothing of Mexican cuisine and Jack ordered for them both: tortilla chips with hot sauce and salsa as an appetiser, followed by wet burritos and refried beans.

'And this will help me go to the toilet?' Eric asked, once the food had been placed on the table.

'If this doesn't, nothing will!' Jack said.

The burritos were filled with beef, shredded lettuce, guacamole, salsa and sour cream, and topped with a red chilli sauce and melted cheese. The food was good and Eric ate not only everything on his plate, but also the leftover beans on Jack's. He'd never before tasted food so hot, and the Tabasco sauce he'd mistaken for ketchup and splashed over his food – against his mother's advice – had only made it hotter. Beads of sweat formed on his scalp, ran down his forehead, neck and cheeks, and left his hair wet and matted.

'Boy that was good! I'm going to eat Mexican food again, Jack. Shall we eat it tomorrow?'

'Let's see how you get on with this first.' Jack looked at his watch and called for the check – and again, five minutes later, after the check hadn't arrived. While they waited, he told Eric to visit the restroom and use the hand blower to dry his hair.

No sooner had they left the restaurant than the waiter who'd served them came running out after them. 'Hey, you forgot to leave a gratuity!'

'I didn't forget: I purposely didn't leave you one!' Jack said. 'I had to ask for water; I ordered a beer from you and you never brought one; and you never once asked us how the meal was! If you think I'm leaving a tip just because you banged two plates of food down on a table, then you can think again. Your whole attitude sucks, man, and if I'm honest, you're the worst damn waiter who's ever served me. I'll tell you what I'll do though: once I get to church I'll pray for you, and ask God to cure that deformity of yours that makes it impossible for you to smile at customers!'

Once his customers were a safe distance from the restaurant, the waiter shouted after them: 'Fuck you, assholes! I hope God kills you!' When Jack turned, the waiter quickly retreated into the safety of the Happy Sombrero.

Jack and Eric walked back to the hotel and found a waiting taxi.

'Where to, gentlemen?' the driver asked.

Jack dug the folded sheet of newspaper from his pocket and

read out the name and address of the church. Under the impression it was located somewhere close to the downtown area, he was surprised when the driver took the ramp on to the I40 and headed west.

'Is the church far?' Jack asked, slightly concerned.

'Twenty minutes, maybe thirty in this traffic,' the driver replied.

'Have you heard of this church?'

'No, I can't say that I have. There are a handful of small churches out there, but I don't know any of them by name – or reputation, for that matter. I'm a Methodist, myself.'

Jack looked at his watch: ten till six. Even if it took them thirty minutes they'd still arrive in good time, but just where they'd be arriving he now wasn't sure. The advertisement in the newspaper had stood out head and shoulders over the other church notices on the page, and led him to believe that the church was a major player in the area. *If you're hungry for an old-fashioned and Heaven-sent Revival,* the notice had read, *then join us this Saturday at 6:30 pm.* It promised a *shower of blessings* on all who attended, and named the guest evangelist as Brother Logan Bloodworth, a man who'd been born again at the age of eight and subsequently led more than two thousand revivals.

Jack hadn't disclosed to Eric – and certainly not to Doc – his true reason for attending the revival, and had probably led Eric to believe the service was for his benefit. It wasn't: it was for the benefit of Jack, specifically his hair. Although he'd tried desperately to convince himself that losing it was no big deal, he knew that it was and always would be. It preyed on his mind the whole time, especially so when he showered and afterwards had to unclog the drain. Being away from Laura and Conrad hadn't reversed the hair loss – not even stabilised it. Every time he imagined himself bald, he shuddered. He saw the revival as a last chance salon, an opportunity to seek a cure at the hands of the supernatural. He had nothing to lose.

Jack's train of thought was interrupted by the borborygmic rumblings of Eric's stomach. Gas and air had now started to move through the boy's intestinal tract, a sure signal that the long-awaited housecleaning was about to commence. The wambling noises grew in intensity until a blast of gas forcibly exited through Eric's rectum and filled the car with the unpleasant odour of rotten eggs.

'Hot dog, Eric!' Jack exclaimed.

The taxi driver said nothing but rolled down the car windows. Eric had been as surprised as anyone by the sudden expulsion of gas from his body. He spluttered his apologies to the driver, who told him not to worry – a lot worse things had happened in the back of his cab.

'Try and sit on them while we're in the car, Eric,' Jack whispered. 'As soon as we get to the church, you can let rip there.'

The taxi dropped them at the church and they stood in the parking lot for a time, while Eric got as much gas out of his system as possible.

'I think I'm okay now, Jack,' Eric said eventually.

They walked into the church and took seats mid-way down the hall, adjacent to the aisle. Jack looked around: the church was barely half full and there were less than five minutes remaining before the service started. The congregation, he noticed, was completely white and looked to be overwhelmingly poor. A few people sat in their finery, but most looked as if they'd either just walked in from ploughing a field or fixing a car engine. A woman belonging to the former category, and wearing a long shiny blue coat, turned around from the pew in front of them and smiled.

'Sir, I don't believe I know you,' she said to Jack.

'That's right,' Jack said.

The lady's smile became less certain, but her manner remained generous. 'Well, happy to have you with us.'

Jack's mind had already wandered off to more important topics – namely his hair – and it was Eric who smiled back at the woman and thanked her. 'That's a nice coat you're wearing, ma'am,' Eric said. 'Is it waterproof?'

'I think so,' she said, 'but I wouldn't like to get baptised in it,' she laughed. She then pointed to two young girls sitting on the other side of the aisle. 'They're getting baptised at the end of the service,' she explained.

At that point the music quieted and the minister of the church walked to a pulpit flanked by national and state flags. He was an old man with a kindly face but, worryingly for Jack, also as bald as a badger. He looked at the programme he'd been handed on entering the church and found his name: Brother James Bruister.

'Welcome, welcome y'all to what I know is going to be a mighty fine night of worship and prayer,' Brother James commenced. 'It's good to see so many old faces here tonight and good to see new ones as well,' he said, looking in the direction of Jack and Eric. 'I also want to thank Brother Logan for agreeing to come to our small church this evening and lead us in praise. If anyone's going to get the Holy Spirit moving among us tonight, it's Brother Logan, and those of you touched by it are welcome to come to the front of the church and commit yourselves to Jesus and be blessed in His name. Also, as this is a special night of worship, any of you with ailments you'd like the Lord to cure, Brother Logan and I will be happy to lay our hands upon you and pray for a healing. Praise the Lord, everyone. Praise the Lord!'

'Amen, Brother James,' the congregation responded. 'Praise the Lord.'

'It's good to hear y'all are in the mood for prayer tonight, and I hope y'all are in good voice too. We've got Brother Wyatt playing guitar tonight, Sister Lurlean on piano and Brother Bill on drums; we'll start our glorification of God with an old favourite of both mine and yours: *Revive Us Again*.'

Everyone stood and the band started to play. Wyatt was a flamboyant guitarist who performed with a windmill action, occasionally falling to one knee and lunging towards the congregation. Lurlean was more restrained and hammered away at the ivories without show, while Bill battered the skins of his drums with an expression of unrelenting hatred.

The hymn ended and everyone sat down. Brother James then invited the congregation to bow their heads in silent prayer. Jack lowered his head and stared at the floor, but was unable to focus on anything in particular – not even the floor. He wondered how much the room at the Union Hotel was costing Doc; how long the water supplies on the bus would last before running out; and how long it would be before the septic tank became full and, if it did fill up, how would they empty it.

And then the silence was unexpectedly broken by the rallying call of a trumpet. The walls of Jericho weren't about to come tumbling down, but Eric's bowels were!

'You okay?' Jack whispered.

'I think I need to go to the toilet, Jack, but I don't know where it is.'

'Okay, hang on until the prayer's finished and I'll ask someone. It can't be too much longer – what do people pray about, anyway? I can't think of a damned thing.'

'Other people,' Eric whispered.

'Other people? Why would anyone want to pray for other people?'

Eric had no time to answer. Brother James drew the silent prayer to a close and announced the next hymn: *Victory in Jesus.* Jack tapped the lady in the shiny coat on the shoulder and asked where the restroom was.

'Immediately outside the hall, sir: first door on your left.'

Eric took off down the aisle in short fast steps, his buttocks clenched tightly together. He had no trouble finding the bathroom, as the door to the restroom was off its hinges and propped against the corridor wall, leaving the stall visible. He went straight to it, latched the door behind him and quickly pulled down his trousers. He was just in time: Montezuma was on the warpath, and he wasn't happy.

Unfortunately for Eric, a combination of factors ensured that his bowel movement would be heard by the entire congregation. (1) The start of the hymn had been delayed while Wyatt replaced a broken guitar string and then spent more time re-tuning his instrument. (2) There was no door on the restroom to prevent sound from entering the corridor. (3) The corridor had magnificent acoustics, and (4) The door between the church hall and the corridor had been wedged open. Consequently, the worshippers heard Eric's every groan and strain, the echo of long unstable farts and the noise of faeces – sometimes solid and sometimes not – splashing into water. And then the smell came.

At first it was no more than a gentle whiff, but the intensity of the smell grew quickly and very soon permeated the entire church – a funk of Biblical proportion both fearful and frightening. The noxious gases released by Eric cleared the back pews of the church as effectively as mustard gas had cleared enemy trenches during World War I, and those sitting there were forced to move forward and seek refuge closer to the front. One such person took Eric's vacant seat and Jack, still unsure of how to behave in a church, forcibly took him by the lapels and threw him into the aisle after he refused to leave voluntarily.

'Play the hymn, will you,' Brother James hissed to Brother Wyatt. 'Now!'

The band started to play, the congregation to sing, and gradually the church reclaimed its aseptic sanctity. If anyone had turned to look behind them, however, they would have seen a small boy moving awkwardly down the corridor with his trousers bunched around his ankles, furtively glancing over his shoulder and pulling pieces of absorbent paper from the notice boards.

The hymn ended and a man called George Herring came to the front and sang a song praising the Lord a cappella. He was interrupted three times by the sound of a toilet flushing and hard bristles scraping a porcelain bowl. To no one's surprise, and with everyone's understanding, George forgot the words twice and returned to his seat just as Eric was returning to his; the former took his seat in failure and the latter in red-faced and breathless triumph.

'Feel better?' Jack asked him.

'A lot better, thanks, but my legs feel like jelly. I hope that taxi man doesn't forget to come and get us: I wouldn't want to have to walk back.'

They sang another hymn – *There is Power in the Blood* – and then, quite fittingly, Logan Bloodworth came to the pulpit. Logan was dressed in a dark suit and wore a red silk tie. He looked sophisticated, but his delivery was self-consciously folksy. He talked about the importance of a person confessing *their* sins rather than those of other people, and the importance of prayer being sinless and fervent, illustrating his message with a homespun homily about an old woman called Loretta, the prayers of a young girl called Becky and a wet map.

'It ain't too late,' he cajoled them. 'Pray to God with fervour and with your hearts open. Ask Him to forgive your sins and allow you to be baptised again in the blood of His son, the Lord Jesus Christ. You can walk to the front this very night and offer yourselves to Jesus and He'll take you. He'll take you in His arms, love and protect you from now until the day you go to Heaven and shake Him by the hand. Believe me, folks, if you do this, ev'ry day of yo' lives will be as happy and rewardin' as Christmas Day itself.

'And those of you already havin' a special relationship with Christ are welcome to step forward and renew your commitment, and when you do, make sure you bring someone with you that you feel is on the verge of steppin' forward but just needs a helpin' nudge to get 'em movin' in the right direction.

'An' those of you here with sicknesses and illnesses, you get your weary bones down here too and let Jesus take care of you. Me and Brother James will lay our hands upon you and invoke the Lord's power to make you well, and confound all those who told you to stop complainin' an' just make the best of things.'

'Hallelujah! Praise the Lord!' the congregation responded chaotically.

Logan Bloodworth then stood back from the microphone, stretched his arms high into the air and started to jabber. Sister Lurlean played a melancholic hymn on the piano and Brother Bill accompanied her by slowly stroking the drums with a pair of wire brushes. Brother Wyatt, however, had put his guitar to one side in readiness for a more important gig – that of translating the tongues spoken by Brother Logan into intelligible English.

It was difficult to judge if Brother Logan had lost his touch or not, for not one person stepped forward to take up even one of his offers. People looked around the church to see if others were on the edge of commitment, occasionally nodding encouragements with their heads, but no one moved. Jack looked at his watch. The taxi would arrive in ten minutes. It was now or never. He took a deep breath and rose from his seat. Eric looked at him in surprise.

'Wait here for me, Eric. I need to talk to Brother Logan about something.'

Eric had no intention of being left alone and grabbed hold of Jack's coat. Having started to fear a revival wash out, a look of relief now swept over Brother James' face, and he smiled warmly as the two strangers approached. Brother Logan didn't come cheap!

'We're here for a healing,' Jack said.

'The boy's bowels?' Brother James asked earnestly.

'No,' Jack said, surprised by the suggestion. 'He's just cleared them out.'

'Is it his hands then?' Brother James said, noticing Eric's washing-up gloves.

'No,' Jack said again, getting a little exasperated. 'It's me.'

'What's your name, son?' Brother James asked.

'Jack. Jack Guravitch.'

Brother James asked him to kneel. Once Jack was positioned, he and Brother Logan placed their hands over his head and Brother James called out to Jesus.

'Lord Jesus, please have mercy on your servant Jack who is kneeling here before you tonight. In need of your help, he is here to commit his life to you and...' Jack interrupted him.

'I don't want to commit my whole life to Him just yet,' he said, 'I'm Jewish. I just want to commit my hair to him, and if He can stop it falling out I'll look to committing myself fully at a later date.'

Brother James and Brother Logan looked at each other hesitantly. This was something they'd have to pray about before continuing, and Logan now unleashed the full power of his tongues. All Jack could hear was gibberish, but fortunately Wyatt was on hand to hear and interpret the words of God. Although Brother Wyatt was born again, his vocabulary had remained untouched by the experience, and his translation of Brother Logan's words was unceremonious.

'God says to fuck off and stop wasting His time!'

Brother James was taken aback by Wyatt's words. 'You sure He said that, Wyatt?' he asked. (He had reason to be sceptical. On a previous occasion, Wyatt had translated similarly strange language as a message from God instructing Brother James to buy him a new Fender Telecaster. Wyatt played beautifully, God had said, but would be able to play more beautifully and please Him more if he had a new guitar.)

'Words to that effect,' Wyatt replied. 'He said He didn't want any truck with a Christ killer.'

Both Brothers James and Logan were surprised by the strength of the words, but in complete agreement with their sentiments. They lifted their hands from Jack's head and Brother James spoke quietly to both him and Eric.

'I think it's best if you both leave the church now,' he said firmly. 'To save you embarrassment, I'm going to ask Brother Bill to escort you to the back entrance. As far as the congregation's concerned, you'll be in the vestry having one-on-one counselling – and Bill, wait there a good ten minutes, will you? If you come straight back empty-handed, we'll never get anyone to step forward!'

Somewhat shaken by this turn of events, Jack and Eric meekly followed Brother Bill to the rear entrance and left the church. They walked to the front of the building and found the taxi waiting for them.

'I don't think we need to mention this to the others, do we, Eric?' Jack said.

'Probably not,' Eric replied. 'You didn't really kill Jesus, did you?'

'No, of course I didn't. But if I ever meet Brother Wyatt again, I'll probably kill him!'

The Honky-tonk Thief

'Do you remember if Doc mentioned the name of this music bar?'

'He didn't say. He just said it was the only one here.'

'It must be this place then,' Jack said. 'I wonder why they call it the Cow Wash.'

It was 8:15 pm and Doc, Bob and Nancy hadn't yet arrived.

Jack asked for a table by the wall that would seat five and ordered drinks – a beer for himself and a Coke for Eric.

'I think I need to use the toilet again,' Eric said.

'Hot damn, kid! There'll be nothing left of you if you go on like this. You know where the restrooms are, don't you – we passed them on the way in.'

On his way, Eric bumped into Doc. 'Can't talk, Doctor Gene. Got to go to the toilet. Jack's over there.'

Doc smiled to himself and waited for Nancy and Bob to catch up. They joined Jack at the table and Bob waved to the waitress to attract her attention.

'I got you a wall table, Bob. I hope you appreciate that.'

'Sure I do, but how I know you ain't done this outta self-interest? If gravy went down my neck tonight an' I fell down dead, you'd have no driver to chauffeur your butts to Miss'ippi, now would you?'

'Hey, Bob, what do you want to drink?' Doc interrupted. 'The waitress is coming.'

'The usual,' Bob said.

Doc placed the order. 'How did your service go?' he asked.

'Fine,' Jack said nonchalantly.

'That's it! Just fine? You're not telling me something, are you? I'll ask Eric when he gets back – he'll tell me. By the way, I told you Mexican would do the trick.'

'Eric will tell you just the same as me,' Jack said. 'I hope to God he gets his bowels cleaned out before we get back to the bus, though. That stuff coming out of his body smells something awful – like it's been stewing in there for weeks.'

'He's a nice boy, isn't he?' Nancy said. 'He's like a good egg cooked sunny side up.'

'He is,' Jack said. 'But he's giving off the smell of rotten eggs at the moment, Nancy, so don't be surprised if the air gets a bit cloudy every now and again.'

'Thank God we're in the Union Hotel, Nancy,' Doc said. 'I think we should close the window tonight though, just to be on the safe side.'

'He's coming back,' Jack said. 'No more wisecracks.'

'I think that's it,' Eric said. 'I hardly did anything that time and it wasn't sloppy. What was your meal at the hotel like, Doctor Gene?'

'It was good thank you, Eric. It turns out the restaurant was desegregated this very morning, so Nancy and Bob were both happy.'

'It's probably because they heard me talking to you last night, Gene,' Nancy said. 'But it's good we're making progress, slowly bringing about change. I'm going to bring Dora with me next time I visit Nashville and take her to the hotel. She'll give them a piece of her mind if they've gone back to their old ways.'

'What's desegregated mean?' Eric asked.

'It's when you join people of different races together, rather than separating them,' Doc said. 'At one time, you, Nancy and I wouldn't have been allowed to sit at the same table as Jack and Bob, because Jack's Jewish and Bob's black. They'd have been discriminated against and forced to eat in different restaurants, go to different schools and sit in different parts of a cinema or church. Nowadays, people wouldn't sit with them because they're both disagreeable people – not because they're racially different.'

'Al'ays gotta get a dig in, don't you, Gene? Never happy less you makin' some po' soul miserable,' Bob laughed.

'They discriminated against Jack in church tonight,' Eric said. 'One man called him a Christ killer, but Jack said he'd never even laid a finger on Him.'

'This sounds more like it,' Doc said grinning. 'What else went on at the church tonight?'

'I can't tell you, Doctor Gene. Jack said I hadn't to say.'

Doc burst out laughing. 'I knew it. I damn well knew you were up to something, Jack. Are you going to tell me now?'

'Nope, and neither is Eric.'

'I bet it was something to do with your damn hair, wasn't it?'

'How did you know that, Doctor Gene?' Eric blurted out, and then turned sheepish when he saw Jack staring at him.

There was a stage close to the entrance where the musicians played. A woman in her early twenties had been singing when they'd arrived at the Cow Wash, but now a man in his late fifties had taken to the stage. His name was Brett Turbine. He had three guitars propped up behind him and was tuning another. He talked to the audience as he did this, telling them stories and laughing easily. His voice was deep and gravelly, fashioned from years of drinking hard liquor and smoking cigarettes, and his face looked like a squat for homeless people.

When he was happy with the sound of his guitar, Brett rose from the high stool he'd been sitting on and started to play. He sang songs about drinking hard liquor, smoking cigarettes and homelessness; songs about cheating women and cheating men; and songs about dying cowboys and crippled children. After each song, he would remind the Saturday night crowd to tip the waitresses who served them and, if they liked what they were hearing, to feel free to throw money into the large plastic bucket at the edge of the stage.

'Man, ain't he the cheery one,' Bob said. 'Next time the waitress comes by I gonna ask for two glasses: one full o' beer, an' an empty one fo' my tears. Only thing goin' fo' the man in my book is his appearance. Least he don't look like the mannequins me an' Marsha saw at the Gran' Ole Opry. Looked like they'd just come outta some beauty parlour an' got clothed in a fancy dress store.

'You heard the story 'bout when Elvis played the Gran' Ole Opry, Gene? He went there once an' never went back. Some ol' guy tol' him to stick to drivin' trucks; tol' him he'd never make it in the big time. Ha! That was back when the Opry was still in the Ryman Auditorium over on Fifth – before it moved out here. An' who you think played piano at the openin' night o' the new one? I'll give you a clue: he were a good friend o' yo's an' mine.'

Doc thought for a while and then gave up. 'No idea.'

'Richard Milhous Nixon his'self. Ha!'

'I need to go to the bathroom, Gene. Where is it?' Nancy asked.

'I know where it is, Mrs Skidmore,' Eric said. 'I can take you.'

'That's very kind of you, Eric; I'd be delighted to have your company.' She looked at Jack and said: 'You could learn a lot from this young man!'

'How come she's always on my case?' Jack asked, after Nancy

and Eric had left the table. 'Is she confusing me with someone else?'

'Who knows?' Doc said. 'It's Nancy's voice, but it's not her speaking the words. You need to keep that in mind. Oh shit! What's she doing down there?'

Brett Turbine had stopped singing and was kneeling by the edge of the stage talking to Nancy, who was in the process of dividing the money in his tip bucket between her and Eric. He stood up and walked back to the microphone and, in a laughing voice, announced to the crowd that he was being robbed by two of the FBI's most wanted and could anyone help. Doc got down there as fast as he could.

'Anyone can take the money, Gene,' Nancy said. 'People are throwing it away. They don't want it anymore.'

Pilfering from Ike Godsey's Store had been one thing, but stealing from Brett Turbine in public was another matter altogether. Doc told Brett to continue his set and promised to sort things out. Eric only too willingly threw his share of the spoils back into the bucket, but Nancy held on to her dollar bills and Doc had to prise them out of her hand. She started to get agitated and Doc saw a cold glint in her eyes, a sure sign of approaching danger if ever there was one. He remembered it had been her birthday the previous day and used it to his advantage.

'Come on, Nancy, they're waiting for you at the table. They want to wish you a happy birthday, sing you a song.'

Nancy relaxed her grip on the money long enough for Doc to take it from her and place it in the bucket. 'Is it my birthday?' Nancy asked incredulously. 'I had no idea. How old am I?'

'We can talk about that back at the table; let's take you to the bathroom first. Eric, you go back to the table and I'll take care of Nancy.' He then took a twenty-dollar bill from his wallet, placed it in the bucket and got Brett's attention. 'When you see us walk back to our table – over at the back there – can you sing *Happy Birthday*? Her name's Nancy.'

'Happy to,' Brett smiled. '– And thanks for taking care of things, Grandpa.'

Eric returned to the table alone, his hands inside the rubber gloves feeling particularly moist. Jack shook his head from side to side in mock-disappointment. 'Not only a snitch but a desperado, too,' he said to Bob. 'Who'd have believed it of one so young and innocent?'

'I didn't do anything, Jack – it was Mrs Skidmore who took the money. I told her we shouldn't do it.'

'Just following orders, eh, the old Nuremburg Defence?'

'I think we're supposed to sing *Happy Birthday* to Mrs Skidmore when she gets back.' Eric said.

'I hate singing that song,' Jack said. 'I hate singing *Auld Lang Syne*, too, and wearing party hats. Hopefully, by the time she gets back she'll have forgotten all about it.'

'I reckon you an' Brett Turbine could be soul buddies, Jack. I cain't see him likin' those things neither.'

As if to disprove Bob's point, Brett immediately launched into *Happy Birthday*, and as Doc and Nancy made their way back to the table, the raucous Saturday night crowd joined in.

Nancy didn't sit down but stood there beaming, lost in the moment and graciously accepting the well wishes of those around her. The song eventually came to an end and Brett spoke into the microphone. 'Happy Birthday, Nancy! If I were twenty years older, I'd sure as hell make you mine, darlin'.'

Altercation in Plaid

They left Nashville the next morning and continued on the I40 towards Memphis. Sweet gum trees replaced maples, and the first cotton fields appeared. Bob stuck to the speed limit and drove at a steady 70 mph; Gene and Nancy snoozed; Jack read the now out-of-date newspaper he'd bought in Nashville; and Eric completed the second book of Chronicles: a further 1,623,021 fatalities.

'The toilet's blocked,' Jack announced.

'Shit!' Bob exclaimed.

'That would be my guess,' Jack said.

''Course it blocked with shit, you damn ninny! I was jus' exclaimin' when I said the word. Who gone an' blocked it?'

'It will be an accumulation,' Doc said. 'We'll stop at the next rest area and empty the sewage holding tank into the dump facilities there. Do you know how to do that?'

'No I don't know how to do that!' Bob snapped. 'I'll have to read the damn manual again!'

'I'll read it,' Jack volunteered. 'I've finished the newspaper.'

'I bet you put it down the damn toilet, didn't you?'

'If you don't quit moaning, I'll stick your head down the toilet!'

'Either you two behave yourselves or you won't be allowed to go on any more trips!' Nancy said. 'I'm not having any falling out on my bus.'

'Sorry, Nancy,' Bob and Jack said in unison.

'It's Mrs Skidmore to you, if you don't mind! Honestly, Arnold, I'm tempted to make them both get out and walk the rest of the way. The sooner I retire the better.'

'You could punish them by making them empty the holding tank,' Doc suggested helpfully.

'That's a good idea, Arnold. Bob and the other one – yes you, I'm talking to you,' she said, looking at Jack sternly. 'You both empty the tank when we stop! Understand?' She then turned to Doc. 'What's a holding tank, dear?'

Two old men stood at the urinals of the rest area, facing forward and studiously ignoring each other. One was dressed in a green plaid shirt and corduroy pants, and the other in a red plaid jacket and Mackinaw wool hunting hat. If death came to either man as slowly as urine left them, one of them at least would be content.

The last time the two men had been in such close proximity was almost fifty years ago when, on the front porch of Oaklands and in the company of Hilton Travis, they'd smoked cigars together. Brandon Travis was the first to finish. He gathered his rucksack and cardboard sign from the tiled floor and exited the restroom without washing his hands. Brandon had been on the road for three days.

Having resigned themselves to an impending lawsuit for the loss of his sister, the administrators of the Oaklands Retirement

Community had seen no further advantage in paying for Brandon to stay in a hotel. At Brandon's insistence, however, they'd given him the cash equivalent of a first-class plane ticket to Memphis, and the taxi fare from there to Clarksdale.

Believing his luck to have changed, Brandon visited a casino in nearby Grantville and there, found that it hadn't: in less than an hour he lost not only his fare at the blackjack tables, but also the remainder of his money. He had no option but to hitchhike home. To give himself an edge over any competition he might face on the road, he tore off the side of a cardboard box and inscribed on it: VIETNAM VET. That Brandon had never fought in that, or any other war, was unimportant.

Brandon had no trouble getting cars or trucks to stop for him, but had the greatest of difficulty remaining in these vehicles for any length of time. He was disadvantaged by a body odour that ripened by the hour, a conversational manner that was sour and expletive, and an unpleasant habit of loudly coughing up phlegm and then swallowing it. Consequently, Brandon's rides had been many but short. He now stood at the entrance to the services touting for a ride to Memphis.

Doc exited the restroom and waited for Nancy. She came out of the ladies' room with her hands wet. 'There aren't any towels in there, Gene. Can you believe that?'

Doc saw no point in mentioning the hand driers that would have been on the wall, and instead gave her his clean handkerchief.

'This is no good, Gene,' she said after a few moments. 'The material's too thin.' She dropped the handkerchief to the floor and proceeded to dry her hands on his shirt.

Doc retrieved the kerchief and took Nancy's arm. As they prepared to leave the lobby, the man standing at the exit started to shout at them. 'Nancy Travis! What in God's name are you doing here? Is that you Chaney, you son-of-a-bitch kidnapper!'

They came to an abrupt halt, and Doc stared disbelievingly at the man he'd only recently stood next to in the restroom. It slowly dawned on him who he was. What kind of plain dumb luck was this? Not for a moment had he ever considered that

Nancy's estranged brother might be the one to derail their escape to Coffeeville. But here Brandon was, exposing their identities at the top of his voice to a crowd that now gathered. Doc was not only speechless in that moment, he was mentally paralysed and couldn't think of a damned thing to say or do!

For once, Nancy's Alzheimer's came to their rescue. She literally had no idea who the man shouting at them was, and screamed at him when he tried to touch her. Her conviction was total and convincing, and when bystanders noticed Doc having difficulty restraining the man, they willingly intervened on his behalf.

'Get your damned hands off me!' Brandon shouted at them. 'That woman's my sister and that man has kidnapped her!'

'I've never seen you before in my life!' Nancy shouted back at him. 'My brother's dead; he died in a tractor accident twenty years ago, and this man is my husband! How dare you say such things? Call the police, Gene. This man's a lunatic; he needs to be locked up in a secure unit!'

'You're the fucking lunatic, Nancy!' Brandon countered.

The grip of the trucker holding Brandon tightened, and Brandon reluctantly had to recognise that public opinion was once again passing him by. He stopped struggling and became placatory. Having recently purloined the wallet of an ancient motorist who'd been kind enough to give him a ride – deciding on the spur of the moment to place it in his jacket pocket rather than the glove compartment as requested – he had no desire for the police to be involved.

Bob had now arrived at the scene. He'd left Jack and Eric to pump out the sewage and headed to the service building with the intention of bumming a cigarette from Doc. He hesitated when he saw the commotion, and then moved casually to Doc's side, to all outward appearances just another face in the crowd. Doc noticed him but avoided showing any signs of recognition, waiting until Brandon's eyes were averted before whispering in an aside for Bob to get the wheelchair from the bus's storage compartment and chloroform from his medicine box. Bob disappeared as silently and inconspicuously as he'd arrived.

Brandon now apologised to the small crowd. The ballyhoo, he explained, had been a misunderstanding, a case of mistaken identity caused by the fragility of his mind: fighting for his country in Vietnam had taken its toll and left him a mere shell of the man he'd once been. He did promise, however, to tell the full story to anyone prepared to give him a ride to Memphis. Unsurprisingly, there were no volunteers and the crowd drifted away.

As Doc and Nancy moved through the door and walked to the parking area, Brandon followed them. 'I know it's you Nancy, and I know it's you Chaney,' he said in a low threatening voice. 'Don't for a moment think this is over!'

Doc had suspected as much, and purposely guided Nancy away from the bus toward an area where cars were parked. He knew Brandon would take the licence plate of any vehicle they climbed into, and that eventuality had to be guarded against. As Brandon followed at a distance, a man with an empty wheelchair followed him, and when no one was looking pushed it hard into the back of his legs and tipped him backwards. Bob then placed a rag soaked in chloroform over Brandon's face and wheeled him to the bus.

'Now what we do?' Bob asked, once Doc joined him.

'I have an idea,' Doc replied, 'but let's get Nancy on the bus first.' He took Nancy to the rear lounge and asked Eric to read her a story from the Bible. 'A nice one, Eric – not one about dead people!'

Doc then went to his box of medicines and rummaged through it until he found what he was looking for. He apprised Jack of the situation and asked him to check for any parked truck with its trailer doors unlocked. 'And try not to be conspicuous, Jack. Make out you're just stretching your legs.'

He went to Brandon's slumped form and listened to his heart through a stethoscope. 'Man, this guy's got the heart of an ox,' he exclaimed. 'How heavy would you say he was, Bob?'

''Bout two-thirty.'

'That sounds about right,' Doc said, and then took out a syringe. He stuck the needle through the seal of a phial, filled the syringe and flicked it with his fingers. He pulled up Brandon's sleeve and located a vein in his arm. He then injected the entire contents.

'How long's he gonna be out fo', Gene?' Bob asked.

'By my calculations, about thirty-six hours. All we have to do now is find a way of getting him out of here. I'd rather we didn't have to take him with us on the bus.'

Jack returned with the news Doc had hoped for.

Jack had strolled around all the trucks, casually stretching his arms and occasionally yawning, but had found all to be secured. He was about to report this to Doc when a truck with Nevada plates drew up, and the driver climbed out and headed for the services building. He walked to the rear of the trailer and found the padlock hanging loose.

Bob and Doc followed Jack to the trailer, Bob pushing the wheelchair. They checked to make sure no people were watching and then opened the door. The trailer was filled with mattresses wrapped in thick polythene. Jack climbed up and pulled the dead weight of Brandon's body while Doc and Bob lifted and pushed.

There was a small walkway between the stacks of mattresses and Jack dragged Brandon's body to the rear of the visible piles and out of sight. Bob helped him arrange the rear mattresses to allow Brandon a comfortable passage, and then rolled a packing blanket into a thin pillow and placed it under his head.

Doc stood watch and then gave Jack $500 to put in Brandon's pocket.

'Why are you wasting your money on him, Doc?'

'The truck's heading to Las Vegas, Jack. If Brandon wakes up with money in his pocket, he won't be leaving there until he's gambled it away! It will give us more time.'

They fastened the padlock and moved away from the truck, and watched from a distance as the driver returned, started the engine and pulled his slightly heavier load back on to the interstate.

'You shoulda been a crime boss, Gene,' Bob laughed. 'You wasted yo' time bein' a Medicine Man!'

'How many laws have we broken now?' Jack asked, slightly concerned.

'Five that I know of, maybe six. It's hard to keep track,' Doc said.

They returned to the bus and immediately left the rest area, determined to make no further stops on the interstate. Doc went to lie down, exhausted by all the excitement.

It was a while before Nancy noticed his absence. 'Where's Gene?' she asked Jack.

'He's resting in the compartment. I think all the unpleasantness got to him.'

'Oh for Heaven's sake!' she said, dismissively. 'There are worse things in life than a restroom running out of paper towels!'

Memphis

They reached Memphis shortly after midday. It was a city that had been in existence for fewer than two hundred years, although the site itself had been occupied for thousands of years more: Native Americans who'd built earthworks in the shape of truncated pyramids long before the Egyptians had ever thought of the idea, and later Chickasaw Indians who lost control of the bluffs, first to the Spanish, then to the French and finally to the British.

'We oughta go hear us some blues music tonight,' Bob said. 'Get us an antidote to all that rhinestone shit we been listenin' to. You up fo' it, man?'

'Sure. We can eat dinner at the hotel and then walk over to Beale St. You're definite you squared the parking with the hotel?'

'They reservin' us a place on the street right by the entrance, an' we got it till midday tomorrow. If there'da been a sport team or musician stayin' in the hotel this weekend, we'da been outta luck, but there ain't, so we okay.'

It had been Doc's idea for them all to spend their last evening on the road in style. The money Nancy had set aside for the trip – the money Doc had taken from her house at the time of her detention – had hardly been touched. He'd paid for gas, meals and two nights at the Union Hotel and that was about it. Whatever was left once they reached Coffeeville, he'd give to Bob: money to cover the costs of his travel to and from Montreal and the hire of the tour bus.

'I went to the toilet, Jack, and everything's back to normal,' Eric said.

'Glad to hear it,' Jack replied.

Eric turned to Doc. 'Jack said yesterday that I was like a human gas ball, Doctor Gene, and that if you'd been smoking a cigarette near me the whole city of Nashville would have blown up.'

'Did he now?' Doc said. 'Nothing like a bit of hyperbole is there, Jack?'

'I call it as I see it, Doc. It's a cross I carry.'

'It's a cross we all have to carry,' Doc said. 'What's Nancy doing back there, Eric?'

'She's looking for people, sir. She says we're missing someone.'

Nancy was always thinking someone was missing, but was never sure who. On each such occasion, Doc would explain to her that there had always been only the five of them and remind her who Bob, Jack and Eric were. She'd accept the explanation without protest but, unless distracted by another matter, would repeat her question within moments. It was a frustrating conversation for Doc, but even more so for Nancy – and Doc never failed to appreciate this.

'Hey, Jack, take the map and get me to Union Street,' Bob said. 'We lookin' for the Peabody Hotel.'

The parking space was there as promised and Bob, now expert in driving the bus, manoeuvred into the opening without trouble. They were greeted by hotel porters, who took hold of their luggage and led them to the reception desk. Doc paid for the three rooms they'd reserved with cash: he and Nancy would share one room, Jack and Eric another, and Bob would have a room to himself. While Doc filled out guest information, Jack went to the concierge's desk and asked where he might find Darla Thomas.

'Usually in that office right there,' the concierge replied, 'but I'm afraid she's off duty this weekend and won't be back until Tuesday morning.'

'Is there any chance you could give me her home phone number?' Jack asked. 'We're trying to find a friend of hers.'

'I'm afraid it's against hotel policy to give out information about employees, sir. Your best bet is to come back Tuesday morning. I can leave a message for her, if you'd like.'

'Tell her I'm trying to find Susan Lawrence, will you? My name's Jack Guravitch.'

'No luck?' Doc asked when Jack returned.

'Nah, she's off duty till Tuesday. I'll have to come back with Eric then. I'll hire a car tomorrow and follow you to Coffeeville and drive back Tuesday morning. I'll need one for when I leave anyway. How far is Coffeeville from here?'

'About a hundred miles,' Doc said. 'An hour-and-a-half's drive.'

'That's manageable,' Jack said. 'What are the plans for this afternoon? Eric wants to see the river.'

'Big plans,' Bob said. 'I ain't tol' you this, Gene, but I've got a surprise lined up fo' you an' Nance – an' the boys'll like it, too. Let's dump the bags in the room an' meet back in the lobby. It ain't far, an' we can ride the Main Street Trolley.'

'What about the river?' Jack asked.

'We can see the Miss'ippi after,' Bob said. 'I hope he ain't expectin' nothin' too special, 'cos it ain't: jus' gallons o' dirty brown water headin' in the same direction – nothin' romantic 'bout it.'

'I don't think he's planning on writing a sonnet about the river. He just wants to see it.'

'I don't want to miss the ducks,' Nancy said.

'Ducks are splashin' right there in the fountain, Nance.'

'I'm not blind, you fool,' Nancy snapped at Bob. 'I want to see them march! Gene, find out what time they march, will you?'

Doc had no idea what Nancy was talking about, or why in fact there were ducks in the fountain in the first place. He returned to the reception desk and prepared himself for a look of non-comprehension when he asked the question. The receptionist, however, didn't bat an eyelid: 'Five o'clock prompt, sir,' she said, 'but you'll need to be here before then if you want a seat.'

Doc reported back and Bob looked at his watch: 'We got plenty o' time,' he said. 'Let's make a move.'

They walked to the elevator and Eric pressed the button. Bob's room was on the fourth floor and the other two on the ninth. 'Lobby in fifteen,' Bob said, when he exited.

Doc and Nancy's room and Jack and Eric's room were on opposite sides of the same corridor close to the stairwell.

The following day, Doc ruminated, they would arrive in Coffeeville, and Brandon would arrive in Las Vegas. He could foresee no further problems.

7

Coffeeville

The Lorraine Motel

The five of them stood in the Lorraine Motel on Mulberry Street. When Martin Luther King had stood on its second floor balcony on April 4, 1968, a man by the name of James Earl Ray was kneeling on the floor of a second-storey bathroom in Bessie Brewer's Rooming House looking at him through the scope of a deer rifle. At one minute past six, a single hollow point bullet blasted its way into King's cheek and sent him to the very same Promised Land he'd been talking about the previous evening.

After the assassination the old motel went downhill at a pace, and was only saved from extinction when it was decided to turn the property into a museum dedicated to the memory of Martin Luther King and the civil rights movement. Through artefacts, photographs, newspaper accounts and three-dimensional scenes, the National Civil Rights Museum told the story of Afro-Americans from the time of their arrival in the American colonies. It detailed the brutality of slavery and the injustices of the Jim Crow laws, highlighted the activities of the Ku Klux Klan and the White Councils, and traced the key events of the civil rights struggle, culminating in the assassination of King.

The knowledge that the three elderly people he travelled with had once played a part in this struggle gave the visit an added poignancy for Jack. It was an experience that also left him feeling confused. Although he appreciated the biological necessity for any old person to have at one time in their lives been young, emotionally Jack had always struggled with the idea. In all the time he'd known his godfather, the man had been an adult; he was now an overweight tub of lard in his seventies. He associated Doc with sitting and chairs, for settling for things that worked rather than trying to change things for an idealistic better, and certainly not with activity.

Jack had known from his father that Doc had been active in the civil rights movement, but Doc had rarely mentioned it. All he'd ever told him was that he was embarrassed by the insignificance of his role, and that all he'd ever taken from the experience was the knowledge that he was a coward. Jack had learned more from talking to Bob than ever he had talking to his godfather: Doc saving Bob from a burning bus in Alabama and the two of them being thrown into jail in Mississippi. If he'd needed proof that such events had indeed happened, Bob was about to provide the evidence.

'You never see'd it, did you?' Bob said to Doc.

'Seen what?'

'C'mon, follow me.'

They'd already toured the exhibits and Eric was concerned they were about to do it all over again. 'What about the river, Otis? I haven't seen the Mississippi, yet.'

'We got time. Jus' need to show Doc an' Nance somethin'.'

They followed Bob to a series of photographs taken during the time of the Freedom Rides, and Bob stopped in front of one taken outside the Union Bus Terminal in Montgomery, Alabama. 'Now you see it?' Bob asked.

'See what?' Doc asked.

'Man, you blind or somethin'?'

'Not yet, but you'll have to point it out to me.'

'Sorry, Gene. Fo'got 'bout yo' eyes, man.' He then pointed to two figures in the photograph: side shots of a man and a woman. The man had his arms around the woman, shielding her from the missiles being thrown by an angry crowd. 'That's you an' Nance, Gene. See it now?'

Doc looked at the images and waited for them to clarify.

'Well, I'll be damned. Hey, Nancy; come and look at this, will you. It's you and me. How in God's name did you know about this, Bob?'

'I see'd it the first time I visited the place. I knew we was there when the photograph was taken, so I looked at it closely. If you wanna know the truth, Gene, I was lookin' fo' myself, but 'steada findin' me I foun' you two.'

Nancy stared at the photograph. 'I don't remember having any trouble in Nashville,' she said. 'Was this happening outside the hotel when we took Bob to the restaurant? I thought you said it had been desegregated.'

'Nancy, this is the Union Bus Terminal in Montgomery, not the Union Hotel in Nashville. The photograph was taken fifty years ago. See how young we both look.'

'I don't know about you, but I look exactly the same. I look like that now, and to tell you the truth I'm not happy about all these niggers gawping at my photograph.' She made a move to take the photograph from the wall and Bob had to restrain her.

'Take your damned hands off me, you fucking nigger,' she shouted. 'Gene, tell him he's fired. We'll get someone else to drive the bus. I'm not having hired help touching me.' She struggled to get free from his grasp and Bob was so shaken by her outburst that she almost succeeded. Jack came to his aid.

'And you can get your hands off me too, Jew boy. You thought I didn't know, didn't you, but I've known all along. You don't pull the wool over my eyes. Jews and niggers always stick together.'

People started to look in their direction, and Doc wondered if they'd have to manhandle Nancy out of the museum. It was Eric who came to the rescue. 'Mrs Skidmore, will you take me to see the river please?'

Nancy's manner changed almost immediately and the old Nancy returned to them. 'Of course I will, honey. We can go now, if you like. She took his arm, and once outside the museum also took Bob's. 'Thank you, Bob. That was delightful. You're always thinking of us, aren't you? Isn't he, Gene?'

'That woman's getting crazier by the day, Doc,' Jack said, as the two of them walked behind the others. 'One minute she's snarling like a rabid dog and the next she's meek as a lamb.'

'I know it,' Doc said, 'but you can't hold her responsible for the things she says as you would another person. You have to bear in mind that she grew up surrounded by prejudice and that, like it or not, prejudice is insidious. It seeps into your pores without you ever knowing it. Nancy fought bigotry her whole life, and for someone from her background that was no easy thing. The illness is pulling her apart, tearing down her defences. She's back walking the Delta of her youth now, and unconsciously tapping into all the hatreds that used to pool there.'

'How are you going to manage when it's just the two of you?'

'I'll figure something out,' Doc said. 'I've been thinking about it for some time now.'

Ducks

They arrived back in the hotel lobby shortly before 4:30 pm and found people already gathering for the extravaganza. Doc and Nancy managed to take two of the remaining front-row seats, and Eric sat cross-legged on the floor in front of them. Bob and Jack, neither of whom was particularly interested in watching the ducks, climbed to the second floor balcony and viewed the proceedings from there.

Shortly before 5 pm, a small flight of steps was placed at the base of the fountain and a roll of red carpet extended from its foot to the elevator door. A man, resplendent in red jacket and dark trousers, introduced himself as the Duckmaster and started to explain the origins of the pageantry the audience was about to witness.

Supposedly, a general manager of the Peabody in the 1930s called Frank returned to the hotel after a weekend shooting ducks in Arkansas with a friend called Chip. They sat in the lobby drinking bourbon that evening and decided to put some live duck decoys into the lobby's travertine marble fountain. The hoot – or quack, as some described it – proved so popular with guests that, in 1940, it was formalised: the hotel appointed a Duckmaster and the ducks began to march. The only thing to have changed over the years was that the Duckmaster was now a black man.

'Y'all ready to see 'em march?' the Duckmaster asked. 'Okay then, start the music!'

John Philip Sousa's *King Cotton March* started to play and the Duckmaster strode to the fountain and marshalled the ducks down the steps and along the carpet to the elevator. The doors opened, the ducks walked in, the doors closed behind them and the music stopped. The audience burst into applause.

'Don't seem right, somehow,' Bob said to Jack. 'Martin Luther King gets his self shot, and fo' what? So's a black man can become a Duckmaster?'

Nancy and Eric had been thrilled to see the ducks march to the elevator and, along with the other hotel guests and tourists who'd come to see the procession, had lapped up the performance. Doc, however, had been overcome by tiredness and slept through it, his snores fortuitously masked by the noise of the ducks and the appreciative laughter of those gathered. Jack shook him awake.

'Hey, Doc, we're fixing to eat and then go down Beale Street. Wipe your chin and let's go.'

'The restaurant doesn't open till six,' Doc said. 'Why don't you go and make reservations?'

Jack did, and returned with the news that he, Doc and Bob would have to wear jackets: Chez Philippe required business casual attire. Doc grimaced, but handed Jack his room card and asked him to get his jacket; he'd stay and watch over Nancy and Eric.

They were the first to enter the restaurant and were shown to a corner table. Even before his eyesight had started to fail him, a bane of Doc's life had been menus: they were too long, too complicated and never simple or straightforward. He'd resigned himself to ten minutes of torture when Bob spoke up. 'I'm gonna have duck,' he said, without even opening the menu.

'That sounds like an idea,' Doc said, and immediately closed the menu. 'How about everyone else? Duck sound okay?'

'Fine by me,' Jack said. 'Duck's my favourite.'

'What's duck like?' Eric asked. 'I've never eaten duck before.'

'Best damn bird you'll ever taste,' Bob said. 'Goose comes close, but duck's got the edge.'

'I'll have duck, too,' Nancy said. 'It used to be one of Dora's specialities.'

'Duck it is, then,' Doc confirmed, and indicated to the waiter they were ready to order. 'Duck all around,' he said.

The waiter looked flummoxed. 'I'm afraid we don't have duck, sir,' he said apologetically.

'What you talkin' 'bout, man? I just see'd five of 'em. All we'll need is two at most.'

'Those were the marching ducks, sir. It would be akin to cannibalism to serve them.'

'How do you figure that?' Doc asked him. 'Are you saying we're descended from ducks or something; that I'm a duck and you're a duck? If you are, it's the first I've ever heard of it. And this is the first French restaurant I've been in that doesn't have duck on the menu.'

'No, sir, of course I'm not. It's just that the ducks are too much a part of the hotel's brand. We haven't served duck in the hotel since 1981. It would be like eating a family pet.'

'You wouldn' mind that, Jack, would you?' Bob said to him. 'I bet Bingo woulda tasted real good.' Jack ignored the remark and re-opened the menu.

'Oh fuck the damned duck!' Nancy said. 'Let's go someplace else and eat barbecue.'

Everyone at the table looked at her in surprise and the waiter hovered uncertainly, unsure how to react. It was Bob who laughed first, and then they all broke into laughter – though not the waiter.

'Why are you laughing?' Nancy asked. 'What's so goddamned funny?'

'Yo' language is what,' Bob said. 'We need to get you a breath fresh'ner 'fore we take you anyplace else, girl. Ha!'

They returned to the lobby and waited while Bob went to ask for the name of a good barbecue place. He purposely avoided the front desk and looked for one of the black bellboys. He saw one pushing a trolley of suitcases into the hotel and approached him.

'Hey, kid, where's the bes' place to eat barbecue an' listen to the Blues?'

'Gutbucket Club on Beale Street, sir. Bes' fo' both.'

Bob thanked him and pushed a five-dollar bill into his hand.

They walked the two blocks to Beale Street and found the club without trouble. It was already crowded and, worryingly for Bob, all the wall tables were taken. Doc pointed to a table set on a raised dais three feet above the main eating area; it had a wooden rail on the nearside to prevent anyone from falling on to the table below it. 'You won't come to any harm there, Bob,' he said.

They made their way to the table and Bob sat with his back to the rail. Doc ordered beers for the men, a small glass of white wine for Nancy and a Dr Pepper for Eric.

'Wan' me to order fo' us all?' Bob asked. 'One thing I know 'bout is barbecue, an' the bes' barbecue is pork.' They agreed that he should.

The food the waiter brought to the table was a mixture of hickory smoked ribs on a slab (dry-rub style), pulled pork, slaw, baked beans, potato salad and bread. It was served with the Gutbucket's own brand of tangy barbecue sauce.

'Will this make me go to the toilet like the Mexican food did, Jack?' Eric asked.

'No, you'll be fine with this. It'll help keep you regular, but no more than that.'

While they ate, they listened to an old bluesman called Blind Mississippi Johnson who played an open-tuned guitar with a metal slide on his small finger. A young man sat next to him, attentive and admiring, on hand for the eventuality that the old man might fall off his chair.

'He good, ain't he?' Bob said. 'Al'ays wished I could play like that but my fingers is too thick. Me an' you should form us a band once this trip's overed with, Gene – live us the rock 'n' roll lifestyle. You up for the idea?'

'No, and I can't see Marsha going along with it, either.'

'You prob'ly right, Gene. You ain't – but I still a good-lookin' man. I could see groupies bein' a real problem: young girls throwin' 'emselves at me an' wantin' to share my bed.'

'You're a crazy old man, Bob,' Nancy said. 'You should know better – and what would your children say about it? They'd be downright ashamed of you.'

'Hey, Nance, you wanna dance? Move those li'l ol' legs' o' yo's an' give 'em some exercise?' Bob shouted. Blind Mississippi Johnson had stepped down from the stage and been replaced by a nine-piece electric and brass ensemble.

Nancy readily agreed and took hold of Bob's outstretched hand. As they walked down the steps to the dance floor, Doc called after Bob: 'Keep her away from the tip bucket, will you?'

'Why does Mrs Skidmore want to dance with Otis when she wouldn't let him touch her at the museum?' Eric asked.

'She has mood swings, Eric. They're caused by an illness she has. That's why she acts strangely sometimes.'

'Will she get better, Doctor Gene?'

'Sure she will. Just a matter of time and taking the right pills.'

'That's not what you...' Jack started to say before catching himself.

'By the way, Eric,' Doc said. 'I want to thank you for what you did this afternoon at the museum. You did well – very well. How did you know to do that?'

'I don't know, Doctor Gene. I think it's because I've seen Mrs Skidmore like that before, and noticed she gets sidetracked easily and then changes back to being nice again.'

'You're a wise young man, Eric, and I'm mighty proud of you,' Doc said. Eric beamed with pleasure and looked at Jack, who beamed right back at him.

'Are you going to dance, Doc?' Jack asked.

'Nah, I can't dance – never have been able to. I don't have rhythm and I don't have the moves. Even Beth refused to dance with me – and that was before we got married. She said my dancing would be okay for a Grateful Dead concert, but not for any place she'd like to be seen in public.'

Bob and Nancy returned from the dance floor out of breath. They stayed in the Gutbucket for another half-hour and then made their way slowly back to the hotel. The air was cold.

As Doc put the key card in the door, Eric said goodnight to them both. He shook Doc by the hand and kissed Nancy on the cheek. 'Don't worry, Mrs Skidmore,' he said, 'You're going to get better. Doctor Gene said so.'

'I wonder what Eric meant by that?' Nancy said to Doc, once the two of them were inside their room. 'There's nothing wrong with me.'

Doc turned on the television and the two of them watched a mindless chat show for a while. A celebrity was graciously allowing the common people of the world into his own remarkable world, describing its unusual wonders and uncommon difficulties: the paparazzi, his diet and fitness regime, the boredom of hanging around film sets, his anonymous work for charity and his wonderful children. Every famous person he talked about was incredible, fantastic, or hilarious – and they were all his special friends. And then he got down to the business at hand, his real reason for being on the show: his new film.

After about twenty minutes, Doc raised himself from the chair and went to the bathroom for some aspirin and a glass of water. The noise of the Gutbucket had given him a headache and he blamed but one person: the trumpet player. It was more likely to have been the lead guitarist, but Doc had an inborn prejudice against trumpets. He saw no reason for them, disliked their blare and wished for a world where trumpets were illegal and police ran amnesty days for owners to hand them in without fear of prosecution.

He was turning these thoughts over in his mind when he sauntered casually back into the room. He was aghast to find the door open and Nancy gone. He pulled on his shoes, made sure he had the key card in his pocket and then rushed into the corridor. Their room was located at its dead end, so the only possible route Nancy could have taken was the one leading to the elevators.

He walked briskly to the elevator doors and checked the buttons that were lit. One elevator was going down and the other heading up, currently taking a breather at the fourth floor. He punched the button and waited. After a seeming lifetime, the door opened and he climbed in. Rather than descend to the lobby, however, the elevator continued to climb and only reversed its direction after it reached the eleventh floor.

Doc walked into the lobby and cast his eyes around for Nancy. He explored the entire ground floor, its bars, restaurants and gift shops, and then the mezzanine. There was no sign of her anywhere. He walked through the main entrance and into the street. Nancy wasn't there, either. He retraced his steps and called Bob and Jack from the house phone, and then waited impatiently for them to arrive.

'She's left the hotel!' Doc told them. 'She's been gone ten – maybe twenty minutes. We have to find her!'

'You check the groun' floor, Gene? You sure she ain't here somewhere?'

'I've checked it and the mezzanine,' Doc answered. 'My guess is that she's gone back to Beale Street, but having said that she could be anywhere. Jack, you move faster than Bob and me: head back there, will you? I'll take the opposite direction and the roads across. Bob, you see if she's gone down to the river. We'll meet back here in an hour.'

The river was quiet and the small park there deserted. Bob stopped a couple of joggers approaching from opposite directions, but neither had seen an old lady. He walked parallel and arterial streets in a three block area and returned to the hotel where Doc was waiting with a similar story of failure.

'Maybe this the way it suppose' to be, Gene. You off the hook, man.'

'As long as Nancy's on it, I'm still on it,' Doc sighed. 'I promised her, Bob, promised her I'd get her to Coffeeville. Another day and we'd have made it.'

'What else can you do? 'Less Jack finds her, we ain't got no options. You call hospitals an' the police gets involved; police gets involved an' we all got questions to answer. I got Marsha to consider, an' Jack his whole life ahead o' him.'

'I know that, Bob... I know,' Doc said wearily, and fell silent.

Jack joined them. He'd found no trace of Nancy, either. He'd returned to the Gutbucket Club, checked with bouncers standing at the doors of other clubs on the street, and slowed when he saw stationary police cars and ambulances to make sure Nancy wasn't the reason for them being there.

'Maybe she's returned to the hotel already, Doc – or maybe she'll return later. There's still a chance.'

'Maybe,' Doc said weakly. 'Let's make one last sweep of the ground floor and then call it a day. There's nothing more we can to do tonight.'

Bob climbed out of the elevator at the fourth floor. 'Call me if she back, Gene.'

Doc promised he would. He and Jack then returned to the room he shared with Nancy and found it as empty as when he'd left it. A thought occurred to Jack.

'Did you check the stairwell, Doc?'

'No, I didn't think to,' he said, hope rising. 'Let's take a look.'

Jack pushed open the door to the staircase and listened. There was no noise, no one treading its steps. He walked down two flights of stairs and then saw Nancy halfway down the next flight, standing stock-still and holding on to the balustrade.

'She's here, Doc!' he shouted.

Doc ran down the stairs, a wave of relief washing over him.

'Nancy, what are you doing down here?' he asked. 'I've been worried to death.'

Nancy made no answer. She remained motionless, rigid, staring unknowing into space. Doc tried to take her hand from the rail, but she resisted with a strength he'd never known she possessed. Her skin was cold. 'Come on, Nancy, let's go back to the room and get you warmed up,' he said. Nancy still didn't reply. She stayed rooted to the spot in a kind of trance, emotionally paralysed. She didn't know Doc and was deaf to his words. She was out of his reach, out of anyone's reach. 'Shit!' Doc muttered.

Jack looked at her and Nancy looked through him. 'If you can prise her fingers from the balustrade, Doc, I'll lift her and carry her up the stairs. Want to give it a try?'

Doc managed to loosen Nancy's grip, and Jack lifted her from the ground and carried her upright, as if she were a statue. Her bladder broke just as they reached the stairwell door and a stream of urine spilled over Jack's jeans. He ignored the warm dampness and followed Doc into the bedroom.

'You might want to clean Nancy up, Doc: she's pissed her pants – and mine too. I think she's scared to death.'

'I will, Jack, and thanks for your help. I can take care of things now.'

'I'll stay for a while, Doc. Make sure she's okay before I leave. I'll phone Bob.'

Nancy had started to move again but like a zombie, and Doc had to coax her into the bathroom. Fifteen minutes passed before they returned to the room. Nancy was dressed in her nightgown. Jack pulled back the covers and together they carefully manoeuvred her into the bed.

'I'll just wash these things in the sink,' Doc said. 'Are you okay to stay with her a while longer?'

Jack sat on the side of the bed looking down on Nancy. Her eyes were open but she was still unaware, as likely in the mountains of Peru as she was a bedroom of the Peabody Hotel. For some unknown reason he leaned forward and kissed her on the cheek. Nancy smiled at him. Her eyes were still as vacant as an old abandoned factory, but she was now smiling. He kissed her again and again, and with each kiss the smiles kept on coming.

It was the first time Jack had fully appreciated the wretchedness of Nancy's being, recognised how the disease had robbed her of her own life while allowing her to live another's. Nancy Skidmore, he realised, was probably a person he'd never even met.

'Poor old sod,' he said gently. 'No one deserves this.'

'You're not trying to make out with my girl, are you?' Doc asked when he came back into the room and saw Jack kissing Nancy on the cheek.

'Every time I kiss her, she smiles, Doc. How strange is that?'

Doc had a couple of pills in one hand and a glass of water in the other. He put his arm behind Nancy's head and raised her towards him. He placed the pills in her mouth and watched as she swallowed each one. 'I think she'll be okay now, Jack. Are you okay?'

'Sure I'm okay, Doc. Why wouldn't I be?'

Jack left the room and closed the door behind him. He stood leaning with his back against the corridor wall for a time, and then slid slowly to the floor. It was then that he burst into tears.

Kudzu

The next morning they drove to Coffeeville: Bob, Nancy and Doc in the bus, and Jack and Eric following in a hired car. Nancy was back on track with no recollection of the previous evening's events. A part of it, however, had touched and remained with her: she now had a warmth-of-feeling for Jack she'd never before experienced.

They headed south on I55 and into Mississippi. They passed houses decorated with artificial cobwebs and skeletons, pumpkins on porches and in yards. Halloween approached.

'What we should do when we get to Coffeeville is have us a party,' Bob said. 'Celebrate Nance's birthday an' Halloween in one. We can make it a farewell party, too. Say goodbye to each other in style.'

Doc couldn't remember passing cemeteries visible from the interstate before, but he noticed them now: there were burial grounds on either side of the four-lane and, closer to Batesville, a coffin manufacturing company standing in its own attractive grounds.

'I don't min' graveyards,' Bob said, 'hell knows I spent 'nough time wanderin' round in 'em when I worked fo' Morris – but I ain't got no time fo' people who build shrines on the sides o' roads fo' friends an' relatives what got 'emselves killed there. To my way o' thinkin', that's jus' plain weird. What's the name o' that woman in England who named herself after a playin' card?'

'I don't know,' Doc said. 'Who was she?'

'That what I aksin' you! She were a princess o' some sort. Got herself killed in a car wreck.'

'Princess Diana,' Nancy said. 'She had a lovely smile.'

'That's her!' Bob said. 'Queen o' Hearts! All 'em flowers stacked outside her house when she died an' people who never even knowed her breakin' down an' crying. Creepy is what it was. Plain creepy.'

'You need to leave the interstate here, Bob. Take the exit marked Highway 227 and head in the direction of Charleston. There'll be a sign for Coffeeville shortly after that. Is Jack still behind us?'

'Yeah, he been tailgatin' me the whole damn way. Boy needs to learn how to drive 'less he got Eric sittin' behin' the wheel. How many mo' miles, Gene?'

'Fifteen, maybe twenty.' He looked at the map Nancy had drawn for him when she'd first discussed the idea of going to Coffeeville. 'Somewhere down here there'll be a cotton gin. We turn left immediately before it.'

They came to the gin and turned on to a red dirt road. They followed it for about two miles. 'There it is, Bob! Turn left here.'

Bob turned and eased the bus carefully up a sloping, potholed drive that continued for a quarter of a mile. As the bus approached the ridge of the small hill, a lodge constructed from split wooden logs with a stone chimney stack came into view.

'Man, look at all this green shit,' Bob said.

Eric also gaped when he saw the plant. (He would have gaped even more had he known that Arthur Annandale had used its properties to treat his father's migraines.) 'What is it, Jack?'

'Kudzu,' Jack said. 'It's a Japanese plant.'

The bombing of Pearl Harbour was the *second* time Japan attacked the United States. The first – and more damaging of the two attacks – had been sixty-five years earlier at the Centennial Exposition of 1876, a World's Fair organised to mark the one-hundredth anniversary of the signing of the Declaration of Independence. Countries from around the world were invited to join the United States in its celebrations and build exhibits in Fairmount Park, Philadelphia.

Japan, happy to be invited anywhere, accepted the invitation and landscaped a beautiful garden for the American people. They filled it with plants from their own country, one of which was kudzu, an associate of the pea family with large leaves and pungent purple blooms. Visitors to the fair were as much taken with the vine as they were with Alexander Graham Bell's telephone, Remington's typewriter or Heinz's Ketchup, all of which were on show for the first time. Unwittingly, the Americans had fallen in love with a monster: Kudzu was uncontrollable.

Insects that limited its spread in Japan had been barred from entering the United States at the time of the Centennial, and once freed from predation the plant flourished. Gardeners who'd used kudzu for ornamental purposes were the first to recognise its danger and immediately stripped the plant from their yards. All might have been well if the US Soil Conservation Service hadn't seen kudzu as an ideal plant for controlling soil erosion and decided to pay farmers eight dollars for every acre of the vine they planted. They came to their senses in 1953, however, and twenty years later the government declared kudzu a weed.

By then, however, it was too late and the damage had been done. No area suffered more than the Deep South. The region's long humid summers and short winters had suited kudzu to the toes of its twelve-foot roots, and overnight the area lost seven million acres to the rampaging vine. It grew at a rate of sixty feet a year, and suffocated anything and everything in its path: it climbed trees and power poles, wrapped itself around deserted houses and left huge areas looking like movie sets for science fiction films or pages from a Gothic novel.

'I hope to God the inside of the house is in better shape than the yard,' Jack said.

It was. When Nancy had resumed responsibility from the management company for the lodge's upkeep, she'd retained the services of a local family to clean the house and oversee any necessary repairs. They were people she trusted, people she'd known her whole life, and she'd instructed her lawyer to pay any bills they sent on receipt and without question. It had never occurred to her, however, that kudzu might march on the property. The plant had never before been a problem in the area, and having decided to allow the surrounding land to revert to nature, she had made no arrangements for the maintenance of the yard.

Doc took a key from his pocket and led the way to the lodge. The door opened without difficulty and they entered a large room with a high-pitched ceiling, intended for both dining and lounging. At one end of the room was a large open fireplace with a protruding chimney breast made from big pieces of irregularly shaped stones. The walls and floor were made from large pieces of sealed rustic pine and adorned with primitive works of art, animal heads and Indian rugs. A door to the left opened to an old-fashioned kitchen, and a corridor to the right led to four bedrooms of approximately equal size.

The air in the house was cool and Jack turned the thermostat to seventy. There was a rumbling and then a whooshing noise as the old boiler kicked into life and the room started to warm. 'The fridge is empty, Doc, and there's no food in the cupboards,' Jack said. 'If you make out a list, I'll drive into town and pick up some groceries. How long do you figure we'll be here?'

'Nancy and I will be staying on, so it depends how long the three of you will be here: how long it takes you to find Susan and when Bob decides to leave.'

'What's the date today?' Bob asked. 'When's Halloween?'

Doc had to think back to Nancy's birthday. The 26th had been a Friday, Saturday they'd stayed in Nashville and yesterday they'd been in Memphis. 'It's Monday 29th, so Halloween's on Wednesday.'

'Okay, We'nsday night's the party then; I'll leave Thursday. I ain't missin' no party!'

Coffeeville was a small town in Yalobusha County with a population of fewer than a thousand people. According to the motto coined for its 175th anniversary, it was a place *where old friends gather*. At one time, it had been the place where Choctaw and Chickasaw Indians had gathered, but they hadn't always been friends.

The town owed its origins to General John Coffee, a friend and business partner of General Andrew Jackson. Coffee had fought alongside Jackson in the War of 1812 and the Creek War, and then become a surveyor. One of his last assignments had been to survey the boundary line dividing Choctaw from Chickasaw hunting grounds and maintain peace between the two tribes. For this purpose, Coffee and his soldiers had established a hill camp overlooking the site of the present-day town, and the settlement that grew around it was named after him.

Although Coffeeville was *of* the map, it was never really *on* the map until the Civil War Battle of Coffeeville in December 1862, when Confederate troops ambushed and defeated Colonel Theophilus Lyle Dickey's Union cavalry. It then promptly fell off the map again and went back to growing yams and cotton.

'It's like a neutron bomb's gone off here,' Jack said.

'Neutron bomb wouldn'ta done this,' Bob said. 'Neutron bombs jus' kill people; they'da lef' the buildin's standin'. Why don't you pull over so's we can take a look roun'?'

Jack's car had been the only moving vehicle on the town's main street. He drove to where Front Street joined Oak, and parked close to a feed and seed outlet. As they walked the length of the deserted main street, it was apparent that Coffeeville had seen better days. There were empty spaces where buildings had been torn down and never replaced, and the charred remnants of a large building that had been lost to fire and then simply abandoned. 'Kinda gap-toothed, ain't it?' Bob said.

Interspersed were a couple of empty shops; a number of small stores selling auto and electrical parts, drugs and gifts; and offices advertising legal, tax and insurance services. At the far end of the street was a General Store – provided that a person's idea of a general store wasn't too general and didn't include food – and a small restaurant.

'Where we gonna buy groceries?' Bob asked. 'Ain't no place here.'

'Let's go to the restaurant and get coffee,' Jack said. 'We can ask there.'

The restaurant was as empty inside as the street had been outside. They sat down at a table and waited while a woman with tattoos on both legs came to terms with the fact that she was no longer alone. The surface of the table was sticky and Jack wiped it with a paper napkin, while Bob moved the ashtray full of cigarette butts to another table.

'How y'all doin' today?' the woman asked. 'What can I get you?'

She seemed relieved when they only ordered coffee. She brought two cups and filled them with a weak filtered brew that had been percolating since the restaurant had opened for business that morning. 'Is it always this quiet?' Jack asked.

'Pretty much,' she replied. 'I'm thinkin' 'bout movin' to Water Valley. More goin' on there. You just visitin'?'

'Passing through,' Jack said. 'Tell me, where can we buy groceries?'

'Piggly Wiggly on Route 7. Takes three minutes to drive there. It don't take more 'n three minutes to drive anywhere in this town. Did I say I was thinkin' 'bout leavin'?'

'Yes, you said you were thinking of moving to Water Valley. Is that a much bigger town?'

'Sure is,' she said. 'Got a population o' more 'n three thousand.'

While Doc and Eric unloaded the cases from the bus, Nancy walked around the house and visited every room. She'd been sure her parents would have been there to welcome them and couldn't understand their absence. Maybe they were visiting Ruby and Homer over in Leflore, or had driven to Memphis to see Daisy. 'Oh my Lord,' Nancy thought. 'We forgot to call on Daisy when we were in Memphis.' Her parents would never forgive her. 'How could you go all the way to Memphis and not visit your own sister?' they would ask her, and she wouldn't know what to tell them. She went looking for Gene: 'He'll know what to say,' she reassured herself. She found him standing on the porch smoking a cigarette.

'Quite a view, isn't it?' Doc said. 'How much of the land is yours?'

A large paddock sloped gently to the edge of woodland extending for as far as the eye could see. Hilton Travis – and later those who'd rented the lodge from the Travis family – would have walked into these woods with rifles in hand and returned with the carcasses of white-tailed deer, wild turkeys and doves and, on one occasion, the body of a man called Homer Comer.

Doc and Nancy walked to the bottom of the paddock where Eric was standing, wearing his familiar bicycle helmet and red gloves. It was a peaceful surrounding and Doc could understand why Nancy had decided to end her days here rather than in Hershey. He turned and looked back at the lodge – a house in any vernacular other than the Travis' – and saw the grandeur of its log and stone simplicity for the first time.

The approach to the lodge had been disfigured by the encroaching kudzu, but the land to its front was free of the vine and its menacing omen. The sun, too, was warmer than it had been all week, occasioning the start of an Indian summer that would last for the next three days. Doc took off his sweater and tied its arms around his waist.

They heard the sound of a car arriving. 'That'll be my parents, Gene,' Nancy said excitedly. 'Don't mention that we never called on Daisy.'

'Daisy who?' Doc asked.

'Don't be foolish, Gene,' she snapped, and then called to Eric. 'Eric, my parents are here. I want to introduce you to them.'

Nancy walked ahead of them, unaware of the disappointment awaiting. 'Oh, it's you two,' Nancy said when she saw Jack and Bob. 'You didn't run into my parents when you were out, did you?'

'Apart from the girl at the checkout, the only person we ran into was a woman with tattoos on her legs,' Jack said. 'I'm going out on a limb here, Nancy, but I'm guessing she wasn't your mother.'

'My mother didn't have tattoos on her legs, did she, Gene?'

'Of course she didn't, Nancy. Your mother was a *lady*.'

Bob took control of the kitchen, while Doc and Nancy settled on a couch and Jack unpacked his bag. Eric went exploring and made a careful examination of each room. He came back with three pieces of information: there was a piano and guitar in one of the rooms; all clocks in the house had stopped at exactly eleven minutes past eleven; and the same genealogical chart he'd seen in Arthur Annandale's house – the one tracing the origins of the British royal family to the House of Israel – was also hanging on one of the bedroom walls. Apart from the piano, which had always been in the lodge, Nancy was unable to explain why these things were as they were, and suggested to Eric he ask her father when he returned. Hilton, however, would never walk through the lodge's door, and the mysteries would remain just that – mysteries.

They ate meatloaf, yams and salad that night. 'You've done us proud, Bob. This is the best tuna fish casserole I've ever tasted,' Nancy said.

'It's meatloaf, Nance, but long as you enjoyin' it, I don't min' what you calls it.' Bob drained the beer from his glass and went to get another.

'Did you get the beer from the funeral home?' Nancy asked.

Bob looked at her curiously. 'I got it from the store, Nance. Why would I go to a funeral home for beer?'

'Well, I'll be! They must have legalised it since I was last here. It used to be you could only buy beer from the funeral home. They used to keep it cold in the mortuary and pay the sheriff to turn a blind eye.'

'What did the town used to be like, Nancy?' Jack asked. 'It was as quiet as the grave when Bob and I were there.'

'Front Street used to hum on a weekend,' Nancy said. 'There was a picture house there, and people would socialise until well after ten o'clock. I remember going with Ruby and having good times. We used to meet boys, and I remember smoking my first cigarette there, too.'

'Did you stub it out prop'ly,' Bob asked.

'Of course I did. Why are you asking me such a stupid question?'

''Cos half the town's burned down,' Bob laughed.

'Most of the towns in this part of the world look as if they've been burned down,' Doc said. 'Either that or the people building them lost interest halfway through and didn't bother to finish up.

The time I visited the Delta, I came away thinking they should sweep all the two-bit communities into a pile and make one decent town out of them.'

'What nonsense!' Nancy said. 'The Delta's the most beautiful place on earth – and, for your information, Coffeeville isn't in the Delta.'

'I'll take yo' word on that, Nance, but so far as Coffeeville goes, I reckon there's mo' goin' on in the Sargasso Sea. One good thing, though: no one's gonna come lookin' fo' us here.'

Just as Bob had spoken, there was a knock on the door and everyone looked at each other nervously.

'I wonder who that is,' Doc asked. 'You didn't tell anyone in town where you were staying, did you?'

'No one,' Jack said. 'I told them we were passing through, didn't I, Bob?' Bob nodded in agreement.

'It'll be my parents!' Nancy said enthusiastically. 'I told you they'd be here. Eric can ask them about the clocks now!'

'Your parents would have a key, Nancy. They wouldn't knock, they'd just let themselves in.'

He walked to the door and opened it wide enough to see who was there. He took a surprised step backward and then pulled open the door.

'Holy shit!' Doc exclaimed. 'It's Dora!'

Wanda and George

'You looked like you'd see'd a ghost,' Wanda laughed. 'Thought you was gonna fall down dead an' leave me standin' there wit' you on my conscience. My mamma woulda 'bout laughed herself silly – ain't that the truth, George?'

'Sure is, Wanda. She'da laughed that laugh o' hers, an' the whole damn house woulda shook. We'da needed a struct'ral engineer to come sort things out.'

Wanda's resemblance to her mother was uncanny. It was difficult to believe that the girl who'd helped serve dinner during his stay at Oaklands was now a grown woman in her sixties, a mother of four and grandmother to six. Wanda was having similar trouble coming to terms with Doc.

'You sure you that skinny boy Ms Nancy brought home wit' her? You looks nothin' like him.'

'It's me alright, Wanda; greyer and heavier maybe, but it's me. I think the years have been kinder to you.'

'In that case, why you mistakin' me fo' some hun'red-an'-ten-year-old dead woman then?' Wanda laughed. 'My mamma woulda had a fit if she'd knowed I was talkin' to you. She never forgive you fo' what you said 'bout her cookin': "Reminded him a dead people," is what she used tell us. You really say that?'

'You said that and you complain about the things I say?' Jack said to Doc.

'I didn't say that,' Doc said. 'Brandon told Dora I'd said it, but I never had!'

'He a no good,' George said. 'Never did like the man.'

'Watch yo' mouth, George. Brandon Ms Nancy's brother,' Wanda said.

'Don't mind me,' Nancy said. 'I didn't go to his funeral after he died, and neither did Ruby.'

'He dead?' George asked surprised. 'Thought the man lived in Clarksdale.' A frown crossed Wanda's brow and she looked across at Doc.

'You haven't seen Ruby, have you, Wanda?' Nancy asked. 'My parents haven't mentioned her for some time now. I hope she's alright.'

'She be fine, Ms Nancy.'

'She alive? I thought *she* were dead. Now I gettin' confused.'

'You bin confused yo' whole life, George; no point worryin' 'bout it now. Mr Gene, can you he'p me in the kitchen fo' a minute?' Doc followed Wanda to the kitchen and closed the door behind him.

'So who's the little girl?' Bob asked.

'B'shara Byrd,' George said with pride. 'She our youngest gran'child an' she stayin' with us while her Mom and Daddy go cruisin' in the Caribbean. Ain't that right, B'shara?'

B'shara Byrd said nothing and continued to suck the wooden beads hanging around her neck.

'That's going to cost,' Jack said. 'Cruises don't come cheap.'

'Doretta – that our daughter – catched herself a good one. Earns a ton o' money tradin' frozen pork bellies in Chicago. Ever' time he comes an' visits he tells me 'bout his job an' what he does, but I cain't says I'm none the wiser. Frozen pork bellies is the only words I can understan'.'

'What you do, George?' Bob asked.

'Works at the cotton gin down the road. Bin there close to thirty years. Ain't much, but it pays the bills an' I ain't got too long b'fore I retires. Dora woulda bin surprised I lasted this long. She thought I'd never 'mount to much.'

'Why she think that?' Bob smiled.

'Years ago, I stole a car as a protest,' George replied.

'What were you protesting?' Jack asked.

'Fact I didn' have one,' George said, a grin spreading across his wide face. 'Dora weren't a forgiver. To her way o' thinkin', once you crossed a line you were crossed it fo' good. Fo' all her Christian values, when it came down to it, she weren't a b'liever in redemption. I jus' thank the Lord I never said nothin' bad 'bout her food – she'da prob'ly killed me. That friend o' yo's got off lucky.'

'That's cos he's white,' Bob laughed. 'White men al'ays gets off lucky.'

'You men,' Nancy said. 'You talk such nonsense!'

'Mrs Skidmore, can I show B'shara Byrd the piano?' Eric asked.

'Of course you can, dear. Do you play the piano?'

'Yes, and I can teach her some notes.'

Eric and B'shara Byrd left the room just as the lucky white man and Wanda returned to it. Doc had confirmed Wanda's suspicions: Nancy was indeed travelling down the same road taken by her mother and grandmother before her. 'That po' woman,' Wanda had said. 'You ever needs he'p, you call me. Travis fam'ly bin good to me an' George – Ms Nancy in partic'lar.'

Wanda and George had been taking care of the lodge since the time of Hilton Travis. In need of someone to oversee the often empty property, and aware of the friction that existed between

George and Dora, Hilton had bought Wanda and George a small house close to the property and paid them a yearly retaining fee. After the lodge and its land had been leased, Nancy had made it a condition of the lease that Wanda and George continue as caretakers. The lodge could be seen from their house, and the unexpected signs of life that evening had attracted their attention.

'B'shara's a real cutie,' Nancy said. 'She's got the exact same eyes as Doretta.'

'I hopin' not, Ms Nancy: Doretta's blind in one eye,' George said.

'Oh my, I didn't know that, George. What happened?'

'Walked into a damned twig, Miss Nancy.'

'There's always something, isn't there?' Nancy sympathised. 'I'm losing my mind – did you know that? I'll get it back some day, but Gene says it's going to take time. That's why we've come to Coffeeville. Gene says I'll get better faster here than I would if I stayed in a nursing home, so it looks like we'll be neighbours for a while, Wanda.'

'They says good things come from bad, Ms Nancy, an' if you losin' yo' mind makes you my neighbour fo' a time, then that the good fo' me… C'mon, George, we need to get back an' leave these people be, get B'shara Byrd to bed.'

'We're having a party on Wednesday night – Halloween and Nancy's birthday rolled into one,' Doc said. 'If you haven't already made plans for the evening…'

'You must come!' Nancy said. 'It'll be like old times.'

'Yes it will,' Doc said. 'You can serve me dinner again.'

'Gene!' Nancy said sternly.

'Wanda knows I'm joking, don't you, Wanda?'

'No one knows when you're joking, Gene. How many times do I have to tell you that?'

'I can understan' now why my Mamma didn' like you,' Wanda laughed.

That night Eric couldn't sleep. He lay there with his eyes open, thinking of the day ahead.

He'd pinned all his hopes on finding Susan, but until this moment had never entertained the idea that Susan might be unwilling or unable to help him. He'd run away from school, lied to people and travelled thousands of miles to find her, but what if she wanted nothing to do with him, what would he do then – just go home? How could he when he had no home to go to? He didn't want to go back to Talbot Academy and he didn't want to go back to the Annandales, either.

He was happy with the people he travelled with, but Otis would soon leave and Doctor Gene and Mrs Skidmore were old people and Mrs Skidmore ill. He couldn't expect them to look after him and they wouldn't live forever. Maybe Jack would help him; maybe, he could live with Jack. Jack, he knew, would live forever.

He started to cry. He missed his parents and wanted them to be alive again. He wanted to taste his mother's cooking and smell her perfume, hold his father's hand and feel safe. He wanted to be a part of a proper family again, for someone to love and take care of him.

He closed his eyes and pressed his hands together in prayer. 'Please, God, make Susan love me. Let me live with Susan.'

Seemingly, God heard his prayer.

Desperately Seeking Susan

The next morning, Jack and Eric left for Memphis.

The concierge remembered Jack. 'I gave Darla your message, sir, and she's expecting you. Someone's in with her at the moment, but if you take a seat I'll let you know when she's free.'

Jack thanked him and was about to turn away when a thought struck him. 'Is this hotel named after the same Peabody they name the radio and television awards after?'

'I believe it is, sir. Why do you ask?'

'I was just curious. *The Mary Tyler Moore Show* won a Peabody Award for excellence in 1977, did you know that?'

'I didn't, but I used to enjoy the show. My favourite character was Ted Baxter.'

'Mine too!' Jack said enthusiastically. The day was getting off to a better start than expected, and he started to feel optimistic. 'Which one was your favourite episode? Mine was...?'

'Are you Mr Guravitch?' a voice interrupted.

'Yes ma'am. You must be Darla Thomas.'

They followed Darla to her office. Darla hadn't smiled when he introduced himself, and he now noticed her broad shoulders. The thought crossed his mind that if Darla had been an employee in the eighties and worn business jackets of the time, with large padded shoulders, she'd have never made it through the office door.

To add formality to the smile-less introduction, Darla now blockaded herself behind a desk.

'You didn't used to be a swimmer, did you?' Jack asked her.

'No, why do you ask that?'

'No reason,' Jack backtracked. 'It's just that I've been thinking about taking up the sport and figured it would be a good idea to talk to someone who's been a swimmer. I ask everyone this question. It's amazing how few swimmers there are in this country.'

'You wanted to ask me about Susan,' Darla said.

'Yes I did. This is Eric Gole, and Susan Lawrence is his cousin. Eric was orphaned recently, and Susan's his last remaining relative. He's trying to find her. Warren Kuykendahl told us she'd come to Memphis and might be staying with you. He said you were a friend of hers.'

'I was... I am... oh, this is complicated. Susan is in Memphis, that's true. I know where she works, but I don't know where she lives.'

'Do you have her mobile number?' Jack asked.

'No, I deleted it.'

'Did you and Susan fall out?' Eric asked.

'Something like that – and I'm afraid it was all my fault, too.' She took a deep breath. 'I wrongly accused her of flirting with my fiancée and threw her out of the apartment. It turned out that it was him who'd been trying it on with her, and after she refused to play ball, and out of spite, he told me that Susan had come on to him. I should have known she wouldn't have done that, but at the time I didn't want to believe he was capable of being unfaithful to me. I loved him. I thought he was the real deal. It was only when I was telling a friend about what happened that she told me he'd made a play for her too. Men! They can be such bastards!'

'So too can women,' Jack said. 'My wife had an affair, too. She became pregnant by the man and told me the child was mine.'

'I'm sorry,' Darla said. 'That must have hurt.'

'The infidelity hurt, but I don't regret I'm no longer with her. You'll get to feel the same way.'

'I know. It's not the first time this has happened to me. I'll survive, but what makes it worse is that I've lost a good friend as well as a fiancée. When you find Susan, will you tell her I'm sorry and ask her to give me a call?'

'I'll be glad to, Darla, but where will we find her?'

'She's working at Graceland, but just where in the complex I don't know. I'm afraid you'll just have to buy a ticket and work your way around.'

They left Darla, and Jack was pleased with himself for not having mentioned her speech impediment. The concierge called out to him.

'Yeth?' Jack said.

'It's the one where Ted's brother turns up,' he said. 'My favourite episode,' he added when he saw Jack's puzzled look.

'What's Graceland?' Eric asked.

'It's the house where Elvis Presley used to live. You've heard of him, haven't you? He was a rock 'n' roll singer with bad dietary habits.'

'I think so. Will we get there today?'

'It's less than nine miles away, Eric: we'll be there in half an hour. We're closer to Susan now than we've ever been. We've almost found her!'

Jack headed down Union Avenue and took a right on to Bellevue Boulevard. Bellevue turned into Elvis Presley Boulevard, and Jack followed the signs for Graceland and parked the car.

They bought tickets and waited in line for a shuttle bus to take them to the large white columned mansion.

'Excited?' Jack asked.

Eric nodded. 'I hope she recognises me. She's never seen me with black hair.'

'I'm sure she will, but will you be able to recognise her? It's been five years since you've seen her.'

'Sure I will. She'll be the most beautiful girl here!'

Jack would have preferred a more detailed description to go on, but Eric never went beyond the word beautiful. Warren Kuykendahl's description of Susan was of equally little value: asking people if they knew of a girl who looked like a bottle of Downy wouldn't get them far.

The shuttle bus arrived and chauffeured them across the road. Unlike their fellow passengers, they had little or no interest in touring Graceland – their only concern was to find a living girl called Susan Lawrence, not to pay homage to a dead rock 'n' roll star.

They stayed with the tour guide and heard how Elvis had been the most popular guy in the world, and always at the centre of jokes, laughter and story-telling. 'I'd be the most popular guy in the world, too, if I bankrolled a bunch of hangers-on like he did,' Jack whispered to Eric. 'A real friend would have told him to lay off the drugs and the fried food.'

They visited the mansion's downstairs living areas, the Jungle Room and the Music Room, and then moved outside to the Meditation Garden, where Presley and his parents were buried. 'Does this remind you of anywhere?' Jack asked.

'Mr Kuykendahl's house. I think he'd like living here,' Eric answered.

'Exactly so!' Jack said. 'They should have called this place Graceless Land.'

The tour guide knew of no beautiful girl working in the mansion called Susan, and neither did any other member of staff Jack approached. He started to head for the exit when Eric pulled at his sleeve.

'We didn't look upstairs, Jack. Maybe Susan's working there.'

'No one's allowed up there, Eric – not even tour guides. Elvis was found dead on one of the bathroom floors and I'm guessing they want to keep that bit private and away from the gawkers.'

They went outside and waited for the shuttle bus to take them back across the road to the other exhibits – Elvis' cars, motorcycles and airplanes; Elvis' years in Hollywood; and Elvis' years in the army. Jack and Eric only glanced at these, but mentioned Susan's name to every Graceland employee they found: 'Her name's Susan Lawrence and she works here. Have you seen her? She's supposed to be very beautiful.' No one had.

They went to the Chrome Grille for lunch. Eric played with his food, seemingly without appetite. 'We're not going to find her, are we?' he said. 'We're never going to find her.'

'Of course we are,' Jack said, though in truth he too was now harbouring the same fears. For the sake of Eric's watery eyes, however, he pretended that he didn't. 'We've still got the other restaurants to check, and also the souvenir shops. She's got to be here somewhere.'

They drew another blank at the restaurants and turned their attention to the souvenir shops. The amount and variety of junk sold was limitless, but in the Elvis Kids' store they struck gold. 'I don't know her name,' the cashier said, 'but there's a new girl working in Gallery Elvis and she's a stunner! I'm not surprised they gave her a job selling the high-class stuff.'

She left her chair and went to the door with them. 'You see the Rockabilly's Diner? Okay, walk past it and Gallery Elvis is the next shop down.'

They walked briskly past the diner and then moved more slowly. Their bravura dimmed, and as they approached the gallery door they became apprehensive. Eric took hold of Jack's hand and Jack squeezed it tightly. Suddenly, Jack stopped in his tracks. 'Jesus Christ, Eric! Look at that,' he said. 'It's a Kelvin-Helmholtz!'

Eric looked up and saw what appeared to be huge breaking waves in the sky. The image lasted for no more than a few seconds. It was the rarest cloud of all.

Susan was standing behind a counter, eating a Snickers Bar and staring wistfully into the distance. She had a slender but shapely body, and facial features that were textbook: wide eyes, a small nose, full lips and high cheekbones. She was the most beautiful girl Jack had ever seen.

'That's her, Jack. That's Susan!' Eric whispered. 'What should I do now?'

'Go talk to her,' Jack said gently, letting go of Eric's hand and nudging him forwards. 'And don't forget to introduce me.'

Eric walked hesitantly towards her, hobnailed butterflies dancing a stomp in his stomach. 'It's me Susan,' he said, timidly. 'Eric!'

Susan looked at the small boy, momentarily confused by the white cycling helmet, red washing-up gloves and dyed eyebrows. Then, she shrieked his name in recognition, dashed from behind the counter and flung her arms around him. 'Eric! Oh my God, it is you!'

Eric's stiff upper lip – still in its formative stage – weakened, and despite his best efforts to the contrary, he started to cry. He held on to Susan and Susan held on to him. They hugged without words, communicated through sobs and soothing noises. Then Susan started to cry.

Jack checked his reflection in a glass cabinet and put a stick of gum in his mouth. A potential customer came into the gallery and left immediately. The manageress of the store returned from lunch and suggested that Susan and Eric take their reunion someplace else, perhaps the Heartbreak Hotel. They walked instead to the Shake, Split & Dip and ordered ice creams.

Susan and Eric sat together and Jack, who Eric had introduced to Susan as the man who'd bought him the washing-up gloves, dyed his hair black and told him the facts of life, sat facing them. 'He's like my big brother, Susan,' Eric said.

Susan looked at Jack doubtfully and then turned her attention back to Eric.

'I was so sorry to hear about your mom and dad, Eric,' she said. 'Jeff told me about how they died. If I'd known at the time, I'd have come to the funeral and stood with you. It must have been so hard going through it alone.'

'My daddy forgave you, Susan,' Eric said. 'I think he'd want me to tell you that.'

'What for?' Susan asked puzzled.

'For tearing the pages out of his Bible.'

'Oh… I'd forgotten about that,' Susan said, a bit sheepishly. 'I used to do a lot of crazy things in those days… but who's looking after you now, how did you find me?'

'No one, Susan. I'm an orphan. I was… I was… I was hop…' He then burst into tears again and Susan cradled him, pulling him towards her so that his head rested on her right breast.

For a moment, Jack envied the boy, wished it was his head resting there, but quickly remembered himself and spoke on Eric's behalf.

'He's got no one to speak of, Susan. His guardians don't seem to care: they enrolled him in a deaf school, believe it or not, and he's run away from there. A friend of mine picked him up close to where your dad's in prison, and he's been travelling with us ever since. He's been looking for you. He went to Hershey and talked to some guy there…'

'Fred?' Susan interrupted.

'I wasn't with Eric then so I don't know his name, but the guy gave him Warren Kuykendahl's name and address, and Warren told us to get in touch with Darla Thomas. I think he wants to live with you, Susan – for you to take care of him. If you can't… then the two of us will figure something out.'

Susan's prompt response surprised him. 'Of course I'll take care of you, honey,' she said to Eric. 'You can live with me for as long as you like!'

Eric's face lit up like a Fourth of July night sky and he quickly wiped away his tears. 'I'll be good, Susan. I promise I will! I won't be any trouble, and when I grow up I'll pay you back – I'm going to be a postman! Thank you, thank you, Susan… and thank you too, God,' he said, looking up at the Shake, Split & Dip's ceiling

He hugged Susan and just as quickly let go. 'Where's the toilet, Jack? I need to use the toilet!'

Jack and Susan were left alone together, smiling at Eric's

abrupt departure. Jack mentioned Darla Thomas, but Susan quickly changed the subject. 'What Eric said about you dying his hair and telling him the facts of life?'

'It makes me sound a bit creepy, doesn't it?' Jack smiled. 'I'll put it in context for you.' He then told Susan the story of the trip and the people they travelled with, sensibly omitting the part where they'd kidnapped Nancy from the nursing home.

'You've shown Eric a great deal of kindness,' Susan said. 'You all have. Thank you.'

'It was no hardship,' Jack said. 'The kid's got a good heart. Are you sure you're going to be okay looking after him by yourself – you didn't seem to give it too much thought.'

'You sound as if you're checking me out as a suitable foster parent,' Susan smiled.

'Your life will change. You know that, don't you?'

'I hope my life does change – it needs to change. And what kind of person would I be if I turned my back on Eric? He's family. I might dance naked for a living, but I know what the right thing to do is. The decision was easy.'

Jack looked at her. 'I could help you get things squared with his guardians, if you like. I can vouch that he hasn't been in any danger or up to no good while he's been missing, and I've got time on my hands to do it.'

'How come you have the time? Don't you have a job?'

Jack told her about Laura and Conrad, and his fall from grace as a television weatherman.

'Wow, that's so cool!' Susan laughed. 'Not the bit about Laura and Conrad, but the way you resigned on air. I wish I could have seen it.'

'You still can,' Jack said. 'Evidently, it's a big hit on YouTube.'

'So what do you plan to do now?'

'I'm going to retrain as a hairdresser. Fortunately, I have funds that aren't affected by the divorce. My father never liked Laura and didn't figure the marriage would last, so he left everything to my godfather, and he's holding it in trust for me – he's Doc, the guy on the bus I was telling you about.'

Susan studied Jack's face for a moment and then smiled. 'It

would be great if you could do that, Jack,' she said. 'It would really help!'

'It's no hardship,' Jack said, and it wasn't. Spending time with Susan would be no misfortune.

'Do you believe in love at first sight, Doc?' Jack asked.

'I'm not sure I even believe in like at first sight,' Doc replied. 'Why are you asking?'

'Because I fell in love with Susan the moment I saw her. I know it sounds crazy, and you'll probably make fun of me, but it happened. It wasn't just her looks, either: it was her voice, her laugh, her smell, the things she said and the way she was with Eric.'

'You don't think you're at all vulnerable at the moment, do you?'

'Vulnerable? In what way?'

'You've lost your job; you've left your wife; the kid you thought was yours isn't; you've grown attached to Eric; you're thinking of becoming a hairdresser... do you want me to go on?'

'I know all these things, Doc, but I don't think any of them has made me vulnerable. If anything, they've made me a stronger person. I'm thinking more clearly now than at any other time of my life. Tell me: what *didn't* I mention about Susan when I was describing her just then?'

Doc thought for a moment. 'Her star sign?'

'Give me a break, Doc! Her hair! I didn't mention her hair. Doesn't that tell you something? In the past, it's always been about the hair. It had to be thick, long and shining. Susan's hair isn't anything like that – it's fine, cut in a pageboy style.'

'So what are you saying?'

'I'm saying that I've matured. I'm seeing the bigger picture. Can't you be pleased for me?'

'If you're sure about this, then of course I'm pleased for you. I just don't want you getting hurt. How does Susan feel about you?'

'I don't know – you don't think I *told* her I loved her, did you? Even I know that would have been the kiss of death. She likes me, though – I'm sure of that – and the two of us are going to take

Eric back home and get things straightened out for him.

'You should have seen Eric when he saw her. The kid burst into tears and couldn't stop sobbing. It was like he'd found his mother again. Susan just held on to him. She didn't have to think twice before she agreed to help him. It was immediate. She handed in her notice then and there, and she's going to put her career on hold until we figure out what to do with Eric.'

Doc smiled, wondering how Susan's career at Gallery Elvis had been going. 'So when are you three leaving for California, and how are you getting there?'

'Saturday. The manager of the store was understanding, but said she needed Susan to work out the week. I'll drive to Memphis with Eric on Thursday, turn in the car and help Susan tie up loose ends. We'll be driving to California in her car.'

'That's the same day Bob leaves – the day after the party.'

'Are you going to be okay with Nancy by yourself?'

'We'll be fine,' Doc said. 'We'll need a fair wind and some groceries, but we'll work things out.'

'I was startin' to b'lieve she were a figment o' the boy's mind,' Bob said. 'Wonder if we'll ever get to meet the girl?'

Doc shrugged. 'At my time of life, I don't need to meet any new people. The main thing is they've found her and Eric's no longer our responsibility. I wonder what they'll do.'

'By the sounds o' things they'll be tourin' the country with a one-song repertoire. What is it they suppose' to be learnin'?'

'It's a song from Jack's rock band days, one that his friend wrote. He and Eric are going to perform it Wednesday night.'

'You gonna sing somethin', Gene?'

'What song would I sing?'

'How 'bout "What a Won'erful Worl'"? Steada doin' the straight version, you could do yo' own ironic renderin'. Ha!'

Doc smiled. 'Do you ever regret not being Bob Crenshaw anymore and having to live life as T-Bone Tribble?'

'Depends on what you mean. The man still me – jus' got to call his'self by a diff'rent name, is all. Sometimes I get sad he's dead, an' cain't take credit fo' what I done with my life, but I'da prob'ly never done those things had he not been dead – if you see what I mean. You think 'bout it, Gene, when Bob Crenshaw was alive all he did was kill people fo' a livin', an' now he's dead, the killin's ended. In that respec' I don't min' him being dead. Why you aksin' me this?'

'It's just that there are times when I think it's my fault he's dead. When we were arrested in Jackson, you got us out of jail by making a pact with the Devil – with Fogerty. And what happened after that? My life continued as normal and yours came to an end; I became a doctor and you became a fugitive, living under an assumed name and having to look over your shoulder the whole time. It doesn't seem right.'

'Figure it this way, Gene. If you hadn'ta pulled me from the bus in Anniston when it was burnin', Bob Crenshaw woulda been dead already. It was my fault we got arrested in Jackson, an' so I did what was necessary. You'da done the same if you'd been me. I ain't got no regrets. Sure, there was bad times 'long the way, but I met some good people. They weren't exactly members o' the Chamber o' Commerce or the Rotary Club – an' most o' what they did wasn't exac'ly legal neither – but even so, they was still salt o' the earth. An' I met Marsha! My life's good, Gene. I ain't got no complaints. Man on the run sometimes ends up with mo' freedoms 'n a man that ain't.'

Doc thought about what Bob had said. 'I think you could be right there. A week ago I shot a dog and kidnapped Nancy, and ever since *I've* been on the run. It's the first time I've ever been on the wrong side of the law and, to tell you the truth, it's been the most exhilarating week of my life. I'm almost sorry it's ending. All considered, I think it's been a damn fine time! Maybe I will sing that song!'

Halloween

The day of the party arrived. 'We need to get ourselfs organised,' Bob said. 'Know who's doin' what.'

'I'll drive to the Piggly Wiggly and buy the groceries and a couple of pumpkins,' Jack said. 'You want to come with me, Eric?'

'You might wanna buy him some Valium while yo' there,' Bob said. 'Kid's goin' roun' like he's on amphetamine or somethin'.'

This was true. Since returning from Memphis the previous day, Eric had been living on Cloud Nine. He'd talked more in these hours than in the entirety of the days he'd travelled with them. He ran rather than walked places, chattered endlessly about Susan and of returning to California with her and Jack. He joined in every activity and insisted on helping with all the chores: he served food, cleared plates, washed dishes, tidied his room and tidied the house. It was tiring just to watch him, even more tiring to be with him. He no longer read the Bible, and explained that he'd finished the Old Testament and was going to take a break before starting the New.

'I'll come with you, Jack. Just let me get my helmet.'

'We need to make a list of the food and drink we'll need for tonight, and another list for the food and drink Nancy and I will need after you've gone,' Doc said. 'Remember, we won't have a car. Let me check what we have in the kitchen and then write down what I tell you, Jack.'

'I can write it down, Doctor Gene. I'll follow you into the kitchen,' Eric said. He went to his room and tore a clean sheet of paper from his notebook and grabbed his pen. 'I'm ready, Doctor Gene. You can start calling things out.'

'What you gonna do, Nance?' Bob asked her.

'I think I'll just sit here and wait for my parents,' Nancy said. 'I feel tired today.'

'You do that, Nance. If you need me, I'll be outside checkin' the bus, makin' sure the oil an' water levels are okay. You wanna give me a hand, Gene?'

'Sure. I'll look through the compartments and make sure we haven't left anything. Just let me finish off these lists and I'll be with you.'

'I ain't in no rush. I'll sit here with Nance and chat fo' a while. You wanna chat, Nance?'

'No, not today, thank you, Bob.'

'In that case, I'll sit here an' say nothin' then.'

Jack and Eric left for Coffeeville, and Doc and Bob went to the bus. 'When I first saw this thing in the church car park, I thought you'd gone and lost your mind,' Doc said to Bob, 'but I have to admit, it was an inspired choice.'

'It weren't so much inspired as what they had, Gene. It was either this bus or a large van with no seats in it. I'da been okay, but it woulda been distractin' havin' an old guy like you rollin' round in the back. Them scratches we got up at Three Top Mountain ain't so bad as I thought; what you think?'

'They'll need touching up but it shouldn't cost too much. That reminds me, I need to settle up with you.'

'What you mean you need to settle up with me? I ain't takin' no money from you, Gene. Man who hired me this vehicle owed me a favour; he ain't chargin'.'

'I don't care – just take it. Nancy set it aside for the journey. It's yours: you can do with it as you please.'

'How you gonna manage without money?'

'I've got money and we've got food. It's not as if I'm going to be here forever.'

'Where you gonna be, then? You ever plannin' on goin' home?'

'Where else am I going to go?'

'You could come stay with me an' Marsha. You an' Nance could live in the cabin if you like. No one'd go lookin' fo' you there.'

'I appreciate the offer, Bob, but I'm not risking your well-being for the sake of ours. Nancy and I will stand or fall on our own terms.'

'It the fallin' that worries me,' Bob said.

Doc looked at him.

'It's okay, Gene, I ain't gonna say no mo'. I figure I ain't gonna see you again though, am I?'

'Of course you are. Now for God's sake take the money and let's go and see how Nancy's doing.'

'I'll follow you in. Jus' need to finish checkin' the oil.' He opened the hood of the engine, pulled out the dipstick and wiped it clean with a cloth. The oil level was fine. He replaced the dipstick and spoke to himself: 'You lying to me, ol' man. I ain't gonna see you again, an' you knows it.'

'Jack taught me this trick for when I start learning to drive, Mrs Skidmore.'

'What trick is that, Eric?' Nancy asked.

'When you pull up at a stop light and there's only one car in front of you, as soon as the light changes you honk your horn at him and...'

'Why would you want to do that, dear?'

'Because he won't have had a chance to move forward and he'll get annoyed.'

'That doesn't sound like a good idea. Why did you tell him this, Jack? What would have happened if the man in front had got out of his car and shot you both in the head?'

'We didn't *do* it, Nancy. I just thought it was a good scenario for a joke. I wasn't suggesting Eric do this.'

'I thought you said I could. Does this mean I can't?'

'Of course you can't, Eric. And before you even think about learning how to drive, you first need to learn how to keep your lip buttoned. Now let's go and carve the pumpkins. Do you want to help us, Nancy?'

'Yes – and thank you for asking, Jack. I used to be good at carving pumpkins.'

Jack and Eric carried the pumpkins outside, while Nancy went into the kitchen to look for a serrated knife and scoop. She joined them on the porch and they set to work. Nancy took a lipstick from her purse and drew a circle around the pumpkin's top, and asked Jack to cut it out and clean the underside of what would become the lid. She then handed the scoop to Eric and told him to scrape out the seeds and soft flesh from the inside, and dump them in the bucket.

'Now what do we do, Mrs Skidmore?'

'I'll draw a face on the side and then one of you can cut it out,' Nancy replied.

They finished the first pumpkin and started on the second. This time Nancy drew a different face on its side, and Jack carved out triangular rather than square holes for the eyes and nose. The mouth took longer, as Nancy had insisted on jagged teeth. Once finished, they took a step backward and viewed their handiwork.

'We've done well, haven't we?' Eric said. 'We could become professionals.'

'If we did turn professional, we'd only have one day's work a year,' Jack said.

'That's one more day than you have at present,' Doc said. 'You should consider it.' He smiled contentedly to himself and then lit the cigarette he was holding.

It was dark, and the stars glistened in the night sky. Eric lit the white candles inside the gourds and Nancy replaced their lids. She stared silently at the flickering lights and watched the shadows dance. 'I'm going to die, Eric. Did you know that?'

'Don't talk like that, Mrs Skidmore! You're not going to die – I don't want you to.'

'Don't want me to what, Eric?'

'Die – I don't want you to die.'

'Whatever put that idea into your head? This is the night of the year when the dead come back to life. I'm expecting all kinds of visitors tonight.'

Eric was spooked by Nancy's conversation and went inside to tell Doc. 'Doctor Gene, Mrs Skidmore says she's going to die and that dead people are coming to visit tonight. Can you go and talk to her?'

Doc put down his beer and was about to step outside when the door opened, and Nancy came into the room with Wanda, George and B'shara Byrd in tow. 'Look who's come to visit us, Gene. It's Wanda and George and they've brought the cutest little girl with them.'

B'shara Byrd was dressed in a pink rabbit suit, and had white whiskers painted on the sides of her face. 'She don' do scary stuff,' George said by way of explanation. 'I bought her a witch face an' hat to wear, but she won' go near 'em. Jus' wan's to be a rabbit.'

George was carrying a case of beer and Wanda two pies – one pumpkin, the other chocolate. 'Where you want these put?' she asked.

'Give 'em to me Wanda an' I'll put 'em in the refrig'rator,' Bob said. 'We got pizza an' hot dogs to start with. Go sit down an' I'll bring some drinks through. What you want – wine, beer, or juice?'

'Wine fo' me, juice fo' B'shara an' beer fo' George, if you will.'

Without looking, Doc slotted a CD into the player and pushed the play button. A cacophony of noise exploded into the room, followed a few bars later by a voice tailor-made for Halloween.

Nancy came running into the room with her panties halfway between her knees and ankles. 'Arnold, turn that damned racket off!' she shouted. 'You know the rules!'

'Who Arnold?' George asked Wanda.

'Arnold her husband what died,' Wanda replied.

'Then why she talkin' to Gene?'

'I'll explain later. I need to go he'p Ms Nancy.'

It took a while for Doc to find the eject button, but when he did and the music stopped, Nancy quietened. Wanda took her by the arm and guided her back to the bathroom, while Doc tried to make out the name on the CD.

'Jack, what's this CD I've just played?'

Jack took it from his hand and held it to the light. '*Lick My Decals Off, Baby* by Captain Beefheart & The Magic Band. What's Nancy doing with this in her collection?'

'It's one of Arnold's,' Gene replied. 'I'm surprised she still has it.'

The evening recovered and the party gathered ground. To a background of *Beatles* music, the revellers filled their glasses with alcohol and their plates with hot dogs and pizza. Eric and B'shara Byrd huddled together on the porch, and Eric brought her a pair of his washing-up gloves to wear. Wanda, Nancy and Doc sat by the fire reminiscing about Oaklands, Dora and the Travis family; while George, Bob and Jack swapped stories and told jokes.

Doc whispered something to Wanda and she called over to George. 'Hey, George, come give me a han', will you?'

'What you wan', Wanda?'

'Gene wan's to toast Ms Nancy with champagne.'

'Why cain't he do it his self? He hurt his han' or somethin'?'

'Ms Nancy all clingy with him an' he wan's it to be a surprise. She'd wanna know what he doin' if he got up an' left.'

Wanda took champagne glasses from the cupboard and George got busy with the corkscrew. 'What in the name o' Sweet Jesus you doin', George? You don' open a champagne bottle with a corkscrew, you use yo' damned thumbs. If only my mamma could see you now. Ha!'

'How I suppose to know that? I ain't never drunk champagne b'fore.'

'Sure you has. Sometimes I think you got shit fo' brains, George – an' fo' the love of God, stop shakin' the bottle!'

There were two loud pops and Wanda came into the room holding a tray. George walked slowly behind her, looking at his thumbs and rubbing them with his fingers. Doc took the glasses from the tray and handed them around. He lifted his glass. 'To Nancy,' he said. 'A belated Happy Birthday. We're glad we know you, and we're glad to be your friends.'

'Nancy,' everyone replied – including Nancy.

'Let's play our song now, Jack,' Eric said. He settled at the piano they'd moved into the room earlier in the day, and waited for Jack to bring the guitar.

'This is a song a friend of ours wrote...' Jack began.

'I didn't know him,' Eric said.

'Okay, wise guy, this is a song a friend of *mine* wrote. We were going to change the words to make it more appropriate, but in the end we decided not to. It's appropriate enough.'

He looked at Eric, and Eric started to play the opening bars.

If I had to live my life again I'd want to be with you
sharing every second of each day
For the love that you have given me is more than I deserved
a love no man could ever hope repay
Take my love as read, there are no words inside my head
to make you realise I'm dead without you by my side
I'll maybe smile or simply nod, play the fool or act the sod
I never felt a need for God when you were by my side

I hope I die before you dear, I couldn't bear to live
in shadows cast by your not being there

There'd be no meaning left to life, no place to hide my soul
just years and feelings no one else could share
Take my love as read, there are no words inside my head
to make you realise I'm dead without you by my side
I'll maybe smile or simply nod, play the fool or act the sod
I never felt a need for God when you were by my side

They then played the first verse again, and afterwards Jack explained the reason for singing the song.

'What Eric and I are saying is that we've enjoyed travelling with you this past week, and that if we ever have to make another trip like this, you'd be the people we'd want to make it with. Thanks Doc, thanks Bob, and a special thanks to you, Nancy, for making it possible.'

Everyone applauded. The two boys had played well together and Jack's words had been unexpected – especially to Nancy. 'What trip is he talking about, Gene?'

Before Doc had time to answer, Jack was introducing him as the next act on the bill. 'Doc's now going to sing *What a Won'erful World*, so let's give the old guy a big hand.'

'Whoa, I'm not singing anything!' Doc protested.

'I knew you'd try squirm outta it, Gene, so I wrote down the words fo' us all to sing. We'll sing it together – you included. You ain't not singin' it!'

Bob handed out his homemade lyric sheets, and Jack and Eric started to play the music. Doc sang the words as best he could from memory – he couldn't see any words written on the paper Bob had given him.

Eric's unbroken voice rang out from behind the piano. For him, the world really was starting to reclaim its wonder. He knew he would never stop missing his parents or wishing they were still alive, but he now no longer felt like the orphan who'd been enrolled at Talbot Academy. He had friends – true, many of them also old enough to be his grandparents – and now the promise of a new family life with Susan. And maybe even Jack. He'd always known that Jack would like Susan.

For Jack, too, life was looking up. The longer his hair grew, the more distant the memory of Laura and Conrad became. A new career in hairdressing beckoned, as well as a possible future with the most beautiful girl in the world and the most naive boy in the universe. He sang the words of the song with gusto and smiled at Eric, who smiled right back at his older brother.

Bob, Doc and Nancy stood together like a trio from light entertainment's yesteryear; three old friends reunited after decades of separation, soon to be torn apart for the final time. Doc knew this and Bob knew this, but neither acknowledged the truth on this perfect evening. The wonder of the world for Bob was having Marsha and a life in Seattle to return to; for Doc, the wonder remained in the moment – this one glorious and unforgettable moment.

Bob's atonal voice dredged the depths of known music, and Doc looked at him and laughed: he couldn't remember hearing anyone sing worse! Bob smiled back and then caught Nancy's eye and smiled at her. She was looking around the room rather than singing; looking, in all probability, for people who were long dead.

If only things could have been different and the world's axis brought back to kilter, the planets realigned and missing constellations restored. If only things could have been different!

'It is a wonderful world, isn't it, Gene?' Nancy asked when the singing ended.

Doc had never before seen such a sad and questioning face. 'Right now, Nancy, it's the most wonderful world there's ever been,' he told her, and kissed her on the forehead. For an instant, he almost believed it.

'Weren't so bad as you thought, was it, Gene?' Bob said. 'I coulda sworn I even see'd a tear in one o' yo' eyes.'

'That's sweat, Bob. I'm a doctor: I should know the difference.'

'You should know a lotta things you don't know. The worl' is a won'erful place – 'specially with me in it. Ain't that right, Nance?'

'Grandpa George,' B'shara shouted. 'Play B'shara Byrd! Play B'shara Byrd!'

'I cain't play B'shara Byrd, honey. I ain't got no guitar with me.'

'That man over there has a guitar. Tell him to give it to you!'

'Hush yo' mouth, B'shara Byrd. Yo' grandpa plays that song fo' you ever' day. You heard it enough times already,' Wanda said firmly.

'I wanna hear it, I wanna hear it!' B'shara Byrd said, stamping her foot on the floor. 'Eric wants to hear it, too!'

'Take the guitar, George,' Jack said, handing it to him. 'I'd like to hear it as well.' George took the guitar and thanked him.

George placed the capo on the fourth fret and retuned a couple of strings.

'Play it, Grandpa, play it!' B'shara Byrd shouted.

'Honey, jus' give me a minute, will you. Okay, now I ready.'

B'shara Byrd she jus' gone three
an' I don't thinks that she likes me
she pulls a face and shows her tongue
then she moons me with her bum

B'shara Byrd has pulled a mood
an' I don't like her attitude
she screams shit an' calls me fart
her hobnail boots dance on my heart

Oh B'shara Byrd
sweet B'shara Byrd

When flowers came an' leaves turned green
we threw pebbles into a stream
we fed the ducks an' rowed a boat
she held my han' when we crossed the road

B'shara Byrd you'll never know
how much I tries to love you so
but it's so hard when you so soft
you catch col' ever'time I cough

Oh B'shara Byrd
sweet B'shara Byrd

Cute as a button with big brown eyes
B'shara Byrd can mesmerise
blackest hair an' platinum smile
B'shara Byrd turns on the style

I hopes you grows up big an' strong
knows what's right an' knows what's wrong
but try not to break too many hearts
when choosin' horses to pull yo' cart

B'shara Byrd danced throughout the song, and once George had finished playing jumped up and down and clapped her hands excitedly. 'Play it again, Grandpa! Play it again!'

'That the bes' damn song I ever heard,' Bob said. 'You write it?'

'It no mo' 'n three chords, Bob. Song wrote itself.'

'Play it again, will you,' Jack asked. 'And Eric, try playing along on the piano. It's just three chords.'

George played the song twice more until Eric figured out the song's structure, and then by popular demand played it again. Doc excused himself and walked out on to the porch. He lit a cigarette and watched through the window: George and Eric playing, Jack harmonising, Bob dancing with B'shara, Wanda laughing, and Nancy happily banging a spoon against a pie plate to whatever rhythm played in her head.

Doc's world was in that room: his oldest friend, as full of the joys of life as he'd ever been; his first love, now damaged beyond repair; his godson, the one person he truly considered family; and the conundrum that was Eric – a small boy who'd become a friend to all. He loved these people, loved them with all his heart, and he allowed himself the rare luxury of believing that they, too, loved him. His creased face broke into a broad smile and then collapsed into sadness.

It had been forty years since the old man had cried, and he felt the tears on his cheeks long before he understood the nature of what was happening. In that brief moment, he experienced happiness.

Crossing the Rubicon

Overnight the temperature dropped, and the morning air was as crisp as an expensive lettuce. When Doc walked into the kitchen, Bob was clearing debris from the previous evening, scraping uneaten food from plates and stacking the dishwasher.

'One o' the bes' parties I never been aksed to leave,' Bob said. 'Had me a good time. How 'bout you, Gene?'

'I must have drunk too much,' Doc replied. 'My head feels like someone's just dumped a truckload of broken glass and concrete into it. Hand me a glass of water, will you?'

'I ain't surprised you hung-over, man. Firs' time I see'd you laughin' long as I remem'er. Remin'ed me o' the times we had at Duke. Them was good days, weren't they?'

'They were,' Doc agreed. 'Pity they didn't last.'

'Don't go gettin' all depressin' on me, Gene. I gotta long drive 'head o' me today, an' I don' wan' the mem'ry o' yo' miserable face stuck in my head.'

'I'll be fine once I've had some coffee. Pour me a cup will you?'

'What am I – yo' damn slave? "Han' me a glass o' water, Bob; pour me a cup o' coffee, Bob." Man, if I didn't know better, I'd say you was one o' them white supremacists. Four days in Miss'ippi an' you a changed man, Gene. Ha!'

Jack walked into the room. 'What's for breakfast, Bob?'

'Hell, you bad as Gene. Ain't even my house an' people puttin' on me.'

Despite his faux outrage, Bob poured coffee and they moved into the lounge to wait for Nancy and Eric. 'Do you want us to move the piano back to the bedroom?' Jack asked.

'Nah, it's fine where it is. It's doing no harm there.'

Nancy was the first to make an appearance, her hair uncombed and wearing the same clothes she'd worn the day before. Her mood, however, was chipper. 'Was it my imagination or was there a pink rabbit here last night?' she asked.

'It was B'shara Byrd dressed as a pink rabbit,' Doc explained. 'Wanda and George's granddaughter,' he added.

'Oh, of course it was. I remember now. She was Eric's girlfriend, wasn't she?'

'She's not my girlfriend, Mrs Skidmore,' Eric said, walking into the room. 'I'm seven years older than she is.' Eric's hair was also uncombed and he too was wearing the same clothes he'd worn yesterday. 'Last night was the latest I've ever stayed up. I did well, didn't I?'

'You sure did,' Doc replied.

'Do you want to play that song again, Jack? We could play B'shara Byrd as well.'

'Not right now, Eric. Doc's got a headache and we need to eat breakfast.' He stood up from his chair. 'Toast and cereal okay with everyone?' It was.

Apart from Nancy, they were all silently aware that this breakfast would be their last meal together, and that once it was over three of them would be leaving. It proved a sombre affair and conversation was stilted. Eric broke into tears and Jack put his arm around his shoulders. 'He hasn't done that thing with his pecker again, has he?' Nancy whispered to Doc. Doc smiled and told her he hadn't, that he was just sad to be leaving. 'He can always come and visit us,' Nancy said. 'We have plenty of rooms.'

While Doc cleared the breakfast table, Bob, Jack and Eric packed their belongings and took them outside. Nancy sat by herself, tap-tapping her fingers to a song no one but she could hear. Once Jack had finished taking his bags to the car, Doc pulled him to one side and gave him a pouch with ten thousand dollars tucked inside it.

'This is part of your dad's estate, Jack; together with details of the account I placed the rest of the money in. You can draw on it at any time, but before you do, check with that lawyer of yours to make sure it won't be included in the divorce settlement. Your dad would turn in his grave if it was. I also need the name and address of your lawyer.'

'How do I get in touch with you?' Jack asked. 'How long are you going to be here?'

'I don't know. It all depends on Nancy. Bob threw my mobile into the river and I don't know the number here. I'll keep in touch with my lawyer and suggest you contact me through him. His details are in the money pouch, too.

'I don't want to get into any big goodbyes while Eric's around, so I'll say it now: I owe you, Jack! We couldn't have made this trip without you, and I'll always be indebted to you. I never had a son, but if I had, I'd be more than happy if he'd turned out like you. Laura never deserved you, but maybe this Susan girl does. I hope it works out.'

'What's the punch line, Doc?'

'There isn't a punch line. That's it.'

Jack put his arms around him. 'There's no need to thank me, Doc. You've always been there for me and you were always there for my father. Besides, this trip's worked out well for me. Do me a favour though – next time I see you, don't pull any more of this soft-heartedness shit. In my book, you and sentiment just don't go together, and that's the way I like it.'

Doc agreed to his godson's request and then pulled away. 'Say goodbye to Nancy, Jack. I'm glad the two of you got to like each other in the end. I wish you'd have known her in her day.'

Eric was in tears, incoherent, unable to say more than a few words before breaking into sobs. He hugged Nancy and kissed her on the cheeks; hugged and kissed Doc and Bob – the man he still referred to as Otis. He thanked them over and again: for looking after him, for helping him find Susan, for being his friends. He told them they'd always be on his prayer list – a list recently swollen by the names of Merritt Crow, Wanda, George and B'shara Byrd – and that he'd write regularly and always remember them.

Jack took hold of Eric's hand and led him to the car before his tears started to flood the house. Just before the boy climbed into the passenger seat, he turned to the three old people waving to him: 'I love you,' he stammered, and then broke into sobs again.

Jack closed the passenger door after him and walked back to

the house. He hugged Doc again, put his arms around Nancy and kissed her on both cheeks, and then hugged Bob. 'How do I get in touch with you, Bob?'

Bob wrote down a mobile telephone number. 'Don't never give this to another person, Jack, an' I'd 'preciate it if you kept my name an' the bus outta the story you tell Eric's people. Make sure you keep in touch, man.'

'You have my word on it, Bob, and once I get settled, I'll call you.' He then walked to the car and started the engine. Just as he was about to drive away, Bob came running towards them.

'Hey, win' down yo' window, kid,' he called out to Eric. Eric did, and stuck out his head. 'Don't go readin' the Book o' Revelations, neither,' Bob gasped. 'Man what wrote it was on mushrooms, an' if he weren't, then he copied it straight from the Book o' Daniel!'

Bob walked back to the house chortling to himself. 'That boy,' he said to Doc and Nancy, shaking his head from side to side. 'Stranges' damn kid I ever met.'

He then turned serious. 'I gotta go, Gene. Watch me while I reverse, will you? An' Nance, give me a hug b'fore I go, girl, an' promise me you'll put a comb through that damned hair o' yo's once I gone. Looks like you been dragged through a hedge or somethin'.'

Nancy laughed and gave him a big hug. 'You're the stupidest man I ever met, Bob Crenshaw. I don't know why Gene wastes his time on you.'

'He ain't got no other person to waste his time on, Nance – that's why. I'm the only one prepared to take pity on the po' soul.'

Nancy went back into the house, while Doc watched Bob reverse down the pitted drive. Bob halted the bus on the road and stepped out.

'Give me a cigarette, will you, Gene? I think I got time fo' one las' smoke.'

Doc shook two cigarettes from his pack, and Bob cupped his hands around the flame of the lighter. They inhaled and exhaled in synchrony.

'This state ain't good fo' us, Gene,' Bob declaimed. 'Miss'ippi al'ays finds a way o' separatin' us. You remem'er what happened las' time we was here? Cain't b'lieve we allowed ourselfs to get drawed back, man.'

'And I can't believe your grammar's no better now than it was then,' Doc smiled. 'Remember me to Marsha, will you?'

'Sure I will. Don't aks me why, but she got a sof' spot fo' you. Hell, if you was black, she'd prob'ly divorce me an' marry you. Thank God you ain't though, an' she partic'lar.'

It was hard keeping the banter up, talking of one thing and thinking of another, and while neither man wanted his cigarette to ever burn away, both were relieved when, at last, Bob dropped his to the road and extinguished the dying embers with the sole of his boot.

He then rested his hands on either side of Doc's shoulders and looked him in the eyes. He saw tears welling there, felt movement in his own eyes. 'All I gonna say, man, is that it's been an honour – a real honour. I glad I knowed you, Gene. Glad you was my friend.' He then pulled Doc towards him and held him.

'For me too, Bob,' Doc choked. 'For me too.'

They remained there unmoving, locked in embrace, reluctant to let go. Eventually, Bob relaxed his hold and kissed Doc tenderly on the cheek. 'Who I gonna drive a bus fo' now, old man?' he whispered.

The bus pulled away and moved down the road. As it neared the bend it slowed, and Bob's arm waved through the open window. Doc waved back, and then watched as the bus and his oldest friend disappeared from sight, disappeared from his life forever.

A malaise as thick but nowhere near tasty as porridge settled over the lodge. The house felt empty and so too did life. Nancy's condition, temporarily alleviated by the activities of the trip and the diversions of others, quickly regained its downward momentum. She wandered the house distractedly, endlessly searching rooms for people already dead, and looking through windows for people who would never arrive. She stopped smiling and started sentences that never finished, asked questions that had no happy answers and veered wildly from one mood to another like a grenade without its pin.

It was now Saturday and still Doc prevaricated. He never doubted that Nancy's fluorescent years were dead, or that her life was now shrouded in shadows of frightening proportions, but the will to take the final step eluded him. He needed a sign; something that would prompt him to take action.

'The sun's shining too hard, Gene. I can hear it – can you?'

'It's making a bit more noise than usual, Nancy, but I prefer the noise of the sun to the sound of the rain.'

'Why isn't Ruby here yet? She was supposed to be having lunch with us, and she's usually so reliable.'

'Maybe she got held up in traffic,' Doc replied. 'Let's take a short walk while we're waiting – head down to the woods?'

Nancy agreed and took his arm. They walked slowly down the paddock and stopped at the edge of the trees. When they turned to look at the lodge Doc saw two white cumulus clouds floating high in the sky, and was reminded of the day Nancy had first poured out her fears and asked for his help. The real Nancy.

'We should go back now, Gene,' Nancy fretted. 'Grandmamma says these woods are full of monsters.'

Doc took hold of Nancy's hand and squeezed it gently.

It would happen on Monday.

That night, Doc built a fire in the grate and the two of them spent the evening sitting in front of the television. He'd increased the dosage of Nancy's medication and for much of the time she dozed. To any outsider peeping through the window, Doc and Nancy would have given the appearance of an old married couple who'd run out of things to say. There would have been no clue that the woman sitting there had less than two days to live.

Doc spent the time carefully sorting through documents and writing letters. His eyesight made progress slow, but it was important that everything he wrote was legible and intelligible. Finally, he put the letters and accompanying documents into envelopes, painstakingly addressed them and affixed sufficient postage stamps for their safe delivery. He then went to the kitchen and took a bottle of Maker's Mark from the cabinet. He poured a generous amount of the bourbon into a glass tumbler, added three cubes of ice, and took it outside to the porch and lit a cigarette. He felt he deserved both.

The next morning, after Nancy had dressed and breakfast been eaten, Doc phoned Wanda and asked for a favour. Wanda readily agreed and arrived that afternoon with George; it was just the two of them, B'shara Byrd having returned to Chicago. While Wanda sat and kept Nancy company, George drove Doc to the post office in Coffeeville.

'That where I works,' George said, pointing to the cotton gin at the intersection of the dirt and hardtop roads. 'When I retires, I ain't gonna look at another cotton seed fo' long as I lives.'

'You don't enjoy your work then, George?'

'Nah. You enjoy yo's when you was workin'?'

Doc only had to think for a moment before replying. 'No. I think I'd have been happier working in a cotton gin.'

'Ha! You don' know what you sayin', Gene. No one likes workin' in a cotton gin. Only reason I works there is to prove Dora wrong 'bout me, an' 'cos I loves Wanda.'

George drove into the deserted town and pulled up outside the deserted post office. 'Push yo' letters through that slot there,' he told Doc.

Doc got out of the car and checked to make sure he had all four letters: one for Nancy's attorneys, one for his own attorneys, one for Jack c/o Tina Terpstra and one for T-Bone Tribble. He pushed them into the box and climbed back into the car.

They found Nancy and Wanda standing at the bottom of the drive looking down the road in their direction. 'I tol' you he'd be back, Ms Nancy; tol' you there was no cause fo' you worryin'.'

Doc got out of the car and Nancy took a firm hold of him. 'Everything okay, Wanda?'

'Ms Nancy got herself in a tizzy, Gene. Thought you'd run off an' left her. I tol' her you an' George had jus' gone to pos' some letters, but she wouldn' settle an' insisted we come lookin' fo' you. She kept sayin' how you hadn' done right by her, lef' without doin' yo' job. I asked her what job she was talkin' 'bout an' tol' her me an' George could prob'ly do it fo' her, but she couldn' remember. You know what she mean?'

'I've no idea, Wanda,' Doc lied. 'I'm going to call out a doctor next week and get him to take a look at her; see if he can come up with any suggestions. Is there a doctor here you can recommend?'

'Call Dr Barefoot: he an' his family been practisin' med'cine in town long as I remem'er. He'll know Ms Nancy. Travis name still stands in these parts.'

Wanda walked with Doc and Nancy to the lodge and George followed slowly in his car. Wanda didn't go into the house with them, explaining that she and George were driving to Jackson to see her sons the next day, and she still had baking to do. 'I'll come by once we gets back, Gene. Say goodbye to Ms Nancy fo' me, will you. I don' wanna go disturbin' her now she all settled.'

Doc turned on the television for Nancy and went to get a magnifying glass. He looked through the telephone directory and found the number for Dr Barefoot. He transcribed it in clear figures and then put the piece of paper in his pocket. It was too early to eat dinner, so he sat with Nancy and stared at the television without knowing what he was watching.

That evening, he cooked pasta with chorizo sausage and tomatoes, and opened a bottle of red wine. Nancy pecked at the food, moved it around on her plate and then put her fork down. 'I'm sorry, Gene, I'm not hungry,' she said. 'I think I'll go to bed now.'

As always, Doc slept badly and woke early. His dreams had been many and disturbed but one remained with him. He was trying to light a cigarette by striking a match against a metal key, but however many times he struck the key the match refused to ignite. And then the key burst into flames and the metal started to bubble and melt. He threw it to the ground and the key fell through the bars of a grate. He lifted the cover and looked into the manhole. The key was resting fifteen feet below him, now shining and pristine but, because of a jumble of exposed electrical cables, impossible to retrieve. It was then he remembered it was the key to his parents' house. He had no idea what the dream meant.

He went into the kitchen and made coffee, and at nine o'clock phoned Dr Barefoot. 'Of course I remember Nancy Travis,' Barefoot said. 'I can come out this afternoon, if you like.' Doc thanked him, but said that Tuesday morning would be soon enough. 'I'll be there at ten,' Barefoot said. Doc thanked him and put down the phone.

Nancy was still in bed, her eyes open and staring. He took clean underwear from her drawer, selected a green sweater and a pair of grey slacks and placed them on a chair. 'Come on, Nancy, time to take a shower,' he said.

He stayed with her in the bathroom while she showered, and dried her with a towel once she'd stepped out of the bath. Nancy stood there helpless and uncomplaining, more reminiscent of a small child than the sixty-eight-year-old woman she'd become. Doc helped her dress and then brushed her hair. 'You're as good as new, Nancy; beautiful enough to break the heart of any man who can't have you.'

Nancy smiled but said nothing. Her world was one of uncertainty; why would she listen to the words of a man she didn't know? She followed him into the kitchen and swallowed the pills he put in her hand and washed them down with orange juice. She ate the slice of buttered toast he prepared and sipped the coffee he poured. The man took her to a chair and turned on the television. She heard the clatter of dishes and the sound of running water. She felt tired, wanted to close her eyes and fall asleep, but the man came back. He was taking her to the bedroom. He gave her more pills to swallow, called her Nancy – was that her name – and lay down on the bed next to her.

Doc watched nervously as Nancy's eyelids fluttered and then closed, listened to her breathing as it grew deeper. 'It won't be long, Nancy. I'm here with you.'

He never expected a reply, but Nancy opened her eyes and looked at him. 'I love you, Gene,' she whispered. 'I married Arnold, but it was you I always loved. Thank you for being my friend.' Her eyes then closed and she slipped into unconsciousness.

'I love you too, Nancy,' Doc murmured.

He waited a few minutes and then took a syringe from a case

and filled it with liquid from a small phial. He found a vein in Nancy's arm and carefully injected the clear fluid. He then lay on the bed next to her again and took hold of her hand, squeezed it, and only let go once he felt the life drain from her body. He rose from the bed and checked her vital signs. There were none. He pulled the sheet over her face. Nancy was gone.

The Day of Rest

For the next two hours, Doc cleaned house. He turned on the air conditioning and switched off the television. He gathered soiled undergarments from Nancy's room, and stripped the sheets from other bedrooms. He did laundry: washed, dried and folded. He emptied the kitchen of perishables and threw them in the garbage. He dumped any remaining tablets into the toilet bowl and pressed the flush. He tidied the lounge, cleaned the kitchen, remade the beds, vacuumed and dusted. He wanted no mess surrounding Nancy when she was found.

He went into the bathroom and ran the shower. He washed, shaved and changed into his favourite plaid shirt and corduroy pants. He took a sweater from a drawer and his jacket from the wardrobe. He checked himself in the mirror and then returned to Nancy's room. He pulled back the sheet from her face and sat down on the bed beside her, remained there motionless. He stared at Nancy's countenance and smiled sadly. She looked serene: the demons that tormented her were gone, and his friend was now at peace.

'We did it, girl,' Doc said. 'We did it.' He kissed her gently on the lips and whispered his final goodbye.

He covered Nancy's face again and closed the door behind him. He went to the dining table and wrote a short letter of explanation to Dr Barefoot, and an apology for burdening him with the consequence of his actions. He then took a paper clip and attached three one-hundred-dollar bills. He placed the letter next to an envelope marked for the attention of the sheriff. The envelope contained the names and telephone numbers of both his and Nancy's attorneys, and a facsimile of the letter Nancy had lodged with her attorney when the state of her mind had been unquestioned. In it, she made clear that dying was her choice and her choice alone, and that Doc's complicity had been reluctant – the action of a dear and devoted friend.

Doc read through his letter to Dr Barefoot, and once satisfied went into the kitchen for the bottle of Maker's Mark and a glass. He walked out on to the porch and sat down in a chair. The sun was shining and the air was warm. He listened to the birds sing and wondered if they were off-key. He decided they weren't – they sang in perfect harmony.

It was a good day to die.

In death, Doc foresaw no consequences, no judgement. Death was *his* get out of jail free card, his escape from eventuality. He filled the glass with bourbon and lit a cigarette. Perhaps because this was his last day on earth, he now started to enjoy it. The porch of Nancy's lodge, he decided, wasn't a bad place at all to die. Certainly, it afforded a better view of the world than his own terrace.

Until Nancy had whispered to him that morning that she'd always loved him, he'd never once in his life been sure of her feelings. In fact, the only occasion he could remember her telling him she loved him was the day he'd agreed to kill her. With Beth it had always been different. He'd never had to promise to kill Beth.

He took a small picture of Beth and Esther from his wallet. He stared at their faces and remembered the short time they'd been a family. He smiled sadly and then returned the photograph to his wallet and lit the last of his cigarettes. He inhaled and watched the ash as it lengthened and fell to the ground, contemplated the smoke as it drifted heavenwards, and then stubbed the cigarette out in the glass ashtray.

He thought about what else in life he'd miss, and smoking was about the only thing he could envisage: he'd miss cigarettes – especially those he smoked with his morning coffee. And maybe bourbon; maybe he'd miss bourbon too. He'd always drunk beer or red wine at home, and the sour mash whiskey of the trip had been a departure from his usual drinking habits. He found that he liked its sharp taste and the fieriness of its sting as it slipped down his throat.

For some reason, he thought of Captain Ahab riding to his death on the back of Moby Dick, and wondered why Ahab had smelled freshly cut grass at that moment and not tobacco smoke or bourbon. Maybe it was because he'd lost his leg in a lawnmower accident, he mused. (Doc had never read the novel.)

He looked around at his surroundings for one last time and then took a small bottle of pills from his jacket and emptied them on to the palm of his hand. He swallowed the pills one at a time and washed them down with the bourbon. He sat there and stared into the distance, started to feel drowsy. He wondered what life would have been like if he'd known at its start what he knew now. Would it have been different? Would he have done better? He heard Bob's voice from deep inside his head.

'You'da still screwed it up, ol' man. You'da been better off as a rhinoc'ros.'

Doc broke into a broad grin and shortly closed his eyes. The glass dropped from his hand and the bourbon spilled on to the floor. His head slumped forward and the drool from his mouth collected in the fibres of his sweater. He snorted twice and then fell silent as he embarked upon the deepest and most uninterrupted sleep of his seventy-two-year-old life.

He was found the next morning, the smile still on his face.

Epilogue

Eric is in his counting house counting out the dead. He wonders how many are in Heaven, and which of them are his parents' friends. He can't think of many. He thinks his parents will prefer the company of his grandparents and ordinary people like them. In his heart, he also knows that Mrs Skidmore and Doctor Gene are in Heaven, and that one day he'll meet them again and introduce them to his parents.

He's finished the books of the New Testament and adds their deaths to those of the Old. He starts with an unknown number of males aged two years and under living in the area of Bethlehem at the time of Christ's birth. They are put to death on the orders of King Herod, who later executes John the Baptist and serves his head on a platter to Herodias, the wife of his brother Philip. He adds the name of Judas Iscariot. There are two versions of his death: one says that Judas hangs himself; the other that he buys a field with the money paid to him by the enemies of Jesus and falls headlong while walking in it, bursts open in the middle and his bowels come gushing out. The last name Eric adds to his list is Antipas, a witness of Christ killed in Pergamum.

Eric totals and then re-totals the number of dead. Only one hundred and seventy-eight of them are named. Once satisfied, he walks into the living room. He no longer wears washing-up gloves.

Jack is practising his skills on a wig, and Susan is putting the finishing touches to a chocolate cake. Jeff is sitting at his computer working on a story about an Indian boy who lives in a slum and wins a popular television quiz show and becomes a millionaire. 'Son of a goddamn gun,' he mutters to himself. 'This is good. No son of a bitch is going to tell me this is derivative!'

Eric clears his throat. He's ready to make his announcement. He has their attention and tells them that the final number is not exhaustive and never can be. These are only the documented deaths; there are others referred to that probably run into their hundreds of thousands.

'Don't keep us all in suspense, Eric. Tell us!' Jack says.

Eric beams proudly. 'Two million, five hundred and seventy-one thousand, one hundred and eight!'

'Jesus Christ!' Jeff exclaims.

The smile disappears from Eric's face and is replaced by a look of disbelief. He's made a mistake. He takes out his pen and amends the total, and then makes another announcement.

'Two million, five hundred and seventy-one thousand, one hundred and NINE!'

THE END

About Us

In addition to No Exit Press, Oldcastle Books has a number of other imprints, including Pulp! The Classics, Kamera Books, Creative Essentials, Pocket Essentials and High Stakes Publishing > oldcastlebooks.co.uk

For more information about Crime Books go to > crimetime.co.uk

Check out the kamera film salon for independent, arthouse and world cinema > kamera.co.uk

For more information, media enquiries and review copies please contact Frances > frances@oldcastlebooks.com